"An oath is a bond, as is marriage, and any such vow. When ye made that oath, ye tied your souls together, and it's that knot that needs be cut, to sever the bond that ties ye. A blood bond, no less. Poor fools." She shook her head.

"I didn't know," Jonathan said quietly. "I had no idea."

"The young never do."

"I . . . I loved him so terribly," he said, blinking against the tears that burned his eyes.

"I know, child," she said in the same gentle voice she'd used years before. "I saw it then, and I see the ruins of it now. And that's why, when ye asked, I answered."

"What must I do?"

"You have t'cut the knot that binds the two of ye as lovers," she said.

"But . . . I don't know what that is. What do you mean?

She reached out and took his hand. *"You have to cut the knot,"* she repeated, then turned his hand over, and tapped on the underside of his wrist.

"You must do it this night, and then you'll be free."

More M/M Romances

Transgressions, by Erastes

False Colors, by Alex Beecroft

Tangled Web, by Lee Rowan

LOVERS' KNOT

An M/M Romance

BY DONALD L. HARDY

RUNNING PRESS
PHILADELPHIA • LONDON

9 8 7 6 5 4 3 2 1
Digit on the right indicates the number of this printing

Library of Congress Control Number: 2009927580

ISBN 978-0-7624-3685-9

Cover design by Bill Jones
Cover illustration by Larry Rostant
Interior design by Jan Greenberg
Typography: Amigo and New Caledonia

Running Press Book Publishers
2300 Chestnut Street
Philadelphia, PA 19103-4371

Visit us on the web!
www.runningpress.com

Dedication

For my parents, Barb and Ted,
who never once told me to put down
the books, with love.

I do love nothing in the world so well as you.
—Benedick, *Much Ado About Nothing*

CHAPTER 1

London 1906

The train whistle shrieked its warning, and Jonathan checked his watch as he hurried down the crowded platform; five minutes until the train departed—he was in time, but just. He tucked the watch back in his waistcoat pocket and scanned the platform ahead, blinking against the smoke of the waiting engines. Ten years living in the city hadn't inured him to the soot and fogs of London, and he rubbed his eyes as he methodically ran through a mental list. Train ticket: in his waistcoat pocket; he was still a little uncomfortable about buying a first-class ticket, though he could afford it now. Trunks: sent ahead by baggage train the day before; he only had a few necessities packed in the portmanteau and small bag a porter carried a few steps behind him. Papers for his cousin's solicitors in Penzance: in a billfolder in the breast pocket of his greatcoat; he patted them to be certain they were there.

"Williams!" a man called on his right. Jonathan started and looked around, taking a moment to locate the source. "Over here." An arm waved out the window of a compartment opposite him, and he hurried across the platform.

"Good morning, Langsford," Jonathan said. "I rather thought you'd be here already." He took off his hat. "Just put the bags in the carriage," he said to the porter. "I'll see to them myself."

"I should think I'd be," Langsford replied as he opened the

carriage door and stepped onto the platform. "I'll take those, man." He took the bags and lifted them into the carriage.

"Thank *you*, sir," the porter said. "Thank you, sir," he said again as Jonathan handed him a shilling. "Have a good journey, sir." He touched his cap briefly and disappeared into the crowd.

Jonathan stepped into the carriage, where Langsford was stowing the portmanteau under the seat. Jonathan slipped off his coat as he glanced around. "A private carriage?"

Langsford straightened up. "Of course," he said. "I certainly tipped the guard sufficiently to insure it. I didn't want to spend the day traveling with a boor of an old general, or, worse, his wife." He sat and stretched out his legs. "Lay out your coat. Perhaps it will dry before we reach Plymouth."

Jonathan draped his overcoat across the seat opposite Langsford and placed his hat on the overhead rack. "I don't think it's terribly wet," he said, and settled in on a seat by the window. "The rain didn't start until I was in my cab, actually." He opened the smaller of his two bags, a slightly battered brown leather case, which Langsford had placed on the seat. "I don't doubt that it will dry." He pulled out a small, tan-covered volume and placed it next to him.

"Reading already?" Langsford asked slyly, raising an eyebrow. "You might at least make a pretence of waiting until we started."

"You'll be asleep before we're out of the City," Jonathan pointed out, "if past experience is any indicator of future behavior."

"Nonsense," Langsford replied, and held up his hand as Jonathan opened his mouth to enumerate the list of train journeys the two had taken in the fifteen years they'd known each other. "No. I know. What book is it this time?" he asked. Jonathan smiled at the change of subject and held up the slim volume. "Ghost stories?" Langsford asked. "Not your usual fare, is it?"

"Guy Mansell-Jones sent it. Dr. James, you see." He showed Langsford the cover. "He thought I'd be interested." Langsford nodded, and Jonathan placed the book on the seat again.

"Odd of Guy to send it over, even if Dr. James wrote them,"

Langsford said. "Neither of us is what one might call a student of the occult or the macabre."

"I don't know," Jonathan said, tucking the book closer to him. "His note simply said I might enjoy these and find them useful."

"Useful? I can't imagine how. Is the house haunted? If so, perhaps we should study up. Guy's quite the occultist, even if we aren't. Perhaps he knows something we don't." He stretched out across the seat.

"My cousin never mentioned anything, and I certainly saw nothing when I was there," Jonathan said thoughtfully. "And how would Mansell-Jones know anything about it at all? He never met my cousin, much less visited him at the farm." He pulled another book out of the case and handed it across the carriage. "He also sent this one; it may be more to your liking. Ersk ine Childers. An espionage novel of some sort." He opened the case wider and began to remove the contents. He unfolded a white silk handkerchief and laid it carefully on the train seat, as Langsford gave the cover a cursory look and ruffled through the pages.

"That does sound interesting." He handed the book back. "I'll look into it after we settle in." Jonathan placed it on top of the other book. He emptied the case, meticulously laying everything on the handkerchief. He placed the last item, an old worn double florin he'd had since he was a boy, on the pile, checked the case again, counted the items, then began replacing them in the case in the reverse order he'd taken them out.

He was folding the handkerchief, corners to center, when Langsford asked, "Did you bring anything to eat?" Jonathan paused. The negative must have read in his face, because Langsford smiled as he jerked a thumb upwards at a brown paper wrapped parcel on the overhead. "Don't worry. I thought you'd forget. I had Mrs. Galloway pack us some sandwiches and beer this morning while you were out. We'll eat after Exeter."

Jonathan finished folding the handkerchief, tucked it in, and closed the case. "Thank you. I suppose I had too much on my mind to think about food this morning." The guard paused at the window and checked the door of the carriage before passing down the train. "I barely made it from the solicitors to the station as it was."

"Still, it's a bit of luck, your mother's cousin leaving you everything, house, money, and all." Langsford crossed his legs and leaned against the carriage wall, the first step, Jonathan knew, to dozing off shortly after the train left the station. "I'll miss you dreadfully if you decide to live down there permanently, being a man of property now."

Jonathan covered his discomfort by standing and shoving the case onto the overhead. "I'm not sure I shall," he said. "I haven't been to Landreath but that one summer, and I don't know that I'll want to sequester myself entirely." The train moved with a slight lurch, and he stumbled. Langsford leaned forward and caught him by the arm before he fell. "Thank you," Jonathan said, flushing slightly. "Everything seems a little off balance this morning."

Langsford sat back in his seat. "Well, you needn't worry that I'll ask anyone else to take your room if you do decide to stay there. Solitude will suit me better than an unpleasant companion." Jonathan sat as the train eased out of the station, and a squall of rain spattered against the window. "Have you decided at least whether you'll be coming back with me at the end of the week?" Langsford asked.

Jonathan shook his head. "No. I haven't thought much past the next few days. I suppose I will, but . . ." he hesitated. "I really don't know. There's no reason to do so, actually."

"Except the pleasure of my company."

Jonathan nodded and looked out the window to cover his momentary embarrassment. "Of course," he said lightly. "It will be *dreadfully* boring without you nattering about the place all day."

"You won't be rid of me quite so easily," Langsford said, stretching out on the seat. "I fully intend to hold you to your invitation. London's a pit in August, and by then I'll be more than ready to join you in your life of leisure."

"Come as often as you like, and stay as long as you like. I have to warn you though: Trevaglan isn't very large, just an old farmhouse, so there won't be any house parties. I'm afraid it will be terribly dull."

"All the better," Langsford said easily. "It will be just the two of us, a pair of old bachelors. We'll loaf about in the sun during the day and play chess and piquet in the evening. You'll complain when I win, and then I will have to throw the next game to cheer you up. Not terribly sporting of you to drive me to such lengths." Langsford leaned forward, his face suddenly serious. "I really will miss you if you decide to stay, Williams. I know you'll accuse me of the worst possible sort of sentimentality, but there it is. We've been together so long I shan't know what to do with myself." Jonathan shifted uncomfortably in his seat, and Langsford leaned back and smiled, tucking his hands behind his head. "There. I *have* embarrassed you. Pick up your spook book and read something really chilling to unsettle you further while I fulfill your predictions by taking a nice long nap." He closed his eyes, and Jonathan picked up the book of ghost stories. "Mind you don't shriek in terror," Langsford said sternly, barely opening his eyes. "I will be very put out if you disturb my rest." He closed his eyes and settled himself in.

Jonathan opened the book and began to read the first story, but found it didn't hold his attention; his mind was running down other tracks. He closed the book and set it on the seat next to him and watched for a while out the window as London steamed by, bleak and grey, the cold April rain dripping from its eaves. After a few minutes his gaze wandered to the fittings and pictures in the carriage and finally came to rest on the man sleeping on the seat opposite him. Langsford's hand had slipped from behind his head as he'd fallen asleep, mussing his sandy hair. Jonathan studied his face, relaxed in sleep: the smile lines around his eyes, the slightly turned up nose, the wide, full mouth, curved in a smile even at rest. Jonathan envied Langsford his ability to fall asleep anywhere at a moment's notice—his own slumber was much more unsettled.

Theirs had been an odd friendship from the start. They'd known each other slightly at Eton, and as did all the boys in his year, Jonathan had idolized Alayne Langsford-Knight, an older boy who'd always been at the center of a large circle, drawing everyone in with his frank good humor, breezing through exams and athletics with the same cheerful ease. Jonathan, quieter and more studious, had watched from a distance, treasuring the occasional contact and notice the older boy chanced to bestow.

When Jonathan had gone up to Cambridge after that terrible summer in Cornwall, Langsford had, to his surprise, renewed the acquaintance almost immediately. They were both at King's, and at the end of the first week Langsford had stopped by his rooms and asked him to dine that evening. They'd gone to a popular public house, and as he gradually overcame his diffidence and shyness under the beam of Langsford's unfailing cheerfulness, Jonathan realized that Langsford had done so to deflect any taint of gossip that might have made Jonathan's first weeks at the university difficult. After Jonathan's mother's death that spring from a short, severe attack of influenza, his father had married with indecent haste, the reason for which became rapidly apparent: Jonathan's half brother was born barely five months after the funeral. The scandal had been tremendous—Jonathan's father had been an MP for a small borough in Sussex. Jonathan had gone straight from Cornwall to Cambridge, and his sister had remained with his father's parents in Norfolk, where she'd lived until her marriage eleven years ago.

The acquaintance, initiated simply as a gesture wholly typical of Langsford, who had never stood for malicious or bullying behavior, had, to Jonathan's astonishment and the amusement of Langsford's peers, quickly developed into an intimate friendship. He frequently spent the holidays with Langsford's family in Yorkshire, and they were rarely apart while at Cambridge. Most thought of Jonathan as the faithful shadow, but after matriculating and going down to London to read for the Bar, Langsford's initial letters had been full of a vague surprise at how much he missed Jonathan's company. Their habit of taking holidays together dated to this period, and they traveled extensively, though never, somehow, visiting the West Country, and when Jonathan followed him to London, it seemed only natural to Langsford that they share rooms until Jonathan established himself in business. Within a year it seemed just as natural that they continue on as they were.

Now, nine years later and because of this inheritance, everything had changed.

Although he hadn't visited Andrew Penhyrddin, his mother's cousin, at the old farm after going up to university, Jonathan had maintained correspondence with him, and they had met yearly at Penhyrddin's club when the older man had come to London from Cornwall. Initially, their meetings had been awkward—they had too many painful subjects to avoid in conversation for there to be any ease in their meeting. As time passed, however, and they fell back into the more comfortable interaction that had been customary for them that first summer, Jonathan looked forward to Penhyrddin's visits.

Still, Jonathan had been a startled when he received the letter from the solicitors in Penzance telling him of the older man's death and informing him that he was the principal legatee of the estate. Surprise deepened to shock when, upon meeting with the representative of the solicitors who'd traveled to London to review the estate with him, he learned that he had inherited not only the house and land, but also over 80,000 pounds, after duties and minor bequests. He was, suddenly and unexpectedly, quite wealthy.

When the will had passed probate, he'd resigned his position at the bank, and in the two weeks since he had buried himself in the legal paperwork surrounding the estate and in planning this journey to take possession of the house. He'd stayed firmly anchored in the immediate present, meticulously reading each document, purposefully avoiding looking beyond this week. And, as was his custom, Langsford had unconsciously touched on the very reason why.

The train jolted slightly through a junction, and Jonathan looked back out the window. He was in love with Langsford, and knew it. He had known, in fact, from the time Langsford had left Cambridge. While Langsford's letters had mentioned missing his company, Jonathan's loneliness had been intense and painful. He had been horrified, having believed he'd buried all such feelings deeply after leaving Cornwall that summer, and the shock of the realization that he hadn't, that such feelings still lived within him, and for Langsford, had played as much havoc with his mind as had the sheer pain of his loneliness. His friends at Cambridge had laughed at his silences, not suspecting the source, and his studies had suffered to the point that the dean of his college had taken him aside and given him a stern dressing down. Jonathan listened, throwing himself into his studies with a passion that bordered on obsession, taking prize after prize, but all the while living for and dreading the weekly letter from London.

He knew, somehow, that Langsford wouldn't despise him for such feelings, but he would pity him, and that would be infinitely worse.

Jonathan folded the white handkerchief, corners to center, and tucked it into his carrying case as the train slid into the long, narrow shed of the Penzance railway station.

The trip had been an uneventful one. Langsford dozed while Jonathan read or sat looking out the window as the scenery whirled past. After Langsford woke, he pulled down his travel kit and handed Jonathan a sandwich wrapped in brown paper and a bottle of beer, and they settled into a companionable quiet as the afternoon wore on. A thin rain spattered against the windows, and the countryside was a soft new green veiled in the grey of the drizzle. They left the carriage briefly at Exeter, stretching their legs, and changed trains at Plymouth. The new train pottered across country, stopping at small towns and cities along the route; they finished a second round of sandwiches later in the afternoon. The train rattled across the Saltash Bridge shortly before dark, and Langsford put down the window so he could lean out and watch the double arches pass. He dozed again after nightfall, but Jonathan sat staring out into the darkness, watching the telegraph poles flash by, gleaming wetly in the brief light of the train's passage.

The train lurched to a stop in the station, brakes hissing, and he stood and shrugged on his greatcoat as Langsford opened the carriage door and stepped out onto the platform. Holding the brown leather case tightly, Jonathan followed, looking around, blinking against the smoke-filtered glare of the electric lights; there had been gas lamps when he'd been there before, but otherwise the place seemed little changed. The roof and trusses of the shed disappeared in the gloom above them. Langsford waved, and a porter trotted up the platform as the steam hissed and billowed around the engine.

"We're expecting someone from the White Hart Inn," Langsford said. "I wired this morning. Please find him and send him to us, and bring someone to handle our bags." The boy touched his cap and hurried away. A harried looking woman from further down the train brushed by, carrying one child asleep on her shoulder, holding another, fretful and crying, by the hand. She called over her shoulder, her voice rich and soft with the music of the region in spite of her weariness. Jonathan shivered at the sound. Two more children, boys, came pelting up the platform, shouting as they passed. "God spare me from ever having children," Langsford muttered as they ran by. Jonathan looked up at him in surprise. "They're delightful in the abstract," Langford explained, "but the reality is a bit more troublesome. As fond as I am of Charles's brood, I'm always glad to get away."

"They're perfectly acceptable as long as they aren't running in packs," Jonathan said, "and I don't think your nieces and nephews fall into that category."

"That may be," Langsford said. "Still, I'm somewhat surprised that you enjoy them so much."

Jonathan shrugged. "Children are simpler than adults," he

said. "They're intrinsically honest."

"Good evening, gentlemen, good evening, good evening," a stout, red-faced man called as he hurried up the platform. "Are you Mr. Williams and Mr. Langsford-Knight?" He wiped his forehead with a large handkerchief as he approached. "Mr. Langsford-Knight, Esquire, that would be, sir, sorry sir. The porter fellow said you was waiting, and if you aren't them, well, I beg your pardon and I'll pass on." He tucked the handkerchief in his pocket.

"Yes," Langsford replied. "We are they. You would . . ."

"Dawkins, sir, Alfred Dawkins, at your service," the man said, puffing and bowing. "From the White Hart, sir, and we'll be taking care of you right, sir. We have supper waiting for you." He straightened, put his fingers in his mouth and whistled shrilly. Jonathan glanced at Langsford, who shrugged. "Will!" Dawkins shouted. "William! Get yer up here and get the gentlemen's bags!" Rubbing his hands together, Dawkins turned back to the two men. "Now, sirs, let William get your bags. And I will take care of you." A young boy trundled a hand cart up the platform, put it down and bobbed his head. "Will, get the gentlemen's bags, and mind you don't damage them. Gentlemen, if you'll follow me, I have a carriage to take you. We're only a short ways, sirs, but damp and chilly tonight, and can't have you walking about in the rain." He started off down the platform as William tucked their bags into the cart. "This way, please, gentlemen, this way, please."

"Unless I'm mistaken," Langsford said conversationally as they followed him down the platform, "you aren't from this part of the county ."

"Right, sir, right you are," Dawkins said; he bowed without interrupting his progress down the platform. "Very astute of you sir, very astute. London born and bred sir, if you please." He led them through the gates into the main station.

"You're quite a way from home, then," Langsford said. Jonathan shot Langsford a glance and sighed; Langsford was fascinated with eccentric characters, and never failed to encourage them in their eccentricities. Langsford simply returned the look, his face all innocence.

"Yes, sir, it is, sir," Dawkins answered as he held the station door open. "My wife's people are from here about. I came out one summer to help with the hotel, and, well, it suited me, so I stayed. Here we are, gentlemen," he said as he crossed the pavement to a small carriage and pulled the door open. "You settle in, and I'll ride up with the cab man." They hurried through the drizzle and climbed in.

Dawkins shut the door. The carriage shook as he clambered up onto the seat, then jerked as they pulled away from the station and clattered down the street into town.

CHAPTER 2

"Sign here, Mr. Williams, and that will be everything we need for the time being."

Jonathan dipped the pen and scratched his signature across the last sheet, blew on it, and handed the document across the desk. Fastnedge, his late cousin's solicitor, scanned the document quickly, then tucked it into the sheaf of papers sitting on the desk. He took off his pince-nez, laid it on the desk, folded his hands, and leaned forward. "Very good," he said. "That should be all for the moment." He hesitated, then said, "I do hope, Mr. Williams, that you will contact us if there is anything you need regarding the estate, or if you have any questions about the late Mr. Penhyrddin's affairs. We will, of course, prepare to transfer any documents to your counsel, and will do so at such a time as you require." He indicated Langsford with a slight gesture of his long, thin hand.

Jonathan shook his head. "That won't be necessary," he said. "Mr. Langsford-Knight is a friend, not my solicitor. I would very much like to retain your services."

"It would be both a pleasure and an honor, sir." Fastnedge sat back, a brief smile creasing his narrow, lined face. He looked unaccustomed to the gesture. "Our firm has been associated with your family for a number of years, and we are delighted to continue. I appreciate your confidence." He picked up the papers and shuffled them, stacking them neatly. He pulled a cord hanging on the wall behind him; Jonathan heard the slight tinkle of a bell in the outer office. The door opened, and a clerk entered. Fastnedge handed him the papers, then turned his attention back to Jonathan. "Have you any questions?" he asked as the clerk left the room and quietly closed the door. "I am afraid I can tell you very little about the farm itself. Mr. Penhyrddin kept the accounts himself. The workers have all stayed on pending your arrival; the estate was authorized to pay their wages, as you know."

"I certainly hope they stay," Jonathan said. "I know very little about running a farm, I'm afraid."

"James Hale is a good man," Fastnedge said. "He will advise you. He and his wife are quite capable. He runs the farm, and she is the housekeeper."

"I remember him, though I don't believe he was married at the time."

"Indeed?" Fastnedge said. "You were here in the summer of '93, I believe."

"'92, actually," Jonathan replied.

"Ah." Fastnedge paused. "Yes," he said after a moment. "'92." He picked up his pince-nez and polished them with his handkerchief. "No. Hale would not have been married then." He tucked his handkerchief and pince-nez in his pocket and stood. "It has been most pleasant to meet you again, Mr. Williams. If I may be of any more assistance, do not hesitate to call upon me." He stepped around the desk and held out his hand. Jonathan shook it; it was dry and papery, as if the man had grown like his documents across the years he'd handled them. Langsford followed suit, and the solicitor escorted them to the door of his office. "Thank you again, Mr. Williams," he said as he opened the door. "Perhaps both of you would do me the honor of dining with me when you return?" Jonathan murmured a polite assent, and Fastnedge signaled to the clerk, who stood. "Good day, gentlemen," Fastnedge said, standing in the doorway.

"This way, if you please, sirs," the clerk said softly. He led them through the front room, toward the door to the street.

Jonathan paused in the doorway and glanced back. Fastnedge was watching him, his eyes sharp and critical, as he unconsciously polished his pince-nez. He nodded slightly, then closed the door to his office behind him.

"Congratulations!" Langsford said, slapping Jonathan on the shoulder as they descended the stairs. "You are now a gentleman of property."

Jonathan snorted. "I certainly don't feel like one," he said. "I'm sure that will all change when I have to start giving orders and keeping the books." The rain of the night before had given way to a clear, warm day, and Jonathan could see the sun glittering on the bay at the end of the street. "You were rather quiet during the entire conversation," he said, as they strolled down the street toward the promenade. "I almost didn't know you were there."

"I thought it best you handle it on your own," Langsford replied. "Make no mistake, I'd have spoken if anything seemed out of order, but the old stick knows his business. I think you'll have no problems if you keep him on."

"I'm glad you think so," Jonathan said. "I was going to ask you."

Langsford leaned on the iron railing and looked out over the harbor. "He'll do well," he said. "A proper gentleman of the old school. Very dependable, very responsible, and *very* staid." He frowned slightly. "Though I must say, he was a bit abrupt at the end. Not quite sure what to make of that."

"I noticed," Jonathan said. "Perhaps he was annoyed by having got the year wrong, the year I was here before, I mean."

"Most likely," Langsford said off-handedly, and stretched. "No matter. Now for a week of leisure for me, and a week—or more—of farming lessons from the redoubtable Hale for you."

They walked along the promenade, Langsford making increasingly outrageous suggestions as to what crops to grow, and Jonathan responding to each with a calm "sheep and hay." They reached the Queen's Hotel just as Langsford recommended butterflies and mahogany trees ("Just think of the time it will save: The collectors can catch the butterflies and build the display cases all in one place!"), and Jonathan took him firmly by the elbow and led him, protesting, into the dining room. They ate a leisurely luncheon, then wandered back through the town toward their own hotel. They had packed their bags that morning before leaving for the solicitor's chambers, and Fastnedge had already made arrangements, per Jonathan's instructions, to have someone come to the hotel to take them back to the farm that afternoon.

"Did your cousin keep a carriage?" Langsford asked. "Or are we to be fetched in a farm cart? I'm certain he didn't own a motor."

"I believe a carriage," Jonathan answered as they turned a corner and walked up the main street in the town, "but he never used it while I was there. I assume we'll travel as he and I did: in the dogcart."

"We have a perfect day for it," Langsford said, "and I must say, I won't miss the smell of fish." He indicated the couple of fishing smacks anchored behind the harbor's breakwater. "Promise me at least that there will be no fish." They started up the hill toward their hotel; the big square tower of a church loomed above them on the hill.

"Only for breakfast, if you like. There are several fishermen who set out from the village, or were, in any case, but that's a mile or so away, and so won't bother you." He glanced at Langsford, a picture of robust health, his face ruddy with the sea breeze. "Such a delicate constitution," he said with exaggerated sympathy. "I'll tell the housekeeper you are to be treated with the utmost care. South facing room. Warm blankets. Weak tea. Gently perfumed air . . . "

Langsford raised his eyebrows. "If you do, you will soon regret it," he said. "I'll throw you in the sea at the first suggestion of it."

"Ah," Jonathan said, "you seem to forget I am a man of property now. I will simply have my trusty men throw *you* in, should you attempt anything of the sort."

"I am suitably cowed by your threat of brute force," Langsford retorted, "and I will have to resort to cunning instead. My mind is subtle and complex. Your fate is sealed."

Jonathan smiled. "In that case my fate is sealed indeed. I will remain dry, and safely on the shore." He looked up the street toward their hotel.

Dawkins stood on the threshold, his arms folded on his belly. The boy who'd helped him at the station the night before was handing their bags to a man bent over the back of a freshly painted and polished dogcart drawn up a little beyond the door. The man's back was to them, his face shadowed as he stowed the bags under the seats.

"Good afternoon, Dawkins," Langsford called as they approached. "I take it this is the man from the farm?"

"Yes sir, it is, sir," Dawkins replied. "Here, young fellow, here are your gentlemen. Turn around quick now, turn around. Don't be having your back turned on your gentlemen."

The man gave one last shove on the bag, then straightened and pulled off his cap. "Good afternoon, sir," he said, his voice a soft, husky burr.

My God, Jonathan thought, frozen with the shock of recognition. *It's Nat.*

Cornwall 1892

He had wandered the fields and cliffs around the farm for weeks that spring, the warm, gentle Cornish air gradually healing the knot in his chest and the ache in his throat. His mother had died shortly before Easter, and when her cousin, who had traveled to Sussex for her funeral, offered to take Jonathan back to Cornwall for the summer, Jonathan's father had accepted with alacrity. The Lent half was finished; Jonathan had matriculated and had been accepted to King's College.

Two days after the funeral, Jonathan was on the train bound for the family home he'd never seen, with an older man he barely knew, whose moods veered between a worried concern for his young guest and a cold, simmering anger. They spoke very little; Jonathan spent most of the journey staring out the window of the carriage, dry eyed and bleak. A man from the farm, a few years older than Jonathan, with the curling black hair and black eyes of the people of the coast, met them at the Penzance station with a dogcart, and they rode quietly through the dusk, around the bay and past small, whitewashed thatched cottages and stone hedges nearly covered with moss and ferns—a farmer's wife had tucked wallflowers in the hedge walls at one point, and they glowed in the last light like stars. When they reached the fields and hills on the other side of the bay, the gorse was in bloom, and the scent lay heavy around him, perfuming the still evening air. His cousin had ridden on the seat with the driver, asking questions about the farm that were answered in a soft lilting tone that Jonathan had never heard before, but which reverberated with something in his blood; he was of these people, taking after his slim, dark-haired, quiet mother, rather than his fair, heavily built, and brash father. Jonathan listened with half an ear, hearing the sound and music of the men's voices—his cousin's accent had softened as he spoke—rather than the words.

At the farm he had been left largely to his own devices; Andrew Penhyrddin was an odd combination of gentleman farmer and scholar recluse and socialized very little with the neighborhood, so Jonathan filled his evenings reading from the old man's library and his days exploring the surrounding countryside. He walked the footpath that led across the black, rocky headland that jutted into the ocean, then down to the cluster of cottages that comprised the village of Landreath at the mouth of its small river, barely more than a stream that tumbled through a wooded ravine from the fertile uplands. He climbed the steep cobbled streets and dawdled on the quay, watching the village women mending the fishing nets or hanging wash to dry, sometimes staying late to see the fishing boats riding the setting sun and cliff shadows into the quay. He skirted the fields where the spring hay was growing, thick and fragrant, explored the small copses scattered across the downs, and lay in the sun on the short turf on the hill behind the farmhouse, watching the clouds chase each other across the brilliant blue dome of the sky.

His favorite retreat, however, was a small beach he found early in his stay, cupped in a cove between two rock outcroppings directly below the farm. The cliffs here dipped to only thirty feet or so above the sea, and late one afternoon, when the sun was hot and the air still, he'd clambered through the gorse and over the rocks down to the sea. The beach was small, a sandy crescent barely a hundred feet wide and ten deep when the tide was full, but completely sheltered from the winds, and completely private. He'd stripped off his clothes and dove into the calm sea, puffing and blowing from the sudden shock of the chilly water, then scrambled back onto the beach to sit on a rock by the surf's edge until he dried sufficiently to dress and climb back to the farm for tea. He came to the beach often, and when the loneliness and sorrow were more than he could stand, wept there until he had no more tears.

The last Sunday in April was such a day. He had received a letter from his father by afternoon post the day before, but hadn't read it until he and Penhyrddin had returned from church services and were seated at Sunday luncheon. It was a short letter, and Jonathan read it while the kitchen maid was serving. He lowered it and gazed blankly ahead for a few moments, then carefully folded the letter, slipped it back into its envelope, and laid it next to his plate.

"I hope all is well with your father," Penhyrddin said, cutting his mutton and taking a bite.

Jonathan nodded, staring at his plate.

Penhyrddin took a sip of water and cleared his throat. "Jonathan," he said. "Are you ill? You've gone quite pale." Jonathan shook his head, but didn't speak. "I don't want to seem inquisitive," Penhyrddin said, "but was there any bad news?"

"No, sir," Jonathan said, not looking up.

"That will do, Rose," Penhyrddin said. "We will serve ourselves now." The maid nodded and placed the dish in the center of the table. "Well, for heaven's sake, lad," Penhyrddin said after she'd left, "don't make me ask more directly. It only embarrasses you, and makes me seem one of the village hens, scratching for gossip."

"My father was married yesterday," Jonathan said in a low voice and then jerked his gaze from his plate to his cousin's face. Penhyrddin had slammed his fork down on the table, and his mouth had gone to a thin, hard line.

"I rather suspected something of the sort was in the offing," he said tersely, "which is why you're here, and not with his people. I would I could have brought your sister here also, but she was already gone."

"You suspected, sir?"

"Yes, as did your mother, poor thing. She wrote me shortly before she was taken ill." He picked up his water glass, his hand trembling. "We were always quite close, even after she married your father. She asked me then if you and Caroline could come and stay here for the summer. She wanted you safely away from home. She was afraid there was about to be a very public scandal."

Jonathan stared at him for a long moment, then looked back at his plate. "May I be excused, sir?" he asked. "I'm afraid I have no appetite."

Penhyrddin's face softened. "Of course, of course. Perhaps you should lie down." He reached over and patted Jonathan's hand. "Heaven knows you've had enough shocks this summer."

"I believe I'll go for a bathe," Jonathan said as he pushed back from the table and stood.

"Do be careful," Penhyrddin said worriedly. "The sea is still a bit chill." He hesitated. "Shall I send someone along with you?"

"No thank you, sir," Jonathan replied. "I had rather be alone, I think. I'll take care."

"Very well, very well. Just don't stay too long."

"No, sir," Jonathan said, and left the room. He crossed through the hall and the drawing room, then down the flight of low steps toward his room, which was located at the end of a wing that had been added on to the original house; his cousin had given him the room to allow him some privacy. He changed from his church clothes into a pair of flannel trousers, a loose cotton shirt, and a waistcoat, and pulled on a pair of stout boots. Tucking a piece of toweling from his bath stand under his arm, he slipped out the low casement window, skirted the barn and outbuildings, climbed the stile, and walked down across the pasture toward the cliffs.

Sheep scattered as he passed them, and he scrambled through the gorse at the cliffs' edge and clambered down the black, tumbled boulders toward the beach. He scooped a handful of water from a spring that bubbled out of the rocks halfway down and drank, then climbed the rest of the way down to the beach. He dropped his towel on the warm sand, and sat and untied his boots. He placed them and his stockings next to the towel, rolled up his trousers, and waded through the few feet of surf out to his rock. He sat, his arms hooked around his knees, staring out across the wide bay toward Penzance, but no tears came.

After a time, he climbed down and waded back to the beach. Still dry-eyed, he stripped, then folded his clothing carefully and placed them on the towel. He waded out in the surf, and when the wave tops reached his mid-thigh, dove into the water and swam straight out from the shore. He swam past the surf line and the rocks jutting out from the cliff; the swell was broad and easy once he was clear of the land. He lay on his back for a moment, catching his breath, then started back to shore. The current had swept him down shore a bit, and he fought against it as he swam around the boulders that broke the swells into foam. His feet touched bottom, and he staggered out of the surf and onto the rocks, then climbed around to the beach, collapsing on the sand next to his clothes and panting for air, his heart pounding. He rolled over and stretched out on the hot sand, the sun warm on his legs, chest, and face. His eyelids fluttered as his breathing grew deeper, and, exhausted by the exertion of the swim and the curious lack of emotion, he slept.

A prod in his ribs woke him, and for a moment he was disoriented, not knowing where he was.

"Well, if this bain't a pretty enough picture for the artist folks to paint." A man was standing over him, silhouetted against the sun. Jonathan scrambled back and grabbed his clothes, pulling them and the towel to cover his middle. The man laughed and squatted down next to him. "Eh, you don' have worry, Mister Jonathan. I'll not be painting your picture, and I haven't any camera." It was one of the farm hands, the man who had met the train the night Jonathan and Penhyrddin had arrived in Cornwall. Jonathan had seen him now and again in the weeks that had followed, but hadn't spoken more than a few words to him.

"Did my cousin send you?" Jonathan asked, torn between pulling on his trousers and clutching them closer.

The man cocked his head. "Now why would he be doin' that?" he asked. "No, I often come down of a Sunday afternoon for a dip." He held out his hand. "My name's Nat Boscawen. We've not been properly introduced."

Jonathan hesitated for a moment, then shook his hand. Nat raised his eyebrows and sat back on his heels. "Of course," he said, "I can't say as the introduction's proper, you bein' naked and all." Jonathan blushed furiously, and Nat laughed. "Well, it wouldn't be gentlemanlike of me to leave you in such a state by yourself. And I'll be wantin' my dip."

He untied the laces of his heavy boots, and tugged them off. Standing, he pulled his rough shirt over his head and dropped it on the sand, then unbuckled the heavy leather belt around the waist of his trousers and let them fall. He stepped out of them and glanced down at Jonathan. "What are you gapin' at, lad? Have you never seen a man naked before?"

Jonathan looked away quickly. Nat laughed again and walked toward the water. Jonathan had seen the other boys at school naked on occasion, but never anyone like this. He watched Nat's back as he walked down the beach. He was tanned dark on the neck and arms, and his back was startlingly white in comparison, broad shoulders tapering to a narrow waist and hips. His buttocks and legs were solid from the work on the farm, muscles moving smoothly under the pale skin. Nat waded into the surf, and a wave struck him at mid-thigh, the water splashing over him. The water had just covered his thighs when he turned, water droplets glittering on his shoulders and in the dark hair on his chest. A thin dark line ran from his navel down to his groin.

"What! Are you not coming in?" he shouted.

Jonathan shook his head. "No," he called back. "I've been in already."

"'Tis no good reason not to now," Nat said. "Shall I come out and get you?" He started to wade back to the shore.

Jonathan scrambled to his feet, still holding his clothes over his middle, unsure as to what he wanted to do, but fairly certain that this man was more than capable of wading out of the sea and tossing him in. He was flustered; he wasn't in the least accustomed to servants being this familiar, either here or at home, and he wasn't sure what course to take. Nat had stopped, calf deep in the surf, his hands on his hips.

"Well?" he said. "What are you waitin' for? Midsummer?"

Gritting his teeth, Jonathan dropped his clothes and walked down the beach to the water. Nat grinned and dove into the waves, surfacing a few yards farther out. Jonathan waded in to his waist, then pushed forward into the water and swam out to where Nat was floating on his back. Jonathan stood, his feet touching the sandy bottom in the troughs between the swells. "That's better," Nat said, standing next to him. "Come, swim out to the rock, and then I'll race you back." He pointed to a rock a couple of hundred yards offshore, the last portion of one of the two outcrops that cradled the beach. The swells from the bay washed over the top of the rock, the spray sparkling in the westering sun. "Don't be getting too close, though. The waves'll do you for sure."

They swam slowly out toward the rock, and when they were about thirty feet off, and Jonathan began to feel the pull from the currents eddying around it, Nat stopped and tread water. "Now," he said. "The last one to shore carries the kit back." And he kicked over and started back toward the beach.

Caught slightly off guard, Jonathan set off in his wake. For the most part he kept his head down, only glancing ahead occasionally when the swell lifted him; Nat was widening the gap between them. He was still tired, he knew, from the earlier outing, and he wasn't a terribly fast swimmer, but he pushed himself; he wasn't about to let this farmhand get the better of him without a fight. The current pulled him slightly out of his course, and he adjusted, aiming right for the middle of the beach.

He was still about fifteen yards out when he saw Nat hit shallow water and stand, just twenty feet in front of him. Kicking harder, he felt a swell lift him, and the breaking wave caught him up and pushed him toward the shore. Looking up again, he scanned the beach, but didn't see Nat on the shore, where he expected him to be. The wave broke, and as he started to tumble in the foam, he realized that Nat was directly in front of him, still wading through the surf. He had just time to shield his head with his arms before he took the other man from behind, right below the knees. Nat staggered backward, falling heavily, and Jonathan was pinned beneath him briefly, his face shoved in the sand and foam. He choked, inhaling seawater, and struggled to get free. Nat rolled off him, then grabbed his arms and pulled him roughly to his feet.

"What were you doing that for?" Nat said angrily. "That'll be some university way they have of winning an honest race?" Jonathan coughed, spitting out water and sand, trying to bend over as he gagged, but Nat held his arms tightly.

"I'm sorry . . ." Jonathan said, coughing. "I'm sorry . . . I didn't mean to . . ." He coughed again, his knees shaking. Another wave hit him and he fell forward; Nat caught him.

"Eh," Nat said, the anger fading from his face. "Bain't your fault, I suppose. Too much water too early in the year." He slipped an arm under Jonathan's and half carried him up the beach. "We'll have to get you used to it." He helped Jonathan sit on his towel, and squatted down beside him. "Are you all right, lad?" he asked gently. "Are you hurt anywhere?"

Jonathan shook his head. "No," he said, spitting out more sand and brushing off his face. "I'm well." He looked up at Nat. "I *am* sorry. Are you all right?"

Nat laughed. "It'd take more than a tumble in the sea to hurt me," he said. "I was practically born in it, and swam before I could walk." He glanced down. "Did you bring a mug or anything for water? I'll fetch some from the spring for you." Jonathan shook his head. "Well, I have a paddick and a cup. It'll have to do." He rooted through the satchel that sat on the sand next to his clothes. "Are you hungry?" he asked over his shoulder. "I mean, once you've done retching up half the sea."

Jonathan smiled. "Yes, actually. I didn't have a noon meal."

"Well, then, no wonder you took a plunger." Nat pulled a cloth-wrapped bundle out of the satchel and handed it to Jonathan. "Here's some bread and cheese. You open it up, and I'll get you some water, and we can have an eat." He pulled a small, battered pitcher and tin cup out of the satchel.

"Thank you," Jonathan said.

"I'd offer ye some of my beer," Nat said, "but like as not you'd be all wobbly-kneed on the first mouthful." He trotted up the beach and quickly clambered over the rocks to the small pool at the spring. Jonathan unwrapped the bundle—a crusty loaf of rough bread and a thick round of hard cheese—and set it on the cloth. He thought for a moment to check if Nat had a knife for cutting it in the satchel, but decided to wait. He looked up; Nat was climbing down across the rocks, carefully balancing the little pitcher of water. With a slight shock, Jonathan realized they were both still naked; he'd forgotten in the confusion of the water and sand. He reached over and began to untangle his trousers from his shirt and waistcoat, then hesitated, suddenly shy at standing up to pull them on.

"What are you bothering with them for?" Nat asked as he sat down beside him and handed him the full pitcher. "Here's your water." He reached over, grabbed the satchel, and pulled out an ivory-handled clasp knife. "Nothin's better than the sun on your skin after the sea. Besides, the sand on you will itch terrible if you should put 'em on now." He opened the knife, cut a chunk of the cheese, then tore off part of the loaf, and handed both to Jonathan. "Here. Eat."

Jonathan bit into the thick, crusty bread, suddenly aware that he was ravenous. The bread was good, plain and homey, and the cheese hard and sharp. They ate silently for a while, and Nat opened an earthenware bottle of beer and took a swallow. He wiped his mouth with the back of his hand, leaned back on his elbows and sighed. "That's grand," he said. He nestled the jar in the sand, tucked his hands behind his head, and lay back against his satchel. "It's a grand afternoon." Jonathan finished his bread and washed it down with a mouthful of water, then sat forward, arms around his knees, chewing on the rind of the cheese. The sun was warm on his skin, the light clear and liquid as it shimmered off the water of the cove. He chewed more slowly, and his eyelids drooped slightly, the warmth of the sun and a full stomach making him sleepy again.

Nat stirred and sat up. "I'm sorry about your Mum," he said, clasping his arms around his knees and looking out across the bay. "It's a hard thing, losing her so sudden."

Jonathan froze, his eyes wide open, all drowsiness banished instantly. "Thank you," he said harshly. He had, for a moment, forgotten his grief under the influence of the sun and the sea and the company, but this unexpected sympathy brought it rushing back.

"Eh, I'm sorry. Me Mum's always sayin' I'm too forward with my tongue," Nat said, glancing at him, "and I'm supposin' she's right. But still, I'm thinkin' some things are best said. Does you no good to ignore sorrow, or pretend it isn't there." Jonathan was silent, burying his sorrow in anger. "I'm also supposin' you're all bedoled for the time, but there's no better place than here for the healin' of it."

It was more than Jonathan could bear. "I appreciate your sympathy," he said, reaching for his clothes, "and thank you for the meal. However, I don't think this is either the time or the place for such conversation. Now if you'll excuse me, I'd like to get dressed." He clenched his jaw and stared straight ahead. "Well?"

"Well what, Mister Jonathan?"

He glanced over; Nat was watching him, a smile quirking the corners of his mouth. "I would like to get dressed," Jonathan said tersely. "Please turn your back."

Nat laughed out loud, falling back against his satchel. Jonathan felt his face flaming.

"Don't you think it's a bit late for that?" Nat said, sitting up again. "But if it makes you feel better, I'll look away." Whistling ostentatiously, he faced the other direction.

Jonathan furiously scrambled into his underclothes, then stood and pulled on his trousers.

"Will you be comin' down here every Sunday, then?" Nat asked over his shoulder. "I need to know if I'll be needin' a bathing costume or some such thing."

"I might, or I might not," Jonathan said as he buttoned his trousers. "And you are welcome to bathe in any state of dress or undress you please." He pulled his shirt and waistcoat on, not bothering to button them, then sat and pulled on his stockings. "It makes absolutely no difference to me."

"Here you go, lad," Nat said, and Jonathan looked up. Nat handed him a boot.

"Thank you," Jonathan said, pulling it on. He tied it, put on his other boot, then scooped his towel up and started toward the cliff. When he reached the first of the boulders, he paused. "Thank you for luncheon," he said stiffly. "I apologize if I was rude."

Nat stood and brushed the sand off his legs as he walked over. "You're welcome, lad," he said, holding out his hand. "And I 'pologize if I was a bit too forward." Jonathan hesitated, then took

Nat's hand, callused, thick and strong, in his. "Good," Nat said, and shook. Jonathan nodded and started to climb the rocky cliff. "Mister Jonathan," Nat called when he was halfway to the top, and Jonathan looked back. Nat stood in the water, hands on his hips, the waves washing about his thighs. "I'll be seein' you next Sunday, then." It was a statement, not a question.

Jonathan stared down at him, naked and gleaming in the golden sunlight, the sea foam swirling about his bare legs. "Yes," he said, then ran up the narrow path to the cliff top.

Cornwall 1906

"Williams?"

Jonathan blinked, realizing his error: Even had Nat still been alive, he would have been in his thirties. This was a boy standing by the cart, holding his cap in both hands and looking at him with a frank, appraising gaze, a boy no older than fourteen or fifteen, though big for his age. It was his size, his way of standing by the cart, the dark, tousled hair and the soft voice, not quite settled into its manhood timbre, but close, that had deceived him. The tightness in his gut loosened, and he exhaled; he hadn't been aware he'd held his breath.

"Williams," Langsford said again. "What is it? Are you all right?"

"I . . ." Jonathan said, unable to look away from the boy. "I beg pardon?" He balled his hands into fists to keep them from trembling. "I'm sorry, what did you say?"

"Are you all right?" Langsford asked again, looking worried. "You're as white as a sheet."

"I'm, yes, I'm quite all right," Jonathan said, still shaken. "I, well, I . . . I just remembered something I'd intended to ask Fastnedge." He looked at Langsford. "I'll, I suppose I'll write him about it this week. It isn't that important."

"The way you look, I should have thought it was life and death," Langsford said, then addressed the boy. "So, you're here to take us, are you lad?" he asked, and the boy nodded once.

"Very good. What's your name, then?"

"Hale, sir," the boy said. "Alexander Hale, though most everyone calls me Alec."

"Hale, is it?" Langsford asked. "Your mother and father work on the farm, do they?"

"Yes, sir," the boy answered.

"Well," Langsford said, when Jonathan didn't speak. "I'm Mr. Langsford-Knight, and this is Mr. Williams. You finish what you were doing while we settle with Mr. Dawkins."

Jonathan stirred. "No, I'll, well, I'll take care of the hotel. You see to the rest of the baggage, would you, please?" Alec nodded. Jonathan followed Dawkins into the cool darkness of the hotel, where he paid the bill. He tucked his billfolder into his pocket. "Dawkins . . ." he started.

"Yes, sir, how else may I help you, sir?" Dawkins asked as he bustled around from behind the counter. "Will," he said as the inn's boy came through the door. "You be getting back and help Maria with setting the rooms straight." The boy nodded and dashed toward the back of the inn. "Now, Mr. Williams, what do you wish, sir? How may I be of assistance?"

"I . . ." Jonathan hesitated again. "It's nothing, I suppose. I just thought I recognized the boy from the farm," he briefly waved a hand toward the bright light pouring through the front door, but I suppose that isn't possible."

"Well, sir, I wouldn't know about that, but I've found they all look much the same, the folk around here, what with them all being related in some degree, or so it seems, don't you know, sir? It's possible you know his cousin or uncle or such up in town, perhaps."

"Yes," Jonathan said. "Perhaps that's it." He crossed the room, Dawkins following behind him, chattering about how pleased he was to have had them stay, and the honor it would if he came again, and if there was anything Mr. Williams needed, simply to send word and he would be glad to be of assistance; Jonathan barely heard the words, and paid them no attention. "Yes, yes, thank you," he said absently. He blinked as he stepped back into the bright sunlight of the street.

"Your carriage, m'lord," Langsford said grandly from the back of the cart, spreading his arms wide and smiling. "Shall we travel on?" The boy—Alec—stood by the cart, still holding his hat. "Thank you, Dawkins," Langsford called. "I will be seeing you again in a week, I believe."

"Yes, sir," Dawkins said from the doorway, touching his knuckle to his forehead. "It will be a pleasure, sir."

"Don't you want to ride on the front?" Langsford asked, and Jonathan shook his head.

"May I help you up, sir?"

Jonathan caught his breath at the sound of the boy's voice; his heart pounded. "No, thank you, I'll manage," he murmured, and stepped up into the back of the cart. He sat down next to Langsford, who had settled in with his arm across the seatback. The boy donned his cap, climbed on the driving seat and, picking up the reins, clicked his tongue to the horse. The horse obeyed, his gait a slow trot clattering on the cobbles. They turned up a side street, then struck the main road, and the horse broke into a faster, easier trot. "I think the first thing you should do after you've settled in," Langsford said as they clattered up the hill, "is purchase new springs for your carriage."

They hugged the shore after they left Penzance, passing outlying houses and a small town, and then climbed away from the coast as they rounded the bay. Langsford attempted conversation for the first mile or so, but Jonathan was preoccupied and answered in short, distracted sentences; Langsford eventually gave up the effort with a slight shrug.

They crossed the uplands in relative silence, the only sounds the creaking of the harness, and cart and the splash of the horse's hooves in puddles left from the previous day's rain. At first, gaps in the hawthorn hedges and stone walls lining the road gave occasional glimpses across the fields to the sea, sparkling in the sun, but a small line of hills rose to block the view as they wound through the countryside. They rode through a few small villages, the smells of baking bread and human habitation mingling on the breeze with the scent of moist earth and sheep that had followed them across the fields. As they passed one farm, a large dog bounded out of the yard, barking furiously; the horse ignored it, and the boy spoke sharply but without urgency, his tone indicating an encounter so customary that neither human nor animal paid any real attention to one another. The dog followed them to a small stone bridge over a rushing stream, its tail wagging, before trotting back to the farm. Shortly thereafter, they passed the narrow road leading down to Landreath on the coast, and a hundred yards further, the lane to Trevaglan Farm.

A small stone cottage stood opposite the turning, its thatched eaves low over its small windows and a tidy garden behind the low hedges that separated it from the road. Smoke drifted lazily from its chimney, and as they approached the turn, the green door opened and an old woman, sixty perhaps, but ramrod straight and dour of face, stepped out. The boy pulled up the horse as she walked down the path. "Good day, Aunt Bannel," he said, doffing his cap.

"Good day, Alec Hale," she replied as she opened the gate in the hedge. He looked at Jonathan. "Welcome home, Mister Jonathan. It's been a longful while since you've been to Trevaglan."

"Thank you, Mrs. Bannel," Jonathan said as he and Langsford stood up. "Yes, it has been." He shifted uncomfortably under that cold, clear gaze, remembering the last time they'd met, two weeks and a day before he'd left Cornwall for Cambridge. She nodded as if she was sharing that memory, then looked up at Langsford. "This is my friend, Mr. Langsford-Knight," Jonathan said, and felt his face grow red, as if she shared knowledge of these thoughts, too.

"Mrs. Bannel," Langsford said and smiled. "It's a pleasure to meet you."

"Is it now?" she answered and looked at him for a long moment in silence. She glanced back at Jonathan, then at Alec.

"Perhaps it is, then." She walked back to the gate, and a lean tabby cat slipped out of the hedge and wrapped itself around her ankles. She closed the gate as Jonathan and Langsford sat, and Alec flipped the reins and they started down the lane.

"Charming neighbors," Langsford murmured, but Jonathan stayed silent.

They bounced down the lane, rounded a small hill. Jonathan was startled at how clearly he remembered every shrub, every stone in the road. Nothing had changed, or so it seemed. The lane wound between tall hedges, and then broke into the open. "We're here, sir," Alec said.

Langsford twisted in his seat. "Williams, it's beautiful," he said, looking at Jonathan. "Hold here, Alec." Alec pulled the horse up, and Langsford jumped down and walked around the front of the cart. Jonathan climbed down slowly and followed him. "It's heaven!" Langsford exclaimed. "You never told me!"

The farmhouse stood on a slight rise at the base of the hill they had just passed. Low, square, and solid, its whitewashed walls and stone slab roof glowed in the midday sun, white and warm grey against the green of the hill behind it. The house faced south, across the pastures that fell gently to the line of cliffs; the sea sparkled to a misty horizon. The small paned windows stood open, and a gentle breeze bellied the lace curtains out the casements. A large barn, wood and plaster with a thatched roof, ran at right angles to the house to help form the square of the old farmyard, and a long, low wing, built of rough stone and also thatched, stretched toward them from the near end of the house. A stone wall, running straight out from the main house, enclosed the rest of the yard, and they could see a hint of color inside the enclosure: flowers, safe from the sheep that dotted the pastures. Woody vines clung to the front of the house—climbing roses, Jonathan remembered; their scent had filled the house that June. At the foot of the rise, a ring of hawthorn trees stood at regular intervals, perhaps thirty feet apart, circling the house and farm buildings on three sides. The nearest stood just the other side of the hedge.

"August is too long to wait," Langsford said. "You'll be lucky if I'm not here to stay by mid-July." He looked over at Jonathan. "Why so silent, man?"

"I'd forgotten how beautiful it was," Jonathan said honestly. "And how much I loved this place while I was here." He smiled up at Langsford. "Perhaps it won't be such exile after all, to live here."

Langsford snorted. "Exile indeed. Let me make my packet, and I'll follow you down quickly enough."

Jonathan opened his mouth to speak, and hesitated. "There could be possibilities closer than London," he said slowly, as if the idea was only occurring to him and hadn't been at the back of his thoughts since receiving the first letter from Fastnedge. "Falmouth, perhaps, or Penzance."

Langsford hooted. "Penzance, with its fish and its staid and proper Mr. Fastnedge? I hardly think so," he said, tucking his arm in Jonathan's. Jonathan's heart pounded, but he made no immediate move to pull away, uncomfortable as he was with being touched. "No, it's here with you for a lazy life, or it's nothing. I won't do things by halves. Alec," Langsford called over his shoulder. "Drive ahead. We'll follow you up." Alec chirruped to the horse, which immediately broke into a quick trot, heading for home and hay. Jonathan moved to free his arm, but Langsford held it a moment longer. "Perhaps Penzance," he said and smiled. "But in the meantime," he gestured across the fields, "paradise."

"Paradise," Jonathan echoed; he knew better.

Alec and the cart had vanished behind the barn. Jonathan and Langsford walked up the lane toward the house and let themselves into the yard through a low wooden gate. A rosemary bush grew just inside to the right, and lavender to the left. A flagged path ran up one side of the yard, bordered by a narrow band of spring flowers between it and the stone wall, and a deeper bed of herbs and blossoms separated it from a neatly trimmed lawn. The path cut across the front of the house to another gate in the wall between the house and the barn; the kitchen garden lay beyond it, Jonathan remembered. Over their heads, swallows wheeled and chattered, ducking in and out of the eaves of the barn.

Jonathan stopped at the bottom of the two steps leading up to the front door. "Do I knock?" he asked. "Or do we just walk in?"

"Frankly," Langsford said. "I'm not quite sure."

"Mister Jonathan!" a man called, and they turned. A large man in his early forties stood by the garden gate, a broad smile on his ruddy, sunburned face. "Though I suppose I should be callin' you Mr. Williams now. Welcome home, lad!" He reached over and unlatched the gate to let himself into the yard. He was dressed in heavy work boots, rough spun trousers, and a loose white shirt with its sleeves rolled up to the elbows.

"Hale?" Jonathan asked. "James Hale?"

"So you remember," Hale said as he approached. "I wasn't sure, it's been so many years." He pulled off his cap and ran his hand through thinning red hair. "It's good to be seeing you again, lad."

"Yes, of course I remember," Jonathan said, and held out his hand. Hale wiped his own hands on his trousers, then shook Jonathan's warmly in both. "I was glad to hear you were still here," Jonathan said. "I'm afraid you'll have a lot to teach me about this place." He gestured to Langsford. "This is my friend, Mr. Langsford-Knight, who will be staying here this week."

"Good afternoon, sir," Hale said, nodding to Langsford, "and welcome. We'll do our best to take care of you right, though I don't know that we'll be up to London standards. But me wife's a good cook, and Meg the kitchen maid, too. Alec and me children mostly work on the farm, but they'll help out, too, if you need a valley or somethin' like."

Langsford smiled. "I'll try to be as little trouble as possible," he said, offering his hand. "I'm used to taking care of myself, for the most part."

"If there's anything you need, just say," Hale said. "Now, Mr. Williams let's get you both settled in. You'll be wanting tea or something to eat. Alec!" he called over his shoulder.

"Here, Dad," Alec said from the garden gate, where he stood surrounded by a small crowd of red- and sandy-haired children peeking over the fence, their eyes wide.

"Children," Langsford muttered.

"*Paradise*," Jonathan responded.

Langsford sighed. "And the serpents therein."

"Get the gentlemen's bags in, and fetch your mother," Hale was saying, "then get the cart put away."

Alec nodded. "Cassie's gone for mother," he said, "and Jamie's taken the bags."

"You'll remember me wife, Rose, too, I'll be bound," Hale said to Jonathan, and the front door to the house opened. "Here she is. Rosie, this is Mr. Langsford-Knight, who'll be staying with us this week, and you remember Mister Jonathan."

Jonathan took an involuntary step backward. "Pritchard."

The woman standing in the doorway dropped a slight curtsey. "It's Hale now, sir," she said. "James and me were married after you left." She met his eye squarely, a tall woman, heavier than he remembered, the smile lines around her blue eyes belied by the thin, hard set of her mouth.

"Then . . ." Jonathan glanced toward the children behind the gate.

"Yes sir?"

"Just that . . . I'm pleased to see you again."

"Thank you, sir. Will you want something to eat," she asked, "or shall I show you your rooms?"

"Our rooms first, please," Jonathan said, glancing at Langsford. "Then some tea in the library, I think."

She curtsied again. "This way, gentlemen." She walked into the house, and they followed her. Jonathan glanced around the dark hall; nothing had changed here, either. A broad oak staircase led to the second-floor gallery. The large drawing room ran the full width of the house on the left, with the doorway to the new wing next to the big fireplace, the library on the right of the hall, at the front of the house, the with the dining room behind it, nearest the kitchen.

She stopped at the bottom of the staircase. "I put your things in your old room, Mr. Williams," she said. "If you wish, I'll have them moved to Mr. Penhyrddin's rooms on the first floor. I've put Mr. Langsford-Knight in the front bedroom."

Jonathan shook his head. "That's perfectly good," he said. "Please show Mr. Langsford-Knight to his room, and have tea for us in half an hour. I can find my own way."

"Yes, sir," she said.

CHAPTER 3

Rose closed the door to the main house behind her and leaned against it. The worst was over, she hoped. For the thousandth time, it seemed, since the solicitor had told them of old Mr. Penhyrddin's will, she wondered what in heaven's name had possessed the man to leave the farm and everything in it to the boy who had brought such misery to her and to this house. She'd begged James to take the hundred pounds Penhyrddin had left them and use it to buy his own land, but he'd refused, saying they'd live better here and put more money away out of wages. She closed her eyes and laid her head back against the door, her mind running down the same paths it had for the last three weeks. Nothing could be proved, nothing had even been questioned at the time, but she knew. All that sorrow, all that grief, locked away for years, and brought out again because *he* was here. And now she had to fix him tea. And then supper after, and breakfast in the morning, every day for the rest of her life. Him and his lugger of a friend.

She opened her eyes. That was a handsome one, that one was, and she'd have to have a word with Meg about him before Meg went and did something foolish. They had enough little ones around the house without Meg bringing in another, and a come-by-chance at that. *God alone knows what keeps her from having a passel of brats, the silly slut*, she thought. Still, the man would only be here for a week, and she'd keep Meg busy in the kitchen and the laundry.

She pushed away from the door and, smoothing her apron, walked down the short passage past the pantries to the kitchen. Meg was cutting cake and placing the slices on a tray, and looked up as Rose came in. Rose eyed her narrowly. Her blouse looked tighter than it had earlier that morning, and the two top buttons were open.

"Well, now," Meg said, laying down the knife. "What's the first look of the new master?"

"Don't 'ee even be trying that on me, Margaret Berryman," she said as she crossed the kitchen. "I know sure enough you were watching as they came up to the house. You finish laying out tea, and take it to the library right away. The gentlemen will be down in a half hour, and you're to be back here before they are." She moved the boiling kettle off the stove and put it on a trivet on the table.

Meg laughed, not in the least intimidated by Rose's manner. "He's a proper one, isn't he?" she asked as she cut chunks of bread and placed them on the tray. "Not the new master, no. He's like old Mr. Penhyrddin, that one. He'll be nose in a book before the evenin's done. But the other, well, that'd be somethin' fine to meet walkin' home of an evening."

"That's what I mean," Rose said, lifting the teapot off the shelf and setting it down so hard that the lid rattled. "There's enough trouble with a new master settling in, without you being mixed up in the middle of it. You'll mind your manners and stay in the kitchen."

"And how am I supposed to lay out the tea things if I'm mindin' my manners in the kitchen, I'd like to know," Meg said as she scooped up the tray. "Even if I am," she said, pausing in the doorway, "gentlemen have been known to come sniffin' around for something to eat late at night, and where would they go but the kitchen?" She hurried up the passage.

Rose put two tea cups on the tray with the teapot, her hands trembling.

"There's naught you can do about Meggy, Mother," Alec said

cheerfully from the window. "There's not a man around these parts she's not set her cap for, and not a few of 'em she's caught one way or t'other." He pushed back from the window and let himself in through the kitchen door.

"What you'd know about that, I'd like to hear," Rose said, covering her discomfort by setting the silver on the tray. "I didn't raise you to be chasing after light skirts like Margaret Berryman, nor to be gossiping about them neither." Alec grinned at her as she crossed the kitchen to the linen cupboard. "Don't you be smiling at me. Shouldn't you be helping your dad?"

Alec shrugged. "We got the cart and the horse put away, and he sent me in to get summat to eat. I'll muck out the cowshed after."

"And you haven't answered my question," Rose said as she folded napkins and placed them next to the silver. "How is it you know about such goings on."

Alec pulled out a knife and cut himself a piece of bread. "Well, it bain't through anything happening, if that's what you're worried about," he said, "though she's been givin' me that eye now and again, as I get taller. Where's some cheese, Mum?"

"Where it always is, where do you think?"

"You're in a temper today," Alec said.

"And I don't need any back talk from *you* to make it worse," Rose said. "Eat your cheese and bread, and get yourself to work. And be quick about it. I don't know if we're going to need you to look after the visitin' gentlemen."

Alec bit into his bread and cheese. "Dad asked him already, Mum," he said around the mouthful, "but he said they didn't need any help."

Rose shook her head. "He may have said so, but you don't know. Foreign folk are peculiar, particularly Londoners."

"If you're needin' someone to take care of the gentlemen," Meg offered as she bustled back into the kitchen, "I might be able to finish up my chores soon enough. Good afternoon to you, Alec."

"You'll do no such thing," Rose said, clutching a napkin tightly. "You'll take that tray out and place it, then you'll get yourself back in here to start on dinner. And that's the last I want to hear on it."

"Mom . . ."Alec said.

Meg shoved the tea kettle back on the center of the stove. "That's a fine response," she said tartly as she walked over to the table and picked up the tea pot. "As if I've ever done anything amiss. All I'll be doing is makin' the gentleman comfortable whilst he's here."

"'*Makin' the gentlemen comfortable!*'" Rose said, throwing the cloth on the table. "You can do as you like in the village on your day off, Margaret Berryman, and in every hayrick between here and Penzance, but you'll not be whorin' around in this house, not while I'm running it, and not with any gentleman that's stayin' here. So just you mind."

"You're a fine one to be lecturin' me, Rose Hale," Meg snapped, planting one hand on her hip and gesturing with the pot in the other. "Scripture says let him without sin cast the first stone, and I think you'd best be watchin' what stones you're throwin' at me."

Before she even realized what she was doing, Rose slapped her across the face, hard. Meg staggered against the table, dropping the teapot, which shattered on the floor.

"*Mother!*" Alec shouted, and ran for the door. "Dad!"

"Don't you dare speak so to me again, Margaret," Rose said, her voice low and harsh, "or you'll be out and living on the streets of Penzance before the night falls. Don't you ever doubt it."

Meg clutched the edge of the kitchen table, her hair pulled loose from her combs. "And don't you ever raise your hand to me again, Rose Hale," she hissed, "or the new master'll hear some things about you that you don't want told."

"That's enough from you, Meggy." Rose turned; James was standing in the open doorway, face like thunder, with Alec standing behind him. "And from you, Rose." He glanced at Meg. "Clean up the mess, Meg, and get back to work." He looked back at Rose. "We'll talk more tonight. Tend to your business. I don't want to be interrupted again this day. Alec, tend to your chores." He walked back down the kitchen path toward the barn.

Rose unclenched her fists. James was a quiet man, a gentle man, but she knew that when he spoke in that tone there was no argument. "Go ahead, Alec," she said, as the boy hesitated in the door. "Go." She looked at Meg. "I'll clean the mess, Margaret," she said quietly. "Finish tea, and use the next best pot. I'll explain to Mr. Williams that we'll be needing a new one."

Meg, stiff-backed with indignation, walked back toward the pantry. Rose knelt and started to pick up the shards of the pot, dropping them one by one into her apron.

Jonathan spent the hours between tea and dinner in the library with Hale, going over the books for the farm; his cousin had been a frugal man and a precise bookkeeper, and everything seemed fairly straightforward. He'd need a few days' study to fully understand the books and to transcribe Hale's notes of the expenditures and income since Penhyrddin's death into the ledgers, but he didn't anticipate much difficulty in the task. Langsford had sat and listened for a while and then, apparently satisfied with what he'd heard, wandered off to take a stroll around the farm whilst the sunlight lasted. He'd returned in the dusk, and finding Jonathan still at the books, chided him to dress.

Rose had seen to the unpacking of Jonathan's luggage and trunks that day; his dinner clothes were laid out neatly on the bed. He splashed some water on his face, dressed quickly, and was adjusting his tie as he met Langsford in the hall. Through the meal they'd spoken primarily about the farm, the stock, and the finances until, over the sweet, Langsford had rebelled and declared that, if they reviewed one more total of wool sent to the Midlands, he'd pack his kit and walk back to Penzance that night. Jonathan laughed.

"If you continue to eat like this," Langsford said as he leaned back in his chair after they'd finished, "you'll be as large as the King by the time I return in August."

Jonathan smiled as he folded his napkin and laid it next to his plate. "I don't think I need worry about that too much," he said. "I believe there will be enough here to keep me busy and away from the table."

"Well, don't spend all of your time indoors," Langsford said as Rose and the kitchen maid entered the room, "at least not until I've gone back to London. I want to do some exploring while I'm here. I saw enough to intrigue me before dinner."

"Certainly," Jonathan said, then looked up at Rose as she stood quietly in front of him. "Yes, Rose?"

"Would you be likin' your coffee in the library, Mr. Williams?" she asked. "Or would you prefer it here?"

"I think in the library would be fine, thank you," he replied. "And dinner was very good. My compliments."

"Thank you, sir. Margaret," she said over her shoulder, "set out coffee for the gentlemen, and then clear this up."

"There's no rush, Mrs. Hale," Langsford said as he stood. "We'll take a stroll in the garden before coffee. It's a beautiful night."

"Yes, sir."

"I walked down across the fields to the edge of the cliffs before dinner," Langsford said to Jonathan. "It looks like there's a nice little beach, right below the house. Perhaps we could bathe there tomorrow? Is there a path down?"

Jonathan hesitated, then answered, "Yes, perhaps. There is a beach there."

"There must be a path down," Langsford said as he crossed the room toward the door. "I saw Alec down there this evening." Jonathan flinched. "He must have been having a bathe before dinner."

"I beg your pardon, sir?" Rose said, pausing in the door.

"I was just saying, I saw Alec down on the beach below the house this evening while I was out for a walk," Langsford said. "I'll ask him to show me the way down tomorrow."

"Alec wouldn't have been swimming there, sir, if you'll pardon me," Rose said in a tight voice. Jonathan glanced up; she was looking straight at him. He looked back down at the table. "No one does, and Alec had his house chores and his dinner to see to."

"Ah," Langsford said. "I see. Well, perhaps it was a trick of the light, then. It was just at sundown."

"Perhaps, sir," she said. "Mr. Williams?" She was still looking straight at him when he met her eye. "When would you like your coffee?"

"Well . . ." Jonathan said, faltered, and fell silent.

"I think in a quarter hour, Mrs. Hale," Langsford interjected smoothly. She nodded, then slipped silently from the room.

"I hope I didn't get the boy in trouble," Langsford said when she was gone. "Like as not it was someone else, though it looked like him." He shook his head. "Regardless, she's not a woman I'd want angry with me. She has you cowed well enough. You'll have to learn to speak up, man."

Jonathan stood slowly and pressed his hands against the tabletop to stop their trembling. "I'm not cowed," he said. "It's . . . just all very strange, being back here again, and in such different circumstances. I expect my cousin to walk in at any time and quiz me on my day's activities, or inquire after what book I'm reading." He smiled slightly and looked around the room. "Odd, for something so long ago to leave so vivid an impression."

"Not at all," Langsford said. "For all it's the end of the earth, this is a rather vivid place." He opened the door to the hall. "And now, before we have our coffee, let us go out and be vivid ourselves in the moonlight, what little there is." He tucked his arm in Jonathan's and led him from the room.

Rose hurried down the passage to the kitchen. He knew. He *knew*. He knew what had happened to her, and that he was to blame for her near ruin, she was certain now. The look he'd given her, the twitch when the other one mentioned Alec . . . she stopped.

Alec. What if . . .

Should she? Dare she? She walked slowly into the kitchen, thinking furiously. She couldn't do anything about *him* being here, about him owning Trevaglan now. They wouldn't leave the farm themselves; James made that clear. But she could make him sorry he'd come back, sorry he lived there. Make him feel all the guilt and shame she'd felt, that had so nearly ruined her, and had destroyed her life. She smiled to herself. She could do it, and she wouldn't risk her situation, or James's place. In fact—sweetness itself—she'd enhance it, to all outside appearances. And she knew well—none better—that appearances were more important than truth, if there was such a thing as truth where that one was concerned.

"Margaret," she said, and Meg looked up from the coffee tray she was arranging, her face wary. "Leave that a minute; the gentlemen will be a little while yet before they need it. Run down to the cottage, and tell Alec to gather his good clothes and his things and hurry up here." Meg stood up, her hands on her hips.

"Oh, don't pull that face," Rose said cajolingly. "I'm sorry I struck you. It was an ill-mannered thing of me to do, as were the things I said." She smiled. "It's a difficult time, with a new master and all, and my nerves are all upsot."

Meg pursed her lips. "If they are," she said, "it will be the first time I've seen them so."

"That may be," Rose said, "or it may not, but as they say, there's a first time for everything. Now run. Don't dawdle. The gentlemen will be wantin' their coffee soon as they're in." She shushed Meg out the door and carefully placed the sugar spoon on the tray. "They'll be wantin' their coffee sure," she said to herself softly.

Jonathan stopped by the garden gate. "No further, I think," he said. "We don't know the land well enough to walk about in the dark."

"True," Langsford said. He pulled a cigarette case from his pocket, lit one, handed it to Jonathan, and then lit one for himself.

Jonathan inhaled the smoke. The pastures lay grey and dim before them; the setting moon, waxing toward half, was muted by thin, high clouds, and the landscape lay mostly in shadow. The trees and hedges were dark blurs, and lighter patches—he assumed they were sheep—dotted the fields. The sea was a black sheet stretched across the world beyond the cliffs, occasionally spangled with the lights of a passing ship or a fishing boat come very late to harbor. A bush-cricket, more determined than his kin, chirped forlornly in the hedge, and somewhere behind the barn a dog barked, its voice cut off as a door slammed. He shivered a little in the breeze off the ocean.

"It is a bit chillier than I thought," Langsford said softly, "and so very still."

Jonathan nodded.

"You will have an adjustment, I think, living here, after being in the city for so long."

"Any change is an adjustment," Jonathan answered, his voice also hushed by the huge silence surrounding them. "If I had moved to Edinburgh, or to Birmingham . . ."

"Heaven forbid."

Jonathan smiled. "True. But to my point, if I should have moved to another city, the adjustment would have been equally, if not more, difficult. This," he gestured across the fields, "is familiar to me. I know this place. The things that would strike most people as the greatest changes—the remoteness, the quiet, the customs of the people—are only surface differences, appearances. *Had* I moved to another city, I would know nothing, be acquainted with no one. That is not the situation here. I know this place. I know these people."

"Do you?" Langsford asked, and Jonathan glanced over. Langsford still looked out over the fields. "Do you know them?" He looked at Jonathan, his eyes shadowed. "Fourteen years is a long time. They have had their lives, created new lives, buried old ones. Nothing is entirely static, Williams. You've changed. Can you truly say you know these people, this place? And that they know you?"

Jonathan was silent.

"You were a boy when you were here before, and a guest. Now you are a man, and master of this place. Do they know you?"

Langsford looked out across the fields again, and took a slow inhalation of his cigarette. "I think they don't." His smile flashed in the dim light. "I'm not even sure you do."

They smoked quietly for a few minutes. "I don't know," Jonathan finally said. "I was startled, when we rode down the lane, how little things seemed to have changed. I felt much as I did when I would return from a visit to Penzance then, or to church." He paused. "Ah. Church. We always attended morning service, or, at least, my cousin always made a point to do so. I suppose I should, also."

"Church of England, I hope," Langsford said. "Not Methodist or anything like."

Jonathan smiled in the darkness. "No, Church of England. Don't worry."

Langsford sighed. "Very well. At least it's familiar mummery, and nothing terribly dramatic." He lit another cigarette. "Go on. You were saying."

Jonathan shook his head. "It was nothing, I suppose. Just that . . . I feel as if I've never been gone, but when I was dressing, I looked in the glass, and . . . a different person was looking out at me. Older. I found it very unsettling."

"I should think it would be," Langsford said, "and I know how you feel. When I'm home at Christmas, I often feel as if I'm fourteen again, on holiday from school." He smiled, another flash of white in the darkness. "Of course, that may be because my father still treats me as if I *am* fourteen."

"I've always thought your father was a wise man," Jonathan said, stubbing out his cigarette on the gravel path.

"Ho," Langsford said, and laughed. "Another?" he asked, and Jonathan shook his head. "Well, if you say you'll do well here, then I'll accept that you will." He looked back out across the fields. "I've not been certain, these last few weeks, and I'm still not. I hope you'll pardon me the familiarity of long friendship. I'm still concerned. I . . ." he hesitated. "I'll be frank, though I know you'd prefer I wasn't, I'm sure. I had rather hoped that

Cornwall would be less inviting, and that you would come down on holidays, while staying up in town. You never spoke of this place while we were at school, so I'd rather come to the understanding that your stay here hadn't been that pleasant."

"No," Jonathan said, shifting uncomfortably; Langsford was venturing dangerously near the truth. "No. Cousin Penhyrddin was a gracious host. I was . . . I was actually left very much on my own when I was here. What boy wouldn't like that?"

"Well, you certainly looked like you'd been through quite an ordeal," Langsford said. "I distinctly remember when I first saw you that term. If I didn't know you better, I would have sworn you'd been in a street brawl at some point. After I came to know you, it was clear that you'd simply had a serious tussle with one of your cousin's books." He stubbed out his cigarette. "He has quite a fine library . . . another secret you'd been holding to yourself. I'm looking forward to examining it."

"I had a fall," Jonathan said carefully, telling a portion of the truth, "a short time before I left for Cambridge. I was out walking one evening, and had a misstep in the dark."

"I see," Langsford said. "That would certainly tend to make one wary about wandering about in the darkness after a large dinner. We'll do our exploring in the daylight, tomorrow, or Monday, if it suits better."

"Yes," Jonathan said, relieved that Langsford had accepted his explanation. "Perhaps we should return to the house? Rose will have the coffee ready, I think."

"Lead on, MacDuff," Langsford said, bowing deeply.

Jonathan snorted. "I believe the line is 'Lay on.' Only Americans say 'lead.'"

Langsford laughed. "Then you lay on, and I'll lead on. Divided responsibilities. It is holiday after all." He turned to follow, then hesitated.

Jonathan asked "What is it?"

"One of the farm hands, I suppose, down in the pasture," Langsford replied. "I can't really tell. More a sense of movement than anything else. It's too dark to see." He tucked his arm in Jonathan's again, and they started up the path. "Obviously someone new since you were here, or he'd know better than to wander about Trevaglan in the dark, dim, dusky night."

Jonathan shook his head. "Obviously," he said drily, as they started up the steps. "You can start on the library tonight, if you like," he said over his shoulder as he opened the front door. "I was here the entire summer and barely brushed the surface."

"You had better things to do that summer than to bury yourself in books," Langsford said, closing the door behind them. Lamplight glowed from the doorway ahead on the right.

"Perhaps," Jonathan said, "though not much better." He stopped suddenly in the door to the library and Langsford, caught off guard, bumped into him from behind.

"Careful there," Langsford said. "Give a man a little warning."

Meg was setting the coffee pot on the low table that stood in between the divan and the fireplace, and glanced up when Langsford spoke. She smiled briefly, and then placed the coffee cups on their saucers next to the silver pot. Rose stood across the room by the window. Next to her, dressed in a white shirt and dark trousers, stood Alec, his hair tousled and his eyes blurred with sleepiness.

"Is there a problem, Rose?" Jonathan asked cautiously.

She smiled slightly. "No, Mr. Williams," she said, and moved slowly around the table. "I asked Alec to gather his things and come stay here in the house, at least for the rest of Mr. Langsford-Knight's stay. I thought perhaps you gentlemen would be in need of more help than just that what Margaret and I could give." Meg sniffed, and Rose shot her a glance; Meg bent her head over her work, laying out the spoons and the napkins.

"I don't think that will be necessary, Rose," Jonathan said. "Langsford . . . Mr. Langsford-Knight and I are accustomed to looking after ourselves. I wouldn't want to take Alec away from his work on the farm."

"It's no trouble, sir," Rose said, smiling again. "I'll speak with

James. I'm sure he can spare Alec for a week, at the very least."

"Dad already asked about it, Mum," Alec said quietly.

"I appreciate your consideration," Jonathan said, measuring his words, and very conscious of Langsford's silence behind him, "but I'm sure our arrival here has already caused enough upheaval." *I can't have this boy in the house*, he thought desperately. He would have enough difficulty just seeing him in the yard or the fields, but laying out his clothes in the morning? *Impossible.*

Rose moved closer. Jonathan could smell the scent of baked bread and roasted beef on her clothes; his stomach tightened at her nearness.

"If truth be told, sir," she said, lowering her voice, "I'd be beholden to you if you'd allow this. You'd be doing me a great favor. Alec has his letters; Mr. Penhyrddin made sure of that, good man that he was. But helping with you and the other gentleman," she glanced over his shoulder to where Langsford stood, "well, sir, it would teach him better manners, I think, and help him move up in the world a bit."

"I . . ." Jonathan looked quickly around at Langsford, who was leaning up against the doorframe, watching him calmly. "I suppose," Jonathan said more firmly, "given that view of the situation, I'd . . . be delighted. Langsford, you have no objection?"

"It will be an act of Christian charity on the boy's part," Langsford said as he pushed away from the wall and strolled across the room, "more than any favor on ours. That smells wonderful, Margaret. No, thank you, we'll pour ourselves." He smiled at Rose. Jonathan's eyes narrowed slightly; Langsford was being his most charming, laying it on with a trowel, as he sometimes said. "Don't worry, Mrs. Hale. We'll take your boy under our wings and stuff his head with such nonsense that by the end of the week he'll not be fit for farm nor factory nor Parliament itself." He paused. "Well, perhaps for Parliament. What do you say to that, Alec. Are you ready to stand for Parliament in the next election?"

"No, thank you, sir," Alec said. "I see enough sheep here in the pastures. I don't need to travel to London t'see more." Jonathan's throat closed at the sound of his voice, and the flash of his smile. *So much like Nat,* he thought.

Langsford laughed as Rose shushed the boy. "Well, perhaps he won't be the one doing the learning," he said. "Williams, we had best be on our mettle this week."

"Yes, we will," Jonathan replied. "Thank you, Rose. That will be all for now."

"Yes sir," she said. "Alec, Margaret, come with me." She started to lead them out through the doors into the dining room, but stopped in the doorway. "I'm sorry, sir, but there is one more thing. I forgot earlier. The good tea pot was broken this afternoon. I fear we'll have to get a replacement."

"Broken?" Jonathan asked.

"Yes, sir," she answered. "I dropped it while we were preparing your tea." Meg gasped, but Rose kept her eyes fixed on Jonathan's. "It cannot be repaired, I am afraid. I didn't want to bother you with this tomorrow, it being the Sabbath."

"Then we can discuss it on Monday morning," Jonathan said, bewildered by the odd turn of the conversation.

"Yes, sir. I'll send to Penzance for a new one, and as it was my fault, I will deduct the cost from my wages."

"We can discuss that on Monday, also."

"Thank you, sir," she said as she closed the door behind her.

"Well, well, well, well," Langsford said, his eyebrows raised.

"Margaret," Rose said as they entered the kitchen, "finish the dishes while they have their coffee, and then clear those things away."

"Rose Hale," Meg speaking over her, "that's the first untruth I think I've ever heard you say. I do have to say my thanks for that, not that it was my fault, dropping that pot because you gave me such a clout as I never deserved!"

"And as I said before, Margaret," Rose interrupted, "'twasn't a proper thing for me to do. Now stop your nattering and let me get on with my work while your do yours. Alec, get your things, and take them down to the little room opposite Mr. Williams' bedroom. You stay there this week, whilst the other fellow is here. Oh, another thing—Margaret Berryman, those pots won't scrub themselves—the gentlemen will be needin' someone to show them around the countryside. You come in after noon meal tomorrow—Margaret, they'll not need much, just a crib, maybe a cold meal that we can lay out—and you take them down to the village, or up to the ruins, or the longstones, or whatever they want to see."

"But, Mum!"

"Tis just for a week, and you'll mind me," Rose snapped. "You'll get your chores done early in the morning, the gentlemen'll sleep late no doubt. Then you'll help Mr. Williams to dress for church, and the other, too, if he needs it—and don't you even think what you're thinking Margaret Berryman."

"I wasn't thinkin' of dressing him, if ye must know," Meg said over her shoulder as she poured steaming hot water from the kettle over the dishes in the sink.

"That's enough of that talk," Rose said, pouring herself a small cup of black coffee and sitting down at the kitchen table. "Off you go, Alec, and I don't want to hear another word out of you."

"Yes, Mum." Alec picked up his kit and ran out of the room.

"You walk in this house, child," Rose called after him, "and scrub your face in the mornin'."

"The young ones are always runnin'," Meg said. "There's nothin' you nor anyone else can do about it."

"Hush, Margaret," Rose said. "I have to think." Meg sniffed and plunged her hands back into the hot water. Rose ignored her and sipped her coffee, then sat forward and smiled slowly. *A good start.* Not enough on its own, perhaps, but she'd think of something else.

"She's lying, you know," Langsford said over the rim of his coffee cup.

Jonathan settled back on the divan and stirred his coffee absently. "Do you think so?" he asked. "I thought . . . well, I don't know what I thought. Something struck me as odd, but I couldn't put my finger to it."

"Decidedly odd," Langsford agreed. "Odd because I don't believe she's an habitual liar. She isn't very good at it." He took a sip of his coffee. "I've seen it at the bar any number of times. Someone who's accustomed to falsehood speaks as if he *knows* what he says is the truth—he's glib, and fairly casual about it. Someone who isn't . . . well, they do exactly what she did. They look you straight in the eye, and calmly trot out their line, thinking if they look away or hesitate, you'll think they are lying, which in fact they are. They betray themselves with every word. Another cup?" He poured another for himself and for Jonathan, then stirred in the cream and sugar. "The thing I wonder is, why? Meg certainly didn't expect it; she gave the game away immediately. I'll bet a shilling she's the one dropped the pot. As you said, it's odd."

"The pot?" Jonathan stared at Langsford blankly. "She lied about the teapot?" He shook his head. "Why in the world is everyone making such a fuss over an idiotic teapot? That's not at all what I meant. You believe she lied about that also?"

"*Also?*" Langsford echoed. "Not also. Whatever else would she have . . . ah." His brow furrowed and he took another sip of his coffee. "That's very interesting."

"I don't see what's remotely interesting about it. It's . . . it's impertinent and annoying, but the way she put it, I couldn't very well refuse." He took a swallow of his coffee and tried to calm himself. Above all, he couldn't show how upset he was. Though normally not terribly inquisitive, that might prompt Langsford to ask more questions, and the last thing Jonathan desired was questions about Alec, and, by extension, Nat. He took a deep breath and smiled. "Listen to us. If anyone is impertinent, it's the two of us. She's simply a mother trying her best to advance the interests of her children. And as for that wretched teapot, she most likely spoke as a responsible housekeeper who didn't want her scullery maid sacked the first day her new employer was in the house."

"I believe you're right," Langsford said thoughtfully. "I certainly can't think of another reason. Or reasons. Still, it is peculiar—"

"Oh, nonsense" Jonathan said. "After you leave, she'll see that there's far more work in the fields than in the house, and to have the boy wasting his time watching me sit in the library and read certainly isn't going to help him in any demonstrable way."

Langsford leaned forward in his chair. "No, I have to disagree," he said earnestly. "Watching you read is extremely educational. I've watched you for years, and have gleaned innumerable social advantages. The proper turning of a page, the precise distance to raise one's eyebrow at a shocking paragraph, exactly how to hold one's tongue between one's teeth when concentrating . . . priceless, *priceless* lessons."

Jonathan sighed. "I believe I'll go to bed now. You're impossible when you get into this mood, and," he said, overriding Langsford's objections, "no good whatsoever can come of the conversation." He stood and smiled. "Have a good night. After church and luncheon tomorrow perhaps we can explore the countryside. That path to Landreath village is quite lovely, and perfect for an afternoon's walk."

"That sounds wonderful," Langsford said as he stood, "though I'm not so certain about the church portion of the day. I hope the vicar isn't terribly dull." He glanced at the clock on the mantelpiece. "Oh, come, Williams. It's just past eleven—far too early for sleep. Can't I tempt you to another stroll around the garden in the fading moonlight?" He smiled ruefully. "We shan't have many more chances for lazy evenings and idle chatter, I'm afraid."

Jonathan's heart pounded, and he stood a moment too long for comfort, torn between the pain of staying with Langsford and that of separating from him, when, as Langsford had said, the time left them was so very short. Then he shook his head. "It's been a beast of a day," he said. "I'd do well to get some rest."

Langsford nodded. "Good night, then," he said, and Jonathan turned to leave. "Williams."

Jonathan stopped. "Yes?" he asked after a pause in which Langsford just stood, looking at him, seemingly searching for the rest of his thought.

"Sleep well," he said finally.

"You also," Jonathan said. "Enjoy your stroll, but do be careful."

Langsford dropped his gaze, then looked up and smiled again. "I always am, it seems. Good night."

Langsford struck a match and lit his cigarette. He'd walked out across the garden to the gate and once again stood looking out toward the cliffs and the sea. He inhaled the smoke and, as he exhaled, looked at the cigarette, trembling in his fingers.

Twice in the last two weeks, including this evening, he'd come just that close to telling Williams of his feelings, and twice he'd been unable to make that potentially devastating revelation. He had six more days and then any opportunity would be gone. He had kept silent for over ten years, and now he had to find the courage to speak—or to remain silent—in only six days.

Six days. It drummed in his head like a funeral march. Six days and he would return to London to the empty flat and a lonely life. He hadn't even been consciously aware how completely Williams had come to fill that life until the news had arrived about the inheritance, and he faced the shocking prospect of Williams leaving. True, Williams had expressed a similar, if lesser, concern, but he had seemed light-hearted about it . . . well, as lighthearted as Williams was about anything. Langsford smiled in spite of his distress. Few of their friends ever saw the dry wit, the gentle humor that would flash out when they were alone, always finding the chink in his argument or his bravado, skewering him neatly, and always accompanied by the sidelong glance and half smile that made Langsford's breath catch in his throat. The thought of seeing that smile but once or twice a year instead of every day, of growing apart, of being without him had so upset his normal equilibrium that he'd finally contemplated the unthinkable: telling Williams that he loved him.

He'd long since ceased to doubt that he was a not a man for women. The knowledge had troubled him greatly, early in his adult life, but with time he had grown accustomed to the thought. From childhood he had felt himself to be different in some indefinable way from the other boys of his acquaintance, and certain conversations his parents had had which he had overheard—a cousin who'd left the country in the wake of the Cleveland Street scandal, two boys expelled from a public school nearby, a well-to-do gentleman in the neighborhood who, in spite of the machinations of several mothers with marriageable daughters, retained a resolute bachelorhood—lingered in his mind in spite of their then-seeming irrelevance to him. At school he had experimented with sex as had any number of the boys in his form, and though he found it pleasurable, the experiences had failed to move him in any profound way. Despite this, he was always quite clear in his own mind that he was at the very core of his being outside the normal walk of life for men, and the relief that he had felt the day his brother Charles's first son was born had been immeasurable; the pressure to marry and procreate and live a life of deceit was, if not removed, noticeably lessened.

He lit another cigarette and leaned on the low, rough garden wall. He wasn't even certain when he had realized that his affection for Williams had changed into something deeper. He had never really spoken with him at Eton, but knew of him slightly, and felt protective when he'd heard his parents speak of the scandal surrounding Williams's father, which had filled the newspapers at the time. Moved by that protectiveness, he had invited Williams to dinner upon his arrival at Cambridge, and once he managed to get more than a word or two out of him, had been surprised and pleased to find him a truly amiable companion, and so their friendship had begun.

Only after he had gone down to London had he started to suspect the truth. Upon arriving in the capital, he had moved briefly on the periphery of thc clandestine—and not-so-clandestine—circles of those similarly inclined, while avoiding the molly houses and the simpering aesthetes who always seemed to want more than he was willing to give. He found the conversations empty and the propositions offensive, and even before the Wilde conviction scattered those circles, however temporarily, he had allowed the few acquaintances to drop. The trial itself had taught him caution.

He found himself increasingly anticipating Williams's letters from Cambridge, and had insisted that Williams spend his holidays in town. His flat at the time, though small, was sufficiently comfortable for those visits, and the two talked late into the night, even after the lights had been extinguished. When Williams returned to Cambridge at the end of the holidays, Langsford had found himself unaccountably lonely—a novel and unsettling feeling for one who had always been and still was very social—so when the time approached that Williams would complete his studies, he had changed lodgings, taking a larger flat, with the intention of inviting Williams to live with him, as had happened.

He had couched that invitation in terms of a temporary situation, an opportunity for Williams to make his start in the city without the bother of finding a place to live; in truth he had hoped that circumstances would work out as they had. Williams had barely been there two months before Langsford had determined that he wanted Williams with him always. Though he had never thought he would be so, he was mawkishly, foolishly, and utterly in love.

He stubbed out the cigarette. *Foolishly in love is the proper description.* While he was fairly certain that Williams shared the same peculiar bent, he was absolutely certain that Williams, while extremely fond of him, did not have the same depth of feeling for him in return. Though open and frank in all matters of his life, from business to his most intimate family relations, save that of the event of his father's second marriage, about which he maintained a cool silence, Williams was almost obsessively reserved about his emotional life, gently but firmly rebuffing any conversational gambit Langsford made about such matters, and displaying a marked embarrassment whenever he made the attempt; it seemed emblematic that they had never in their long friendship called each other by their Christian names, had never once breached that simple wall of social intimacy. So he had ceased to try, striking an increasingly fragile balance between his love and desire for Williams and his satisfaction with simply having him always in his life. He had walked that narrow line successfully, he thought, for the nine years they had lived together.

And now he had but six days either to speak his heart and risk the rupture of that friendship or to remain silent and allow any chance to fade with time and distance. Not for the first time he wished he had spoken out, and firmly, when first he realized the depths of his feelings; the rejection then, though painful, would have been more bearable than this uncertain agony and, in any case, would have been long since past. But he hadn't. He had been too selfish to be honest. *Foolishly in love, indeed.*

He tossed the cigarette stub into the pasture and turned to walk back to the house. As he did so, he once again caught a glimpse of movement out of the corner of his eye, and, squinting into the darkness, thought he made out the figure of a man standing down by the cliffs, at a low dip just before the headland.

"Ho," he called. "Be careful there, man!" He wasn't sure if what he saw was a man or simply a shadow of the rocks. "What are you doing there?" he shouted, but received no response. He crossed to the gate and stepped through into the path, but, looking again, could see nothing but the dim landscape stretched before him. If indeed there had been someone there, he was gone now. He latched the gate behind him and walked up to the house.

CHAPTER 4

"Good morning, Mr. Williams. I've brought you your tea."

China clinked on the bedside table, and Jonathan stirred and blinked against the morning light that poured into the room with the chiming of the curtain rings. He squinted against the brightness; Alec was silhouetted against the window. He pushed back against his pillows and, though he was wearing a nightshirt and undergarments, pulled his bedclothes up tightly against his chest. He shivered slightly, his heart pounding. Seeing the boy at the hotel had been a shock, and last evening in the library disturbing, but being alone with him, particularly in his room, was unsettling in the extreme.

"Good morning, Alec," he said, trying to sound in the least normal. "Thank you for the tea."

"You're welcome, sir," Alec said as he crossed the room. "Mum and Meggy are fixing breakfast for you and the other gentleman." He stopped at the foot of the bed; Jonathan held the bedclothes tighter, feeling foolish as he did so. "Will you be needing some help laying out your clothes and such?

"No," Jonathan replied quickly, appalled at the thought of Alec helping him dress. "I'll be quite fine, thank you. Perhaps you could help Mr. Langsford-Knight."

"Oh, he's been up for 'bout an hour," Alec said. "He said I should come down and help you."

"Considerate of him," Jonathan muttered. He looked up.

"Well, there's nothing else for you to do here. You can go help your mother or father now."

Alec looked doubtful. "Yes, sir. I'll ask Mum if there's anything more she needs to have done. But in any case, I'll be back in a minute with some hot water for your shaving."

"Thank you," Jonathan said, relieved that Alec would be gone, however briefly.

Alec smiled ruefully. "I'm afraid I won't be much help with that, either, no more than pickin' out your socks. I don't shave yet myself, and Dad says it's a good thing. He's said I'll have to grow a beard, since I'm so click-handed with a knife that a razor'd be foolish. I sure wouldn't trust myself shaving you. I would probably cut you, and myself too. A fine pair of slice abouts we'd be then if I . . ."

Knife. Blood. Hands on his face. Jonathan struggled to take a breath. "I'm perfectly capable of shaving myself," he said harshly. "I certainly won't need your assistance for that."

"I'm sorry, sir," Alec said, looking at the floor. "I didn't mean no harm." He looked up again, his face earnest. "I just say things sometime, and don't think about 'em beforehand. Mum says I'm too forward with my tongue, and she's prob'ly—"

"Get out!" he gasped. "Just get the damn water and get out!"

Alec fled.

Jonathan threw back the bedclothes and swung his legs over the side of the bed. Shaking, he picked up the tea and swallowed some quickly, burning his tongue and throat and spilling some in his lap as he did so. He put the cup down and sat, his head in his hands, elbows on his knees, as he struggled to control his panic. The shock of the pain from the hot tea had taken his breath away, but brought him to his senses.

He was behaving like an adolescent fool. The boy was not at all to blame for his face, or his voice, or the fact that he had been given the task of waiting on him. He certainly didn't deserve to be abused so by a complete stranger. Jonathan took a deep breath. Whether he liked it or not, he had a responsibility to the boy, indeed, to everyone who lived or worked on the farm . . . *my farm*. He picked up the tea again and carefully took a sip. For a moment he was surprised at how good it was, delicate but with a bite, but then he remembered that his cousin had always been very particular about his tea, as he had been about all of his creature comforts.

Calmer, he stood and crossed the room to the dressing table. When he'd arrived the day before, he had been absurdly pleased that the room hadn't changed in the least. The furniture, the rugs on the floor, the wallpaper, even the books on the bookshelf by the fireplace were almost exactly as they had been fourteen years earlier—in fact, several of the books were those he'd bought or had sent down while he was here and had left behind in the confusion of packing at the end of that summer. He had been surprised to find them still here, surprised that he'd even remembered their titles, and felt slightly guilty about abandoning them. He stood quietly for a while, his fingertips brushing the bindings, remembering reading one in the shade of a hawthorn one hot afternoon in July, another in this bedroom on a stormy evening a short while later. Again he had been surprised how vivid and clear those memories were, as if focused through the feel of the leather and the slight scent of dust that always seemed to cling to his books.

He put his tea down and pulled out his old leather case. He set it on the dressing table and opened the small inner side pocket. He pulled out the handkerchief, carefully unfolded it, and took the rest of the items out one by one, counting them as he did. Other memories crowded his mind this morning, but not memories of words on paper, or lazy summer afternoons redolent of climbing roses and filled with birdsong; he resolutely shoved those aside. What was past was past. He packed the items back into the case in reverse order—a small ritual that always calmed him, though he knew not why—counting as always, and folded the handkerchief, corners to the middle, corners to the middle, corners to the middle, then tucked it in with the rest.

He crossed to the chest of drawers that stood against the wall by the door and pulled open the drawers. Rose Hale or Meg had unpacked his trunks—or Alec had, a thought that made his skin crawl, Alec touching his clothing—and had placed them as made sense to them, but was not as he always sorted them. He straightened his bedclothes, then carefully pulled his clothing out and laid it on the bed. When he'd emptied the chest, he began replacing the items as suited him, unfolding them and refolding them as he did so: neckties, handkerchiefs, and collars in the upper right drawer, undergarments in the second, stockings and shirts in the third, trousers in the bottom. The upper left remained empty, as it always did. As it always had, since he'd lived here before.

He had just pushed the last drawer in when a soft knock sounded on the door. He crossed quickly to the wardrobe, shuffled through the contents and slipped into his dressing gown. "Come," he called.

Alec entered, carrying a steaming copper kettle, both hands on the handle. "Here's your hot water, sir," he mumbled, his eyes on the floor. He edged past Jonathan without looking at him, and placed the kettle on a pad on the dressing table. He tried to leave, but Jonathan blocked his way.

"Alec," Jonathan said, and the boy stopped, folding his hands behind him, his head down. "I want to apologize for my behavior earlier." Alec glanced up, then looked back down again quickly. "Look at me please." The boy slowly looked up, clearly expecting a reprimand. "I apologize. That was very ill-mannered of me. I can only beg the excuse that I'm a poor sleeper, and mornings are not my best time of day."

"Yes, sir," Alec said, bobbing his head once.

"I would suggest, in the future," Jonathan said, stepping aside, "that you carry a lion tamer's chair if you bring me my morning tea. It will stand you in good stead." The boy's mouth opened slightly, as if uncertain of Jonathan's meaning. Fighting his nerves, Jonathan smiled. "I'd suggest the whip also; however, I fear I'd give you too much cause to use it."

Alec smiled hesitantly. "Yes, sir."

"Now," Jonathan said. "Mr. Langsford-Knight and I will be attending church services this morning. Please prepare the dogcart or the carriage, or whatever Mr. Penhyrddin used to use for such occasions. It was the cart when last I was here."

"The cart it was, sir. Mr. Penhyrddin, he didn't go about often, and didn't much use the carriage, only in winter."

"Very well," Jonathan said, "the cart." He looked at the clock on the bureau. "We'll leave in an hour and a half, after we've eaten."

"Yes, sir," Alec started out of the room, then paused in the doorway. "Will you," he asked, and hesitated. "Will you be needing any help dressin' or anything, sir?"

Again, Jonathan fought down the panic that rose in his chest. "No," he said, forcing his tone to be light. "You have more than enough things to do about the farm. I can take care of myself, thank you."

"Yes, sir." Alec closed the door behind him.

Jonathan sank onto the bed and dropped his head in his hands. "It will get easier," he said aloud. "I will become accustomed to it, and it will not be this difficult."

He didn't believe it.

Cornwall 1892

He had spent the week following that peculiar Sunday on the beach debating with himself as to whether he would return as he'd said, or not. That evening he had determined he wouldn't; while he wasn't, in his own opinion, a snob or terribly class conscious, he didn't think it appropriate to socialize with a hired farmhand. He could hear his father's voice in his mind, asking what his future associates at Cambridge would think. Jonathan knew just the tone he would take: pompous and condescending, with all the acid rigidity of the recently rich toward people whose class they had but a few generations ago occupied themselves. He would stay in the house next Sunday.

The next morning he decided he would go, his father be damned. *He* had little room to talk about social niceties, given his recent behavior. *Why shouldn't I befriend whomever I will?* he argued with himself. While Nat was certainly not the sort of man he'd associated with at school, he seemed a decent fellow, and, thus far, the only person who'd made the slightest overture of friendship in the time he'd been in Cornwall. And, Jonathan admitted to himself, he was more than a little lonely. Accustomed as he was to the crowds of boys at school, and his sister and mother at home, the prolonged solitude he'd initially treasured upon his arrival was wearing on him. His cousin, though a pleasant man, was hardly a lively companion for an eighteen-year-old boy. He would go next Sunday.

That state of affairs lasted until shortly after breakfast.

He'd decided the previous evening to explore an old Iron Age village in the hills behind the witch's cottage (he didn't know if old Aunt Bannel was really a witch, but it suited his fancy to think so, living as she did in a small stone cottage, alone except for a large deaf-mute man not many years older than himself). His cousin had encouraged him, being a scholar of that period himself, and had drawn him a map of the site, outlining some of the more interesting points to see. Jonathan had decided he'd take a meal along.

After breakfast he hurried down to the kitchen to ask the cook to pack some cold meats, boiled eggs, cheese, and bread—and whatever else she had about the place—into a hamper for him to take along. Although he didn't want to carry a great pack with him, he was determined to make it an outing—at the back of his mind he thought of it as practice for the following Sunday, wherein he would provide the meal and thus have a bit more of the upper hand.

He burst into the kitchen to find Nat leaning against the

garden door frame, talking with Rose Pritchard, the kitchen maid, who turned and bobbed her head when Jonathan entered. Brought up short, he stammered out a response to Nat's greeting; his flustered manner made Nat smile even more widely. Taking refuge in a lofty tone, Jonathan ignored him and asked after the cook, who, it seemed, had gone down to Landreath to bespeak some fish for the next day's dinner—and, Jonathan thought to himself, for a bit of a gossip in the village. He told Pritchard what he required and was leaving when Nat spoke.

"I'm glad to see you've recovered your appetite, lad, after having eaten a good chunk of the shore yesterday."

Pritchard snorted, but smothered an outright laugh, and Jonathan, face flaming, responded with a curt "Yes," before retreating.

He would *not* go next Sunday.

And so he wavered through the week. He would go—Nat's comment was just a joke between two men, equals, and was certainly no reason not to continue the acquaintance, quite the opposite in fact. Then, he would *not* go—Nat was mocking him behind his back with the kitchen maid, of all people, and should at the very least be ignored, if not outright censured for his disrespect.

He spent more time around the farm during the week than was his wont, reading in the garden, sitting on the stone walls surrounding the yard, or walking through the pastures and hayfields where the men were working. He'd frequently see Nat in the barn or about the fields. Nat always greeted him with a friendly nod, as did the men who worked next to him.

He decided, yes, he would go.

Thursday, after he'd passed by the men on his way down to Landreath village on an errand for his cousin, he'd heard a quiet comment, too low to be understood, followed by Nat's laugh.

No, he would not go. That was final. The man really was beyond the pale, in all ways.

The next evening, returning from an after-dinner walk, he came upon Nat unexpectedly, standing at the edge of the cliff. Though Jonathan was but a few yards off, Nat didn't notice him at first, but stood looking out to sea, his face and shirt golden in the late sunlight. Jonathan stirred slightly, and Nat looked over at him and smiled.

Yes, he would go.

The following Sunday dawned clear and warm, and after breakfast Jonathan practically ran to the kitchen to ask the cook to prepare him something suitable for tea when he went down to the beach that afternoon. Pritchard was there again—fortunately Nat was not—but didn't comment or even pay him much attention while he gave particular instructions to the cook for what he wanted when he returned. What Pritchard might have said when he left Jonathan didn't want to know, nor did he even really care.

He fidgeted throughout the church service, to the point that his cousin nudged him with his elbow and told him, in a hushed tone, to be still and pay attention. He fidgeted the whole ride back to the farm, ate his midday meal quickly, and left the table as soon as he could politely do so. He changed out of his good clothes and into his everyday wear, tucking his shirttails in as he dashed to the kitchen to gather his food, and then ran down across the pastures toward the cliffs.

He stopped several yards from the cliff's edge, caught his breath, then walked slowly and nonchalantly toward the head of the path that wound down to the beach. His shoulders slumped when he reached the edge of the cliff; the beach lay below him, empty.

Stifling the bite of disappointment, he clambered through the brush and down the cliff's face. Upon reaching the beach, he tucked the satchel with his food between two rocks that lay well above the tide line. He paced for a bit at the surf's edge, hesitating to undress and swim before Nat arrived, that is, if Nat arrived. He stripped off his boots and socks and waded out to his favorite rock, but was unable to keep his eyes on the horizon; they kept wandering back to the cliff's edge.

Finally, about three quarters of an hour after he arrived, he gave up waiting. He dug into his pack for the metal mug he'd asked Cook to pack, and climbed to the spring on the cliff to fill it. After he drank, he filled it and brought it back to the beach for when he ate after his swim. Then he stripped off his clothes, folded them neatly and tucked them next to his pack, and dove into the surf.

The water was warmer than he'd anticipated and he swam out toward the rock outcropping from which he and Nat had raced the preceding week, stopping again when he felt the currents swirling around him. He floated a bit, rising and falling on the swell, then stroked against the current toward the beach. When he was about half of the way back he heard a voice hallooing from the shore, and he pulled up. Nat was climbing down the path, a small sack in his hand. He waved with the other, and Jonathan, suddenly shy now that Nat had come, waved back. He swam in until his feet touched bottom, then stood, still a bit uncomfortable being naked around another person.

Nat apparently had no such delicacy of feeling: He stripped off his clothes as soon as he reached the beach and, leaving them in an untidy heap near Jonathan's, dove into the sea and swam straight out to where Jonathan waited. He stood and shook the water out of his hair, a big smile on his face.

"I'm glad ye came, lad," he said, and promptly hooked his leg behind Jonathan's and ducked him under.

Sputtering and furious, Jonathan caught his footing and surged up out of the water, taking a wild swing at Nat, who ducked it easily, grabbed Jonathan's arm, and pulled him off his balance to push him below the surface again. Jonathan staggered, then rushed at Nat and shoved him as hard as he could. Laughing, Nat fell backward, grabbing Jonathan and pulling him under at the same time he fell. Nat regained his footing first and hauled them both to the surface, then, catching Jonathan under his arms, lifted him and tossed him back toward the shore. Grinning by now, Jonathan moved as if to push Nat again, but instead dove under the water and caught both of Nat's legs as he passed between them, lifting as he went, and tumbled the bigger man as he tucked and dodged and shot back to the surface. Nat broke the water a few feet distant, facing the other direction, and before he could turn, Jonathan leaped on his back and knocked him under again. Nat twisted in his grip and pulled them both up, laughing and coughing, and held Jonathan's arms in a tight grip while he struggled to get free.

"Eh, ye *do* know how to enjoy yourself," Nat said when Jonathan finally stopped fighting him. "I was beginnin' to wonder!"

"Yes, I do," Jonathan said, and immediately threw his arms around Nat, hooked his leg, and pulled him under again.

"And *that* will teach me to think you've given up," Nat said when they surfaced again. "I'll have to be more wary."

"That you will," Jonathan said, laughing. "A truce?" he asked, holding out his hand.

"A truce," Nat said, and took it. "But just to make sure . . ." he pulled Jonathan off his feet and, as lightly as if he'd been a bundle of wood or an errant lamb, tucked him under his arm and dragged him, squirming and protesting, up to the shore.

"Is that what you call a truce?" Jonathan asked as they toweled off by their clothes.

"The best kind there is," Nat said. "One where I have the upper hand."

"We'll see about that."

"And what'll ye do?" Nat dropped to the ground and stretched out in the sun.

"I'll think of something." After a moment's hesitation, he spread his towel and lay down also. "You'll just have to watch, won't you?"

"Oh, I'll watch out for you, make no doubt," Nat said, rolling onto his side and hiking up on one elbow. "You foreign folk bear watchin', and you probably most of them all."

Jonathan snorted. “Foreign folk indeed. My mother is kin to half the people around here.” He caught his breath a moment. “Was,” he said, suddenly sober.

Nat reached over and tousled his hair. “Is, lad,” he said gently. “Once you’re kin, you’re always kin. Don’t you fret.”

Though the week before the other man’s forward offer of sympathy had affronted him, today tears filled Jonathan’s eyes at the gesture, and he turned his head away. He had been alone too long with his sorrow and had no defense against genuine kindness.

“ ’Tis all right, Mister Jonathan,” Nat said, and touched him on the shoulder. “ ’Tis a natural grief, and nothin’ to be shamed of.”

The tears flowed faster, and Jonathan curled up in a ball as great wracking sobs shook his body. Nat sat cross-legged on his towel, saying nothing until the worst had passed, then handed Jonathan a piece of ragged cloth. Jonathan wiped his eyes and blew his nose, then apologized.

“For what?” Nat asked. “Seems to me you have enough sorrow in your life, and to share it will only make it easier to bear.” He reached around and pulled a sack out of the pile of his clothes. “And nothing makes it easier than having something to eat or drink.” He pulled two bottles of beer out of the sack. “Here,” he said, handing one to Jonathan. “I brought this, figuring you’d be along. Let’s drink to your mother and then eat.”

Jonathan took the earthenware bottle and pulled the top off. Nat raised his.

“To those that are with us still,” he said, “even though they be gone.”

Blinking back more tears, Jonathan raised his bottle, and then took a swallow. The beer was rich and nutty, and stronger than that which he’d had when he’d snuck away with his friends at school on late-night adventures in the town. It warmed his throat and stomach as he swallowed. He raised it again. “To those who are with us now.”

“Ay,” Nat said. “To those present.”

They spent the rest of the afternoon in quiet companionship, neither saying much, Jonathan enjoying the warmth of the May sunshine on his skin and the nearness of someone in whose company he felt more comfortable than anyone he'd met in a long while. He'd never known anyone so completely unselfconscious; the man lay sprawled naked on his back without, it seemed, the slightest worry that someone from the house might come upon them. Jonathan was a little less secure; he kept his clothes near him, and started at every noise, which made Nat laugh, gradually loosening Jonathan's nerves. Nat dozed as the afternoon wore on, and Jonathan sat and watched him as he slept. He was fascinated by the man's body, solid yet graceful; it was like looking at the great cats sleeping at the zoo, but present and immediate, not caged and watched by hundreds of curious passersby. It felt both intimate and dangerous, and when Nat woke and opened his eyes and smiled at him, Jonathan's breath stopped.

They dressed in silence as the sun began to set, then climbed the path to the pastures above. They parted at the garden gate with a handshake and few words, Jonathan to dinner and his cousin's library and books, and Nat to his lodging down in Landreath village. And when they met the next evening by chance, out along the cliff path, it seemed natural to continue along together, and to sit in the dusk and speak of the events of their day. The following evening they met by choice, and the day after shared the noon meal as well, sitting out under the hawthorn trees that ringed the house.

Andrew Penhyrddin had no little concern at the growing friendship between the two, though he thought that it was doing the boy good. Jonathan was more talkative at meals, and when Penhyrddin saw the two walking together in the fields, or lying in the sand on the beach, Jonathan and the farmhand laughed as much as they talked; Jonathan's laughter wasn't a sound he'd heard since the boy had arrived. Still, he was aware of the difficulties that might arise, and spoke to Jonathan the next Sunday at dinner. Nat Boscawen, he said, while a good worker, had a hot temper, and no small reputation as a rough man when crossed. If he had deeper concerns—something Jonathan could never determine, even after reading his cousin's diaries upon inheriting, which meticulously chronicled the events of that summer and the older man's thoughts about them—he kept them to himself, but Jonathan was always peripherally aware that Penhyrddin was watching them.

That Nat could explode without warning was not news to Jonathan. He'd seen the man stand up and punch the solid barn door three times with his bare fist when a piece of equipment—Jonathan couldn't even decipher its purpose—jammed, and Nat had difficulty clearing its workings. And one day he showed up at the farm with a swollen eye and bruises on his arm and chest. When Jonathan asked about them that evening, Nat's face had grown stormy; he shouted that it was none of Jonathan's damn business and had turned abruptly and walked off toward the village.

Jonathan spent the next day brooding in his room, but shortly after dinner, there was a tap at his window. Nat stood in the twilight, looking embarrassed and uncertain for the first time in their acquaintance. He'd come to apologize, he said. One of the men in the village had taunted him for "playing nursemaid to a grown boy," and Nat had thrashed him, though taking a few blows of his own. Jonathan had stood on his side of the window, not knowing what to say, until Nat said, "Come out and walk with me. It will do us both good." Jonathan scrambled out the window, and they climbed the hill behind the house and lay side by side in the short, fragrant turf as the moon rose.

As naïve as he knew himself to be, Jonathan was perfectly well aware of his feelings. He'd often had a passion for other boys at school; that was the way of things—close, intense friendships that lasted a month, at most a year, jealousy over the other boy's attentions and time, all of which lasted until the next new friendship blossomed. He had never descended to vice, though he had listened to tales told by the older boys with the same abhorred fascination as the other boys his age. He knew those feelings would pass, as they had for countless others in similar circumstances, and as he had been slower to mature physically than the boys in his form—he still didn't shave more than once every few weeks—he assumed that the feelings also would take more time and that one day he would meet a girl to marry, and this would be behind him. Nat would fade like the others, and most likely more quickly, given the difference in their situations.

The next day being Sunday, Jonathan had prepared to go down to the cove, but Nat met him and his cousin at the garden gate upon their return from church. Penhyrddin sent Jonathan off to change, but before he was finished, knocked on his door. Handing him a few coins, he said that Nat had planned an afternoon's outing. The old man seemed worried, but bade Jonathan behave himself and sent him on his way.

Jonathan burned with curiosity, but Nat refused to say a word about their destination. They set off in the direction of Landreath, and the end of a brisk walk found them on the small stone quay at the foot of the main street. The tide was in and most of the fishing boats rode at the end of their mooring lines, but one was tied up to the quay. An older man, grizzled and bearded, was on board, as was a man about Nat's age. The younger man's face was discolored to the point that it was difficult to know what his natural complexion was; his lip was cut, his nose swollen, and both eyes blacked.

Nat was all cheerfulness, and introduced the two men by their Christian names and climbed aboard.

"Come along, Mister Jonathan," he said. "This is your treat for today. We'll take you out across the mouth of Mounts Bay, if the wind is fair."

Jonathan was hesitant, but Nat urged him, so he clambered down off the quay and into the boat. It wasn't one of the heavy fishing smacks that jostled each other in the cove, but was a far cry from the pleasure boats with which he had but a nodding acquaintance. Sturdily built and weather beaten, it smelled of tar and paint and old fish; its sails were a faded blood red. They cracked as they caught the wind, causing the boat to heel as the older man wove his way through the other boats. Despite his gruff appearance, he seemed to be enjoying himself immensely, and chuckled frequently for no reason that Jonathan could see. The younger man crouched sullenly by the mast, tending the ropes that managed the sails. Jonathan had a growing suspicion as to who that man was, a suspicion that was confirmed when, as they cleared the headland and the boat rose to the deep swell off the ocean, Nat leaned back and stretched his legs in front of him.

"So, Thomas," he called, and the younger man looked back. " 'Tis not so bad to be nursemaid to a grown boy, now is it."

The older man at the tiller guffawed, and Jonathan felt his face flame.

Thomas stood and gripped the mast. "You just watch your lip, Nat Boscawen, or you'll get yours the next time."

Nat and the older man laughed as Jonathan sat in silent mortification.

"Now, Tom, you mind your manners," Nat said. "Don't worry about him, lad. Tom's me cousin, and we've been beating each other since we were children." He glanced over his shoulder. "That'll teach you to insult me and my friend when you're slewed, Tom. Never could fight when he was drunk," Nat said in an aside to Jonathan. "And he always forgets that I can."

Jonathan sat, quietly miserable, until the magic of the wind and the waves wove their spell around him, and he began to enjoy himself in spite of the embarrassment he felt. Even Tom gradually unbent, goaded into laughing at himself under the good natured jibes of his cousin and the older man—his father and Nat's uncle, as it turned out. By the time they'd returned to the cove and the quay, Jonathan was ravenous in spite of the food that Nat had brought along, and with the money Penhyrddin had given him stood the other men supper in the small public house in the village. He won the cheers of the entire room when he beat Tom at a game of darts; Tom claimed he couldn't see straight out of his blackened eyes, which caused everyone in the room to jeer and catcall until he conceded an honest defeat.

Jonathan had had two beers with his meal, and Nat insisted on making certain he returned safely home, in spite of having had at least twice that amount himself. They climbed the footpath, laughing and talking, at one point having to sit by the edge until they caught their breath. Jonathan couldn't help laughing, and every time Nat tried to get him to stop—"Now you be serious, Mister Jonathan, or your cousin will give me no end of trouble for leadin' you astray"—Jonathan would set off in a fresh wave of giggles. Their laughter eventually wore itself out, and they just sat, grinning at each other. Finally Nat stood, pulled Jonathan to his feet, and, linking their arms, started them off toward home.

"Here ye are, lad," Nat said, stopping when they were still a distance from the house.

"Thank you," Jonathan said. "I had a wonderful day."

"As did I," Nat said and held out his hand. "As did I. You're a good friend, Jonny."

Jonathan thought his body couldn't contain the happiness he felt at that moment. He took Nat's hand in both of his. "As are you."

Cornwall 1906

Rose looked up from the stove as Alec came back into the kitchen. "Margaret," she said, "finish the toast. Be certain it doesn't burn." She brushed her hands on her apron, then took Alec by the arm and pulled him aside. "Well?"

"He asked me to get the cart ready to take him and the other gentleman to church," Alec said. "He wasn't even started to get dressed, so I don't think he'll be needin' breakfast for a little while."

"What was he like?" Rose asked, tightening her grip. "Was he cheerful, or no?"

"He was short like when he first woke up," Alec replied, looking confused. "But he was fine this last, and 'pologized for bein' angry before."

"Did he now," Rose said with some satisfaction. "He was angry, was he? What did he say?"

"He said he didn't need no help, and I should just get him his shaving water." He looked up at her, then back at the floor. "When I went back, he said as mornin' wasn't his best time of day, and he was sorry for being angry first thing."

"And that's all?" She glanced over at Meg at the stove, all ears, no question, for all she was pretending to mind the breakfast.

"Well," Alec said, "he did joke about it. He said I should bring a lion tamer's chair and whip next time."

"That's a thought," Rose said, releasing his arm.

"Can I go, Mum?" he said. "I have to get the cart and horse ready to take him and the other gentleman to church."

"Yes, go," she said shushing him away. "And don't forget you're to take them around after you get back."

"But, Mum!"

"You'll do as I say. Now get ye goin', and don't give me back talk."

"Yes, Mum."

She went to the window and watched as Alec disappeared around the back of the barn, and smiled to herself as she brushed her hands off on her apron. *Not his best time of day, indeed,* she thought. *Now to breakfast.* She paused, wondering if Alec would be done setting up the cart in time to wash and wait at table, then shook her head. Time enough for that.

"The toast is ready, Rose."

Rose snapped back to the present. Meg stood by the kitchen stove, eyeing her curiously.

"Then put it in the warmer so it stays good," Rose said, meeting her look. "And get to work on the herring and the eggs."

Meg didn't move, but stood there, the same look on her face.

"You get to work, Margaret," Rose said sternly. "That breakfast won't get done with you standing there and staring like a half-witted goose. You shouldn't have started that toast before you finished the rest of the meal."

Meg bristled. " 'Twasn't me that started the toast early, Rose, and you well know it." She paused, that sly look coming back to her face. "Seems to me you've other things on your mind 'sides fixin' a meal for the gentlemen."

"Indeed I do," Rose said sharply, bustling over to the stove and crowding Meg out of the way. "I have to take care of two London gentlemen with none to help me exceptin' a back talkin' boy, for all he's my own son, and a village girl who wouldn't know how to behave around proper folk if her life depended upon it."

Meg's face grew stormy and she drew a breath to retort, but Rose cut her off. "There, now, Margaret," she said in a more conciliatory tone, "let's not start this again. We've no need to go breaking up more crockery to prove a point. Just you go and make sure the table's set. Mr. Langsford-Knight will come down soon, and it won't do no good to have everything at sixes and sevens when he does."

Meg sniffed—Rose ground her teeth at the sound—and hurried off down the passage to the dining room. When she was gone, Rose exhaled. *I'll have to be more careful*, she thought as she crossed the kitchen to get eggs out of the pantry. Meg had eyes, and a sharp nose for gossip, and for all she was a fool where anything in pants was concerned and couldn't stop her mouth from running once it got started, was fast as fast could be in figuring out the lay of the land where people and their secrets were concerned. *I'll have to be a bit slower in leading things along.* She stopped in the pantry door and rubbed her eyes. It wasn't as if she didn't have all the time in the world to do it—

"Good Sabbath to you, Rose Hale," a woman said behind her, and she turned.

Aunt Bannel stood in the doorway from the garden.

Rose was instantly wary. Meg might nose secrets out, though fully half the time she got the wrong end of the stick, but Aunt Bannel had no need of nosing about, nor of listening to idle gossip. She knew those secrets, all of them, everything to do with anyone in the village and the surrounding countryside, if one believed the gossip *about* her. And Rose did. It was no coincidence that she came calling the morning after the new master arrived; Rose was certain as if she'd read it in the Bible. And though she had wished a good Sabbath, Rose knew better: Mistress Bannel of Breawragh Cottage kept more than one Sabbath. Few spoke of it, and none in other than whispers about the fire on a winter night when such things seemed more likely, but everyone knew, and none crossed her word, not even the Vicar, who, unlike most in that position before him, had been born and raised in Landreath before going away to study at University.

Rose smoothed her face into a smile of bland welcome. "A good morning to you, too, Mistress Bannel," she said, crossing from the darkness of the pantry toward the woman standing in the door. "What may I do for you this morning?"

Aunt Bannel just stood, silent, hands folded in front of her, watching.

"Would ye like some tea?" Rose asked, turning back to the stove and putting the big copper kettle on the fire. "We're all of a muddle, what with the new master and his foreign friend here, even though we've been expecting him." She turned back and started; Aunt Bannel had entered the kitchen and was standing by the big table. "I'll have the tea ready in a minute or two. The water's already hot." Rose faltered under the unblinking stare of the older woman. "I'll . . . I'll just go about getting breakfast for the gentlemen if you don't mind. We can have a chat whilst I'm working."

She hurried over to the pantry and took half a dozen eggs out of a bowl on the shelf. Hands shaking, she turned to go back to the kitchen and started violently, dropping two of the eggs to smash on the flagstone floor. Aunt Bannel was standing in the door to the pantry, her face in shadow, her figure filling the doorway and backlit by the morning sunlight pouring past her from the kitchen.

"Lord's mercy," Rose breathed. "You gave me a fright."

"So I did," Aunt Bannel replied, glancing down at the floor. "So I did."

"'Tis no worry," Rose said, forcing her voice to normal volume. "I'll clean it up shortly, or have Meg. The chickens have been laying something a prize this spring, and we've no shortage." Balancing the remaining eggs carefully, she took two more out of the bowl, and stepped around the mess on the floor. She stopped a few steps from the door.

Aunt Bannel didn't move. "Tell me, Rose Hale. How fares the new master of Trevaglan this Sabbath morning?"

Nettled in spite of her fear, Rose drew herself up to her full height. "He fares as well as the old master did, as does anyone who comes into this house. And if you hear otherwise, Moereven Bannel, I'll say to you and to their face that they're a liar."

"Indeed," Aunt Bannel said, and walked back to the kitchen.

Rose followed her, clutching the eggs to her bosom, and as she did so, the door up the passage opened, and Meg's footsteps sounded on the flags. She was talking before the door even closed.

"La, la, la, bain't he a fine gentleman," she said as she clattered down the passage. "'Tis no problem that the breakfast isn't ready yet,' he said and gave me such a smile, 'for I'm a full half hour early before time.' Such manners he has and such a—" Meg stopped dead on the threshold to the kitchen, her eyes darting from Aunt Bannel to Rose and back again. "Good morning, mistress," she said in a lower tone and dropped a slight curtsey toward the older woman.

She knows what's what, Rose thought, *for all she's the greatest fool in three parishes.*

"I dropped two eggs in the pantry," Rose said as she placed

the remaining eggs in a bowl on the table. "Would you be a dear, Margaret, and clean it up for me whilst I finish the breakfast?"

Meg opened her mouth to protest, then, with another glance at Aunt Bannel, nodded silently.

"When that's done you can take the tea in to Mr. Langsford-Knight. Mr. Williams will be a while yet, dressing."

"Yes, Rose," Meg said as she bobbed toward her.

"There's eggs waiting under the tickey-tickies that want collecting, Margaret," Aunt Bannel said as Meg started toward the pantry. "We'll clean out the old while ye bring in the new."

Meg looked uncertainly at Rose, who nodded.

"There are seventeen of them, Margaret," Aunt Bannel said. "Take the basket, and be sure to bring them all."

Rose waited, temper mounting, until Meg was safely out the door and off through the garden gate, then spun and planted her hands on her hips.

"I give ye the respect you're due, Mistress Bannel," she said tightly, "seein's how you've brought all my children safe into this world, and helped me keep 'em alive and healthy, but I don't much like you givin' orders in my kitchen, and I don't care if ye know it."

"Would ye rather Margaret Berryman hear what I come to say to ye this morning, Rose Hale?" the older woman said as she moved slowly across the kitchen toward her. "And then the half of the town that'll listen to her tittle-tattle?"

"Then have your say, and have done with it," Rose said. "I have work to do, and can't spend all this morning waiting, even for you."

"Just this, Rose Hale. You take care which path you choose. There's more at stake in Trevaglan than your sorrows, and full well you know it." The light in the room seemed to dim as the old woman drew closer to her. "You'll not cross me or mine, nor, if you're wise, your own ghosts. You know not what you're doing."

Rose backed away until she caught up against the kitchen table. "I'm listening to an old woman babble nonsense in my kitchen," she said, her voice cracking, "instead of seein' to my work."

"Then you're as great a fool as Margaret," Aunt Bannel said, drawing back, "and I wash my hands of ye."

She turned to go, then stopped. The light in the room brightened. She stepped up to Rose and reached out with one hand to touch her cheek; Rose flinched away at the contact.

"Two eggs, smashed at once," Aunt Bannel said softly, glancing over Rose's shoulder toward the pantry. "Such perfect, perfect things, destroyed in an instant. My poor, darlin' child."

CHAPTER 5

"Piquet? Or chess, perhaps?" Langsford asked. "A quiet evening is in order, after the fleshpots of Landreath." Jonathan looked up from the book he was reading and smiled as Langsford crossed the library from the hall door. Meg was laying out the coffee on the table.

They had walked down to the village that afternoon after luncheon, Jonathan having firmly declined Rose's offer of Alec as a guide. Jonathan was a bit surprised that she had acquiesced immediately; he'd anticipated some resistance on her part, but she simply nodded and returned to the kitchen. The day had been beautiful—warm and sunny, with a light breeze blowing off the ocean—and the two men had strolled along the cliff path and down to Landreath, tucked under the headland.

They wandered the two streets of the village and looked out across the beached fishing smacks, then had a beer in the village's only public house. The three loungers in the room went silent when they entered, but the woman behind the bar, a big blowsy creature with a cast to her eye and very few teeth, greeted them cordially. Langsford introduced himself and Jonathan and said they were in from Trevaglan Farm. When he mentioned Jonathan's name, one of the men murmured a comment to his companion, but when Jonathan looked around, none met his eye; they all looked steadily at the table in front of them. After they left the pub, Langsford had teased him that word of some untold or long past scandal had preceded his arrival and that the locals were gossiping, but Jonathan hadn't risen to the bait; again Langsford had shown his usual unerring accuracy, and Jonathan had no desire to explore or explain what incidents the people of Landreath might hold in their long memories.

They'd climbed back around the headland by a different path, and came to the farm from behind, climbing the stiles in the stone hedgerows and crossing pastures still damp in places with the morning's heavy dew. Tea had followed, then dinner—Langsford had napped between, while Jonathan sat in the sun in the garden, reading—and now coffee.

"Neither, perhaps," Jonathan said in answer to Langsford's questions, and indicated the chair opposite him. "You told me earlier that I'd force you to un-gentlemanlike behavior should we play, and rather than throw such temptations in your path, perhaps conversation will suffice."

Langsford sighed as he settled into his seat. "More chatter?" he said, stretching his feet out toward the fire burning in the grate. "At this rate, Williams, we'll have talked each other out by Wednesday, and will sit, stony faced and silent, until it is time for me to take my leave."

"That might have been," Jonathan said, laying his book on the table beside him, "but we've engaged the Vicar and his wife to dine with us tomorrow evening. That will give us meat for chewing on for at least two or three days."

"True, true," Langsford said, nodding. "That should be interesting. I believe I actually noted an original thought somewhere around the fourth or fifth paragraph of his homily." He crossed to the table and poured himself a cup of coffee.

Jonathan had been surprised that morning to discover that Dr. Deane, who had been vicar fourteen years before, was still there—Jonathan had thought him quite elderly when he had lived at the farm before, but now he seemed no older than he had then. Deane had expressed himself delighted at Jonathan's return, and, after a few words of sympathy about Penhyrddin's death, had accepted Jonathan's invitation with apparent pleasure.

"I'm looking forward to it," Jonathan said as Langsford took his seat again. "He's something of a scholar, and, as I recall, very good dinner company, as is his wife. My cousin invited them often. About the only people he did, now that I think of it."

"A scholar, is he?" Langsford asked, and took a mouthful of his coffee. "Well, well."

"Yes," Jonathan replied. "History, as well as divinity, if I recall correctly. Oxford. Magdalen College."

"Well, that would explain why there was only *one* original thought." Jonathan clicked his tongue disapprovingly and Langsford held up his hand. "Don't worry. I will behave myself impeccably." Langsford leaned forward, elbows on his knees. "So. Conversation. What book held you so enraptured? Something edifying, I suppose."

"Moderately so," Jonathan said. "The Sonnets."

"Ah." Langsford smiled. "*Shall I compare thee to a summer's day? Thou art more lovely and more temperate . . .*"

Jonathan felt the color rise in his face and he looked down. "No. Not that one."

"*Let me not to the marriage of true minds*, then. Come, confess. That was always a favorite of yours."

Jonathan said nothing, but nodded. That had been, in fact, the sonnet he had been reading when Langsford had entered the room.

"*Let me not to the marriage of true minds admit impediment,*" Langsford said. "*Love is not love which alters when it alteration finds, or bends with the remover to remove.*"

Something in Langsford's tone changed, and Jonathan glanced over; Langsford was looking at the fire. "*Oh no,*" Langsford continued quietly, "*it is an ever fixed mark, that looks on tempests and is never shaken.*"

"Do you think that's true?" Jonathan interrupted, then stopped, aghast at having blurted the question. Langsford looked at him, his eyebrows raised. "I mean, it's a lovely thought," Jonathan said quickly, trying to find a way to make it an academic question and not a personal one, "but is it true, do you think? Or merely a poet's fancy?"

Langsford opened his mouth to speak, then looked at the fire again. "I don't know," he said finally. "I should like to think it true. There are many different aspects to the word: the love of a parent for a child, a husband for his wife, or a man for his brother, or . . . or his friend. I suppose we cannot know what he meant precisely, as we don't know of whom he was speaking when he wrote."

"No, I suppose we cannot," Jonathan echoed.

Langsford looked back at him, and their eyes locked. The silence lengthened, though Jonathan was certain the pounding of his heart must be audible throughout the house.

"Williams," Langsford said, and swallowed. "I—"

A slight cough sounded at the library door, and Jonathan jumped as if a gun had gone off directly behind him. Alec stood in the doorway.

"M'sorry to interrupt, sir, but is there anything else you'll be needin' tonight?"

"No, no," Jonathan stammered, more unnerved by the conversation than by Alec's unexpected presence. "There's nothing more you need do. Get to bed now."

"Yes, sir."

"Before you do, Alec," Langsford said, "there's a book on the table in my bedroom. Would you bring it down for me, please?" Alec nodded and hurried out. Langsford looked back at Jonathan and smiled. "Perhaps a literary evening would be best."

"Perhaps, yes," Jonathan said quickly, and scooped up the slim volume of Shakespeare. He crossed to the bookshelves lining the wall behind his chair and tucked the book back in its place. "What book were you reading that you left upstairs?" he asked over his shoulder.

"You'll think me most remarkably silly," Langsford replied, "but I was reading Dr. James's ghost stories."

"Really?" Jonathan said. "How do you find them?" He

scanned the shelf for something a little less fraught than love poems, and settled on *Pride and Prejudice.* His cousin had been a confirmed Janeite, much to Jonathan's amusement at the time. Jonathan had preferred Walter Scott.

"That's the silliest thing about it," Langsford said.

Jonathan sat and laid the Austen in his lap. "What is?"

"Well, they're well written, of course, and viewed in the plain light of day, nothing to cause undue alarm. But late last night, read only by candlelight, they were completely unnerving." Langsford looked sheepish. "I had the distinct sense that someone was watching me, and felt positively compelled to draw the curtains, so strong was the feeling. I just managed to refrain from bolting the shutters. Never mind the fact I was on the first floor, and no one could look in."

"How very odd."

"Silly, as I said." Langsford shrugged. "I slept rather badly, too. That will teach me to . . . *good God!"* Langsford stood suddenly, dropping his coffee cup on the carpet.

"My God, what is it?" Jonathan exclaimed, startled.

"That boy's outside, looking in at the window," Langsford said, his face pale. "What in the world is he about?"

"Alec?" Jonathan asked.

"Yes, sir?" Alec said. He stood in the doorway, book in hand. "Here you are, sir. I hope this is the right one."

Langsford glanced from the boy holding out the book to the window and back again. "Yes, lad. That's the one," he said, and took the book. "Thank you."

"You're welcome, sir. Will you be needin' anything else, Mr. Williams?"

"No, thank you, Alec, that will be all."

"Well," Langsford said after Alec left the room. "We have just had a lesson in the power of atmosphere and suggestion over the rational mind." He stooped and picked up his cup and placed it on the table. "Empty, fortunately. In any case, here I sit, a completely rational being, and because I see the reflection of Alec's face in the window pane, I leap like a started rabbit. If I were a more credulous or a more superstitious man, I'd swear to any who asked that I'd seen a ghost. Coffee? Or brandy, perhaps?"

"Coffee, please," Jonathan said, and Langsford poured two cups.

"I wonder how many ghost sightings are just such a circumstance," he said as he handed Jonathan his coffee. "I mean, those that people truly believe to have witnessed, not simple fabrications to frighten their neighbors."

"A good many, I should think," Jonathan said, and sipped his coffee. He made a slight face. "It certainly seems to have shaken you. You forgot the sugar." He crossed to the tray and dropped a lump in his cup. "Do you believe in them?"

"Do I believe in what?"

"Believe in ghosts."

Langsford laughed. "You might as well ask them if they believe in me."

"Interesting point," Jonathan replied as he crossed toward his chair. He paused by Langsford's chair and looked at the windows flanking the fireplace. *Odd,* he thought. *The hall door doesn't reflect in either. How peculiar.* He put his coffee on the mantle and drew the curtains over the right-hand window.

"And here we see how silliness is a contagious thing," Langsford said, lifting his cup in a mock toast.

"I am merely protecting my carpets," Jonathan said firmly as he crossed in front of the fireplace to the other window. "Your cup is full now, and I wouldn't have you startled." He glanced out the second window before drawing the drapes and shivered. Silliness or not, the sense of being watched, once suggested, was indeed contagious; the fading moonlight on the lawn and the shadows under the hawthorns were eerie, even though there was nothing out of the ordinary to be seen. He drew the curtains. "And you haven't answered my question."

Langsford frowned in response. "It's an odd question, if you think about it," he said. "Rather like 'Do I believe in God?' or

'Do I believe in America?' I have no doubt either exists, even though I've never seen them. Enough people have—or claim to have—to allay any doubts I may harbor." He paused. "Well, enough have seen America. I question the sanity of those who have clamed to have seen God, at least those who have claimed it in the last century or so."

Jonathan smiled. "I sometimes question the sanity of those who claim to have seen America."

Langsford's smile flashed across his face. "America does seem a rather unlikely thing, doesn't it? But then, many things are unlikely, and yet prove true. Should one not believe in them, simply because they are unlikely? Or should one try to believe six impossible things before breakfast—or in this case, before retiring to sleep? Why not ghosts?"

"I certainly did when I was a child," Jonathan said, and sipped his coffee. "Or rather, I *wanted* to believe it."

Langsford nodded. "Yes," he said. "There was a great deal of hopefulness involved at the time for me, too. Later, of course, I simply pretended to do so in order to terrify my sisters. What monsters children are."

"Some children, in any case," Jonathan said pointedly.

"Oh, I'm guilty of that crime as any prisoner brought before the bench," Langsford said. "But to get back to your original question: Do I believe in ghosts? I cannot say. I believe that there are many things that are as yet unknown to us, that time will show as being perfectly real." He took a swallow of coffee and then held up the cup. "Coffee was unknown to our ancestors, and yet here we sit, sipping it as a matter of course. Scientists make new discoveries every day. Will disembodied spirits be one of those? I don't know." He put down the coffee cup and held up his book. "Do I believe in the horror of Dr. James's vengeful spirits? No, I do not. I can only think that, once free of the body, the soul has better things to do than lurk about, frightening those still on this plane of existence."

"I certainly hope you're right."

Langsford laughed. "This is a most peculiar conversation," he said. "And in any case, I'm sure neither of us has anything to worry about, unless perhaps your cousin would object to your bringing me along and rattling on about such things in his library."

Jonathan shifted uneasily in his chair. Penhyrddin no doubt slept quietly in the churchyard. Of others, Jonathan was not so certain, though he truly did not credit such nonsense. "My cousin would have no objections. Such things fascinated him."

"Then we will continue this conversation tomorrow evening." Langsford stifled a yawn. "And now you'll have to forgive me. Between the fresh air and sunlight today and my unsettled sleep last night, I'm quite weary, in spite of my nap."

"Sleep well tonight," Jonathan said, rising.

"I'm certain I will," Langsford said, and retrieved his book. "Good night, Williams."

"Good night."

Jonathan poured himself another cup of coffee and picked up the Austen, but soon found he was unable to concentrate on the printed words. His eyes kept wandering to the door through which Langsford had just exited, and as the fire burned low, he gave up the attempt. He laid the book aside and stared blindly into the glowing embers.

Twice since they'd arrived at Trevaglan Langsford had seemed on the brink of some communication, and twice he had drawn back. Last night was less certain, but tonight Langsford had been clearly about to share a confidence, and had been prevented only by Alec's fortuitous interruption.

Jonathan bit his lip. He'd been an idiot to acknowledge the sonnet. Langsford was no fool, far from it. That last, telling comment about the love of a man for his friend confirmed that. He bit down harder until the pain caused his eyes to water. He had been so careful, always, not to hint, not to indicate in any way how much he loved Langsford, but Langsford had clearly seen through his evasions. And now, just at the moment that he might be free of the unbearable weight of that daily silence, and love safely from a distance, Langsford, in his compassion and sympathy, had seemingly decided to bring it into the open, to share his knowledge of Jonathan's secret, and, most miserable of all, be understanding about it.

He could not bear it.

The only course he could think to take was to act as if the moment had not occurred and to give as little opportunity for Langsford to bring up the subject as possible. He would try to behave as if nothing untoward had happened, as if this was just another holiday, and at the end of the week they would both return to London. Brushing away his tears, he rose and returned the book to its place on the shelf. *I'll bring him hot chocolate in the morning,* he decided. He always did on holiday, and then would sit on the edge of Langsford's bed and talk. Perilous, perhaps, in these circumstances, but an old and established pattern that would raise no questions, and perhaps divert more than one. He smiled slightly. Langsford was never at his sharpest in the morning, and if there was ever a safe time to be alone with him in conversation, the chocolate hour, as Langsford called it, was most certainly that time.

Deep silence wrapped the house as he walked down the passage to the kitchen to tell Meg or Rose to prepare the chocolate in the morning, assuming there was any in the house, and to clear the coffee trays, but he found the kitchen dark and empty. *Odd.* He retraced his steps, pausing by the library door. The flickering shadows thrown by the dying fire and his lamp startled him; one looked like a man standing by his chair. Chiding himself for his suggestibility, he crossed the hall and the drawing room. As he walked down the steps to the passage leading to his bedroom, he noticed that his door was slightly ajar and that a dim light flickered against the jamb. He pushed the door open quietly. Rose stood by the open window, her back toward him, and a candle in her hand. A small fire burned in the grate.

"Yes, Rose?" He remained in the doorway, thoroughly disconcerted at finding her here, at being alone in the room with her.

She spun and fell back against the wall, her hand to her breast, the other holding the candlestick like a shield. Her eyes were wide and dark, and her free hand flew to her mouth.

"I'm sorry," Jonathan said, taken aback by the violence of her reaction. "I had no intention of frightening you, I assure you."

She drew a deep breath, and hurried across the room. "You did startle me a bit, sir," she said rapidly. "I was just in to see that Alec was settled in and to turn down your bed"—she gestured toward the bed; the quilts were folded back and his nightclothes laid out on top of them—"and I didn't hear you come in."

"Thank you," Jonathan said. "Alec is settled in? I don't understand."

"Yes, sir," she said. "I've asked him to sleep in the little room across the hall, in case you'll be needing anything in the night."

Jonathan frowned. "I'm sure that won't be necessary, Rose."

"I'm sure it won't either, sir," she said, her eyes darting around the room, "but might we discuss that in the morning, if you please? He's asleep now, and he does have morning chores in addition to seeing to you gentlemen." She sidled toward the door, and he stepped aside. "Thank you, sir," she said and slipped past him.

"The coffee things are in the library, Rose," he called after her. "You can see to them in the morning, if you like. Oh, and also, please prepare some hot chocolate for Mr. Langsford-Knight before breakfast, if we have any in the house. I will take it to him myself."

"Yes, sir, we do," she said, "I'll see to it in the morning. Good night, sir." To his astonishment, she bobbed a curtsy before hurrying up the three steps to the drawing room.

Jonathan closed the door behind him, relieved at her going, but puzzled. The woman had seemed positively terrified. He glanced around the room but could see nothing that would have so upset her. He wasn't at all pleased that she was having Alec stay in the house, and he was fairly certain she knew it, but that wouldn't cause this headlong flight from the room. *Very strange.* He set the lamp on the dressing table and crossed to the window. Warm as the day had been, the evening sea breeze was cool, and he didn't want the window open all night.

He stood by the window for a moment, looking out across the pasture toward the sea. The moon had set, and the faint starlight did little to illuminate the pastures; the sea was a grey blur beyond the black line of the cliffs. He pulled the sash down, and, just as it closed, noticed something on the sill outside. He raised the window again and picked the object up.

And dropped it immediately, as if it had burned his hand. He staggered across the room and vomited violently into the wash basin, his stomach heaving and black spots dancing in his vision. He clutched the dressing table until the spasms passed, then wiped his mouth with one of the towels. Hands shaking violently, he picked up the lamp and crossed back to the window and knelt. Pale gold against the dark carpet, a small bundle of straw tied with a scarlet thread lay where he had dropped it. He picked it up and threw it into the fire, then turned to the basin and vomited again.

Cornwall 1892

The day spent sailing had cemented their friendship, and Jonathan never again questioned whether he would meet Nat either at midday or after the day's work was done.

The other farmhands were amused, but pitied the boy who'd lost his own mother and gained a stepmother in such rapid succession. Penhyrddin, still somewhat concerned but willing to chance that Nat's company would help the boy, spoke with Hale, the new foreman on the farm, about arranging Nat's work to allow him more free time. He would, he said, hire an extra hand to make up the work if need be; he felt the money was worth the good it did.

Hale wasn't pleased—he thought Nat got away with far too much as it was, and Penhyrddin was aware he felt so—and spoke against his master's wishes but once in that conversation, then consented. So on Nat's free afternoons the two rambled across the countryside or lay in the sun on the beach. Nat wasn't always free of an evening, or even on some Sundays—he had family responsibilities in the village, he said—but when he was, he'd tap on Jonathan's window, and they'd spend the evening out under the hawthorn tree nearby, talking in whispers or, more frequently, simply lying on their backs, looking at the sky.

At dinner one Saturday in mid-May, Jonathan begged permission of his cousin to forgo Sunday services the next day. He said he had a mind to visit an ancient site about five miles distant, a trio of standing stones with a massive lintel above. Nat knew the way, he said, and he'd already spoken to Cook about preparing food. Jonathan actually had little interest in the stones themselves; his hopes lay in spending the entire day out of doors with Nat. When his cousin hesitated, Jonathan played his trump card: The trek would take them past the ruins of the Iron Age village, which Jonathan hadn't seen, his earlier plan to do so having fallen through. Perhaps, if they made good enough time in the morning, he and Nat would be able to explore both the ruins *and* see the standing stones . . .

Penhyrddin wasn't at all fooled by Jonathan's avowed fascination with ancient stones and villages, but again he felt that any change was an improvement over the silent, sad boy he'd been for the first weeks of his stay. And if the boy was being sly and thought he was getting away with it, well, why not. What harm could come of it? He only made Jonathan promise to be back before dinner or, at the worst, by nightfall.

The weather had promised fair for the next morning, and Jonathan woke earlier than was his custom. Throwing back his covers, he jumped out of bed and opened the window; the sun was up and the sky was bright, with only a few high thin clouds; the air was warm and still. He dressed hurriedly, then ran down the hall and through the house to the kitchen. Cook and Rose were already there and preparing the morning meal, and Jonathan worried at them so to hurry that Cook finally shooed him out of the room, saying he'd get his food when it was ready and not before, so shouldn't he just get out from under foot and let them finish their work?

He moped impatiently about the library until he heard the chime for breakfast, then, sitting with his cousin, bolted his food as quickly as propriety would allow. Then he was off to the kitchen again as soon as he finished.

Nat was there, lounging by the stove and talking to Rose. She looked none too pleased to be interrupted, but Nat just laughed and told her that their gossip would have to wait until he returned; he had nursemaid duty to do and had best be about it. He grinned at Jonathan as he said it, and Jonathan smiled back. It had become a joke between them, and rather than be embarrassed by it, Jonathan treasured the teasing.

"Here is your food," Cook said as she bustled in from the pantry carrying two satchels. "Ye said ye didn't want no proper picnic, Mister Jonathan, so I didn't pack the hamper." She placed the satchels on the big table in the middle of the kitchen. "I've set in enough for the two of ye, but ye just be careful with my goods, Nat. Mister Jonathan's a gentleman, but ye, ye lazy shift about, ye wouldn't know good things it they took your nose off. I don't want no broken crockery come the end of the day."

Rose picked up the two bags. "This one here's yours, Nat," she said, handing him the larger of the two, "and this one's yours, Mister Jonathan."

Nat hoisted his bag. "I'll take care, Gran," he said—Jonathan had had no idea he was the cook's grandson—and handed the second pack to Jonathan. "And if I don't, I'm sure the young master here will take it out of my hide."

"Well, someone should," Cook huffed. "Now you two get out of my kitchen and let me get to laying out Mr. Penhyrddin's luncheon."

"Ay, Gran," Nat said. He bowed to Rose. "And a good day to *you*, Miss Pritchard."

"Hmph," Rose said as she followed them to the door. "You just get yourself and the young man back in one piece, Nat Boscawen, and soon. You've better things to do with your time than pokin' around in old stones."

"I'll be back when we're back," Nat called over his shoulder as they headed down the garden path. "Eh, women," he said to Jonathan. "They've no idea there's things more important than crockery and courtin' and babies."

Jonathan stopped. "Courting?" he asked

Nat looked back at him and laughed. "Course, courtin'. Thing is, ye say two nice words to a woman and she thinks ye fancy her." He opened the garden gate. "Come on, Jonny," he said, when Jonathan made no move to follow him through. "We won't make five miles and back if ye just stand around."

Jonathan walked after him slowly, and they started up the lane toward the high road that ran from village to village across the countryside. Nat told him of his latest go around with his cousin Tom—"Damn fool's been throwin' darts every day for two weeks, claimin' he's going to challenge you to a match"—and Jonathan smiled half-heartedly at Nat's outrageous descriptions of Tom's lack of skill. *Courting.*

They reached the top of the lane and skirted the Witch's Cottage, slipping through an opening in the hedge. The door was open and smoke drifted from the chimney, but they didn't see anyone in the front garden. As they rounded the small stone shed out back, however, the deaf-mute who lived with the old woman poked his head out and made a sound. He was a big man, perhaps five years or so older than he, and dressed in rough working clothes. Nat stopped, and Jonathan, after a few steps, did also. Cripples and idiots of any sort made him uncomfortable, and though the man wasn't physically deformed, Jonathan felt awkward whenever he chanced to meet him.

"Good day, Justus," Nat said and doffed his cap. The other man saluted him, then made an odd gesture with his hand. Nat nodded and pointed off in the direction they were headed, and said the single word "Stones." Justus Bannel nodded several times, looked at Jonathan, then looked back at Nat and raised his eyebrow. He made another gesture and pulled a wry face; Nat laughed out loud.

"What are ye findin' to laugh at that gets you out of bed on a Sabbath morning, Nat Boscawen?" Jonathan looked over at the house; the Witch looked out at the open casement.

Nat bowed to the old woman and pulled his cap on. "Your own boy it is making me laugh, Aunt Bannel. For me, the young man and I had a fancy to visit the stones at Cargwyns." He pulled Jonathan forward. "Aunt Bannel, may I present Mr. Jonathan Williams of Trevaglan Farm. Mr. Williams, the Widow Bannel of Breawragh Cottage an' her son, Justus."

"Enough of your foolish bosh, Nat Boscawen," the old woman said, and turned her gaze on Jonathan. "Good day to you, Mister Jonathan. 'Tis time we'd met, I think."

Jonathan took off his cap and bowed slightly, murmuring something about the honor of meeting her, but the woman's cold gaze out of dark eyes under level brows affected him much like being called up in front of his school master for transgressing the rules. He twisted his cap in his hands and looked at the ground. Witch or no, the sharp, lined face, iron grey hair pulled back in tight bun, and the hard, unsmiling mouth certainly looked the part, as did the feeling that she looked into him, rather than at him, and knew his thoughts, his secrets, and his fears. She frightened him.

"Well," Nat said, dropping his hand on Jonathan's shoulder, "We'd best be on our way, if we're to make it there and back by dinner."

"This bain't a good day for travellin', Nat," Mistress Bannel said, her eyes not leaving Jonathan's face. "There's a storm comin' in, and it'll be a banger. The clouds are bankin' up already. You'd do best to go no further than the hills behind me, if indeed you go that far. You'll get caught in the storm if ye go farther, and no good can come of it."

Nat frowned. "I talked to my gran 'bout it this morning, and she said the rain wouldn't fall till late. Yours bain't the only family that can read the weather, Mistress Bannel."

Her eyes shifted back to Nat, and Jonathan exhaled. "Your gramfer had that gift, lad, not your gran, nor you. She's a good woman, but wouldn't know a storm was comin' if she was out standin' in the rain. And ye, you'd pay it no attention if ye did, if it crossed your plans."

"You're not wrong there, I s'pose" Nat said. "I'll keep an eye, and turn back if it threatens." He tugged Jonathan's arm, almost pulling him off balance. "C'mon, lad. We have some distance to make if we're to be back before the weather breaks.

Jonathan stumbled after him up the footpath that wound across the fields and up the hill behind the cottage. He swore he could feel her eyes on him as he hurried to keep up with Nat and, pausing at the top of the rise, he looked back; small in the distance, she was still in the window, watching, and her son by the small shed.

The footpath dropped through a wooded ravine, and he ran down the slope and caught up to Nat just as he crossed a narrow log bridge across a small stream. Jonathan slipped on the moss-covered log, and caught the rough wood handrail to keep from falling into the stream. He called out to Nat to wait, then scrambled up the side of the ravine to where Nat stood waiting.

"You heard the old woman," Nat said. "Hurry, hurry or you'll get wet. Well, keep up, or you'll get caught out in the rain." He started up the path at a quick pace. "Nosey old bird thinks because she birthed half the parish that she's the mother of all of us."

"We don't have to go all the way to the stones, if you don't want to," Jonathan said, gasping for breath. "We can stop anywhere and just sit for a while."

"You said you wanted to see those damn stones, and you're goin' to see 'em," Nat snapped over his shoulder, "if we have to walk all five miles both ways in the pourin' rain to do it."

Jonathan stopped. "Well, you can go see them yourself, if you're that determined," he shouted. "Don't let me or anyone else stop you. Go on back to the farm if you've better things to do."

Nat spun, strode back down the path, and grabbed Jonathan by the arm. "'Twas your idea to go see 'em, and you'll damn well go."

Jonathan twisted in Nat's grip, but couldn't get free. "I don't care about them," he said, struggling. "I just wanted to spend the day away. With you. Let me go, damn you, you're hurting me!"

Nat released him and stepped back, a smile tweaking at the corners of his mouth. "Why, Mister Jonathan, I don't ever think I've heard you swear before."

"I never have," Jonathan said, rubbing his arm.

"I'm a bad influence, then."

"You are."

"Well, then," Nat said, "I'm a bad influence that has the day in front of him, two knapsacks of food, and a companion who, when he isn't swearin' a streak, is as good a company as I could wish for. What else could a man want?"

Jonathan glowered up at him. "To stop gabbling, perhaps, and start walking."

"Done," Nat said, and started up the path.

Jonathan stood for a moment, debating whether to follow or to go back to the farm. When Nat disappeared around a bend in the path without looking back, he scooped up his picnic bag, and ran after him, catching up just as they broke out of the wood and into the bright sunlight of an open meadow. He hiked his satchel up on his shoulder and matched Nat's stride.

"You're a terrible nursemaid," he said, not looking up at Nat.

"Best in all Cornwall," Nat said.

"That's a sad statement on Cornwall," Jonathan replied, trying to keep a serious face.

"Well, we get the poorest charges here, ye see," Nat said. "All these foreign folk."

Jonathan shoved him, though not hard. Nat grinned and shoved him back, and Jonathan staggered.

"Is that how a Cornish nursemaid treats his poor charge?"

Nat grabbed him in a headlock and squeezed. "Indeed it is, lad." Laughing, he set off across the field, Jonathan following a few steps behind.

The path led near the ruined village that Jonathan had used as bait to get his cousin to let him go this morning, and they took a detour to poke amongst the hillocks and pits that were scattered across the hilltop behind the stone walls, broken and overgrown, that ringed the hilltop. There wasn't too much to see; one or two of the pits had been excavated by amateur archeologists at some time past, exposing the ancient stonework, but most of the site was covered with the short turf of the fields, broken by the tops of the grey walls that made up the bones of the village, with little but the regular pattern of rings to show where the huts of the occupants had stood.

The item of real interest, his cousin had told him, was a man-made tunnel—he called it a fogou—that burrowed under a large mound on the hill top. Though Nat said he had played there often as a child, they probably would not have found it if Jonathan hadn't brought the map Penhyrddin had prepared. The entrance was low, barely three feet tall, and a massive stone lintel, covered with lichen and overhung by grass and half hidden behind some gorse, spanned the opening.

After they'd tucked their packs under the gorse bush, Nat crawled into the tunnel, and Jonathan, hesitant, followed him. The tunnel was dark and dank, with rough stone walls and a ceiling of huge stone slabs, all covered in moss. The air was musty, and the sunlight penetrated but a little way in. About fifteen feet in, Nat stood, and in the dim light Jonathan could see that the narrow tunnel had opened into a large, curving passageway that disappeared into darkness ahead. He shivered in the damp.

Nat struck a match and held it up. The ceiling wasn't much taller than his head, all single stone slabs spanning the full width of the chamber. "It goes on another fifty feet or so," he said, his voice echoing weirdly. "I don't suppose we brought any candles?"

Jonathan shook his head. "What a pair of explorers we are. Come on anyway. I have plenty of lucifers."

"No," Jonathan said. "Let's come back another day with candles, and warmer clothing."

"Oh, don't be such a bearn. It's not too far, though there isn't much to see. Damn." Nat shook the match out and struck another. "Come ahead."

Reluctantly, Jonathan followed Nat into the darkness.

"When we were children our folks said that the piskeys lived in this place, and would steal us away if we came here," Nat said. "They said 'twas a haunted place, and to keep away." His smile flashed in the match light. "That didn't keep us, of course, nor did it keep them away when they were small." They rounded the bend in the tunnel, and the light from the entrance faded until it was a slight green glow behind them. The tunnel then bent to the right, and the last light vanished.

"It ends just up ahead," Nat said as they rounded the curve. "Here we go. There's another tunnel off somewhere along here, with a room at the end, but I don't see it. We'd need more light." In the dim light of the match, Jonathan could see the end wall, the stones set in a slight curve to wrap around to the other side of the passage. Nat stooped over something on the floor. "A ticking pallet. Someone's been camping here. Can't say as I'd want to spend the night myself. Eh, might as well head out." He stood and shook out the match.

"Nat," Jonathan said after a moment. "Light a match, I can't see anything." There was a slight scuffling in the dark. "Nat?" Jonathan said again, and then screamed when two hands grabbed him. He tried to pull away as Nat laughed, but was held tight.

"Don't you worry, Jonny," Nat said. "I can find my way in the dark here, even still. Just hold my arm, and I'll lead you out."

He grabbed Nat's arm, and they started walking slowly in the dark, Nat in the lead. They'd gone about four steps when Nat staggered back against him.

"What is it?" Jonathan whispered when he recovered his balance.

"I might be mistaken," Nat said and struck a match, "but I'm pretty sure it was the wall."

"Give me the matches," Jonathan said. "You aren't to be trusted."

Nat laughed. "Don't be foolish."

"Then let's get out of this place. Please."

"Yes, sir," Nat said mockingly, and taking Jonathan's arm, led them back to the entrance.

They crawled out through the low entry and out into the brassy sunlight. Jonathan shivered in spite of the heat and brushed his trousers off as Nat collected their bags. When Nat handed him his satchel, he reached out and touched Nat's shoulder.

"You hurt your head," he said.

"Did I?" Nat touched his forehead and looked at his hand. "I hope the wall came off worse in the deal, but I'm thinkin' it didn't."

"Let me look at it," Jonathan said, but Nat waved him off.

"'Tis nothing to take on about," Nat said. "I'll have Gran or Rose see to it when we get back to the house. If we cross a stream I'll wash it off. We'd best be going."

Nat struck out down the hillside opposite the way they'd climbed, and they joined the footpath farther along. Occasionally they left the path, staying near the small river which eventually ran down to Landreath; Nat said the headwaters started in the hills where the stones of Cargwyns stood, and the direct route was faster than following the footpath. When they reached the plateau the travelling was easier, as the land was gentle and rolling, with an occasional deeper valley, but the day was hot and still, unusual for May.

The path dropped again into a ravine and crossed the river, barely more than a deep stream, ten feet or so across. A small cataract plunged over the stones at the head of the glen and into a deep pool overhung by shrubs and trees. The air was cool, and the rush of the falls soothing. Nat stooped over the water and scrubbed his face, and Jonathan dropped his pack and sank into the soft grass growing on the bank by the pool under a willow. Nat climbed back up and kicked him in the foot.

"C'mon, Jonny," he said. "We've another mile and a half to go at least, and the day's wastin'."

"Can't we just stay here?" Jonathan said, shading his eyes against the filtered sunlight. "This is a nice spot."

Nat snorted. "We've been through this once already," he said. "You wanted to see the stones, and see 'em you will."

"Well, I've changed my mind," Jonathan replied, putting his hands behind his head and leaning back. "I'd rather stay here. It's too hot to keep walking."

"Is it now," Nat said, and sat beside him. "Are ye too much of a lady to go walkin' on a hot afternoon?"

"A lady is it," Jonathan said. "I'll give you lady," and without warning jumped on Nat and pushed him over onto his back.

Laughing, they rolled around in the grass for a few minutes, but in short order Nat had gained the advantage and pinned Jonathan under him. "Well, ye may not be a lady," he said, sitting back on Jonathan's hips, "But ye're certainly no wrestler, lad." He looked around the glen. "Aye. This looks as nice a place as any to spend an afternoon lazin' about." He grabbed Jonathan's wrists and pinned them above his head. "We can stay here if you've a mind to. I could do with a good dip myself, come to think of it."

Jonathan's heart raced. Nat's weight on his body, his helplessness before the other man's strength, and Nat's face smiling down at him frightened him—or rather, not frightened, but aroused in him an emotion he didn't recognize, and his inexperience combined with the sensations coursing through his body made him fear them. They looked into each other's eyes for a long, fraught moment, and Jonathan struggled for breath. "Aye, that'd be good," he said finally, lapsing for a moment into a lilt that matched Nat's.

"Well then," Nat said quietly, almost tenderly, "we'll stay here a while, won't we. We could do worse." He brushed Jonathan's hair back from his brow, and for one terrifying moment Jonathan both hoped and feared that Nat was going to kiss him.

Instead, Nat rolled off and stretched out in the grass next to him. "Ay, a nice dip'll do both of us good. 'Tis a hot day, make no mistake."

Jonathan lay quietly for a moment, then asked nervously, "Should we swim then?" He knew better than he knew his own name that he dared not undress.

Nat stretched and sighed. "There's no rush," he said. "We've the whole day, and jumpin' in the water without coolin' down a little first might be unhealthy."

Jonathan could not have agreed more.

Ten minutes later, however, when Nat sat up and started to undress, Jonathan's rebellious body was no more ready to cooperate than it had been.

"Aren't you comin' in?" Nat asked as he stood and dropped his trousers.

"In a little bit," Jonathan said, desperately looking at the waterfall and the trees, anywhere but at Nat standing naked in the dappled sunlight.

"Well, don't be long about it," Nat said, squatting down next to him. He cuffed Jonathan lightly on the head, then stood and waded out into the stream. He dove under, and surfaced again in the middle of the pool. "C'mon, Jonny," he called. "The water's somethin' rare."

"In a little bit!" Jonathan said again, and Nat started to climb out of the water. "All right!" Jonathan said and sat up. "I'm coming." Nat slid beneath the surface of the water again.

Jonathan untied his shoes slowly and pulled them off, then his stockings. He unbuttoned his shirt and slipped out of it, folding it carefully. Still sitting, he wriggled out of his trousers and folded them up, and then his undershirt joined the pile. He sat in a panic, hugging his knees, then stood and walked down toward the pool, staying near the brush that clung to the rocks. Nat ducked under again, and Jonathan seized those few moments to drop his undergarment and dive in. Within minutes the cold water achieved what all of his desperate wishes had not, and he swam over to where Nat stood under the little waterfall.

"Well, 'tis about time," Nat said. "For one who says he bain't a lady, you certainly went all missish of a sudden."

"No," Jonathan said. "I'm just a bit more proper than you, you great clumsy lout."

"Proper is it?" Nat said and dove for him, but Jonathan was ready for him and ducked aside. Nat hit the water with a huge splash, and Jonathan scrambled up onto the rocks at the base of the falls.

"Ay, proper," he said, crouching low as Nat started slowly toward him.

"I'll give ye proper, boy. A proper thrashing, that is."

Nat lunged for him and Jonathan sprang from the rock in a clean dive over his head. Nat switched his direction, but his hand slid off Jonathan's leg as he grabbed for it. Jonathan broke the water cleanly and stroked to the far side of the pool, then stood and jumped to one side quickly. As he'd expected, Nat had followed, and almost caught his arm, but Jonathan wiggled free and put some distance between them. Nat crouched, and the two circled each other slowly.

"You know I'll catch you, Jonny," Nat said with a wicked smile, and made a feint. "You might as well give up now and save yourself the trouble."

"And what'll you do when you catch me?"

Nat lunged again, and Jonathan darted to the side, but Nat changed directions quickly and got a firm grip on Jonathan's wrist.

"Why, just this," he said, and pulled Jonathan over and ducked him. He pulled him up and said, "Lout, am I?"

"Yes," Jonathan sputtered. "A great clumsy lout who likes to ballyrag his betters."

"Hoot!" Nat shouted, and laughed. "And who's my better here? None that I see."

"Then you'd better be getting glasses, you old grandad," Jonathan said. He planted his feet as best he could and shoved, and they both went down.

Nat recovered his footing first. "Grandad, is it?" Nat bent and scooped Jonathan up in both arms. "And you're my little babby, I suppose. Well, time to baptize the babby," he said, and heaved Jonathan into the center of the pool.

Jonathan surfaced, and Nat grabbed him again. "Stop," Jonathan coughed. "Just a moment."

Nat held Jonathan steady until he stopped coughing and brushed some water weeds off his face. They dropped down into the water and sat, breathing heavily and smiling, when Nat suddenly pulled Jonathan into a rough, tight embrace. "Eh," Nat said, and held him at arm's length. "Who'd have ever thought I'd grow so fond of ye. You were such a sad piece when I met your cousin and you at the train that day."

Jonathan felt his face redden, and he looked away.

"There, now," Nat said. "Ye had reason to be sad, and still do, but we'll not talk of it any more this day." He stood and held out his hand. Jonathan took it, and Nat pulled him to his feet. "Come. Gran's sure to have fixed us a feast, and she's as sure to give us the devil if we don't eat all of it."

Nat rooted through Jonathan's satchel as Jonathan pulled on his undergarments. "Missish," Nat muttered, but held up his hands in surrender when Jonathan threatened to throw all of Nat's clothing into the stream, since he could do without them.

Cook had indeed prepared a feast: cold roast chicken, biscuits wrapped in a linen cloth, a crock of fresh butter, jellied eels in a jar, hard boiled eggs, pasties, cold baked potatoes, ginger fairings and lardy cakes, and a crock of fresh milk ("You're a growing boy," Nat commented, and Jonathan threw a biscuit at him, which Nat caught and immediately crammed in his mouth.) Nat's held a similar bounty—albeit a larger quantity—and two bottles of ale, as well as yarg cheese, which Jonathan detested, but Nat relished.

"You can save the milk for later, Jonny," Nat said, handing him one of the beer bottles. "Just don't tell Gran that I'm leading you into sin and degradation."

By the time they'd unpacked the food, both men had dried in the warm air, so they dressed, and then fell to eating with a will. Jonathan talked about school, and that he was going up to Cambridge in the autumn, about his sister, and, diffidently, about his father's unseemly haste in marrying after his mother's death. This last had been difficult to discuss, but Nat looked so concerned—and not a little angry—that Jonathan gradually told the tale, though holding back his cousin's suspicions about the situation. Nat reciprocated, telling about his own father, who'd died when Nat was a boy, lost at sea with Nat's older brother when their fishing boat went down in a gale. Nat had only been five at the time, but his mother made him swear that he would never go to sea but work the land instead, and as soon as Nat was old enough, she had spoken to old Mr. Penhyrddin, to get him a place at Trevaglan. And so the afternoon wore on.

The sun, which had filtered down through the branches of the trees all day, dimmed as they were finishing, and the still air felt even more oppressive than it had that morning when they'd been walking. Nat glanced up and frowned.

"Clouds are comin' in," he said. "Looks like the old woman was right. It's a thunderer and no mistake. We'd best get movin' if we want to make it back before it breaks." He grabbed his satchel and started to shove the jars and linens and such back in and then stopped. "What's this," he asked, and pulled an envelope out of the bottom of the satchel. He tore it open, pulled out the note inside, and looked at it.

Jonathan stopped packing his things. "What is it?"

Nat's mouth went to a thin hard line, and he shoved the paper and the envelope back into the satchel. "Nothin'," he said. "Just some damn foolishness of Rose's, I suppose. Never you mind."

The food felt like lead in Jonathan's stomach. *Courtin'. Damn foolishness of Rose's.* "Is anything wrong?" he asked.

"*No*," Nat snapped. "Nothin's wrong." A gust of wind shook the trees over their heads, and Nat shoveled all that was left of his food back in the satchel. "C'mon, boy," he sharply. "We don't have time to doodle about." He picked up his pack and started up the path back the way they'd come.

Jonathan followed more slowly, and by the time he broke out of the wood, Nat was some distance ahead. The clouds had rolled in from the southwest, heavy, dark, and threatening, and a cold wind struck him as he left the shelter of the trees. Jonathan ran to catch up to Nat, who was watching the sky with a worried look. As they crossed open fields and climbed through hedgerows, the clouds grew darker, and the air a dense, murky green.

They had come perhaps a mile when the first heavy drops hit them.

"Damn," Nat said. He pulled open his satchel and rooted through it. "Quick, Jonny," he said, "Give me that cloth of yours. Gran didn't see fit to pack me one."

"What for?" Jonathan asked.

"Just do it," Nat said.

Temper rising, Jonathan wrenched open his pack and pulled out the linen. "There," he said, and threw them at Nat, who shoved them inside his shirt. The rain started coming down harder.

"The milk, too," Nat said. "The jug!"

"The milk?"

"For God's sake," Nat said and tore the satchel out of Jonathan's hands. "Just give it to me, ye damn fool." He pulled out the milk jar, opened it and poured out the contents, then wiped the inside with one of the cloths. "There's a shepherd's cott just down the comb," he said, and dug around in his trouser pockets. "We'll stay there until the storm passes." He hunched over and pulled out his match safe, and, shielding it from the rain, wrapped it in the clean cloth, shoved it in the jar, and sealed it. "Come on," he said. "It'll get worse sooner than you think." He grabbed the satchels and started down the hill.

"I want to go back to the farm," Jonathan shouted. Lightning flashed, and a few moments later the thunder ripped through the air.

"What kind of city-bred, lubber-headed idiot are ye?" Nat yelled. He ran back and grabbed Jonathan's arm. "You won't last five minutes in this. Either the lightning will get ye or you'll fall and break your neck, if I don't break if for ye!"

"Let me go!" Jonathan cried, struggling to break free.

"Sweet Jesus in heaven help me," Nat shouted over the downpour. "You don't need a nursemaid, ye lunatic, ye need a damn keeper!" He pulled Jonathan down the hill after him.

They dropped into a small valley, and the wind lessened but the rain came down harder. Staggering through the downpour, they caught up against a small wood. "It's down here," Nat shouted. Jonathan struggled, but the grip on his arm was like iron, and he was dragged along. The cott loomed out of the rain a few minutes later, a small stone hut with a thatched roof and a wooden door, tucked under a small knoll at the edge of the wood. Nat dropped Jonathan's arm to try the latch, and Jonathan made his escape, running back up the hillside. He'd only gone about ten paces when Nat tackled him.

"Ye fucking idiot!" Nat yelled, and jerked Jonathan to his feet. "I've a mind let ye kill yerself then."

"Let me go!" Jonathan screamed, struggling and hitting at Nat. "Let me go, you bastard!"

Nat slapped him hard, and Jonathan went down. He staggered to his feet and started to run again, but Nat caught his wrist and jerked him around. He grabbed Jonathan by the shoulders and shook him. "Have you lost your mind?" he shouted in Jonathan's face. "What is the matter with ye, boy?"

"Are you courting Rose Pritchard?" Jonathan yelled back, the rain streaming down his face.

Nat pushed him away. "Am I *what?*"

"Are you courting Rose Pritchard?"

"What is it to you if I am, ye fool boy?"

"It's nothing to me!" Jonathan yelled.

"Then why do ye ask such a damn fool question?" Nat shouted.

"I don't know," Jonathan sobbed. "I don't know."

Nat stared at him through the rain, then took a step nearer. Jonathan backed away but Nat held out his hand. "Easy, Jonny," he said, and slipped his arm around Jonathan's shoulder. "Easy lad." Jonathan grabbed Nat's shirt and pulled in against his chest, shaking with the sobs. Nat held him tightly until Jonathan's crying eased, then tipped Jonathan's head back. "C'mon, lad," Nat said quietly. "Let's get you inside." Jonathan only sniffed and nodded.

Nat led him back to the cottage, his arm still around Jonathan's shoulder, pausing only long enough to scoop up the satchels the lay in the grass outside the hut's door. He pushed the door open and pulled Jonathan inside. The darkness inside was complete; there were no windows, just the wooden door banging against the wall in the wind. Jonathan stood in the middle of the small room, shivering, while Nat dug through the satchel. He pulled out the milk jug.

"I just hope the lucifers are dry," he muttered, "else it's goin' to be a long, cold afternoon."

He opened the jug, pulled out the cloth wrapped inside, and shook the match safe out to the floor. He wiped his hands dry, then pulled out a match and struck it—it lit. Shielding the flame with his hand, he hunted around the small fireplace and found the stumps of some old candles in holders on the rough wood mantel. These he lit, then shook out the match.

Jonathan retreated against the opposite wall, shivering more and more violently in the cold gusts that blew through the open door. He stepped aside when Nat came to close the door, keeping his distance and not looking him in the face. Nat paid him no attention, but took one of the candles and searched until he found some kindling and small sticks in a corner. He laid these in the fireplace, and in a few minutes had a small fire crackling. He crouched by it, feeding it sticks and, as the fire grew stronger, chunks of turf that were stacked by the hearth.

Jonathan coughed at the smoke, and Nat looked over his shoulder. "Aye," he said, "it's a poor excuse for a chimbly, but beggars and choosers and all. Just pray the roof don't leak." He stood and held his hands out to the fire. "C'mon, Jonny. Get over here and warm yourself." Jonathan didn't move. Nat crossed the room, ducking under the low beams, and took Jonathan by the arm. "My God, boy," he said, "You're cold as a dead thing, and shaking." He tugged gently on Jonathan's arm. "Come over by the fire."

"I'm fine," Jonathan said, trying to keep his teeth from chattering. "Just let me be."

"Jonny," Nat said, and Jonathan looked away. Nat took his chin and forced him to look in his eyes. "Lad. Even if I was courtin' someone, 'twouldn't make no difference to you and me. There's things that are outside such foolishness, and you bein' my friend is one of 'em." He smiled. "The parson'd no doubt say it's the Devil quotin' scripture for his own purpose, but you're Jonathan to my David, and nothin' and no one will change that." Jonathan looked away again, not believing him, and Nat shook him by the shoulders gently. "Rose Pritchard may have set her sights on me, but so've others. None's caught me yet, and none will, I'm thinkin'. So come now. There's bound to be some blankets in here somewhere."

Still shivering, Jonathan took one of the candles and helped hunt. There wasn't much to search. The hut was barely twelve foot square, with a dirt floor and rafters open to the thatched roof. Jonathan found an old straw pallet in one corner and dragged it over in front of the fireplace, and Nat found some musty wool blankets stuffed in a niche in the wall. He draped one around Jonathan's shoulders, but Jonathan couldn't stop shaking, so Nat put both of them around him. The room had started to warm up, but the rain still poured down, and drafts whistled under the eaves and down the chimney.

"We have to get out of these wet things," Nat finally said, "or we'll both come down with the grippe." He stood and started peeling off his wet shirt, and when Jonathan hesitated, crouched down next to him. "Just think of what it'll do to my reputation as Cornwall's finest nursemaid if you up and die on me, Mister Jonathan. Have pity on a poor man."

Jonathan smiled in spite of himself. He dropped the blankets and stripped down quickly, then wrapped himself in one of the blankets, handing the other back to Nat. Nat hung their clothes from pegs on the walls and rafters, then sat next to Jonathan. They huddled together in front of the fire, but in spite of the blanket, rough against his skin, Jonathan's shivering grew worse. After a few minutes, Nat turned to him.

"Two's warmer than one," he said, "and the holes in one blanket'll be blocked by the other—"

"No," Jonathan said, his mind blank with panic. Wrestling in clothes had nearly undone him, and he knew he wouldn't be able to prevent his body from reacting to Nat's nearness, nor would he be able to hide it. Exposure must certainly follow, and with it Nat's derision and disgust. He started shaking even more violently, though for a completely different reason than the cold.

Nat didn't even respond. He simply dropped his own blanket, pulled Jonathan's off, and then wrapped both around them. When Jonathan tried to pull away, Nat wrapped his arm around his shoulders and pulled him back. "Now sit still, ye fool, or I'll knock you down and lay on top of you until ye do."

Faced with this threat, Jonathan sat still, but angled his body away from Nat slightly, hoping that he could shield his growing arousal. They sat, arms wrapped around knees, side by side, and, warmed by the fire and Nat's body, Jonathan's shivering slowed and stopped. Nat leaned forward and tossed another chunk of turf on the fire. When he settled back down, Jonathan leaned against him slightly, terrified of Nat's possible reaction, but drawn by the heat of Nat's body and his own intoxication with the feeling of their skin touching down the entire length of their bodies.

"I'm sorry I was such an ass," he whispered.

"Eh," Nat said, "I'm used to it."

Jonathan glanced over. "Are you now."

"Aye," Nat replied, his mouth twitching in a smile. "It's one of the things I like most about you. Empires rise and fall, but I can always depend on you to do somethin' foolish."

Jonathan elbowed Nat's ribs, and Nat smiled at him. Jonathan's heart started racing, and though he desperately wanted to look away, he could not. His mouth went dry, and he fought for breath. His own smile faded, and he started to tremble again.

Nat leaned in and kissed him.

It was a gentle kiss on the cheek, but a jolt ran through Jonathan's body. He looked at the fire and froze, and felt Nat go still beside him. Jonathan couldn't move, dared not move, and the silence in the room grew palpable, broken only by the crackle of the fire and the muted rush of the rain on the thatched roof. Jonathan sat, desperate, not knowing what to do, or even what he wanted. Lightning flashed around the doorway and the thunder crashed directly overhead. Jonathan jumped, and then the silence fell again.

Slowly, imperceptibly, he leaned back against Nat. He heard Nat exhale and felt a tremor run through his body. He turned his head slightly toward Nat, not looking at him, but keeping his eyes fixed on the fire. Nat kissed him again, this time on the edge of his jaw, directly below his ear. Jonathan exhaled a shaky breath and turned his head a little further, gasping when Nat kissed him again on his cheek. Jonathan closed his eyes and, trembling, his breath erratic, turned a little more. Nat kissed him again and again, small, delicate kisses traveling along the line of his jaw. Jonathan tipped his head back, and their lips met.

Every inch of his body burned at that touch, and Jonathan leaned into the kiss. Nat's arm slipped around his waist and his own wound around Nat's head. Nat's lips parted slightly, and he mirrored that movement. He felt the pressure building in his body, and when Nat's tongue lightly brushed his lips, the pressure exploded, and he clung to Nat as spasm after spasm shook his body. He gasped for breath and Nat held him tightly, each movement of Nat's hand or lips or body on his skin setting off more convulsions.

"Cooo, Jonny, cooo," Nat said softly. "Easy, easy."

Still shaking, he buried his head against Nat's neck and shoulder and held onto him as a deep chuckle rumbled through Nat's chest.

"Eager little soldier," Nat said, rubbing his cheek against Jonathan's hair.

Jonathan pushed away. "Oh, my God," he said, staggering to his feet. "What have I done?"

"Jonny!" Nat said. "It's all right."

"No, no, no!" Jonathan cried as he stumbled across the hut. "No. No!" He wrenched the door open and ran out into the pouring rain, falling to his knees in the deep grass. Aghast at what had just occurred, great, wracking cries tore through him, and he covered his face with his hands, both to muffle his cries and to hide his shame.

"Jonny," Nat said, kneeling by him and touching his shoulder. Jonathan pulled away, falling to the ground and scrambling back on his haunches. "No, lad, no," Nat said, holding his hands out, "I'm sorry, Jonny, I'm sorry. I didn't mean to . . . I'm sorry." Jonathan pressed his hand to his mouth to control his crying, and Nat's face crumpled. "I'd never do anything to hurt you. I'm so . . ." Nat looked down and his shoulders shook, and then looked back at Jonathan; his tears, like Jonathan's, were washed away by the rain. "I'm sorry." Nat lurched to his feet; Jonathan just stared at him. "You can come in again, Mister Jonathan. I won't touch ye or come near ye. I'm sorry." He walked back toward the hut.

"Nat," Jonathan called, and Nat turned, his face a mask of misery. Jonathan climbed to his feet and walked slowly toward him; Nat just stood, biting his lips, his eyes red and swollen. Jonathan stopped just inside arm's reach.

"I'm sorry, Jonny, truly, I . . . "

Jonathan touched his fingers to Nat's lips; this time Nat was the one who flinched. "No. I wanted . . . I thought . . ." He laid his hand on Nat's chest. "I'm just frightened. And . . ." he looked away, "and ashamed."

"I know," Nat said softly, and reached out hesitantly and brushed the hair back from Jonathan's forehead. "I don't want you to be so. Believe me."

"I do," Jonathan said, and laid his hand on the side of Nat's face and kissed him, hesitant, still frightened, but wanting him desperately even while knowing it transgressed everything he'd been taught. The rain poured over them as Nat's arms went around his waist and pulled him in against his body. He tangled his fingers through Nat's hair and felt the beating of Nat's heart against his own chest. Nat broke the kiss, then kissed Jonathan's lower lip over and over again, his tongue brushing against his lip at each kiss; Jonathan gasped at every touch, and pulled tighter against him. Nat slid his hands up around Jonathan's head; dark eyes looked into black, and Nat kissed him again, crushing their mouths together in hunger and need. Jonathan parted his lips, and as Nat's tongue slipped between them he felt his knees give, and he clung to Nat, his hands meeting behind and digging into Nat's back.

"Aren't we an addled pair," Nat murmured, his lips brushing Jonathan's as he spoke each word, "standin' out in the rain when there's warmth and a fire not ten feet away."

"Aye," Jonathan breathed, and kissed Nat again. "I said you were a terrible nursemaid."

Nat guffawed. "You'll be the death of me yet, Jonny my boy," he said. "Then let's us get inside." He twined his fingers through Jonathan's and led him back into the hut.

They dried the worst of the water off with their shirts, and Nat threw some more turf on the fire. They huddled together on the pallet, side by side as they had before, but, chilled through, Jonathan was shivering again, and Nat pulled him in front, wrapping his arms around him. Tentatively at first, Jonathan leaned back, and relaxed when Nat tightened his embrace and kissed him on the hollow of his shoulder.

"I think I wanted ye from the moment I saw ye stretched out there on the sand asleep," Nat said softly, punctuating his sentence with kisses along the back of Jonathan's neck; each touch made Jonathan gasp, and he lay his head back on Nat's shoulder. "Of course,"—Nat rubbed his cheek against Jonathan's head—"that was before I knew what a great stubborn duffer ye were."

"Stubborn!" Jonathan struggled to get free, but Nat just held him tighter.

"Aye, stubborn. But by the time I figured that out, well, there it was, too late to do anythin' about it." He kissed the edge of Jonathan's ear. "Ceptin' this."

"I don't know what I thought, really," Jonathan said, pulling Nat's hand to his lips and kissing it. "Except that you were a forward, fresh thing that didn't have a civil tongue in his head."

"Oh, it's civil," Nat said, and ran his tongue up the back of Jonathan's neck.

"Yes," Jonathan said breathlessly. "I suppose it is." He shook his head slightly, and leaned forward; Nat pulled him back, but Jonathan resisted.

"What is it, Jonny?" Nat asked.

"I . . ." Jonathan bit his lip. "What we're doing is wrong."

Nat was silent for a moment. "By whose light?" he asked.

"The Bible," Jonathan said, "and the law, and . . . and nature."

"Aye," Nat said, "I suppose if ye look at it that way, ye might have a point. But tell me this, Jonny, does it feel wrong?" He tightened his embrace again. "Does it feel like it bain't natural?" Jonathan hesitated, then shook his head. "Them other things, they're just men's words is all, and for every word you can find against something, you can find a dozen others for it. All I know is that time's short on this earth, and we shouldn't waste what

God saw fit to give us, like He gave you me, and me, you. It mayn't be right, and it mayn't be natural, but it's good, bein' here with you, and that's all I know."

"Yes," Jonathan breathed. He turned in Nat's arms and laid his head against Nat's shoulder, reaching up for another kiss. "It is." Their lips met again, and Nat lowered him slowly to the pallet, until they were stretched out and wrapped in each other's arms, their legs intertwined. They kissed gently, lips caressing, and Jonathan pulled back. "Have you . . ." he said, " . . . have you ever done this before? With someone else?"

Nat looked away. "Aye," he said slowly. "I have. Once or twice."

Jonathan bit his lip. Nat looked back at him, his worry evident in his eyes, and Jonathan looked at the fire.

"Are there . . ." Jonathan whispered, "can . . . is there . . . more?"

A soft smile spread across Nat's face. "Oh, aye, Jonny," he murmured, leaning down to kiss him. "There's more."

Jonathan lay with his head on Nat's chest; Nat stroked his hair. He had been clumsy and nervous at first, but Nat had led him gently through their lovemaking. It had been nothing like he had expected, awkward and uncomfortable, natural and exhilarating all at the same time. They had dozed afterward, and when they woke the fire had burned low and the rain had softened to a drizzle. The storm had passed.

"You were right," Nat murmured, his voice vibrating through his chest, "when you said that the law was against us."

Jonathan looked up at him. "Do you mean . . ." he said, and looked away. "Do you not want to . . . to be together again?"

Nat laughed soundlessly and kissed the top of his head. "No, lad," he said. "No, indeed. Having loved you now I could no sooner give you up than I could give up my own name. No, we'll just have to be careful is all."

Jonathan laid his head back on Nat's chest. "I love you," he whispered, and immediately wished he'd bitten his own tongue out before saying such a thing.

"Eh?" Nat said. "What's that?"

Jonathan pulled back, confused and embarrassed. "Nothing," he stammered. "It was nothing."

Nat drew him back down and held his head so Jonathan had to look at him. "What was it you said, Jonny?" he asked softly.

"I . . ." Jonathan felt his face flaming. "I said I love you."

Nat smiled. "I know. I heard you the first time," he said. "I just wanted to hear ye say it again." Nat pulled him close and kissed him, and all thought vanished from Jonathan's mind; he existed in a space bound by the touch of Nat's lips and body on his and the overwhelming emotion flowing through him. The kiss ended and he settled back into Nat's arms. "I never thought I'd say it to anyone," Nat said quietly, "least of all another fellow, but I love ye too, Jonny. I do indeed." He chuckled again. "Seems I was wrong in sayin' none would catch me. You've caught me fair."

Jonathan felt a tear trickle down his cheek. He laid his hand against Nat's chest. "What do we do?" he asked.

Nat pressed his lips against the top of Jonathan's head. "We be careful, is what," he said. "If we're found out and it's proved against us, it's prison for me and disgrace for you. One of the *advantages*, if ye can call it that, of bein' the gentry." Nat sighed. "No. We just be careful."

"Should we not meet like we've been doing?"

"No," Nat said, shaking his head. "That'd raise as many questions as if I'd kissed you in the farmyard in broad daylight. We carry on just as we've done. Everyone knows as we're friends, so it'll not be strange. But for this," he ran his hand down Jonathan's back, and Jonathan shivered at the touch, "we'll have to slip out at night, and find such a place as we can." He turned on his side and hiked up on one elbow. "If I see you durin' the day, I'll tell you where to meet me. If I don't . . ." He pulled at the pallet and tugged a piece of thread and some straw from it. "If I don't, I'll leave this on your windowsill, and you meet me, and we'll go." He made a twisting motion and held up a small bundle of straw tied with a piece of the thread. He laid it on Jonathan's heart. "Here, love. This'll be my sign to ye that I want ye to come to me."

Cornwall 1906

Rose stumbled as she ran down the steps to the kitchen, but caught herself before she fell. *What had he seen? Did he know? Why did I leave it there? Would he find it?*

Hands shaking, she set the lamp down and leaned heavily on the table with her palms flat against the smooth surface. Aunt Bannel's words from that morning came back to her: She would do best not to cross her own ghosts, nor Bannel's will. She knew full well what the old woman meant; she had trained to be midwife under her—and all that that position held with it—until Nat Boscawen had come into her life, and she had pursued him in spite of the warnings of her family and Bannel herself. The older woman had dismissed her then and left her to be kitchen maid at Trevaglan. At the time she'd been delighted—Nat worked on the farm and she'd seen him almost every day, if only from a distance while he worked the fields—but in the years since had come to rue her haste. All that might have been, gone in an instant.

What is done, is done. Calmer, she stood and smoothed her apron. It was behind her, or so she had thought until Jonathan Williams had returned, and in so doing had dredged up all the anger and pain that had been her entire life that summer and the years that followed, until time and habit had dulled the emotions. *His fault*, she repeated to herself, *all his fault.* She had suffered the loss and the shame, and he had gone off to university, as free as you like.

Well, she thought, *he isn't free anymore.* It was well past time he shared the anguish she'd lived through. And he did. She could see it in his face whenever he looked at Alec, could read it in the way he couldn't meet her eye. *Good. Good.* She had lived through the guilt and shame, and now he must do the same.

Still . . . the straw on the window. What did it mean? Should she have left it laying there? She shivered again, frightened. Some things were best left buried, and that was one of them. "*Her own ghosts,*" Aunt Bannel had said. And none so haunting as Nat's.

The kitchen door opened and Rose started, almost dropping the lamp. Meg stood in the doorway, her hair mussed and her color high in the dim light.

"And what are you doin', comin' in at this hour of the night?" Rose said quickly, covering her fear with a scolding tone.

"I was just out for a breath of fresh air," Meg said, closing the door behind her. "And what would you be doing here still at this hour?" she asked.

"Seein' to things that you should have done if you hadn't have been out for air, though it's the first time I've heard it called such in my life," Rose said.

"Were you now?" Meg asked, and sauntered across the room toward her.

"Yes," Rose answered, circling around the table. She lifted a shawl off the hook by the door; her hands were trembling again. "There are still the coffee things to clean from the library, and mind you don't sleep in through breakfast."

Wrapping the shawl around her shoulders, she slipped out the door and into the darkness.

CHAPTER 6

Langsford tossed the book aside, threw back the bedding, and swung his legs over the edge of the bed. In spite of his weariness, he'd been wakeful and had hoped to lull himself to sleep with reading. He glanced at the book beside him on the bed and grimaced; perhaps ghost stories were not the best choice in bedtime literature, particularly given his experiences the night before and his conversation with Williams that evening. He slid his feet into his slippers and crossed to the wardrobe. He shrugged on his dressing gown and wandered aimlessly around the room, absently touching items on the dressing table and the chest of drawers: his shaving mug, a small carved box, a candleholder—all the while replaying the evening in his mind.

He had almost said it, had had the opportunity and the words laid before him, and but for Alec's interruption, would have done so. *A marriage of true minds.* Not in the literal sense, perhaps, but in a figurative manner, would that not describe them? They lived together in greater felicity of mind than had most of the wedded couples he knew, and were even treated as such, in an odd way, by many of their acquaintances. An invitation for one rarely arrived without its match forthcoming for the other, and frequently a single invitation included both. Jonathan's reading that sonnet had caused hope to flare briefly in his heart, and he, though hesitant, had thought to take the chance.

Langsford sighed and drew back the curtains. Opportunity he

may have had, if only briefly, but in that moment, even as he began to speak, Williams had not looked encouraging, or even curious. He had looked terrified, trapped like a rabbit facing a stoat, as if the ruin of everything lay in Langsford's next words, as indeed it did.

He opened the window and the cool air flowed into the room, redolent with the smells of the sea and the damp earth. He shivered and drew his dressing gown closer around him.

He would not make such an error again, nor give in to such a selfish impulse. He would hold his tongue, respect Williams' wishes, unspoken though they were, and not burden him with the discomfort of rejecting his clumsy protestations of a love that was clearly not what he desired. This was the very least he could do in kind, repaying Williams'—*damn it*, Jonathan's—years of reticence and companionship. He smiled again. Not for him the role of Orlando, pinning his love for Rosalind on every tree in the forest, but rather Antonio, sacrificing his own life to secure Bassanio's happiness. He'd never have thought it possible.

He returned the dressing gown to the wardrobe and slid beneath the bedclothes, retrieving the book just before it fell to the floor. He opened it to a page at random, found the beginning of that story, and began to read again. Gradually, weary from the turmoil of the day and lulled by the muted rush of the distant surf and the call of an owl, his eyelids began to droop. The book slid from his hand, the candle guttered and died, and he slept . . . .

He found himself standing on the top of a hill. The wind howled around him, and the black clouds raced across a silver-grey sky. The trees thrashed in the wood below, but the hilltop was bare of them; only cold white stones broke the earth, brightening and dimming as the moon sporadically appeared from behind the fleeing clouds, then vanished again, and dark bushes, rattling and whipping in the wind.

He knew he dreamt, that he did not actually stand in this place, but the landscape was vivid and real to him nonetheless. He could feel the turf beneath his feet yield to his step, hear the moan of the wind as it whistled and eddied around the rock walls that sprawled across the hilltops, and feel the bite of that wind through his nightclothes. Despite this last, he was not cold—the wind was hot and oppressive, as if blowing straight from some infernal furnace and lashing the earth with its fury.

He searched the hilltop for shelter, ducking behind the drystone walls that formed small rings, but the wind followed him wherever he went, plucking at his hair and tearing at his clothing. He cursed as he trod upon sharp rocks or sticks, and once stumbled and fell to his knees at the very edge of a deep pit.

He tried to find a way out of the maze of stone circles and walls down to the shelter of the wood below him, but all paths led to the top of the hill, and if he tried to leave one and walk directly down the slope, he found himself once again climbing toward the crest.

Gradually, though the wind's roar had not abated, he began to hear other sounds blending in, moans and cries, coming, it seemed, from under the earth. They grew more distinct as he drew closer to the hilltop, and though he knew himself to be terrified, he was unable to keep from climbing higher. Voices, two voices, they seemed, growing in volume until one screamed in pain.

Then utter silence. The wind stopped as if a door had been closed, and a great stillness fell over the entire hillside. And then a tiny sound, barely audible, of footsteps on damp earth. He tried to flee, but terror rooted him to the spot. A brief sob echoed hollowly from under the earth, and a breeze whispered across the hilltop, rustling the grass and bushes. The weeping grew louder, and as it did, the wind grew stronger.

Suddenly, with the abruptness of a stage magician's conjuring, a man appeared, seemingly from the bowels of the earth. Silhouetted against the sky, he was tall and strongly built, and in his hand he carried a shuttered lantern.

The gale smote the hilltop again, but this time with bitterest cold. He staggered under its blast, and the man leaned into it. To his horror, the dark figure walked directly toward him. Again he tried to run, to escape, or to hide, but was unable to move. As the figure drew closer, he could hear it weeping. It passed within feet of him, never noticing him standing there, the lantern held aloft in one hand, the other covering its face, all the while sobbing bitterly. It, or rather he, for it was indeed the spectre or figure of a man, stumbled around the edge of a wall and vanished from his sight.

In an instant, he stood in the pastures below Trevaglan, a dozen yards from the line of gorse and brush that marked the cliff's edge. For a moment he thought he was actually there, that he had walked in his sleep only to awaken shortly before stepping off the cliff and falling to the rocks below. But the air was warm and still, balmy and heavy with the scent of newly mown hay, and when he looked at the sky the constellations of summer wheeled above his head in a clear, velvety black heaven. The land slumbered, as did the house; only one light shown in its windows, in the low wing that jutted out from the main block—Jonathan's room, or one near it. He saw no living thing. The pastures were barren of sheep, and no scuttling in the grass betrayed the stirring of small creatures searching for food. A deep silence lay over the scene; neither cricket song nor bird cry broke that great stillness. Only the sea called, endless and hungry, washing over the rocks far below him.

Then, in spite of the warmth of the night air, a chill ran over his body, prickling his flesh and making the hair on his arms stand on end. Over the rush of the waves he heard the sound of a man weeping. A light appeared around the bend of the road, bobbing as it made its way nearer. The weeping grew louder, and he knew that far from escaping the man on the hilltop, he stood waiting in his path. The horror of his situation washed over him, but in the way of nightmare he was unable to move; he could only wait whatever fate brought to him. His limbs were leaden, his mind numb.

The man crossed up to the house and briefly paused at Jonathan's window, then, weeping more loudly, staggered across the lawn, climbed the wall dividing the garden from the meadows, and stumbled along the path leading from the house to the cliffs and the village beyond. As on the hilltop, he seemed not to see Langsford, and though he passed within yards, never noticed his presence. The lantern hung by his side now, and he walked with his head bowed, looking neither around nor before him. Moved by an obscure sense of pity for the man's grief, he struggled with his fear and overcame it; he called out, asking if he might help, but the man walked on, heedless.

Just as he reached the lowest part of the path before it climbed over the headland and plunged down to Landreath, where it skirted the very edge of the cliffs with neither boulder nor bush protecting its edge, the man stopped. Langsford sensed rather than saw another figure in the shadows of a tree that covered the way; he couldn't remember if the tree still stood or not. The man seemed to be arguing with the shadowy figure; he could hear no sound, though the pair stood a scant twenty yards from him. The man leaned into the shadow, then turned abruptly to leave. The other figure caught his arm, and the man pulled free. He lifted the lamp and shouted again—he could see the twisting of his features in the dim light—and then suddenly the other figure leapt forward and pushed him.

He felt the blow hit his own chest, felt himself stumble backward, and felt the ground disappear below his feet. His arms flew wide as he clutched at the air, and the lantern slipped from his grasp, and as he fell and fell, he sensed an overwhelming feeling of horror and remorse and regret, and wished he could kiss Jonathan one last time. The surf thundered below him, ever nearer, the light from the lantern spread across his vision, and he fell to the ocean's hungry depths . . .

He sat up abruptly, clutching his counterpane, his face and body bathed in sweat. Still in throes of the nightmare, he recoiled against the head of his bed; the figure with the lantern stood beside him. He gasped for breath and pushed back harder.

"I'm sorry, sir," Alec said, "but I knocked and knocked and

you didn't answer. It's Mr. Williams, sir. There's somethin' wrong, and he won't speak."

Langsford shuddered and relaxed for a moment, then sat bolt upright.

"What's that you say?" he asked. "What's happened?"

"I heard a scream and woke," the boy stammered, "and when I went to see if aught was wrong, he just stared at me, but like as he didn't see me. I don't know what it is."

He threw back the bedclothes and leaped from the bed. "Show me."

They fled down the stairs and across the drawing room. Langsford stumbled in the darkness down the steps to the passage, but caught himself, and burst into Williams' room with Alec on his heels.

Williams sat in the bed, the pillows and bedclothes tossed about him, his eyes wide and staring and his mouth working, though making no sound.

He took the lamp from Alec, who stood trembling by the door. "Go," he said. "Get your father. Quickly."

Alec ran up the passage, and Langsford walked slowly toward the bed.

Williams neither moved nor gave any indication he saw or heard anything. Sweat covered his face, and his eyes, always dark, were black as he stared across the room. His breath came in short quick gasps. Langsford placed the lamp carefully on the bedside table. The air in the room was stale, and smelled as if Williams had been ill.

"Williams," he said softly. "Williams. Do you hear me?" He sat on the side of the bed, but Williams neither looked nor indicated he heard him at all. "Williams," he said more urgently. He touched Williams' arm, gently at first, but when there was no reaction, he took him by the shoulders and shook him. "Jonathan," he said desperately. "Please, say something."

Williams made no reaction at all, but just sat, trembling, his eyes still wide. Langsford stood and paced around the room, running his hands through his hair. "Williams!" he shouted. "Wake up, man!"

Nothing.

He felt himself on the edge of panic. Williams had never been a quiet sleeper; when he'd first moved into the flat his nightmares and tendency to talk in his sleep—and weep in his sleep—had worried him so that he had suggested that Williams see a doctor, advice which he had firmly refused. Those nightmares had faded with time, but nothing in all the years they'd lived together prepared Langsford for this . . . nightmare of nightmares. He sat on the edge of the bed again and touched the side of Williams' face.

"Please, Jonathan," he pleaded. "Wake up."

Running footsteps sounded in the hallway, and he stood. Alec dashed into the room, with Hale and Rose following closely behind.

"Is he well?" Alec asked breathlessly.

"What is it, Mr. Langsford," Hale said over the boy's question, and moved to the other side of the bed. He was dressed in his night shirt and his boots, his hair mussed with sleep. He sat on the edge of the bed. "Mister Jonathan," he called. "Do ye hear me, lad?" Williams made no reaction, and Hale looked across the room at Rose, standing in the doorway. "It looks like the terrors," he said. "Go get some brandy for Mr. Langsford. He'll most likely need it." She nodded once and left.

"The terrors," Langsford repeated slowly. "What do you mean, the terrors?"

Hale frowned. "Alec had them when he was a babby," he said. "Frighted the wits out of both of us, it did—we even thought someone had cursed him or the like—but Aunt Bannel said 'twas nothing to worry about, so long as he slept after. How long has he been like this?"

"I . . . I don't know. About a quarter hour, I suppose," Langsford answered.

"Aye, Dad," Alec said, "or not much longer."

Hale nodded. "Then 'tis almost done." He looked back at Langsford. "If it's the terrors, he'll just drift back to sleep, and rest through the night. Tomorrow, I'd say, he won't remember any of it."

"What are you talking about," Langsford demanded angrily. "Terrors, and sleeping, what is this?"

"I'm tellin' you all I know, or all I can guess," Hale said calmly. "Was he shakin' and thrashin' about when you came in here?"

He swallowed his fear and answered as best he could. "He was trembling. He's calmer now."

"Alec?" Hale asked.

"He was tossin' his pillows about when I first came in, Dad," Alec answered. "That's when I run to get Mr. Langsford. I didn't know what else to do."

"You did right, lad," Hale said.

"What the *devil* are the terrors?" Langsford asked.

"I don't know, rightly," Hale answered. "Some say as it's demon possession, others that it's a haunt. Nonsense, I say. But whatever they are, Alec had 'em, and was just like you see here." He nodded at Williams, whose eyelids were drooping. "They happened now and again, and then just faded away."

"They happen to children," Rose said, and they all looked to where she stood in the doorway, holding a glass and a decanter of brandy, "and to adults, sometimes, them that harbors a guilty conscience, or so they say." She crossed the room and placed the brandy on the chest of drawers. Like Hale, she was dressed in her nightclothes, with a shawl around her shoulders. Her hair was undone and fell halfway down her back, sandy brown shot with grey. "Like as not he'll have no memory of this." She unstopped the decanter. "Will you be wantin' some brandy, Mr. Langsford-Knight?"

"Yes, please," he said. Hale had been correct; his nerves were shattered, and a restorative was definitely in order. "But Williams isn't a child, nor has he a guilty conscience. He's . . . he's the best man I know, and has never done a thing to cause harm to anyone."

"Perhaps that's so, then" Rose said mildly, and handed him the brandy.

"That's enough of that, Rose," Hale said sharply. "Most likely he's weary from his journey, and the shock of Mr. Penhyrddin's death." He looked at Langsford. "You'll pardon my bein' nosy, Mr. Langsford, but has he ever had trouble sleepin' before?"

"Always," Langsford said without thinking, then amended himself. "That is to say, he's always been a light and restless sleeper, and sometimes . . . well, that's all."

Hale nodded and sat back. "Then this is not so strange as might seem."

"Perhaps not to you," Langsford said, "but I've never seen anything like it." He took a swallow of the brandy; it burned his tongue and warmed him, and he felt his trembling lessen. Setting the glass on the table, he looked once more to Williams, who had closed his eyes and settled back against the pillows. To all appearances he was sleeping quietly. "And you say he'll not remember this?"

"Alec didn't," Rose said, "though he was a child, and not a grown man."

Langsford nodded. "Then I don't want him told if he doesn't ask," he said. "If this happens again, or if he needs a doctor, then yes, of course. I will tell him myself. But now, no." The three others nodded their agreement, and he looked around the room. "This room smells stale, and like a sickroom. We should open the windows, if only briefly." He stood.

"No," Rose said abruptly, and he and Hale stared at her. "What I mean is, don't you worry yourself sir. I do agree, and will see to them myself." She moved quickly to the window nearest Williams' bed, and drew back the curtains. Langsford adjusted the bedclothes to insure Williams was warmly covered, and Rose threw open the casement. She leaned out the window, and drew a deep breath; he couldn't blame her, as the air in the room was terribly close and stuffy. Then she crossed to the second window and opened it also. "I'll have Margaret clean and air the room thoroughly tomorrow, sir," she said as she pushed back the curtains.

"Thank you," Langsford said, and a thought struck him. "But I'd like Williams' things moved into the room adjacent mine." Hale and Rose glanced at each other. "This may well be an isolated incident," Langsford said, "but should it occur again, I would like him to be nearby, so I might watch him. I'm not so certain I like his being off here by himself if that is the case. He might do himself an injury, and though I am grateful in the extreme for Alec's assistance, I would not want to put the full burden again on his shoulders. Alec can stay in one of the attic bedrooms, which will be more convenient for him in any case."

Hale had been nodding his head, but Rose said, "If I might say, sir, if he should chance to walk in his sleep, he might do himself an injury on the stairs."

"As well he might here," Langsford said. "No, my mind is made up. I'll think of some excuse to explain the shift, if he does not remember waking tonight." He looked over again at Williams, whose face was now calm, and his breathing deep and regular. "Please. None of you need stay any longer. I'll watch over him tonight, for a little while at least. Thank you for helping."

"Of course, Mr. Langsford-Knight," Hale said, rising. "'Twas no trouble at all. Are you sure you'll be all right, though, by yourself?"

"Yes, of course," he replied. He glanced at the clock; the hands stood at half past three. "You need your rest more than I do mine."

"Well, then, good night," Hale said. "Come, Rose. 'Tis soon enough we'll need to be awake as it is."

Alec lingered in the doorway for a moment after his parents had left. "If you need me, sir," he said, "I'm just across the hall. I . . . I wish I could be of more help."

Langsford smiled at him. "You did everything exactly right," he said, "and I'll depend upon you tomorrow to help me convince Mr. Williams to move his room."

Alec blushed and nodded, as had any number of younger boys when Langsford had praised them while at school. Langsford smiled at the memory, then bit his lip in thought.

The boy was clearly not Hale's son.

"Go on now," he said. "Get yourself to bed."

Alec nodded, and hurried off down the hall. Langsford closed the windows; the air in the room had cleared but had grown quite chill. As he lit a small fire in the fireplace, he wondered how he had not noted the difference between Alec and the rest of the Hale children; it was obvious enough, just in coloring. The other children had Hale's paternity stamped on them with no doubt—all were as red-haired as the man himself. Rose, whom he'd never seen without her hair pulled up tightly, was equally fair. Alec was as dark-haired and dark-eyed as Williams himself.

Langsford froze in the act of placing another log on the hearth. *No,* he thought, *it isn't possible.* He looked at his friend, now sleeping soundly in his bed. He picked up the lamp and held it near Williams' face, studying his features. Alec's and his eyes, he knew, were of the same hue, a dark brown bordering on black—Langsford had never seen eyes so dark again until meeting Alec that afternoon in Penzance.

He stood upright. Williams had gone white upon seeing the boy standing by the dogcart that first day. He was invariably uncomfortable in the boy's presence, rarely looking directly at him. Langsford put the lamp down and paced around the room. It couldn't be true. James Hale wouldn't stay on here if it were, nor would Rose. How could they? The shame would be too great. How could she face him if it were true?

"They happen to children," she had said of the terrors, *"and to adults, sometimes, them that harbors a guilty conscience, or so they say."*

"Oh, dear God," he said. He sank into an armchair that sat in a corner of the room and stared at Williams. The time was right; Alec was not quite fourteen, though tall for his age, and Jonathan had been here . . . fourteen years before. *Hale must not know, must never have guessed.* And Rose's insistence that Alec work in the house and accompany them about the countryside, in spite of

Williams' clear wishes otherwise, could be, would be, the act of a woman demanding that a man acknowledge . . .

His son.

Langsford groaned and buried his head in his hands. Small wonder Williams had always been so reserved about his time here, had never spoken of his summer in Cornwall except in the most general terms, and then only speaking of his cousin Penhyrddin. Small wonder that he avoided all marriage entanglements, not, as Langsford had supposed, because he loved men, but because he had a bastard child, and that would be certain to come out should he ever engage to marry. Small wonder he maintained a complete silence regarding his father's precipitous marriage that summer: He was guilty of the same failing, and could not criticize where he himself had fallen so far short of the mark. For all his father's dastardly behavior, Williams *pere* had married the woman he had so nearly ruined, no matter that he had treated his first wife disgracefully and no matter how damaging the scandal. Williams *fils* had not.

Them that harbors a guilty conscience.

He rose and crossed the room, poured himself a large measure of the brandy, and drained it off at one swallow. Williams couldn't have been so unfeeling, so reckless, so lacking in honor as to behave thus. It was unthinkable. He looked at the man sleeping quietly in the big bed. He had been a boy then, barely eighteen. Langsford poured another brandy. Rose was a house servant, a village girl. Williams' family would have never permitted him to marry her, regardless of whether she was carrying his child or not, particularly given the publicity around his father's hasty marriage and the birth of Williams' half-brother immediately following. No. They would have bought her off, made some settlement, and married her to anyone they could in an effort to hush it up. Rose herself, knowing she faced disgrace, would have agreed. Even Hale, presented with the unmistakable evidence that the child was not his, could have been talked over, or his silence similarly purchased. Penhyrddin was wealthy, Williams' father no less so. But Hale must not have known who the father was, or he would not, *could not* have greeted Williams so amicably. Rose had held her tongue, then, and most likely would continue to do so.

He took another swallow of the brandy and leaned his head on the mantel. How could he have been so wrong, so blind? He shook his head. All the great myths and all the poetry written said that love was blind, and that there was none so blind as them that would not see. He had never seen, had never wanted to see. Williams had held this secret for all their years together. And when Langsford, great fool that he was, tried to pour out his unnatural love, had reacted as any normal man might: embarrassment and revulsion. God, he was a fool, fortunate only in that Williams held him in enough esteem and affection to thwart those attempts and thus maintain their friendship, rather than denouncing him to his face and ruining him.

He crossed to the chest of drawers and picked up the brandy decanter, then extinguished the lamp. Williams' face was golden and peaceful in the flickering firelight. *No,* he thought, *Williams didn't act without honor fourteen years ago.* He'd been forced to that course of action then by a family determined to avoid another scandal, and now, far braver than he himself could ever have been, had come back to face her he had wronged, and the child he had sired.

"I love you," he said softly, knowing he would never say it again, to Jonathan or to anyone. "I always have, and I always will." Then he quietly closed the door and walked up the dark passageway.

CHAPTER 7

Jonathan put the tray on a hall table and knocked on Langsford's door. *A normal holiday morning,* he said to himself again. A shared cup, a brief conversation, then breakfast in the dining room. He checked the tray again. The hot chocolate steamed in a small pot covered with a cozy, two cups—warmed on the stove—on saucers sat next to a plate of Langsford's favorite biscuits, smuggled along in his own trunk from London as a surprise, and a small pitcher of warm milk, in case the chocolate was too strong, were laid out nicely. He had sampled the chocolate in the kitchen before bringing it up, and it was very good.

Receiving no response, he knocked again. Alec had said Langsford had not yet risen for breakfast, which Rose and Meg had confirmed when he hurried to the kitchen to check on the preparations for the chocolate and breakfast. Odd, because Langsford often woke well before he did, if only to read in bed. Alec had particularly stressed that Langsford still slept, and had hovered so about, asking if Jonathan was well, and had slept well, and if he needed anything at all, that Jonathan had finally had to chase the boy from the room so that he might wash and dress.

Surprisingly, he *had* slept well. He had thought, after cleaning out the washbasin and preparing for bed, that he would lie awake all night, as he often did when memories of Nat intruded, and particularly after finding the token on his windowsill—*how in the world had it come there,* he wondered, *and what could it possibly mean?* He knew the people of the land to be a superstitious lot and that corn tokens were common in the folklore of the place, at least according to his late cousin, but that so specific a thing should appear on his own windowsill had been harrowing . . . at least in the late hours of the night. In the clear light of morning it seemed far less fraught with portent: a peculiar coincidence, no less upsetting, of course, but less freighted with meaning. And to his astonishment this morning when he awoke, he had fallen asleep almost immediately as his head touched his pillow and had slept soundly and deeply through the night, untroubled by the nightmares that so wracked him at such times as he thought at length of that summer at Trevaglan.

Still not a sound from inside the room. Perhaps Rose and Meg had been mistaken, and Langsford had dressed and gone for a morning walk, as was sometime his custom when on holiday. He knocked again and called Langsford's name, then cautiously opened the door.

Snoring softly, Langsford lay sprawled face down on top of the bedding in his nightclothes. The curtains were still drawn; the room was dim and smelled strongly of brandy. He crossed the room, drew back the curtains quietly and opened the casement, instinctively glancing at the sill as he did so—nothing lay there. As he crossed to the second window he saw a nearly empty brandy decanter sitting on the bedside table and a small wineglass lying on the carpet below Langsford's outstretched hand. He picked up the glass and placed it on the table next to the decanter, then threw open the second set of curtains, causing the rings to chime loudly, and made a great fuss opening the window (that sill, too, was bare of any token). Langsford stirred and groaned.

"Good morning," Jonathan said with a ruthless cheerfulness. He crossed to the hall and brought in the tray, setting it on the chest of drawers with a great rattle of crockery. He closed the door loudly, and turned to Langsford, who had rolled over and was shielding his eyes against the bright morning light pouring through the windows. "How are we this morning?" Jonathan asked. "Did we sleep well?"

"We were sleeping beautifully," Langsford grumped as Jonathan poured two cups of the chocolate. "At least we were until some great ass interrupted our sleep at the break of dawn with the morning tea."

"Not tea," Jonathan said, and put the chocolate pot down on the tray with a clang. Langsford winced. "Chocolate. And it isn't the break of dawn, it's fully nine o'clock in the morning."

"In civilized climes that's fully the middle of the night," Langsford retorted. He sniffed. "Chocolate?"

"And biscuits," Jonathan said, handing him a cup, "if you think your stomach can manage it."

"My stomach isn't the problem," Langsford said. "Your cousin kept a very fine cellar." He sniffed the chocolate and took a small sip. "My head, however, is a completely different matter."

"I should think it is," Jonathan said, settling into an armchair that stood in a corner of the room. "What on earth possessed you to drink so much, and so late?"

"It seemed a good idea at the time," Langsford said, not meeting Jonathan's eyes.

"These things usually do," he said, and took a sip of his chocolate. "It's only upon later examination one realizes that perhaps a more moderate course might have been preferable."

"Indeed it does." Langsford moved to sit up, winced again, and settled back against his pillows. "And don't look so smug. It's very unbecoming."

"I will bend my entire mind to the task," Jonathan said smugly. "But it's difficult, you know, when handed such an opportunity."

"Make the effort," Langsford said with a grunt, and took another swallow of the chocolate. "This is quite delicious."

"Yes, it is," Jonathan said. "Biscuit?"

Langsford groaned. "God, no."

"So much for your stomach," Jonathan said. "Might I be smug about that?"

"No, you may not," Langsford replied. He paused for a moment. "How is your stomach this morning?"

Jonathan frowned. How in the world had Langsford tumbled to that? "It's quite well," he said cautiously. "Why do you ask?"

"You looked a bit . . . pale last night when I left you," Langsford said. "I thought perhaps dinner might have disagreed with you."

"Not at all. And we're discussing your stomach, not mine," Jonathan said, steering away from any inquiry along that line. He indicated the brandy decanter with his cup. "You haven't answered my question. What prompted this debauch so late at night?"

"I had difficulty sleeping," Langsford replied. "I went back down again quite late. I thought perhaps a touch of brandy might help."

"A touch might have," Jonathan said wryly; had Langsford heard him being ill in the night? "A full bottle is another story altogether."

"You needn't tell me that," Langsford said. "I'm quite painfully aware of the fact." He took another swallow of the chocolate, and then looked at him queerly, Jonathan thought. "How did you sleep last night?"

"Quite wonderfully well," Jonathan answered firmly, "though I can't imagine why it's such a topic of fascination with everyone this morning. First Alec, then Rose, and now you, even in your crippled state. Surely there are better things to discuss."

"The discussion of another person's concerns is always fascinating," Langsford said. "It makes one forget one's own." He held out his cup. "Might I have more, please?"

"I should be Dickensian and say no," Jonathan answered, as he poured out the rest of the chocolate, "but I shall take pity on your orphaned state. Also, it's been my experience, as I'm certain it has been yours, that one's own concerns hold only the slightest interest to anyone else. Most people are completely self-absorbed." He handed the cup back to Langsford. "Drink it quickly before it cools."

"As quickly as I am able," Langsford said.

"Don't tax yourself."

"Williams," Langsford said after a moment, "would you do me a great favor?"

"Of course," Jonathan answered. "What do you wish?"

"As I lay here awake last night—"

"Prior to your debauch," Jonathan interrupted.

"Prior to my debauch," Langsford said sternly, "and I'd thank you to let me finish before entering any commentary into this discussion."

"I'm so sorry," Jonathan said. "A great favor, you said?"

"Yes." Langsford glanced out the window and, Jonathan thought, looked embarrassed.

"What is it?"

"As I lay here last night, unable to sleep, I was thinking back over the years," Langsford said, "given as I am, so you claim, to great sentimentality . . . ah! No interruptions!" Jonathan held his tongue. "I was recalling our early holidays on the Continent, or to Scotland, when we . . . we used to lie awake and talk half the night."

Jonathan bit his lip. "Yes?"

"Well, given that your endless prattle always put me to sleep immediately," Langsford said hurriedly, overriding Jonathan's exclamation, "and given that there is a bedroom next to this one with a communicating door . . ." He paused. "Might it be a terrible inconvenience if you, well, slept in the next room for the remainder of my stay here?"

Jonathan crossed to the window and looked out. A fog bank was forming off the coast, in spite of the sunlit promise of the morning. He remembered those nights painfully clearly; they had been among the happiest of his life, helping heal his heart between the devastation left behind in Cornwall and the ache of his love for Langsford, who had just moved to London. Trying to recapture them for these last few days would make the parting even more painful; he could not face it.

"We aren't undergraduates any longer," he said lightly. "I doubt I could find topics sufficiently tedious to lull you to sleep."

"You could tell me of your lessons in the husbandry of cattle," Langsford said. "Five minutes only and I'd be off."

"Perhaps that's so," Jonathan said. "I . . . well . . . I will ask you again after breakfast, whether you still wish me to do so." He nodded at the decanter. "This may just be Cousin Penhyrddin's brandy talking."

"If it is," Langsford said, rubbing his temple, "I wish it wouldn't talk quite so loudly."

Jonathan walked back to the chair. "You shouldn't fault the brandy. It really isn't to blame. As I recall it was a very nice brandy." He was about to sit when an object on the opposite wall caught his eye. "Good heavens. Have you brought your kite with you?"

The kite in question had been an object of amusement to Jonathan and embarrassment to Langsford since they'd become friends at Cambridge. Jonathan had first found it tucked behind Langsford's wardrobe shortly after their return from the Easter holidays one year, and when he questioned Langsford about it had been both delighted and touched to learn that Langsford had had it since he was a boy, and that his mother always packed it in his trunks when he returned to school—though Jonathan, having met that supremely practical woman the Christmas before, privately questioned her supposed role in the story.

Of course nothing would do then but that they take it out and fly it, which, to Langsford's even greater embarrassment, had led to a kite-flying craze that spring in their house. From then on his fate had been sealed, and every spring Jonathan would not rest until they had routed out the kite, patched its tears and worn places, and over Langsford's loud—and painfully insincere—objections, traveled to Hampstead Heath or St. James' Park, and there, among children and their nannies, sent the thing winging skyward like a scarred and battered warrior staggering into his final battle.

"Well," Langsford said, his face reddening, "I thought that perhaps you would be disappointed, should you miss the opportunity to . . . well . . . things have been at such sixes and sevens this last several weeks . . . and travelling here, and possibly having none down here . . . For God's sake, man, stop laughing!"

Jonathan hiccoughed and gasped for air. "I do apologize," he said, then laughed again. "Actually, no, I don't. You wonder why I accuse you of sentimentality!"

"I think it in remarkably bad taste to mock a dying man," Langsford said, causing Jonathan to laugh even harder. "Barbarian."

Jonathan sank back into his chair, laughing still as Langsford sat frowning at him. He smiled in response. "I'll tell Rose to bring my things and put them in the next room."

"Thank you," Langsford said. "That is most kindly done."

They sat for a long moment in silence, simply looking at each other, but Jonathan felt none of the tension he had the night before. He felt simply . . . sad.

"I *shall* miss you terribly," he said finally, "and you may remind me I said so whenever I bring up your sentimental nature in the future."

Langsford nodded and looked out the window. "I shall do both," he said. "Both miss your company"—he looked back and smiled wickedly—"and remind you of this."

Jonathan stood. "I will deny it, of course," he said. "I think it only right." Langsford laughed in return. Jonathan placed his cup on the tray. "Shall I have breakfast brought to you here?"

"Please," Langsford said fervently, "though I would prefer if you had Mrs. Hale bring it up. I sincerely doubt I could face Meg and her flirtations in my present state."

"So you've noticed that, have you?" Jonathan asked. Langsford nodded glumly and noted it would be difficult to miss, and Jonathan smiled again and opened the door. "I will see you at luncheon then," he said, and opened the door, "or sooner, if you need me to defend your honor. Oh. Don't forget, the vicar and his wife are coming to dinner this evening."

Langsford looked thoughtful. "Perhaps he can absolve me of my sins."

"He's only here for the evening, Langsford," Jonathan said, "and even with God's grace, he is only human."

"You had better be off before I start throwing things." Langsford moved quickly to grasp one of the pillows, then grimaced again. "Perhaps I shall stir myself and have a walk after breakfast. It might blow the clouds from my head before dinner."

"That sounds like an excellent idea," Jonathan said. "I will see you in a little while." He closed the door and walked down the stairs. Langsford cradled the cup in his hands and sipped the hot chocolate, which by now had cooled considerably. How like Williams, he thought, to remember such a thing in spite of the many demands crowding his mind, from the minute details of the estate and the journey to the devastating presence of Alec at the farm. And still, with all of that, he had brought him the chocolate in the morning, just as he had for years when they were on holiday.

He drained the cup, and then gingerly sat up. His head pounded and the room spun a little if he moved too quickly; he had not had that much to drink since he was at University, and even then had been moderate in his habits. Last night was an aberration, and one he had no intention of repeating any time soon. He had behaved precisely like a jilted lover, though the jilting was only in his own imagination. *Fool.*

He swung his legs over the edge of the bed and paused, gathering his wits for a moment before attempting to stand. He wasn't sure if he was still slightly intoxicated or not; he'd only slept five hours at the most, and couldn't recall precisely how much he had drunk. He turned his head carefully and looked at the decanter. It had been three quarters full; barely an inch stood in the bottom. *Too much, clearly.* He put the cup and saucer on the tray and picked up one of the biscuits. Cream, his favorites. Williams must have brought them with him from London; he doubted they had them here in the kitchen. He put the biscuit down as a soft knock sounded on the door.

"One moment," he called, and quickly slipped into his dressing gown. He tied the sash as he crossed the room and opened the door; Alec stood in the hallway, holding a tray. Langsford stood staring at him for a moment before Alec spoke.

"I brought your breakfast, sir. Mr. Williams said you'd be wantin' it in your room today."

"Yes, yes of course," Langsford said quickly, and stood aside. "Just . . . put it on the table, if you would."

Alec set the tray down and began an attempt to set the table. "You needn't bother with that. I can quite take care of myself." Alec nodded and walked toward the door. "Alec," he said, and Alec looked back at him. He studied the boy's face, still somewhat round with youth, but growing into the contours that would stamp him through life. He tried desperately to recall what Williams had looked like while a boy at Eton, but could not remember; Williams as a man colored all of his perceptions, and to his knowledge had no photographs from those days. While the boy didn't look like Williams in any demonstrable way, his eyes were so similar—deepest brown set under dark brows and lashes—that he could not shake the thoughts that had occurred to him the night before.

"Yes, sir?"

"Ah, yes," Langsford said. "I've spoken with Mr. Williams, as your parents and I discussed last night, and they are to move some of his things to the next room, as we planned, at least for the duration of my stay. Again, not a word, do you understand?"

Alec nodded. "Will that be all then, sir?"

"Yes," he said, "I believe that is all I need." The boy started to leave, but again Langsford stopped him. Although he knew he couldn't ask the boy any direct questions—he might not even suspect his true parentage—he burned with the need to know more. "Have you always lived here?"

Alec nodded again. "Yes, sir. I was born here."

"And . . . how do you find it?"

"Beg pardon, sir?" Alec asked, looking puzzled.

"I mean, do you like it here?" he said, feeling like a fool. "Do you ever wish to travel, or go to school, or anything like?"

Alec's face cleared. "I suppose I should like to see London someday," he said, "and America, and cowboys and such like. But school, sir, well, I can read and write fair enough, but more than that just don't seem to come to me." He grinned. "Mr. Penhyrddin was always after Mum and Dad about me goin' to school, bein' as he was a scholar and all."

"Was he now?" Langsford asked. While not direct evidence, this was strongly circumstantial; why else would the old man be concerned about the education of a farm hand's child? "Why . . . do you suppose he did so?" he asked cautiously.

Alec shrugged. "He was always queer for his books," he said, "and he said we could read 'em if we pleased, so long as we washed our hands before. Not that it did much good for me. Cassie, me sister, she's the bookish one in the family. Mum says she's the one with the brains, and all I got was a mouth that gets me in trouble. Mr. Penhyrddin thought Cassie might do well at school, or even University, if you can imagine them takin' the likes of us."

"Perhaps she shall," Langsford said. "I'll speak to Mr. Williams about it."

"Please, sir, no," Alec said, taking a step closer. " 'Twouldn't be proper. I was just talkin', and didn't intend nothin' by it."

Langsford laid his hand on the boy's shoulder. "Then I won't say anything of where I heard it," he said, and Alec relaxed. "Mr. Williams is a bit . . . queer for his books, too, and I'm sure would be delighted to help any of your family better themselves. This will be our secret. Agreed?" Alec looked relieved. "And to make it a bargain . . ." He held out his hand, and after a moment's hesitation, Alec shook it. "There. You've done well in telling me this. Now, go, get to your chores, or your mother will give you the devil for troubling the gentry."

"Oh, aye, that she will," Alec said, blushing and smiling; Langsford recognized the look: hero worship blended with the dawning pride of being treated as an adult. "If there's anythin' else you need, you just let me know."

"I'll do that," Langsford said. "Now, off you go." Alec started to run from the room, then stopped himself, and with another smile over his shoulder, walked out and closed the door behind him.

Langsford crossed to his dressing table and splashed cold water on his face, then soaked a cloth and laid it across the back of his neck. The throbbing in his head lessened, but he cursed himself for not bringing any headache powders; he could ask, he supposed, but his headache was his own fault, and so he would suffer the consequences of his foolishness without them. He wandered to the window and leaned on the sill, looking out across the fields. A fog bank lay off the coast, pale in the sunlight, fingers reaching toward the shore. He would have to take his walk sooner rather than later, in case it drew closer.

He ate his breakfast slowly, his thoughts retracing the last day's events. He would have to tread carefully for the remainder of his stay, neither pressing too closely for Williams' confidences about the boy, nor acting in such a manner that would preclude those confidences should they come naturally. He sincerely doubted that the latter would occur—if Williams had maintained a silence for the entire span of their friendship, he certainly wouldn't speak now.

As he shaved, he began, for the first time, to look forward to his return to London, though not, certainly, because he anticipated any pleasure in the journey or its destination. But the daily routine of the chambers and his social round would occupy his mind as a soporific, until such a time as he would be able to thoroughly bury his feelings for Williams. He knew, intellectually, that he would experience a great wrench upon returning to the flat; every room, every piece of furniture, every living memory would remind him of what he'd never had, nor would ever have again in any sense. Many of the items in the place had been Williams' purchases; he would have to make a list of them upon his return, and ask Williams if he wished them to be shipped down to Cornwall.

He put his razor down abruptly and grasped the edge of his dressing table, fighting back the pain that twisted his heart and drove the breath from his body. His eyes burned with tears, and he rated himself for them; he had not wept since he was a boy, and he had no intention of doing so now. He would handle this methodically and practically, and not surrender to emotional excess. *At least not here, not now.* He mastered himself, and washed his face.

Forgoing a tie, he dressed in tweeds and a knit waistcoat, a bit warm for the day perhaps, but suitable if he were caught out in the fog, or if the day turned out to be chillier than it looked. He wrapped a few biscuits in a pocket handkerchief and tucked them into his waistcoat pocket.

He touched the kite on the wall briefly and smiled sadly. *The last flight, in all likelihood.* He kept it only because Jonathan took such great glee in chaffing him about it, and in flying it every year. The object on the wall before him wasn't even the original kite Williams had found in his room at Cambridge so many years ago. That one lay in rags and pieces of splintered wood in a box in his wardrobe in the flat, irreparably damaged as the result of a collision with a tree one particularly windy day in St. James' Park. He had taken the pieces to his tailor and had the man duplicate it as exactly as he could, down to weathering the fabrics and matching the threads used to sew on the patches. An artist of his earlier acquaintance had built the frame, mimicking the repairs on the original pieces. The next year he had produced it as the weather turned fair in April, and the delight on Williams' face had been worth the effort and the expense. He had never told Williams of the substitution, fearing that, should it not be his own childhood kite, the outings would cease, and that he would not allow. He maintained the fiction of the kite and his own embarrassment at its existence simply because the moment the thing was aloft, the years fell from Williams' manner like winter garments on the first warm day of spring, and for an hour Langsford could see the boy

Williams had been, before Cambridge, before Eton, before they had even met. He brushed his fingertips gently along the kite's tail, then left the room.

He stopped briefly in the library; Williams was working on the estate books with Hale, reviewing crop and herd projections for the coming year. From there he found his way to the kitchen and confirmed with Rose that Williams had given orders for some of his clothing, sufficient for a week, and his personal effects were to be moved to the room adjoining his. Meg was busy by the stove, so he didn't speak too plainly, but gave sufficient indication to Rose that Williams indeed had not remembered the disruption of his sleep and that he, Langsford, had not enlightened that ignorance.

Evading Meg's flirtations—he was fairly certain that Rose would have something to say to her about *that*, judging from the set of her jaw—he left the house by the kitchen door and wandered through the kitchen garden. Two of the Hale children were busily pulling weeds from around the fresh green sprouts poking up through the ground, but he couldn't, to save his life, remember their names. They had been introduced to the entire family the day they had arrived at Trevaglan—beside Alec there were four children, two boys and two girls—but only one he recognized by name: the bookish Cassie, who, at twelve, seemed indeed a serious, thoughtful child. He wondered briefly why Rose had Alec assisting her in the house, rather than the girl, then recalled her request that first evening. Still, if her parent wished for her a better education than she could receive here, radical as the thought was, she would do best to bring her to her employer's attention.

Although, of course, she was Hale's daughter, and for the moment Rose Hale seemed to have other priorities of a more immediate and pressing nature, in consideration of garnering her employer's attention.

He skirted the yard, and struck out through the pastures toward the cliffs.

"I think that will be enough for this morning, Hale," Jonathan said, and closed the ledger book. He took his glasses off and rubbed his eyes. "There's more to this than I thought possible." He tucked his glasses in their case, and put them in the desk drawer.

"You're almost caught up, Mr. Williams," Hale said, standing. "Once we get everything entered, you'll have no problem. Mr. Penhyrddin, he didn't have to mind the business so close as he did, but he liked it."

"He certainly did," Jonathan said, and sighed. "I spent two full weeks in London just reviewing the papers the solicitors brought, and I still have a great deal to go through."

"'Tis good for a man to mind his own affairs, he used to say, be it the farm or the business in the city," Hale said. "He spoke to me some about that, too, upon a time, but it made me head spin. I told him I'd be best with the farm, and he could look after that sort of thing."

"At least it's fairly predictable," Jonathan said. "This"—he gestured at the papers spread across the desk, notes on the farm's past performance and expected output for the coming year—"is a completely foreign language to me."

Hale laughed. "Then you mind the money, sir, and I'll tend to the livestock."

"Agreed," Jonathan said. "I'll meddle as little as possible."

Hale nodded and left, and Jonathan sat for a moment, his hands flat on the desk. He'd joked with Langsford on the quay at Penzance about sheep and hay, but the reality and complexity of the farm's business had surprised him. Sheep and hay, yes, but also wheat, rye, chickens, eggs, pigs, milk, butter, cheese, cabbage, potatoes, apples, strawberries, cider—Andrew Penhyrddin had clearly believed in spreading his nets wide in terms of agricultural production and sold as far afield as London itself. When Hale added pasturage, fallow fields, fertilizers, sea weed, arable lands, granaries, shippons, and similar terms, which Jonathan understood not in the least, his head began to spin.

"Clearly, I will have to assemble my own dictionary," Jonathan said aloud to the empty room, "as well as studying the almanacs." He began sorting and organizing the papers—bills of lading, letters from wool factors, and similar minutia—when Rose entered the room. "Yes, Rose?" he asked, still somewhat uncomfortable at being alone with her.

"Is there anything in particular you wished this evening for dinner, sir?" she asked.

Jonathan shook his head. "I think you are more familiar with Dr. and Mrs. Deane's likes and dislikes than I. Please prepare whatever you think might please them. I'm certain it will be quite satisfactory." She nodded, but as she left, a thought struck him. "Rose," he said, and she paused in the doorway. "Is there a breeze this morning?"

"I beg your pardon, sir?" she said, her face impassive.

"Is there a breeze this morning," he repeated. "A good wind."

"I believe so," she said, glancing at the window, "though I don't know as I'd call it a wind."

"Very good," he said with some satisfaction. "Thank you." He collected the papers and began to them in neat piles. "Mr. Langsford-Knight and I will be in for luncheon about noon. You needn't exert yourself overly much. Something simple, cold, will be most acceptable." She nodded and moved silently down the hallway.

Jonathan took the papers and carefully placed them in pigeonholes in the secretary that stood against the wall, counting them as he did so: bills, expenditures, letters from factors, each neatly placed. Penhyrddin had, at least, been extremely methodical in his record keeping up until his death, and Jonathan found little need to alter his system; he had, however, upon reviewing the papers, folded and stacked them more neatly than he had found them. He placed the pens in their holders, stoppered the ink bottle, and closed the desk. Locking it, he tucked the key inside a small wooden box on top of the secretary, then left the room and went up the stairs.

He knocked softly on Langsford's door, and, upon receiving no answer, he slowly opened it, feeling more than a little intrusive, but the room was empty. He crossed quickly and stood in front of the kite, hesitating for a moment before plucking it from the wall. He smiled. As was Langsford's custom, the kite was ready for flight, with a knotted cloth tail and a large ball of string attached to it. He inspected it for tears or signs of wear—not that he had to look closely to find wear. The patches they'd put on it last year seemed to have held up; the original fabric, a faded red muslin, had become, across the years, a threadbare frame for a patchwork quilt of repairs, and the old wooden cross members had been glued and reinforced several times. Tucking it under his arm, he hurried out of the room and downstairs.

The day was chillier than he had supposed it would be, with a stiff breeze blowing off the sea, and he stood for a moment on the front step, debating whether he should go back and get his overcoat. The fog bank he'd seen earlier had moved in, spreading across the horizon and encroaching upon the coast; the first tendrils had slipped through the bent and weathered trees that topped the distant headland the other side of Landreath's cove, little more than a mile away. He remembered the dense fogs that he'd encountered years before, and hurried down the steps and the path; he'd best find Langsford immediately, or they would be attempting to fly a kite without being able to see it at all.

He carefully latched the garden gate behind him—old habits died hard, particularly one so strictly inculcated that earlier summer—and crossed the lane that led to the main road. He rounded the end of the barn and walked down the slope along its seaward end. Two of the men were cleaning out the bays in the ground floor of the barn where the cows came each morning for milking, and he called to them, asking if they'd seen Langsford, though he felt slightly childish for carrying the kite while they were laboring. They replied they had seen Langsford strolling toward the cliff path some half of an hour earlier, and that he had not yet returned.

He thanked them, and, somewhat concerned, hurried down the hill and across the pasture toward the cliff path. Langsford was, of course, neither familiar with the terrain, nor did he know how quickly the fogs could wrap the region in impenetrable mist. Even those native to the district were cautious in such a situation; as many had discovered, making a misstep on the narrow paths overlooking the sea was perilously simple—he knew this himself from bitter memory.

He paused briefly on a small hillock and scanned the area, but caught no glimpse of Langsford. Even more alarmed, he strode quickly through the pasture to the footpath, hoping that Langsford was simply sitting in a sheltered spot and out of sight. The breeze off the sea had lessened, but had grown more damp and chill as the fog crept closer. He called Langsford's name once, twice, and upon the second heard an answer, faint and far away. He called again, and again heard answer, away to his right, and he followed the path to the line of bushes and stones at the cliff's edge. He heard his named called again, and he glanced down.

His breath caught in his throat; Langsford stood on the sand near the water's edge, not five feet from where he had lain the first day he'd met Nat. He tried to speak, to call back, but found no words would come.

Langsford waved, small and foreshortened with the distance. "Come down," he called. "It's quite a lovely beach. I can't imagine why no one would bathe here."

"It isn't safe," Jonathan shouted back, shaking, "particularly with the fog. Come back up here, and quickly."

"With the what?" Langsford called.

"The fog," Jonathan answered, pointing out to sea. The fog bank lay just offshore, and its outliers had crept over the headland; the first wisps swirled past him as he watched.

Langsford looked over his shoulder. "Nonsense!" he yelled back. "It's perfectly safe. Come down and let's explore it a bit."

Jonathan shook his head. Though not given to such presentiments, he felt increasingly that some disaster was looming, independent of his own memories of the place, and that Langsford, for no reason he could define, stood in deadly peril. A chill ran down his spine, one not caused by the approaching fog, and he felt the hair on his arms prickle and stand on end. Whatever was coming was imminent and very near.

"Langsford, don't be such a bloody ass!" he shouted, his fear sparking anger in his voice. "Get up here this instant."

"Very well, very well," Langsford called. "There's no reason to get all shirty about it." He seemed to look about briefly. "Where's the path? I certainly don't want to climb back up the way I came."

"This way," Jonathan replied. "To the left of the large black rock."

"That doesn't narrow things down much, you know," Langsford said, laughing.

"It isn't a joke," Jonathan shouted, his sense of dread increasing with each moment. "Hurry *up,* for God's sake!"

"I'm hurrying as best I can," Langsford shouted back, irritation sounding in his voice. "I would be more successful if you'd be bit more precise than saying 'Take the path by the large black rock.' There are dozens of them here." He lifted his head and looked to his right—Jonathan's own left—and said, "Oh, there it is. Thank you. I don't know how I could have missed it." He started down the beach, away from the path to which Jonathan had directed him.

"What are you doing?" Jonathan cried. "That isn't the way."

There was a path of sorts there, it was true, but less a path than a narrow ledge across the cliff face, petering away to nothing about ten feet below a slight dip in the cliff top, shortly before the headland jutted out into the ocean; Nat had often climbed there to dive from the rock face into a deep pool gouged across the ages by waves undercutting the cliffs. At best of times it was treacherous—Jonathan had never attempted the feat himself—but now, in the damp atmosphere, it would be deadly, even if it had led eventually to the headland.

"Langsford, you idiot, that isn't the way!" Jonathan shouted.

"Nonsense," Langsford called back as he clambered over the rocks by the beach. "It's as clear as day, even in this weather." He started out across the cliff face, bracing himself with his left hand against the stone that sloped steeply away from the sea.

"There's no way up there," Jonathan yelled, running toward the cliff's edge. "It doesn't reach the top."

"What's that?" Langsford called, pausing halfway up the face.

"There's no way up there!" Jonathan answered, terrified. Whatever was causing his dread was here, was now. "Go back to the beach. I'll come for you!"

"Well," Langsford said, turning carefully on the narrow path, "if you'd done that at the first, we could have avoided all this shouting back and forth, you great silly fool."

Langsford was facing the cliff, leaning against it and holding with both hands, when his body suddenly lurched, and he seemed to lose his balance. Jonathan screamed his name, and stood horrified, unable to do anything, as Langsford's arms spun for a moment as he tried to regain his balance, and then he fell backward and plummeted into the sea twenty feet below.

Langsford hit the water hard and immediately plunged below the surface; the impact forced the air from his lungs and he was momentarily dazed by the pain across his entire back. He had just sense enough not to inhale, but the searing need for air brought him to a full awareness of his predicament. He began to struggle toward what little light he could see above him—he hoped rather than knew which way the surface lay—and broke into the air with a sob. He coughed heavily, spitting out water he hadn't even been aware he'd swallowed, then, gasping, tried to float on the surface and recover his breath. A wave broke over him and dragged him under again. His clothes were waterlogged and heavy, weighing him down, and he shed his jacket and bobbed back to the surface. He had just time to prepare for the next wave, and as it swept over him, he realized that should he be dashed against the cliff base, he would never survive.

Floundering, he swam into the waves and away from the shore—he could hear the waves breaking against the rocks, but could see nothing. The fog had come in and blinded him completely. He could not even tell which way the land lay except for the direction of the waves. The rush of wave against rock and sand echoed weirdly through the mist, surrounding him on all sides; he was, he realized, probably still within the cove, if he was fortunate, but on two sides lay the rocky cliffs and only one the comparative safety of the small beach.

Something dark loomed out of the blinding white of the fog and he swam toward it: a rock, its surface just above the top of the swells. He clambered onto it; the barnacles and shells which encrusted it cut his hands, but he clung to it while trying to catch his breath. He cursed his stupidity for ignoring Jonathan's warnings, but had thought that surely Alec would be more familiar with the best path to the cliff top, and so had followed his gestures.

No time for that now. Even the slight breeze cut through his wet clothing, and he began to shiver. If he stayed here much longer, he would not have the strength of mind or body to get back into the cold water, should he determine which way to swim. *Nothing to do but scream for help*, he thought. So he did.

Williams' voice immediately sounded behind him, and he twisted around on the rock.

"Where are you?" he shouted. "I can't see for the fog."

"I'm on the beach," Williams called, this time to his right. He shifted again.

"I can't see you," he called back. "The damn fog's too thick."

"What do you mean?" Williams' voice echoed, this time behind him again. "I can see you quite well, though I don't know for how much longer."

"I mean what I said: I cannot see anything for the fog," Langsford said. "Are you certain you're seeing me, and not just a rock, or something in the water?"

"I am seeing a rock," Williams replied, "and you're on it. You're about thirty yards offshore. Are you all right?"

"I've been better," Langsford shouted back, "but all things considered, I'm well. Nothing broken, I believe, but I'm damned cold."

"Can you hold on until we can get a boat to you?"

"I might be able to hold on," Langsford answered, "but you'll never find me in this soup, and the risk to the boat it too great. This is a delightful rock, but it is definitely a one-man affair. I doubt I have room to entertain guests—" A wave broke over him.

"Langsford!"

He coughed and spat out the water. "I believe that also answers your question. The tide appears to be flowing, and judging by the growth on this rock, I will be underwater before any help could arrive."

"Can you swim in?" Williams' voice echoed through the mist. "Shall I come to you?"

"For God's sake, no," he called back. "Then there would be two of us here. Keep talking and I will try to swim toward your voice." He desperately hoped he could make good on that plan; Williams' voice seemed to come from all directions at once, and he had no clear idea any longer where the shore lay. "Can you still see me?"

"Yes," Williams answered, "though I don't know how long that will hold true. The fog is getting thicker."

"Direct me if you can," he said. Another wave swept over the rock, and when it passed, he slipped into the water on what he hoped was the landward side.

After the frigid air the water felt almost warm, but he knew this was deceptive—if he was in the water too long the cold and his clothing would certainly draw him under. He swam toward the sound of Williams voice, adjusting the course to his shouted instructions. He didn't answer, but saved his strength and his breath for his swimming. At one point he apparently shifted directions; Williams frantically called for him to swim to the left, that he was heading for the cliffs and not the beach. He altered his direction, but apparently the wrong way—panic sounded in Williams' voice as he screamed left, left, not right. Grimly, doggedly, he kept on, knowing he was tiring. The current and the waves dragged at him, and he slowly felt a lassitude creeping over him.

Another wave broke and pulled him under, and he struggled weakly to regain the surface. When he did, he listened for Williams' voice, but the only sound he heard was the rush of the water. He swam again in the direction he thought correct, and another wave pushed him from behind. He rode its power, managing to stay afloat, but the next one pulled him down again. This time, however, he touched bottom, and tumbled against the hard packed sand of the sea floor. He pushed against it and upward, and as he did, a hand grabbed his arm and dragged him into the air.

"I'm here," Williams said, pulling him toward the beach, now visible ahead of them. "I'm here."

He coughed. "I'm certainly glad you are."

He felt Williams' arm encircle his chest, and he resisted not at all as he was pulled along. His feet touched bottom, and he struggled to stand, losing his balance as another wave struck them, and dragging Williams down with him. He had no strength left—*foolish way to die*, he thought idly, killing his beloved with him—but was pulled upright and hauled the last few feet out of the surf and onto the sand.

Jonathan staggered out of the water, half carrying and half dragging Langsford with him. They collapsed on the sand at the very edge of the surf, Jonathan gasping for air and Langsford coughing beside him, seawater trickling from his mouth.

Jonathan struggled to his knees and carefully rolled Langsford on his back. "Are you all right," he asked, terrified. Langsford's breathing was labored and his eyes were closed. "Langsford!"

Langsford opened his eyes. "I am . . . here . . . well. Are you hurt?" he asked weakly. "I feared I'd finished you as well."

"Dear God, no," Jonathan said. His hand trembling, he brushed the sand gently from Langsford's cheek. "But I thought you were going to die before my eyes."

"Nonsense." Langsford laughed faintly, which set off another coughing spell. He recovered, and reached up and patted Jonathan's cheek. "Now, now. You know I have better manners than that." He coughed again. "After all, we were at school together. One doesn't die in front of an old school chum. It simply isn't done."

"You idiot," Jonathan said, and, without thinking, pulled Langsford into an embrace and clutched him tightly, rocking back and forth on his knees. After a moment, Langsford's arm closed around his neck, and they held each other as the waves surged around them. A shiver convulsed Langsford's body, and Jonathan released his hold. "I have to get you up to the house," he said. "Can you walk?"

Langsford was silent for a long moment and then whispered, "I don't know. I really don't. I can walk, I'm certain, but I doubt I could manage the climb." He shivered again.

"Come," Jonathan said, "I'll help you." He slipped his arm under Langsford's back and helped him sit up.

Langsford rolled and tried to get to his knees, but fell back to the sand. "You're damn well going to have to carry me, Jon," he said, then broke out coughing again.

"Mr. Williams!"

Jonathan looked behind him; Hale and the two workers who had been in the barn were scrambling down the cliff path.

Jonathan stood. "Hurry!" he shouted. "We need your help." He knelt by Langsford, who was shaking constantly now. "The men are here. We'll get you up to the house."

"I . . . fervently hope . . . so," Langsford managed through chattering teeth.

"What happened, Mr. Williams?" Hale panted as he ran up. "We heard you shouting, but couldn't find you right off. We never thought to look down here."

"Langsford fell from the cliff," Jonathan replied.

"Pushed," Langsford said. "I was pushed."

He's delirious, Jonathan thought, and knelt by him in the sand. He looked up at the three men who stood, waiting for his orders. "You, Bolitho, isn't it?" he said, pointing to one of the men, who nodded. "Get up to the house. Tell Mrs. Hale to run a warm bath. Not hot, but very warm. Hale, you two help me get him back to the house. He's hurt and can't make the climb. Hurry, man," he said, and Bolitho ran back up the beach.

"I'm not hurt," Langsford said, struggling into a sitting position. "I can try to walk."

"You'll not try," Jonathan snapped. "You'll be helped if I have to truss you up and have them carry you back tied to a pole. You two take him," he said to Hale, "one to a side. When we get up to the house, send Alec for a doctor immediately."

"I don't need a doctor," Langsford said fretfully. "A little seawater never hurt anyone."

Jonathan stared at him in horror, stricken dumb for a moment. "You shut up," he finally stammered harshly. "You'll have a doctor whether you like one or not. Back to the house. Now."

The two men helped Langsford to his feet, and, supporting him in spite of his protests, walked with him across the beach to the path. Jonathan followed a few steps behind, fretting at every step, every stumble. What had possessed Langsford to come to the beach, and then to ignore his direction and climb up what was obviously a difficult, dangerous route?

They made the top of the cliff by degrees, stopping when Langsford clearly could not continue, but Jonathan grew more and more anxious at each delay. The fog was thickening, and the air growing chillier by the moment. Bolitho, carrying a pair of heavy wool blankets, met them as they crossed the pasture. He handed one to Jonathan and wrapped the other around Langsford's shoulders. He fell in with Jonathan as they walked, and said that all was being readied for them up at the house. Other than this brief report, they made their way in silence; Jonathan was shivering himself in his wet clothes in spite of the blanket, and had little desire for conversation, so great was his anxiety for Langsford's well-being.

Rose met them at the kitchen door with two glasses of brandy. "The bath is ready, Mr. Williams," she said, "and I've set out dry clothes for the both of you. There's a kettle of hot water in the bath, also, if the water's not warm enough. Here, James, sit him by the stove and let him catch his strength a moment, before you try the stairs." She gave Langsford his brandy, and guided his shaking hand to his mouth. Meg hovered in the background, a steaming cup of tea in her hands. "Sip it gentle there, sir," Rose said softly. "None too fast for you, or it'll do more harm than good." She looked at Hale. "What happened to him?"

"I don't right know," he said. "'Twas all over by the time I got there."

"He was on the beach, and fell from the path when he tried to climb back up," Jonathan said. He drank the brandy in one swallow, and coughed as it burned his throat. His shivering lessened as its warmth spread through his stomach.

"From the path?" Rose asked. "And how could he do that? He'd break himself on the rocks, not take a soaking."

"He was climbing on the diving rock," Jonathan said, and Rose went white. "I've no idea why he went that way." He put the glass on the table and shrugged his blanket to the ground. "Enough talk. Hale, help me get him to the bath. Rose, send Alec for the doctor."

"The doctor's all the way to Penzance," Meg said, scurrying over and collecting the blanket. "Is there aught I can do?"

"Damn," Jonathan said, and Meg looked shocked. "Yes, there is. Run up the road and fetch Mistress Bannel. She's as good as any doctor I know." Meg bobbed a curtsy and hurried out the door. Rose still stood, silent and pale, her hand clutching the back of a chair. "Send her to me as soon as she's here. We'll send for the doctor if she thinks it necessary or if he worsens." She nodded. Thinking better of it, he said, "Never mind that. Have Alec take the cart and bring the doctor back, regardless."

He caught the men halfway up the stairs. Langsford was clearly stronger, but still shivering violently in his wet clothes.

"Take him straight to the bath," Jonathan said to Hale. "Bring our clothes to me there."

"I think you might ask me *my* thoughts on the subject first . . ." Langsford said, showing the first signs of spirit since he collapsed on the beach.

"I wouldn't listen to you if you told me," Jonathan replied, and Hale winked at him as he helped Langsford to his feet.

The bath, a small room off the back staircase, was clouded with steam, and Jonathan was disoriented for a moment, thinking himself back on the cliff in the fog. "Can you undress yourself?" he asked Langsford, then, not waiting for an answer, said, "Never mind. Hale, get the clothes." Hale nodded and then closed the door behind him.

"Sit," he said.

"This is entirely unnecessary," Langsford said, then, taking one look at Jonathan's face, sat on a small chair tucked in the corner of the room. "I'm perfectly capable—"

"Of almost killing yourself," Jonathan interrupted as he knelt to untie Langsford's shoes. "Your lips were blue, for God's sake."

"I'm sure I made a very striking picture."

"The only thing striking in this entire situation," Jonathan said as he tugged off one shoe, "will be me striking you, if you don't keep quiet and do as I say."

"I must say, this violent streak is a new manner for you, Williams," Langsford said.

Jonathan pulled off the second shoe and rocked back on his heels. "I've never been more frightened in my life," he said simply, and knew it to be true. He had been in fear for his life before, had felt helpless before another's anger and violence, but never before in his life had he experienced such utter terror and powerlessness as he had at that moment when Langsford struck the water. He knew he'd be seeing it in his dreams over and over again; that was how his dreams ran.

Something of this must have shown in his voice or his face, for Langsford smiled at him. "Neither have I," he said sincerely. A shudder wracked his body again.

"You need to get into the bath. Stand up and let's get you out of those clothes."

Langsford braced himself against the wall and stood, but he was shaking too much to unbutton his waistcoat. Jonathan brushed his hands aside, tugged the buttons open, and pushed it back over Langsford's shoulders. He moved to undo the braces, and Langsford objected.

"Shut your mouth," Jonathan said. "Now is no time for such modesty. You can undo the trousers yourself if you're so delicate." His own hands were shaking too much to undo the shirt buttons—at this point, he frankly wasn't certain if it was the chill of his own wet clothes or his nervousness at undressing Langsford causing them to tremble—so he simply tore the shirt open, scattering the buttons on the floor.

"This was my favorite shirt!" Langsford protested.

"Every shirt is your favorite shirt," Jonathan said, wrenching open the cuffs. "I'll have Meg repair it. I'm certain she'll be delighted. Face the other way, please." He peeled the wet shirt off; Langsford moved stiffly to assist him. "Now then, your trousers."

"I hardly think—"

"Your trousers or I will indulge once again in my violent streak."

Langsford fumbled with the trouser buttons, his back still to Jonathan.

"Turn around," Jonathan said, his voice cracking. "I'll get them."

"They're done," Langsford said quickly. "They're done." The trousers dropped to the floor, and Jonathan stepped back and looked away, not wanting to meet Langsford's eyes or look at his body, so very near, outlined in the wet undergarments; he would not have been able to maintain the slightest composure had he done so.

Langsford faced him. "Williams," he said, "at the risk of adding accusations of melodrama to the existing charges of sentimentality, you . . ." He looked away. "Damn it, man. You saved my life," he said, the bantering tone utterly gone from his voice. He looked back. "I can't think how to thank you."

Jonathan felt his cheeks burn. "Anyone would have done the same."

"Anyone would have," Langsford said quietly, "but you did. Thank you."

Jonathan looked up, and their eyes met. "How could I possibly have done otherwise?" he asked softly, and, after a long moment, looked away again. He drew a shaky breath. "Now, into the bath. Take my arm if you need."

"I can manage, I think," Langsford said, his voice equally unsteady. *"Good God!"* he cried when his foot, still in its stocking, touched the water. "It's *scalding."*

Jonathan brushed the water with his fingertips; it was warm, but by no means terribly hot. "Only because you're so cold," he said. "Go in easily. Slowly . . ." Langsford placed one foot in the water, and gasped. "There. There. That's good."

Langsford put his other foot in, then, supported by Jonathan's arm, sank slowly into the warm water. "My God," he said. "I feel like I'm being boiled." He rested his arms on the edge of the tub and looked up at Jonathan. "You're next, as soon as I've finished," he said. "I'm looking forward to your suffering as much."

"You certainly won't be here to see it," Jonathan said.

"I thinks that's remarkably unfair of you," Langsford said, and then, in a serious tone, "At the very least, get into some dry clothing."

"I will," Jonathan said, sitting down in the little chair. "Are you certain you're all right? I can have Hale or one of the men stay with you until you are."

"And complete my humiliation?" Langsford said and shook his head. "No, I don't need a nursemaid, other than you."

Nursemaid.

Jonathan covered his flush by standing. "Then I'll be off. I'll bring your clothing, if Hale hasn't found it." He stepped toward the door.

"Williams," Langsford said, holding out his hand. "Thank you."

Jonathan took it in his, and then, biting his lips against further speech, quickly left the room.

CHAPTER 8

The passage door had closed behind the men, Meg had gone for Aunt Bannel, and Rose was alone.

She stood for a time in the middle of the kitchen, staring into space, and then slowly crossed to the old rocking chair by the stove, where the foreign lugger had sat for a few minutes to warm himself while she gave him his brandy.

Brandy.

Though she rarely touched spirits, if ever there was a time she needed some, this was that time. She picked up the decanter and hesitated for a moment—it was Mr. Penhyrddin's best, and so not for her or any of the house to drink—then poured a small amount in the glass that sat on the kitchen table.

She sipped the liquor; its unfamiliar warmth burned her throat as she swallowed. She quickly drank the rest and set the glass down, and then sank into the rocking chair.

"The diving rock," he'd called it—an old name. Boscawen's Leap, they said now in the village, the fools. They knew nothing about it.

But why had he been there? No one had dove from that place for years, ill-omened and haunted spot that it was, not even the boys from the village, not after old Mr. Penhyrddin had forbidden it following Nat's death. Orders had turned to custom had turned to stories, and the beach and the great rock that overlooked it had been shunned by all.

Until now . . .

Until a foreigner, who, blast him, was aware that no one went there, who had been told, though not in hard and fast words, that the place was not to be trifled with, had gone down on the beach, and then ignoring the path up to the pasturelands, had climbed out to the place he had fallen. That they had fallen. First Nat, and then this one, Jonathan Williams' great friend.

She heard running footsteps on the path outside, and she stood abruptly and moved to the center of the room. Cassie and young Jamie burst through the door, panting from their run.

"Is it true, Mum?" Jamie said breathlessly. "Is the London gentleman drowned?"

"He didn't say he was drowned," Cassie corrected him, as was her custom with the younger ones. "He said he fell into the sea."

"Did he break anything then? Is he broken and bloody? Can I see?" Jamie asked, tugging on Rose's sleeve.

"That's enough," Rose said sharply. "There's no one drowned and no one bloody. And you'll mind yourself, or you'll be in trouble if your father hears of you spreading such nonsense. Who was saying such things?"

"Dick Bolitho," Cassie said promptly.

"We weren't supposed to tell!" Jamie cried.

"Well, I'll be talkin' to Dick Bolitho, then," Rose said.

"Now you've done it, you gabber," Jamie said.

The passage door to the house slammed. "The one's in the bath," James said as he entered the room, "and he should be well, but it was a close thing."

"What happened?" Rose asked.

"I don't rightly know," he said, slowly scratching his head, "save that Mr. Langsford-Knight fell in, and Mister Jonathan pulled him out again. Though what either of them was doing there, I don't know. We'll hear soon enough, I suppose, if they feel it right to tell us."

"I *told* you he didn't drown," Cassie said primly, and Jamie frowned.

"Did you now," James said. "And what do you know about it, miss?"

"I . . ." Cassie said, looking at the floor. "I just heard that the gentleman was hurt some."

"Is that so?" James looked at Rose. "Has Alec gone for the doctor?"

"No," Rose answered. "No, I haven't sent him yet."

"Best be about it," James said. "Well, Cassie, seein' as how you're so good at nosin' things out, you go and find Alec and send him to me right away." Cassie ran from the room.

"Mr. Langsford-Knight's in the bath, then," Rose said, and James nodded. "Dick didn't say that Mr. Williams had been in the water, too. I'd best set the old bath up in his room." She crossed to the stove and picked up the large kettle. "Jamie, you run and get Dick Bolitho and send him up here to me. If he's going to be prattling, he might as well be of some use."

"I'll get it," James said. "Dick was working in the barn and is in no fit state to be in the house." He cuffed Jamie gently on the head. "You come with me and help me set it up."

"Can I go to the beach when we're done?" Jamie asked. "I want to see."

"No!" Rose dropped the kettle on the stove top.

"Rose," James said.

Rose crossed the kitchen in a fury, knocking into the rocking chair and sending it flying. She grabbed Jamie by the arm and shook him.

"You'll not be going there now or ever," she said. "If I catch you so much as near that place I'll give you such a pass that you'll not sit for a week!"

"Rose!" James shouted. "Let it be! Jamie, you'll do as your mother says, and not set foot on that beach, nor go near it."

"Yes, dad," Jamie mumbled, rubbing his arm.

"Come along, lad," James said. "We have work to do. You can help me with the bath."

Jonathan had just buttoned his shirt when there came a light tap at his door.

"One moment," he called, and pulled on the heavy knit sweater Rose had laid out for him. He stepped around the large copper bathing tub that stood in the middle of the floor. "Come in."

"Beggin' your pardon, Mr. Williams," Meg said as she peered around the edge of the door, "but I've come for your wet things. We'll see if we can get them cleaned for you."

"Yes, yes, come in." Jonathan indicated the pile of sodden garments in the corner. "I shouldn't worry about them, though. I doubt they'll be worth anything when you're done."

Meg sidled into the room, a large wicker basket in her arms. "Well, Mr. Williams, you never can tell," she said as she knelt and began to place his clothes in the basket. "We're both good with a needle, Rose and me, and if it isn't sayin' too much in my own praise, I can scrub a stain out better than any in Landreath." She stood. "Are Mr. Langsford-Knight's things in his room, sir?"

"No, actually, they're still in the bath, as is he," Jonathan answered. "You can get them later, after he's done."

"Will he be all right, sir, do you think?"

Jonathan nodded. "I believe so," he said, "though I'll feel better after the doctor has a look at him. He seemed in good spirits when I left him."

"That's a relief to my mind," she said. "He's such a nice gentleman, and it'd go to my heart to have anything bad happen to him."

Jonathan suppressed a smile; Langsford had had a similar effect on chambermaids, cooks, and parlor maids the entire time he'd known him, even those of a far less susceptible nature than Meg's. "That's very kind of you," he said, "and I'll tell him you said so."

Meg blushed. "Why, thank you, Mr. Williams," she said. "I'll be taking these things downstairs now." She nudged the door open a bit wider and stepped into the hallway. "Mercy," she said. "I nearly forgot. Mistress Bannel's here to see to the gentleman, sir. She's in the kitchen now."

Jonathan caught his breath. In the flurry of activity, he'd forgotten that he'd sent for her. The request had been purely reflex on his part, as he knew it to be for all the folk in the neighborhood. None would question why he had given the instructions, so accustomed were they to do the same in any similar crisis, even though Jonathan had, if they had paused to give it any thought, barely spoken with her in his life.

"Please tell her I will see her in the library," he said, "and tell Hale he can have the bath cleared away whenever is convenient." Meg nodded and scurried away down the passage toward the back of the house.

He followed her part of the way and tapped on the bath door. "Mrs. Bannel is here," he said in response to Langsford's reply. "We'll come up when you are ready to see her."

He walked slowly down the main stair. As little as he wanted to do so, with Langsford still in the bath, he'd have to see the old woman alone. He knew eventually it would have to happen, given their proximity as neighbors, but he had hoped to delay that meeting until such a time as he was more accustomed to life here, until the emotions and memories had softened with use. Unfortunately, that choice was gone.

He stopped abruptly in the library doorway; Mrs. Bannel stood in the center of the room, her hands folded in front of her.

"Good morning, Mr. Williams," she said. "I hope you're well this day."

He involuntarily looked at the clock on the mantel; it wanted five minutes until twelve. The entire event had taken less than two hours.

"I believe so," he said and stepped into the room, trying for an air of normalcy. "I am more concerned about my friend, however. Thank you for coming." He gestured to a chair. "Won't you sit down? Mr. Langsford-Knight is still in the bath, so it may be some few minutes before we can see him."

"I've seen men in such a state before," she said, and Jonathan felt the blood drain from his face, "but perhaps the gentleman might be embarrassed." She sat in a straight-backed side chair near the large writing table. "I have taken a great liberty," she said. "I told Rose Hale to not send for the doctor just yet. From aught that Margaret told me, assumin' she had half the tale true, you'll most likely not be needin' him, and it's a long journey over to Penzance and back, all for a look and a nod."

"I am extremely concerned for him," he said, "and I would like to have the doctor examine him, also."

She nodded. "Wise p'rhaps, to err in caution, and not foolhardiness." She looked at him intently. "And how fare you, Mister Jonathan?" He flinched at her form of address, and felt a moment of vertigo, imagining himself not in this library, but in a smaller, darker room, smoky and dim.

"I am . . . quite well, thank you." he said, meeting those cold, hard eyes. "I was not in the water so long as he, nor did I fall from . . . the rocks."

"So I heard," she said, "so I heard."

They looked at each other in silence, and Jonathan remembered, painfully clearly, that this was her way: never to ask, but to wait and watch, until what she wanted was given to her. He had stayed silent fourteen years ago. He would not speak now.

"May I offer you a cordial?" he asked. "Or some refreshment?"

"I am quite well, thank you."

"Do you mind if I have a glass of wine?" he asked. "The day has been . . . most upsetting."

She nodded her acquiescence, and he poured himself a glass from the decanter on the table. The stopper chattered against the neck as he replaced it, and he consciously attempted to stop his hand from trembling as he picked up the glass.

"I should think that it would be," she said. "For you."

By chance his back was to her when she made this comment, and he was still bent over the low table. He stood slowly; if he would not be goaded by her silence, he would most certainly not respond to barbed speech. He was suddenly and unexpectedly calm. He turned and smiled a small, tight smile.

"Indeed it was," he said. "I only hope that he takes no serious injury from it. Which, of course, is why I have asked you here, and will send for the doctor."

"I really don't think a doctor will be necessary," Langsford said as he walked into the room. He had dressed in white flannel trousers and a jumper, and Jonathan was momentarily exasperated; he looked as if he was about to step onto a cricket pitch, instead of having just been pulled out of the ocean. "Mrs. Bannel," Langsford said. "I cannot thank you enough for coming out of your way to help me. I do sincerely hope that this will be a social call. Is that for me, Williams? Why, thank you very much." He plucked the wineglass from Jonathan's hand as he passed and pulled a chair up next to Mrs. Bannel. "I do hope you forgive me if I sit down. Although I feel much better than I did an hour ago, I'm still a little weary." He leaned in and continued in a confidential tone. "I actually do like sea bathing, but I prefer to do it at a time of my choosing."

Mrs. Bannel fixed him with the same frosty look with which she had heretofore pierced Jonathan; he was mildly amused to see that Langsford's charm made no impression on her whatsoever. After a full ten seconds' silence, she said, "Indeed?" And waited.

Clearly though momentarily nonplussed, Langsford sat back in his chair, and then smiled warmly. "Why, yes," he said. "Unexpected bathing can lead to unexpected consequences—some pleasant, such as your visit, and some unpleasant, such as the unfortunate state of Williams's and my clothing."

"Indeed," she said again, after another longer and even more uncomfortable silence.

Jonathan stepped into the gap; he had a strong desire to end the conversation and get her out of the house, and Langsford had turned on this spit long enough. "It seems I've asked you here to no purpose," he said. "We both seem to have recovered more quickly than I had anticipated when I asked you to come. Are you certain . . . ?" He indicated the wine decanter, and when she shook her head in a slight but decided negative, poured another glass for himself. "I am terribly sorry for the inconvenience. If you would like, I will ask Rose to prepare you something to eat, or, if you prefer, you may . . . ah . . . join us for our noon meal." He stumbled over the last; the flow of his talk had led him naturally into the invitation, and it wasn't until it was half out of his mouth that he gave actual thought as to what an hour of table conversation with this woman would be like, even with Langsford present to keep topics on a safe and neutral ground. "It would seem," he finished lamely, "that your original reason for coming has . . . well, been resolved."

"Has it now?" she said. "You may be the best judge of that, or ye may not." Langsford looked faintly startled. "You, young man. Tell me what happened, and tell me without your whiffle-headed prattle."

"With all respect, Mistress Bannel . . ." Jonathan started tersely, but Langsford interrupted him with a laugh.

"No, Williams," he said, "she is absolutely correct." He raised his glass to her. "Quite simply, madam, I ignored the good advice of my friend and followed the bad advice of another, and paid the consequences."

Jonathan frowned. "Bad advice of another?"

"Yes," Langsford said, and crossed one leg over the other. "I thought that, maternal prohibitions notwithstanding, Alec would know the path up from the beach better than you, and so instead of continuing to look for your path, which in the fog was quite hidden, I followed his suggestion, and took what appeared to be the clear way up."

"What do you mean?" Jonathan asked, puzzled. "Alec wasn't there. I was quite alone."

"I beg pardon?" Langsford said. "He was standing behind you when first you called to me. He must have moved while we were shouting back and forth. When I began to look for the path, he was standing at the low spot in the cliff, and indicated the way." He took a sip of his wine. "Perhaps for him the climb would have been possible, but it was irresponsible of him to expect me to make it."

"Langsford," Jonathan said slowly, "he wasn't *there*. I haven't seen him since before breakfast." He was nervous about Bannel's silence as Langsford spoke; she was watching him closely, her eyes half closed, so still she might have been a wax figure sitting in a museum.

"How very odd," Langsford said, "though perhaps the fog prevented you from seeing him." He gestured to the windows, which were a solid blank grey. "I had more than a little difficulty with that myself. But regardless, when I realized how narrow the ledge had become, and you told me that you believed there to be no way to the top at all, I turned, and was . . . that I fell. You know the rest. Thank heaven you were there," he finished quickly.

Jonathan started to speak, but was interrupted when Rose came to the door.

"Margaret's setting up in the dining room, Mr. Williams," she said, "a cold meal as you requested. We've also put some beef tea over a spirit lamp for you, Mr. Langsford, in case you should want something warm." She looked at Jonathan. "There is more than enough for two, if you'll be wantin' some also, Mr. Williams."

"Thank you, Mrs. Hale," Langsford said. "That is most kind of you."

"You're welcome, sir," she said. "Will you be dinin' downstairs this evenin'? I wasn't certain if after takin' such a fall you'd be dinin' in company or not."

"Company?" Langsford asked blankly.

"Dear god, the vicar," Jonathan said. They stared at each other in shock. He had completely forgotten that Dr. Deane and his wife were coming to dinner that evening. He looked at the clock—a quarter hour after noon. "I'm afraid it's a bit late in the day to put them off entirely," he said. "You needn't, if you would prefer a quiet evening. I can very easily make your excuses."

"And miss the wisdom of Magdalen College unfolding before

our eyes?" Langsford said. "Not for the world."

"Perhaps I should insist on your staying above stairs," Jonathan said with narrowed eyes, "if this is any indication of how the evening will proceed. I will simply tell them you're deranged from the fall."

"Tell them I'm seeing people who aren't there, and you'll have strong evidence."

Jonathan coughed and flashed a glance at Rose. Alec and the beach were a sensitive subject, and not one he wanted brought up again; Langsford could have no clue of the repercussions a chance comment linking the two might trigger.

Langsford nodded slightly, saying, "Set me a place at the table, Mrs. Hale. If I am weary at the end of the meal, I will excuse myself before coffee. I'm sure they will understand."

"Yes, sir," Rose said. "If you change your plans, please let me know."

"Thank you, Rose," Jonathan said.

"Rose Hale," Mrs. Bannel said, still looking at Jonathan.

Rose stopped in the doorway. "Yes?" Rose said, and Jonathan realized it was the first time since she'd walked into the room that she'd looked at the older woman, or even acknowledged her presence.

"Is Alec about the house today?" she asked. Jonathan and Langsford's eyes met, and Langsford raised his eyebrows slightly. "I didn't see him when I come down. Of course, the fog was that thick."

"I believe he was with Ratchet up in the back pasture this mornin'," she said. "One of the cows was come to calf, and Ratchet likes him along. He has the touch with them."

The old woman nodded. "Aye, he does. Well, perhaps another day I'll see him."

Without a word, Rose nodded her head, and walked quickly from the room.

"The mist's a queer thing," Mrs. Bannel said idly. "What it hides, and what it shows."

"Indeed," Langsford said.

She stood, and Langsford rose from his seat. "You'll hurt worse tomorrow than you do today," she said to him, "and you need to spend this day at rest." She reached up and touched his cheek, then his forehead, and then his other cheek. "If he's feverish in the morning or at any time," she said to Jonathan, "I've left some willow tea with Rose Hale." She folded her hands in front of her. "I doubt you'll need it though. You haven't the feel of it."

"Thank you, Mrs. Bannel," Langsford said.

She crossed the room toward the door, and Jonathan followed her. He motioned for Langsford to stay where he was. "Are you certain I cannot offer you some refreshment," he said as they entered the hall. "If not with Langsford and me, in the kitchen with Rose and the family?"

She shook her head as she led him down the hall toward the kitchen. When she reached the door, she turned. He stopped abruptly, then moved to open the door, but she held up her hand. "He's not told you all," she said, "nor have you, me. 'Tis of little importance, perhaps." She pushed open the door. "Or perhaps not. When you have need, child, come to me, as you did then."

Chapter 9

"Williams?" Langsford called, rummaging through the items on his dressing table. Brushes. Comb. Mirror. Shaving things. *Damn*. He pulled out his portmanteau again. "Williams!"

"Yes?" Williams called from his room. "What is it?"

"I cannot find my cufflinks. Have you an extra pair?" He ran his hand along the lining, but felt no extraneous bumps. Perhaps they had fallen out of the case and had lodged in one of the pockets . . . nothing. He crossed to the communicating door between their rooms, rapped, and entered. "I've searched everywhere," he said, exasperated, "and I cannot find them. I must have left them at home, though I was certain I packed them. Damned annoying. Have you an extra set? I don't want to use a paper clip or anything ridiculous, but if you don't have a set I'm up against it."

Williams was in front of the dressing table mirror, tying his tie. "Look in the top drawer of the chest of drawers. They should be there."

"Wonderful," Langsford said. "That's twice today you've saved my life."

"That's no laughing matter," Williams said. "Bother."

"It most certainly is a laughing matter," Langsford said, walking up behind him and catching his eye in the mirror. "It's either laugh, or fall on your breast and weep tears of undying gratitude, and I certainly wouldn't want to spoil your shirt. What's a bother?"

"Don't be an ass," Williams said, pulling fiercely at the tie. "This tie is the bother. It simply won't tie properly."

"Shall I have a go at it?" Langsford asked. "If I can't weep undying tears, I can most certainly valet you for the evening."

"Did I not just tell you not to be an ass?" Williams said peevishly. "I believe I did. And no, I don't need any assistance, thank you."

"Yes, you did, I believe, but I'm a bit hazy on the whole concept. My delicate condition, you know." He walked over to the chest, opened the drawer, and examined the contents. "I must say, Williams, you are the most meticulous man I know, worse than any sailor. Everything in its place . . . but . . . no cufflinks." He slid the drawer shut and leaned against the chest. "I must have something. If the vicar is properly dressed—and I dare say he will be—I'm afraid we shall suffer an irreversible eclipse before the glory of Oxford, and I shall be cast into the outer darkness with the proverbial wailing and gnashing of teeth. Or worse: shipped to Basingstoke. Now *there's* a fate that teems with hidden meaning—"

"Not there?" Williams said, and crossed the room, the tie apparently forgotten for the moment. "Don't be ridiculous. Of course they're there. I always have two pair."

"I know," Langsford said, stepping aside. "I've come to depend upon it."

"What in the world . . ." Williams said after one quick look in the drawer. "This isn't everything. Rose only brought essentials. I suppose she's assuming I'll move back down to the other room. I'm not so sure I shall."

"Frailty thy name is woman," Langsford said. "And I shouldn't blame you if you stayed up here. A bit cramped, that room."

"I suppose it is." Williams began working at the tie again.

Langsford leaned up against the doorframe. "What sort of fellow is this Deane, by the way? And his wife. Is she the large, hearty, run the village sort? I can't abide them; I suffered enough of that as a child."

"*Damn* this thing . . ."

"Here. Enough of this. You're loaning me your cufflinks, assuming I can find them, so let me tie your tie."

Williams sighed and moved to the middle of the room, and lifted his chin. For a moment they looked in each other's eyes, then Langsford dropped his gaze to the tie. He'd had enough emotionally fraught moments already today and had no desire to risk any more.

"It's not really a bad job," he said, his fingers shaking slightly, "just a little uneven." He quickly pulled the knot apart while risking a glance at Jonathan's face; his friend was looking straight up at the ceiling. "You know," Langsford said, "this *is* rather like being undergraduates again, and preparing to dine with the head of the College. We've come full circle."

"I believe you talked less as an undergraduate," Williams observed.

"Ah, no conversation while I am working," Langsford retorted. "I'll slip and cut your throat."

"That would only happen if you were shaving me."

"Well, I will strangle you, then."

"That would be a wonderful show of gratitude for saving your life."

"I thought that wasn't a laughing matter!"

"Then why are you laughing?"

Langsford stepped back and looked at the tie; this was definitely not one of his better efforts. "I'm laughing because I'm thinking of the consternation you would cause among the general population if you went out looking like that. Come along, give me another try."

"Langsford?"

"Hmm?" Langsford said as he tugged the knot clear again. He pulled the ends so they matched.

"You said the queerest thing on the beach today. It's rather caught at my mind all afternoon."

Langsford felt his cheeks grow warm, and he concentrated on

the first pass of the knot. *He noticed I called him by his Christian name*, he thought, although why Williams should think that queer, and not simply put it down to the strain of the moment, baffled him. He stole another look at Williams, who was still looking at the ceiling, now with a puzzled frown. "What was it I said?" Langsford asked.

"Well, when I told Hale you'd fallen, you said no, that you had been pushed."

"I said what?" He pulled the tie a little too hard, and the knot slid too far. "*Blast*." He stepped back. "I actually said that?"

"Yes," Williams said. "I thought it odd at the time, but didn't put too much stock in it. I actually thought you were delirious. Have you finished?"

"That's completely understandable," Langsford said, relieved that it was something directly related to his accident, and not other, more delicate topics. "I'd have certainly thought the same, had our situations been reversed. No, I haven't finished. Third time pays for all." He undid the tie again and started from the beginning. "I might have thought that, but I never imagined I'd actually said it."

Williams tipped his head slightly. "You thought that? Whatever would make you think something like that?"

"Well, here's the strange thing," Langsford said, frowning. "Queer, as you said. As I told you this morning, I had difficulty sleeping last night, and I had some rather odd dreams." He carefully pulled the bows of the tie. "The pertinent one is that I dreamt I was pushed off the cliff—"

"What!" Williams exclaimed, stepping back just as he released the tie.

"I don't think I'm clairvoyant," Langsford said, studying the tie critically. "In fact, I'm about as sensitive as a stick, and it wasn't me who was pushed off, it was another fellow, or rather, he was pushed and I did the falling—oh, damn, you know how dreams are, all muddled up." He leaned against the door frame again. "What I'm saying is, I must have been thinking about that dream just when you said that, and I blurted it out." He frowned. The thing is, it *had* felt as if he had been pushed. He hadn't been overbalanced; he'd actually been leaning *into* the rock face when he'd suddenly fallen backward. He simply wasn't sure now if he'd been remembering the sensation from the dream, or if it had actually felt like hands pushing him back and away from the cliff. There was no way he could really know.

"But that's not possible," Williams said, looking concerned. "There was no one there. There could not have been."

The clock struck the three-quarter hour.

"Of course there wasn't," Langsford replied, "which shows what a peculiar reaction one can have to such events. What's more important to me at this point is the cufflinks. We can talk this all over after Magdalen and Lady Magdalen have left."

"Rose must have left them in the top drawer of the chest of drawers in my room downstairs," Jonathan said. "Shall I get them for you?"

"No, don't trouble yourself," Langsford said. "You still have to finished dressing *and* straighten your hair. I'm one ahead of you there. I'll find them."

He dashed down the main stairs. A lifetime of experience with country clerics had taught him that they fell into two distinct camps: those who arrived ten minutes early to dinner, and those who arrived three quarters of an hour late. He felt most strongly, just from their short meeting at the church door on Sunday, that Deane fell into the former category—nothing dreamy and absentminded about him.

He hurried across the drawing room and down the passage to Williams' room. Placing the lamp on top of the chest of drawers, he pulled open the right-hand top drawer, where Williams always kept such items. White studs and cufflinks, black studs, eye glasses, and a cigarette case he had given Williams as a Christmas gift five years ago all gleamed in the lamplight . . . but no black cufflinks. *Odd.* Williams had been certain he'd brought them. He opened the center, knowing what to expect—handkerchiefs, ties, and shirt collars, all precisely folded and placed, but again no cufflinks. He pulled the left-hand drawer open, though he knew Williams, as one of his quirks, never kept anything in that location, but as he tugged on the handle, he heard a rattle. He shifted the lamp, and there they lay: black cufflinks in an otherwise empty drawer. He plucked them out and pocketed them, then picked up the lamp and pushed the drawer closed. As he did so, he caught a glimpse of something else a little further back. Curious, he opened the drawer again.

A small rectangle of cardboard, perhaps six inches by eight inches with words printed on it, lay toward the back of the drawer. He picked it up and looked more closely at the inscription: a photographer in Penzance. He turned it over.

The photograph was a fairly typical thing, an embossed cardboard backing mounted with an oval photo in the center. What surprised him was that one of the two men pictured was Williams, a young Williams as he remembered him upon meeting at Cambridge when he had first arrived. He was wearing a shirt and bow tie, a waistcoat and jacket, and sitting in a chair in front of a standard photographer's studio background of slightly blurred clouds. Langsford recognized the look on his face immediately: Williams trying without success to look serious for the photographer, but unable to suppress the gleams of delight that escaped his control.

Another man, dark-haired and dark-eyed, sat beside him on a slightly higher level, his arm casually draped around Williams' shoulders, a man more roughly dressed, with a workman's shirt open at the collar and a heavy jacket, but wearing a similar expression—a happiness that overwhelmed all attempts at sobriety, a sense of mischief shared.

They sat close, clearly comfortable in each other's company. Williams' right hand rested on the dark man's knee, and his left just touched the other's hand where it lay on his chest. Written on the bottom of the picture was one word: "Us."

Langsford felt a hollowness in his stomach that had nothing to do with hunger. Who was this other man? The face was familiar to him, but he couldn't quite place it. He doubted it was anyone from Eton, not in a photograph from Penzance, and definitely not in those garments. *Although*, he thought, *it's possible*; Williams hadn't spoken of a school friend visiting, but he rarely spoke of that summer at all. But who it could be he couldn't think; recognition hovered just behind conscious thought in his mind, but refused to come into the light.

He started to replace the photo in the drawer, but, increasingly uneasy as to its history—he'd never seen it the entire time he'd known Williams—he kept it. He'd ask about it if there was time, or after Deane and his wife left, if they arrived before he had a chance.

"Williams . . ." he said as he entered his room.

"Did you find them?" Williams called from the other room.

"Yes, I did," he answered, "I also found . . ."

"Good," Williams said. "They'll arrive in a few minutes."

Langsford walked toward the connecting door between the rooms. "I've also found . . ." he said again, but as he did so, the bell at the front door rang.

"Good Lord," Williams said, hurrying into the room. "They're here. Do you need any assistance?"

"No," Langsford answered. "You go down; I'll be there momentarily."

"Good, good," Jonathan said, and hurried out into the corridor. "What was it you found?" he called from the stair.

"Nothing of importance," he answered. "We can talk about it later."

"Very good."

He studied the photograph, trying again but failing to think where—and if—he had seen the second figure in it, then placed it on his dressing table. With shaking hands he busied himself with his cufflinks.

"You have outdone yourself with this, Mrs. Hale," Langsford said as he finished the last of his dessert, brandied peaches of a delicacy he had not expected to find in a farmstead on the Cornish coast. *But then*, he thought, *her meals have been excellent from the start of our stay.*

"Thank you, Mr. Langsford-Knight," she said; she and Meg had waited on the table. "It was a favorite of Mr. Penhyrddin's, and I thought it might suit."

"Indeed it did, Rose," said Dr. Deane, laying his napkin on the table. "Andrew *was* fond of them, and I thank you for that good memory."

"You're most welcome, Vicar."

Dr. Deane and his wife had proved another unexpected pleasure for Langsford. Assuming that he would have to endure a long, slow, and tedious dinner, weighed down with village gossip and minutia, he had instead found Deane a brusque and matter-of-fact man, intelligent, well read, and very much up to the mark on national events.

His wife was an even greater surprise: they found, within the first quarter hour, that they were distantly related through his mother's family. Mrs. Deane was a keen and clever conversationalist, not in the least what he had anticipated, and to his astonishment, a confirmed universal suffragist, though by necessity of her position, not a terribly vocal one.

They had a lively debate on the subject through the first half of the dinner, with Mrs. Deane taking a stand for suffrage, he, for the point of argument, opposed, with Williams and Dr. Deane straddling the middle ground. To his chagrin and delight, she had bested him in the discussion, carefully leading him along a path until he was practically forced to say that women ought not vote because they lacked sufficient education and knowledge to make a rational decision—something he most certainly did not believe—at which point she smiled sweetly and said, "I cannot think, Mr. Langsford-Knight, that you mean to say that *I* am insufficiently knowledgeable to cast a vote for the leaders of our country, as I do for our local offices. And I, surely, am not amongst the best educated of my sex." Rather than be ill-mannered, he quite honestly acknowledged her equal with, or, indeed, superior to, many of the men of his acquaintance in possessing the qualifications for the vote, and retired from the field.

The rest of dinner was spent in general conversation about the parish, the farm, the surrounding villages, and, to a lesser degree, about their lives. Deane had been born and raised in the area, and had gone up to Oxford for his degree. It was there he had met his future wife, the daughter of one of the dons; they had married, and for the last thirty-five years he had been tending to the spiritual needs of the land of his birth. Such topics took them through dessert, when Rose said that coffee was laid out in the drawing room, and port in the library.

"I think," Jonathan said as they rose, "given that your wife is the only lady in company tonight, that we might dispense with port, gentlemen, and join her immediately?"

"Not on my account," Mrs. Deane answered. "If I might shock Mr. Langsford-Knight, may I suggest that I join you in the library? It would be much more interesting than languishing alone in the drawing room, pleasant though it is."

Langsford offered her his arm. "Mrs. Deane, I believe there is nothing you can say or do that would shock me," he said gallantly. "However, I would be more than delighted to give you every opportunity of doing so."

"Rose," Williams said, "would you have Meg bring the coffee to the library, please?"

"I am so glad you were able to join us," Mrs. Deane said as she took Langsford's arm. "I was quite afraid that, given your accident this morning, you would not feel well enough."

Langsford looked at her in some surprise. "I beg your pardon, Mrs. Deane?" he asked as they walked from the room.

"Oh, dear," she said, "I'm afraid I've phrased that rather badly. I was of course extremely relieved to hear that you escaped serious injury. Please accept my apology."

"There is no need to apologize," Langsford said. "I'm simply startled that you'd heard of it at all, and not only heard of it, but had been privy to the details."

"You will find, sir, that there is very little that goes on in this parish that does not, with lesser or greater speed, come 'round to the vicarage kitchen," Deane said as he followed them into the library. "And from there it is but a short leap to my wife's ear."

"Williams," he said, "it would appear that we are indeed the subject of village interest."

"*Richard*," Mrs. Deane said, "you mustn't give the gentlemen the impression that I listen to gossip." She turned to Langsford. "Being Richard's wife does include hearing much of the happenings of the wives and families in the parish. If they don't feel they can speak directly with him, they will often come to me."

"I think that's a perfectly natural circumstance," Langsford said, and led Mrs. Deane to the chair by the fire. "May I offer you some coffee?"

"Thank you, Mr. Langsford-Knight," she replied. "You are most kind."

Rose and Meg quietly moved the wine tray and the cigar humidor as Langsford busied himself at the coffee tray. He poured the cup, then, at an assenting look from Mrs. Deane, added milk and sugar.

"Few things in this world travel faster than the telegraph that comprises the conversation of the wives of this county," Deane said as he settled into a chair opposite his wife, "although I will say, the news would have traveled even more quickly had you been injured." He lifted his glass. "We are, of course, much relieved that such is not the case, I can assure you."

"Not so well relieved as I," Langsford said, and sat at on end of the sofa. "Had it not been for Williams, things would have turned out quite differently."

"Nonsense," Williams said, and leaned against the mantelpiece. "You would have swum in just easily by yourself, had it not been for the fog."

"It was a rather unpleasant day," Deane said. "We've had quite a run of fog this year. Most unusual." He settled back and crossed his legs. "However, the whole situation turned out well. It would have been dreadful to have another tragedy at that spot, particularly so soon upon your return, Mr. Williams."

A rather uncomfortable silence fell over the room, and Langsford looked at Williams. He was pale, his mouth pinched, and he said nothing.

"Another tragedy?" Langsford asked, turning to Deane. "I'm afraid I don't understand."

"Oh, yes. I quite forgot myself," Deane said, and leaned back in his chair. "A very sad case. A young fellow, a worker here on the farm, fell from the cliffs late one night quite near where your accident happened. He was not so fortunate as you, I'm afraid, and they found him on the beach the next morning." He shook his head. "Terribly sad. Apparently he'd had a bit too much to drink that night—not uncommon, I'm afraid—and fell as he was coming back to the farm from the village. He must have lost his footing and stumbled off the edge. He was a bit of a wild lad, true, but a good worker, and I think might have grown out of his troublesome ways."

"It must have been most difficult for you, Mr. Williams," Mrs. Deane said sympathetically. Langford looked back at Williams, who had turned red, but nodded slightly.

"Did you know this poor fellow, Williams?" Langsford asked. He was surprised. Williams had never spoken at all about this, and though they had not become friends until after that summer, he thought that such a subject would have been at least mentioned. He thought of the photograph that lay on his dressing table upstairs. *Us.* Might that have been the same man?

"Yes, actually," Jonathan said quietly. "He worked here on the farm."

"You and he were such good friends," Mrs. Deane said. "I've long regretted I didn't have the chance at the time to express my sympathy. I'm certain you were disappointed that you had to miss the funeral." She smiled sadly. "Although it might have been difficult, I know, particularly after losing your dear mother such a short time before."

"I wasn't aware you were acquainted," Williams said quietly.

"Oh, yes," Mrs. Deane replied. "I knew her fairly well when I first came here. She married your father not long after, of course, but we kept up quite a correspondence for a number of years. I still have her letters, if you would like to see them."

"I should like that very much," Williams said, brightening a bit. "I haven't many from her myself, and I would count it a great favor."

"Then I shall send them over immediately," Mrs. Deane said. "You needn't worry, though. There is nothing in them that would cause you terrible embarrassment, though I think I might hold back the letters written during her confinement, when you were born."

"I do believe I will pass those by," he said wryly. "There are some things one simply does not wish to know."

Mrs. Deane laughed quietly. "Of course. A bachelor like you would hardly be familiar with the details of such things." She placed her coffee cup on the table. "I have a thought. Please come for tea, this week or next. Propose yourself, and I will give them to you when you come. I should very much like to have a nice talk. I was so shocked when Andrew—Mr. Penhyrddin, that is—told us of her death." She turned to Langsford. "Did you know Mrs. Williams, Mr. Langsford-Knight?"

"No," Langsford said. "I didn't meet Williams until he came up to Cambridge that autumn. I never had the honor of knowing his mother."

"She was very kind," Mrs. Deane said, "and so sudden and unexpected a passing." She sighed. "But then, there was so much influenza that year."

"Quite the epidemic we had around here," Deane concurred. "We were all very much relieved when you recovered, Mr. Williams."

"Were you ill that summer?" Langsford asked, looking at Williams.

"I . . . why, yes," Williams answered, meeting his gaze steadily.

"I had quite forgotten about it."

"Two full weeks he was bed fast, right before he left for Cambridge," Deane said. "Penhyrddin was most concerned. Nursed him by himself, as a matter of fact."

"I believe my cousin was a trifle over cautious," Williams said. "I don't recall being terribly ill, but I do recall him telling me quite sternly that I was to stay in bed. It was most trying for me, actually. It was a beautiful summer." He moved to the wine tray. "May I offer you some more port, Mr. Deane?" he asked. "Mrs. Deane, more coffee?"

As Williams saw to his guests, Langsford sat back on the sofa and sipped his port. He was puzzled. Williams had, as he recalled, not looked terribly well that first week or so in Cambridge, but he had not seemed like a man recovering from the influenza. He had been pale, true, but he had also carried fading bruises and scratches about the face and neck, marks from the fall he said *he* had taken. Nothing whatsoever about a farmhand's fall. *Odd.* Perhaps the Deanes were mistaken in their recollections of the event, and Williams had, for reasons of courtesy, not wished to embarrass them by contradicting them, but Langsford thought not—Mrs. Deane's memory had more than once gently corrected her husband in his various anecdotes at dinner, and Deane himself had no small eye for detail.

The conversation turned to more general topics, and after an hour Mrs. Deane rose.

"This has been a rather trying day for you both, I am afraid," she said, "and we shan't trespass on your hospitality any longer." She held out her hand to Langsford and he took it briefly. "I do hope we shall see you before you return to London, Mr. Langford-Knight," she said. "I've very much enjoyed making your acquaintance."

"I should be delighted."

"I'm terribly disappointed that you are here so briefly," she said, as they walked to the front door where Rose and Meg waited. "Will you be returning soon?"

"I plan on being here for the month of August," he replied. "That is, of course, if Williams will have me."

"A pity you won't be here for Midsummer," Deane said. "The festivities are quite interesting, left over from pagan times, of course, but fascinating. Thank you, Meg," he said, as she helped him into his overcoat. "I do hope to see you in church this week," he said pointedly. "We have missed you the last two."

"Yes, Vicar," Meg replied. "I'll do my very best, sir, but you know, with one thing and another, a body can't rightly remember where one is, and—"

"Alec is bringing your carriage up, Vicar," Rose said, and Langsford suppressed a smile at the neat way she'd cut off what clearly might have been a rather lengthy series of embarrassing excuses on Meg's part.

"Thank you, Rose," Deane said. "We will see you Wednesday night, I trust?"

"Yes, sir."

Mrs. Deane gave her a penetrating look. "And are you well this evening, Rose?" she asked.

"Yes, Mrs. Deane," she replied calmly. "I am quite well, thank you."

"Ah," Mrs. Deane said. "That is good."

Again a brief and charged silence followed the short exchange—even Meg seemed momentarily quelled—and Langsford had a strong sense of there being undercurrents eddying around him, things unspoken that were understood by all in the room except him, and he recognized the feeling that had been dogging him all day: that these people, all of whom had neither seen nor heard from Williams in almost a decade and a half, in some ways knew him better than he who had been his constant companion through all of those intervening years. He remembered their conversation of two nights ago, but now, instead of believing that Williams had changed from the boy who had summered here into someone that the folk on the farm knew not at all, he felt as if Williams belonged to them, was one of them, and that he stood outside their circle, watching but not understanding. The quiet, dark-haired man talking pleasantly with a country vicar and his wife seemed to be someone he neither knew nor understood, a man with secrets unshared, about which he dared not ask. He shivered.

They walked the Deanes down to the garden gate as Alec arrived with the gig, its top up and its lanterns lit against the fog. Williams assisted Mrs. Deane into her seat, and sent Alec to fetch a rug for her.

"Are you certain you will have no difficulty getting home?" Langsford asked Deane quietly. "It's a dirty night."

"No, no, none at all," Deane answered, swinging up next to his wife. "I might lose my way," he said as he picked up the reins and nodded toward the horse, "but my old girl will get us home safely enough."

Mrs. Deane patted his arm. "That's most rude of you, Richard," she said. "You know I never give directions while you're driving."

Langsford and Williams laughed, and Deane simply shook his head.

"Be careful when you marry, Mr. Langsford-Knight," Deane said. "A clever woman might not drive you home, but she will, in all likelihood, drive you to distraction."

Alec arrived with the rug, and Williams helped Mrs. Deane arrange it comfortably. She thanked him, and Deane slapped the reins. The gig disappeared into the fog, and he and Williams walked slowly back up to the house.

"Well," Langsford said, "that was far more pleasant than I had anticipated. It would seem your neighborhood contains more than farmers and fishermen."

"Yes," Williams said absently. "They're very good company."

"A cigarette before turning in?" he asked.

"No, I think not," Williams said. "It's a bit too damp and cold."

"True."

They entered the house and walked to the library without

speaking. Langsford poured them each another glass of port, and they settled into the two chairs that flanked the fireplace. Langsford took a sip, and studied Williams' face; he was watching the flames with a pensive look, apparently unaware of Langsford's scrutiny. The clock on the mantelpiece ticked loudly in the stillness, and once again Langsford was assailed with a sense of absence, or even loss, as if Williams was unconsciously withdrawing to a place that he could not follow. They had often spent entire evenings together with barely a word spoken, but it had been an amicable silence, a silence where conversation continued without speech, with a language instead of long custom and habit providing a companionship more satisfying than idle chatter could hope to furnish. This restraint, this closing of doors and windows, left him feeling lost and adrift.

"It would seem—" he said, and Williams started, spilling a little of his wine. "I'm sorry; I didn't mean to alarm you."

"No," Williams said quickly. "I'm sorry. I was just thinking how little they'd changed. It surprised me. I had expected them to be different, somehow."

"In all likelihood, they haven't changed considerably since you were last here. They lead a similar life to that which they lived then, except that their children have grown and have families of their own, while you have changed a great deal."

"Have I, do you think?" Williams asked. "I'm not so certain . . . "

"You've been to university," Langsford said, "and have worked in the City, and, most telling of all, have been around me for all the years since. That in itself is enough to have utterly degraded your finer sensibilities. They must be bitterly disappointed in you."

"If they are," Williams said, glancing across at him with a half smile, and Langsford drew an easier breath at the familiar expression, "and if they should say so, or express any such opinion, however remotely, I will lay the blame entirely at your door. Having met you, I'm certain they will understand and forgive me any lapses."

"I don't doubt it for a moment," Langford said cheerfully.

"By the time I return in August, Lady Magdalen—who is quite entertaining actually, and I must stop calling her by that name—will have taken you firmly in hand and improved you all out of recognition. Or at least, one can only pray she will."

"I sincerely hope she does," Williams said, and took a sip of his wine. "Perhaps," he continued thoughtfully, "given that you are relations, however distant, I will encourage her to write a letter to your mother, recommending that *she* take a similar interest in *your* improvement. I'm sure she would be most interested, now that my moderating influences on you will be necessarily lessened."

Langsford narrowed his eyes. "It's true, then, what the radical papers say about the landed gentry," he said, delighted at Williams' return to normalcy. "You are a cruel and heartless race, and should be divested of your privileges."

Williams sighed. "Ah, the undeserving poor. They are so ungrateful."

"Yes, we are," Langsford said. "We are bomb throwing anarchists, every one of us, and thrive on sensation and spectacle. However, I believe I have had more than enough sensation for one day." He stood and stretched his limbs; old Mrs. Bannel was correct: He would feel the pain of today's mishap more tomorrow than he did now.

Williams rose also, a look of concern crossing his face. "Of course," he said. "I'm so terribly sorry. I, well, it's not that I'd forgotten, but I am afraid it didn't occur to me that you might be exhausted."

Langsford shook his head. "I wouldn't say I'm exhausted, but I am a bit fagged." He crossed to the table and moved to put down his glass, and then hesitated. Relations were normal again, but the question of the man in the photograph still gnawed at him, a nagging curiosity that he had worried at through dinner, like a sore tooth that one prods constantly with one's tongue to see if it did indeed still hurt. "An odd coincidence, don't you think," he said lightly, "that I should fall at the same place as that other fellow." His glass rattled against the tray as he put it down. He looked back at Williams, who was still standing by his chair, his face devoid of expression.

"Yes," Williams answered, looking away and draining his glass. "Yes, it is. But a coincidence with a more fortunate outcome."

"Yes, thanks to you," Langsford said. He knew he ought not to pursue the question any further, that he was treading on very delicate ground, but he could not seem to stop himself. "Were you . . . very great friends?" he asked.

Williams rested his hand on the mantle. "We were . . . acquainted," he said stiffly. "I don't know that I should have called us great friends . . ." He stopped speaking, and Langsford thought of Mrs. Deane's saying just that thing. Williams looked down into the fire. " . . . that is to say, he worked on the farm, and was . . . was good company, I suppose." He looked back up and met Langsford's eye. "Any lasting friendship would have been impossible, of course, but he was a good enough fellow. It was a great shock to everyone when he was found."

"I'm sure it was," Langsford said. "Such a thing always is."

Williams nodded. "Yes," he said. "I had put the entire incident from my mind, I'm afraid, until this morning, when I saw you down on the beach. It all came back in a rush."

"Small wonder you were upset, then," Langsford replied.

"Quite," Williams said. He looked at the clock. "But it's late, and it has been a long and difficult day. We could both do with some sleep."

"Yes, I suppose we could," Langsford said, and Williams relaxed slightly. Then, though he was evenly balanced between wanting to know and wanting to remain ignorant, he asked, "Was he the fellow in the photograph?"

Williams dropped his glass, and it shattered on the hearth. "What photograph?" he asked, his eyes wide and dark.

"Have a care," Langsford exclaimed, startled by the violence of Williams' reaction.

Williams took two steps toward him. "What photograph?" he

repeated tersely.

"The photograph in your drawer," Langsford replied. "I found it when I went for the cufflinks. I apologize. I didn't mean to pry."

"There is no photograph in that drawer," Williams said, his voice shaking.

"It wasn't in the usual drawer," Langsford said. "The cufflinks weren't there, and so I checked the others. They were in the left-hand drawer. The photograph was there also."

"That's impossible," Williams said. "I . . . it isn't possible."

"I apologize if I trespassed upon your privacy," Langsford said, puzzled by Williams' insistence that the photograph hadn't been in the drawer. There clearly existed some deeper meaning to the thing than he had had originally conceived, but to completely deny its existence made little sense, and was widely divergent from Williams' usual calm, logical way of dealing with even the most difficult situations. "I certainly didn't intend anything of the sort, so there's no need to get shirty about it," he said. "It must have been tucked all the way back in the drawer and you missed it, or perhaps you left it here before. I brought it upstairs to ask you about it, but the Deanes arrived and I—"

"I'm telling you, there is no photograph," Williams said, raising his voice. His entire body was trembling, and his fists were clenched by his side. "There can't be."

"There most certainly is," Langsford said, thoroughly exasperated. "It's sitting on my dressing table. Go look for yourself."

"You're lying," Williams said.

Langsford stared at him, aghast.

"There is no photograph," Williams repeated, his voice cracking, and walked quickly across the room. "I don't know what you think you found, but that photograph is . . . there is none. Good night." He slammed the door behind him as he left.

Langsford stood in the center of the room, stunned. They had had rows, of course, and disagreements—no one who had been friends as long as they had been could possibly avoid it, unless they were positively angelic, and he knew he certainly was not—

but never, in all their years of acquaintance and intimate friendship, had Williams so much as raised his voice, much less insulted him and then stormed from the room. He felt as cold and numb as he had that morning, when Williams had pulled him from the water, but infinitely worse: This cold was in his heart, and the numbness his mind; he could neither feel nor move.

The door opened and he stepped back, unprepared to face Williams again, but it was Meg who entered the room. She started and gave a brief cry.

"Mercy, sir," she said, "but you gave me a fright. I heard the door close, and thought both of you gentlemen had gone upstairs and to bed." She made a slight motion as if to leave the room. "I'll come back again when you're done."

Langsford shook himself out of his stupor. "No, no, no," he said, and waved to the coffee pot and cups sitting on the table. "Don't let me interrupt you."

"Thank you, Mr. Langsford-Knight, that's very kind of you," she said, and bustled about the room, picking up the coffee cups and spoons and depositing them on the tray. "Why, you've broken a glass."

"What?" Langford said. "Oh, ah, yes. I'm afraid we've made quite a mess."

"'Tis no bother," Meg said. "I'll fetch a broom and clean it up. Have a mind you don't step on it and hurt yourself."

"No," Langsford said, the glass already swept from his mind. "I'll take care."

She chattered on as she knelt by the hearth to pick up the larger pieces, but Langsford paid her no attention; he poured himself another glass of port and wandered to the window. *What on earth could have upset Williams so much that he would react so violently to my mentioning the photograph?* He and the man had been friends and the latter's death had to have been upsetting, but there was nothing in the photograph to warrant that angry, vehement denial of its very existence. Through his own eyes, colored as they were with his feelings for Williams, the photograph seemed to speak volumes, though the words printed on the pages of those volumes were as erroneous as his own assumptions about the direction of Williams' affections had been. To anyone else the image would have been simple: two friends recording a moment in a day, a day of great pleasure, judging from the looks on their faces, but nothing more. Nothing about the thing suggested more, nothing that would have triggered that ferocious outburst.

He became vaguely aware that Meg had stopped moving around the room, but she had stood in front of him for some moments before he was able to focus on her, or what she was saying.

"I'm sorry, Meg," he said. "I'm afraid I was woolgathering. What did you say?"

"You don't need to apologize, sir," she said, smiling up at him. "Why, it's a wonder to me you're still on your feet. I just said that I'm just glad you weren't badly hurt this mornin' when you fell from the rocks."

"That's very kind of you," he said, automatically smiling.

She looked down and blushed, and he wondered briefly if she could do so on demand, as the great actresses could weep true tears whenever they wished.

"I thank you sir," she said. "It was such a fright when they brought you in, all wet and cold, your face so pale that I'll never get over it. I was afeared we'd lost you as we did the other poor man."

"You were here, then, when he died," he said, his attention now fully focused on her.

"Oh, no, sir," she said, looking up at him through her lashes. "I was just a child then, and still livin' with my folk." She took a step closer. "I wasn't more than nine or ten years old then."

"Ah," he said, disappointed; he had hoped she could tell him something, anything, about the man.

She took a deep breath and sighed; her bosom stretched her blouse tightly against the buttons, and he was fairly certain that had been the intended effect. "No, I was a girl, then, but I did see him in the village and around and about. A fine young lad, and gone so young." She stepped closer again. "A terrible waste of a life, the parson said, and I'm sure he was right . . ."

Langsford stepped around her—she had practically backed him into his chair—and poured himself another small measure of port. Perhaps, if he asked the right questions, she would be able to give him some information, though he felt an absolute cad to play on her obvious interest in such a way. But she was the only person in the household he thought likely to answer him.

"He and Mr. Williams were friends, I've heard," he said carefully, not wanting to give any slight indication of his reasons for asking. "He must have been quite distressed. He's never spoken of it."

"Oh, yes sir," she said, busying herself with the coffee things. "Quite the David and Jonathan, me mother said when she saw them together, and had a good laugh about it, Mr. Williams' Christian name bein' Jonathan as it is. Quite the great friends they were. All the summer long, they'd go trampin' about the countryside when Nat didn't have his work to do on the farm. It did Mr. Williams good, she said, to help him through mournin' his poor mother, though of course she called him Mister Jonathan, as everyone did then."

Nat. He had a name to go with the face. He felt a pang of jealousy at that, more than when the man had just been a face on a photograph in a drawer. They had been close friends, devoted apparently, if the girl was telling the truth and not exaggerating. He felt a fool, but he envied them the freedom of that summer, and wished, somehow, that he had been part of it. He frowned a moment, puzzled. He could not understand where Rose Hale fit into the picture that was building in his head, but she must have; Alec was an indisputable fact. He dared not ask any questions along that line, however. Impossible as it seemed, the young woman chattering away in front of him apparently had no idea of that secret.

" . . . and when he died, me mother said, Mister Jonathan

was laid up with grief somethin' terrible," Meg was saying. "He didn't leave his room for four full weeks, they said, but locked himself away for sadness."

"I beg pardon?" Langsford said, once again startled out of his thoughts.

"Oh, yes," she said. "It was right before he went off to the university that Nat died, and when he did, Mr. Williams, poor lad, just closed himself away in his room and wouldn't see no one but old Mr. Penhyrddin."

"I'd understood that he had the influenza . . ." Langsford said carefully.

"That may be," Meg said, "or it may not, I can't say. But me mother thought 'twas grief of his loss, on top of his good mother dyin'. It broke her heart to hear of it, Mother said." She sighed. "Many a heart was broke when that poor man fell, me own included, just a little. I had a tender pash for him, I did, the first of my life."

"Had he no wife, then?"

"No, he was free as a bird," Meg said, standing and brushing her hands on her apron, "and like a bird, he flew to many a nest, so they say. He broke a heart or two before he fell, my mother said, and there's those around these parts that show it." She looked up at him slyly. "You'd not have to travel far to see that, though." She paused, a mean little smile on her face. "Or so me mother said."

Understanding smote him like a thunderclap, and he stood, dumbstruck.

Alec isn't Williams' child at all. In her small-minded, gossiping way, Meg was broadly hinting at the truth, though he couldn't think why she should risk her place here by doing so. And the truth about Alec was that he was the child of the man who had fallen from the cliffs fourteen years ago. That was why the photograph had looked so very familiar. He was startled, in retrospect, at just how very much the son resembled the father: the same face, the same mouth, the same eyes . . .

His heart pounded. Williams had seen it immediately. Of course he had. He'd known the man, had been friends with him. And then saw the face of the man again in the son, a face so similar that it had shocked him speechless when he had seen it that day in front of the hotel. *That* had been the reason for his reaction, and, most likely, his discomfort at seeing the boy every day: Williams was seeing the ghost of his long dead friend.

Friend. They had been friends. Devoted friends. Jonathan and David.

He hadn't been wrong.

Oh, he'd been egregiously mistaken about Rose Hale and Alec, but he hadn't been mistaken about Williams. He'd been correct ever since he'd first realized that, while he loved Williams, Williams did not love him in return.

And now he knew why.

He loved another. He loved a man lost years ago, a grief piled on his earlier grief, and it had broken him and left him longing for something he could never have, a love that could never be returned.

Or replaced.

"Mr. Langsford-Knight? Are you all right, sir?"

"What is it," he said, suddenly and intensely focused on her. "What did you say?"

"I was wondering if you were feeling ill, sir," she said, her voice faltering. "You looked all taken queer of a sudden."

"Yes," he said. "I was. The day has been a long one." He took her firmly by the arm and led her to the table where the coffee service lay. "Don't you worry about me. You take these things and clean them up, and then hurry yourself up to bed. I'll just rest here for a while until this turn passes." He stepped away. "You have a pleasant night's sleep."

"Oh," she said, her disappointment showing clearly in her face as she picked up the tray. "Thank you, sir. Are you certain there isn't anything else you need?"

"Quite certain, thank you, Meg," he said. "You have been most solicitous and kind, and I appreciate it."

"Yes, sir," she said. "Good night."

He grasped the mantelpiece before she had even left the room, his knuckles whitening as he gripped it more and more tightly. *Fool. Great bloody fool,* he swore to himself. *Twice an idiot.*

Williams had never shown the slightest romantic interest in any of the young men of their acquaintance, or any of the young women, for that matter. He had never shown any interest in anyone. He'd been friendly, charming, and pleasant, an excellent companion, and a considerate and conscientious man in all things. But never once, in fourteen years, had he ever looked at anyone with anything approaching the heat of a deep passion; he'd always been cool and reserved with others, and warm, but still reserved, with him. Williams had always loved this lost man.

He lowered his head to the mantel. Small wonder Williams had reacted so passionately to his ill-mannered intrusion into that long privacy with the finding of the photograph and his blundering, impertinent questions about it. It was evidence, it was proof, it was, in all likelihood, the single link to that time, that joy, that he possessed, and he had carried it with him ever since, keeping it—and his heart—locked carefully in the top left drawer of a chest.

His eyes burned again with tears, but this time he let them flow. He couldn't stay at Trevaglan. He had interfered with a cavalier indifference to Williams' sensibilities and had trespassed too deeply to ever forgive himself. He didn't know how he could face Williams in the morning, but knew he must.

He wiped his tears with the heel of his hand. Just one more morning. He would return to London in the afternoon.

CHAPTER 10

Jonathan pulled the library door closed behind him; the pictures hanging on the walls rattled with the force of the blow. He walked quickly down the hall, pausing only to pick up a candle and holder that stood, unlit, on the table at the base of the stairs. He ran part way up the steps, gradually slowing as he approached the top. The hall stretched out before him, dark except for the steady light of a lamp that burned on a wall shelf between the doors of his and Langsford's rooms. He lit the candle with a taper, then walked back to Langsford's door. He was terrified to turn the knob. Whatever photograph Langsford had found could not be that of him and Nat. He had destroyed that picture before leaving for Cambridge, he was certain.

But what other photograph could it possibly be? He had been to a photographer but once that summer, and there had been just the one photograph taken. And yet Langsford had been certain he was in that photograph. Penhyrddin had perhaps obtained another photo, of his father and he perhaps, or a photograph of him and a friend from school, but neither made sense. Langsford knew his family well, and anyone from school or the University would be equally familiar to him.

He released a shaky breath. There had been one photograph, but the photographer had printed two copies, one for him and one for Nat. His cousin had, in all likelihood, been given Nat's at some point in the last several years, and had placed it in his chest of drawers. He turned the knob and entered the room. A fired burned low in the grate, more ember than flame, and the room was warm with the smell of the fire and of bay rum. He lingered in the middle of the room, the scent triggering memories of their first travels in University. He loved the way Langsford smelled.

He had noticed it first during his second year at Cambridge. They were traveling for his first visit to Langsford's family in Yorkshire at the Christmas holidays. The weather had been damp and rainy, and the train crowded. They had been crushed in the corner of a second-class carriage, and as they travelled north the gentle rocking of the train and the steamy heat of the compartment had lulled them both to sleep. He had awoken after a short nap, but Langsford had slept long, and had gradually come to rest with his head on Jonathan's shoulder. Drowsy and relaxed, Jonathan had dozed for most of the journey, comforted by Langsford's weight leaning against him. In later years the slightest hint of the scent could recall that memory and transport him instantly to that carriage, and looking back, he had realized that this was the moment that he had first loved Langsford, and all of the times of joy and longing had grown from that journey.

He crossed the room slowly. Even in the dim candlelight, he could see the dark rectangle of the photograph on the top of the dressing table. He was afraid to pick it up, afraid to turn it over and look at it, afraid to see Nat's face looking out at him after all the years. He didn't need to see the picture to remember it exactly; he had spent hours at night, after they'd made love, looking at it. He'd often tucked it in a book when he sat out under the hawthorn on the lawn, and would slip it next to the page he was reading, so that, with a glance, he could look at Nat any time he wished.

He had burned it two weeks after Nat died.

With a rush, he picked up the picture and turned it over.

The photograph itself was smaller than he remembered, but hadn't faded in the least. Even in the candlelight he could pick out every detail of Nat's face: the dark eyes, the full mouth, surprisingly soft and gentle, the slightly crooked nose and half smile. Nat hadn't shaved that day, and Jonathan shivered as he recalled the roughness against his skin when they had kissed that night. But to his surprise, he didn't feel the panic or nausea he thought he'd feel at the sight or the memory—perhaps seeing Alec so frequently across the last few days had armored him against any distress. They were painfully similar in aspect, though Alec had a softer and more diffident expression. Perhaps it was his youth, or perhaps his upbringing; he had no idea.

He studied his own face for a few moments, wondering that he had ever been so young, so completely unaware of what life was bringing, and so very, very happy, a delight and wonder without alloy, pure and, he had thought, simple. Out of long past habit his gaze dropped to the cardboard backing, just below the oval of the photograph itself.

His heart lurched and pounded so furiously he thought it would burst, and he dropped the picture as if it was once again on fire. A wave of dizziness rushed over him, and he clutched the dressing table for support. Nat's picture had had no inscription. His had. This one did, and in his own hand.

Us.

Cornwall 1892

As June spread its warm languor across the countryside, Jonathan and Nat met almost every night. A word or a glance during the day would suffice, and after the household was asleep, Jonathan would slip out of his window and run across the lawn to the shadow of the hawthorn tree where Nat waited. On the occasions that Nat's work on the farm kept him in the distant fields, or Penhyrddin kept Jonathan occupied in the house, Jonathan would find, after retiring for the night, a small bundle of straw tied with a thread tucked on his windowsill.

They dared not risk being discovered, and so they were cautious, always travelling away from the farm itself and finding a remote and secluded place, in a hidden glade in a wood, or an abandoned barn or cot. Nat had been correct, as Jonathan well knew: The law was against them, and discovery would mean social disgrace, at the very least, or prison.

Nat's favorite place was the fogou in the ruined village on the hill. Jonathan disliked it intensely; the damp chill of the stone oppressed him, and he preferred any of the other places to this one. Nat liked it because, of all the places he knew, this was the least likely to be found or disturbed. To appease Jonathan he cleared out the small side chamber, which he had found again on a later exploration, and brought a ticking mat that he laid on oilskin on the ground. Candles set in niches in the wall banished the darkness, and when the chamber was lit they discovered a rough, fire blackened hearth in one corner. Whether by design of the original builders, or by a chance flaw in the roof that allowed it to draw, a fire lit there burned cleanly, and Nat made certain that a ready supply of peat and deadfall wood was stacked just inside the entrance. Jonathan brought some older blankets from the attics of the farm, and admitted that, though it made him uneasy, it was the safest place for them to be together. Wrapped in Nat's arms, their skin warm against each other, the chamber lit by the flickering light of the fire and the candle flame, he was able to put aside his discomfort and lose himself in his lover's scent and taste and touch.

The time they spent during the day—sitting together at the midday meal, walking along the cliff path after dinner, or, most treacherous of all, lying on the beach in the warm sunshine of a Sunday afternoon—was difficult. The temptation to look too long, to smile too fondly, to touch, was almost overwhelming, and in an unspoken agreement, they met less often, lest they unwittingly betray themselves and raise suspicion in the minds of those around them. They did not avoid each other, but Nat gradually resumed his full work in the fields, and Jonathan engaged his cousin in conversation about the farm or the history of the region, or spent his days reading or wandering about the countryside, as he had when he had first arrived. But now his feelings were vastly different to what they had been at that earlier time; every tree, every stream, every rock, bush, and creature was part of a web that wove itself around his soul, and at the center of that web, in the deepest place in his heart, he was happy beyond the power of his comprehension.

Their nights, at first, were frantic. Nat would pull Jonathan into the utter darkness under the hawthorn and kiss him desperately, seemingly unable to restrain himself. Jonathan, more frightened, more timid, ignited at Nat's touch, and, drunk with sensation, was barely able to keep his senses long enough to escape to the hills. When they reached their retreats, he gave himself to Nat fully and without hesitation, as if the walls that had surrounded him—walls of propriety, of social restraint and disapproval—had been shattered, or, more accurately, had never existed. And as they grew to know each other's bodies and hearts, as they explored the sensations both physical and emotional, the flaming, mindless passion of those first encounters was tempered and leavened by tenderness and warmth, with low whispers and muffled laughter as they kissed under the starlit skies.

They lay, one warm night in the middle of June, in Jonathan's favorite place: the remains of a small, tumble-down shelter dug into the side of a hill in one of the upper pastures. Little more than two walls and a square, turf-covered floor, it commanded a view down across the fields and the farmstead and out to the ocean beyond. It was difficult to find; the mossy stone walls were overhung with old lavender and rosemary bushes that had been planted years before, and now, leggy with age and neglect, spread along the top of the wall like rambling shrubs, filling the warm, still air with their scent. They also shielded the small hollow from view, and, with the stone walls embracing two of the sides, a passerby would have to be on top of them before he would see them. But still they took no chances: They lit neither candle nor fire while they were here, but spread blankets on the grass in the starlight and made love by touch rather than by sight. The crushed grass beneath them added its scent to the night, mingling with the lavender and the clean smell of Nat's sweat, creating a perfume so intoxicating that Jonathan forgot that any world existed outside the bounds of this small place.

"Jonny," Nat said, and kissed him on the top of his head. "We'd best be going back. 'Tis late."

"I know," Jonathan said. He gently kissed Nat's chest, then laid his head down upon it again. "I wish we could stay here all night."

"I know, love," Nat answered, "I know. I, too. It tears me to have to leave you before morning. Tears me so, that I want to keep you with me and tell them all to be damned."

"We can't," Jonathan said.

"Ay," Nat said and sighed. "I know. That would lead to a greater evil than me pinin' for you as I work in the yard."

"Pining for me?" Jonathan said, and looked up, his chin resting on Nat's chest.

"Oh, I pine for you somethin' powerful," Nat said. "There are days, truth be told, that I can't eat more than twice my usual midday meal, and other where I fear that my longing for you has made me so weak that I'm sure I must have gained a stone five."

Jonathan snorted. "Some beloved you've turned out to be," he said, and slapped Nat's chest gently. "You're supposed to suffer a terrible collapse when away from my side for more than an hour, and I am supposed to come in at the last moment before you expire and revive you with a kiss. Like this." He slid on top of Nat and leaned down and kissed him. Nat wrapped his arms around him and pulled him down.

"You'll revive me, sure enough," Nat said. "You've brought me to life more times than I thought anyone could. You've bewitched me, and when I kiss you I don't know anything else." Nat kissed him again and rolled over on top of him, their legs intertwined, and their arms locked around each other.

Jonathan's head fell back and Nat kissed his chin, then his throat, then the hollow of his neck. Jonathan gasped at each touch of his lips. Nat pulled back, and Jonathan looked up at him, a deep black silhouette against the velvet night.

"I daren't go any further, darlin', or I'll not be able to stop," Nat said huskily.

"Then don't stop," Jonathan whispered.

Nat kissed the end of his nose. "There's time and enough for that," he said. "We've all summer at the least."

"Then stay, just a moment longer," Jonathan said.

"No, love," Nat said, "though it kills me to deny you anythin'. There'll be time after the bonfire. We'll stay all night then, though we'll have to be canny about where we lie. There will be folk enough about the countryside that night."

"The bonfire?" Jonathan asked. "What bonfire?"

"St. Golawan's fire," Nat said. "Tis later this week."

"What's that?"

"What's that?" Nat repeated, sitting up. "A poor showing of your blood and family, you not knowing. The Feast of St. John at midsummer."

"I know the Feast of St. John," Jonathan said.

"Likely not as we do here." Nat looked out across the dark fields. "'Tis an old tradition, from long before the Christians came, or so they say. We light the great fires on the hilltops, and we dance in the midsummer night. Those that would protect themselves against witchery and evil leap the fire, and animals are brought for blessing.

Jonathan shivered and moved closer. "It sounds like superstitious nonsense," he said.

"Some might think so," Nat said, "but they'll not say it." He wrapped his arms around Jonathan and pulled him in close. "And whether nonsense or not, come with me afterward, and we'll stay the night in the hills."

Jonathan bit his lip. "Do we dare?"

" 'Tis a time of such things, though less so now than in the old days," Nat said. "The couples dance and those that become betrothed leap the fire too, as good as calling banns." He laid his head against the top of Jonathan's. "'Tis a time when those that love declare it, and sanctify it." He kissed the top of Jonathan's head. "Would I could leap with you, Jonny me boy, but it wouldn't be right." He laughed softly. "Could you imagine Parson Deane, if I should ask him to speak the banns for you and me? He'd send me to Bedlam."

"Do you think we could stay the night?" Jonathan asked, half hopeful, half fearful.

"I don't see why not," Nat said. "We'll be late, certain, with the fire, and next day we'll just come in with the mornin'." He tightened his arms and kissed the back of Jonathan's neck. Jonathan gasped and leaned back. "Think, to wake up with ye, instead of lettin' you go back to your bed alone."

"I know," Jonathan said, terribly tempted by the possibility. He'd imagined it often, and had had such wild fantasies as travelling with Nat to Cambridge, or to London, and taking a room in an inn or hotel, if just for one night. Any place closer was too great a risk. The thought brought him back to reality. "But they'll talk, won't they? The people in the village?"

Nat was silent a moment. "Ay, that they might," he said, "if we just slip off and don't come home. There'll be some that'll talk." He rested his chin on Jonathan's shoulder. "I'll have to think. But for now, love, we have to be goin' back."

Jonathan sighed. "I suppose we should," he said, and turned in the circle of Nat's arms. "It's just harder each time to go." His lips found Nat's in the darkness, and they kissed again, softly at first, then harder and deeper; Jonathan slowly pushed Nat back on the blanket and rolled on top of him. His fingers entwined in Nat's hair and he kissed Nat's mouth, then down his neck, along his shoulders, and down to his chest. Nat's breathing was ragged and unsteady, and Jonathan slid back up and kissed his lips.

"Not just yet, though," he said.

They walked in silence down from the hills, so close their shoulders brushed when the ground was uneven, and they welcomed the chance contact. They passed the hayfields, the hay thick and tall and nearly ready for the scythe, and climbed the stiles into the pastures that surrounded Trevaglan. The wild lilies bloomed in the hedgerows, unseen in the darkness, but filling the warm, still air with their scent. An owl called from a distant copse and was answered from a nearby oak tree. The waning moon had set early, and over all, the stars burned in the black sky, the great light river of the Milky Way meandering on its course between the constellations.

They stopped behind the threshing barn, as they always did, and, as always, did not risk more than a touch of the hands before parting. Jonathan watched as Nat vanished in the darkness toward the cliffs, then hurried around the barn and toward the house. He closed the gate carefully—in the deep silence of the night, even the soft click of the latch sounded like a pistol shot—and started across the lawn.

He stopped abruptly. A light shone in his window, alone in the entire house. He'd left none burning when he'd gone to meet Nat; he was extremely careful to maintain the visible fiction that he'd retired and directly gone to sleep. Yet the window glowed with a soft light.

He crept up to the house slowly and peered through the window pane. The lamp burned on the top of the chest of drawers, where he'd placed it when he'd returned to his room after supper, but he was certain he had extinguished it before leaving. He tugged the casement open and stepped over the low sill and started across the room toward the lamp.

"Good evening, Jonathan," a man said behind him. "Or perhaps, more accurately, good morning."

Jonathan spun about. Andrew Penhyrddin was sitting in the armchair in the corner of the room, his face in shadow.

"I hope you'll forgive my intruding," Penhyrddin continued, "but I recalled something I wished to discuss with you, and I came down. I suppose it could have waited until morning, but I wished to speak with you privately." He crossed his leg. "I was most concerned when I found you gone, and so decided to wait until your return."

"Good morning, sir," Jonathan stammered. "I . . . I . . . it was late and, I . . ."

" . . . was unable to sleep, and so thought you would take a walk?" Penhyrddin finished calmly. He shifted in the chair.

"Yes, sir," Jonathan said faintly. "I couldn't sleep."

"I understand completely," Penhyrddin said. "I often feel the same myself, and find that a turn about the garden helps calm me, and readies me for sleep."

"Yes, sir," Jonathan said, his voice shaking. How much had his cousin guessed? Had he seen him leaving? Or far worse, had he seen Nat?

"I would take care, however," Penhyrddin said, rising from the chair, "not to wander too far afield in the darkness. There are pits and ravines in the countryside here about, and one unfamiliar with the land might be injured."

"Yes, sir," Jonathan said. "You said . . . you said you wished to speak to me, sir?"

"Ah, yes. I did." He crossed the room toward the door. "This Thursday there is a festival, a local custom, but one in which our family takes part."

"The bonfire, sir?" Jonathan asked.

"Yes, on Golawan's Eve," Penhyrddin answered. "Of course, Boscawen would have mentioned it."

"Yes, sir," Jonathan said quickly. "He did, just in passing."

"Indeed." Penhyrddin stopped in front of him, and Jonathan met his eyes briefly before looking away. Even in the dimness of the lamplight he feared his cousin saw too much, and that he dissembled too little.

"He would not have mentioned that it is customary for the owner of Trevaglan to light the fire on the hill behind Breawragh Cottage," Penhyrddin said. "I will do so, and I hope you will join me. Our family is scattered, and you are near kin." He paused, and Jonathan looked up. "There are nearer, of course," Penhyrddin said with a slight smile, "but none with whom I particularly care to associate in this."

"Yes, sir," Jonathan said. "I'd be honored."

"Good boy," Penhyrddin said, patting him on the shoulder. "I think you'll find it an enjoyable event." He opened the door. "It is . . . not uncommon for the revels to go quite late. There are those who do not return home until the next day. Few pay attention, so long as proper discretion is observed."

"That . . . is good to know, sir," Jonathan said, after a few moments of silence.

Penhyrddin nodded. "It is." He began to leave, then turned back. "As for your walks before bed: be cautious. The risk of injury, though not extreme, does exist."

"Yes, sir."

"Very good," Penhyrddin said. "Have a pleasant night's sleep." He left and pulled the door closed behind him.

Shaking, Jonathan sank onto the bed. He was certain that Penhyrddin either knew or guessed about his trysts with Nat. This frightened him, but what unsettled him more was that the older man seemed to tacitly approve, or, if not approve, intended to take no steps to prevent them meeting, so long as he and Nat were discreet and did not draw attention to themselves.

Was it possible? Penhyrddin had never attempted to stop their friendship, aside from an early caution concerning Nat's temper, though he had not seemed to encourage it, either. Like so many other times across the summer, he had simply let Jonathan do what he would, so long as he was home for meals and attended church on Sunday mornings. Beyond those two things, the older man, while not ignoring him, seemed to have adopted an attitude of benign neglect, talking with him when they were together, but demanding little if anything else of him.

Jonathan began to undress, his mind running back across his interactions with his cousin. Though their daily lives intersected but tangentially, he never felt that Penhyrddin resented his intrusion into that secluded life, which, upon reflection, surprised him. Penhyrddin visited not at all with the other farmers around the county, nor, being of a lower social class, did he associate with the gentry. The only people that actually dined with them, and then only occasionally, were the vicar and his wife, and those visits were never returned; indeed, an invitation was never forthcoming—peculiar, when he thought about it.

His cousin, to all appearances, had no friends but they, and no close ties with their other relations scattered across the area, relations with whom his mother had kept correspondence, but one neither frequent nor intimate. And yet Penhyrddin had, without hesitation, invited him to come and live there for the entire summer, had insisted on it, and having done so, adapted his own life with a calm serenity that had been so natural that Jonathan had never questioned it.

A curious man.

He folded his clothes carelessly and placed them on the armchair; he'd put them away in the morning, or, if he didn't,Rose Pritchard would. He would have to talk to Nat, and quickly, and warn him that they needed to be more cautious, that Penhyrddin at least suspected, and if he did, unobservant man that he had always seemed to be, others might also.

At this he paused. If Nat knew that his employer, no matter how lenient, was aware of their illicit meetings, he might break off the relationship. Penhyrddin would never broach the subject publicly, wishing to avoid the scandal, but Nat might not want to risk even the slightest whisper of a rumor, and the subsequent chance of dismissal.

He slipped into bed. *Had* Penhyrddin guessed? His comments certainly seemed to indicate that this was the case. Moreover, he seemed to have given them an implied permission to stay out the entire night after the Golowan's Eve fire. There seemed no other possible explanation for the comment. *This* he would tell Nat, but in such a way as to make it sound as if the conversation had been general, a dinnertime chat about the peculiar customs and habits of the countryside, and not the odd, circuitous conversation it had been.

He blew out the lamp and settled back into his pillows, but sleep was long in coming. The panes of the window had started to pale to grey from black when he finally slept.

He spent most of the next few days indoors, penned in by his caution and the weather. Clouds had gathered the morning he slept late after the peculiar interview with Penhyrddin in his room, and the rain had been a light, steady drizzle since that afternoon. Penhyrddin's solicitor, a thin, dry man whose name Jonathan missed at first introduction, had brought some documents to review, and Jonathan had moped about in his room while the two men monopolized the library. Dinner had been a particular torment: The solicitor might have been an excellent man at law, but he was a deadly dull dinner companion. Jonathan struggled through the meal to stay awake; the solicitor's quiet monotone and his own lack of sleep the night preceding made for a potent soporific.

He had seen Nat but once, the rain precluding their meeting at night. They had shared a midday meal the day following, sitting in an open doorway on the first floor of the chall barn. The fresh, wet air, the scent of the cattle below, so pungent and unpleasant when he had first arrived at the farm, but the impact of which had mellowed with his stay, and Nat's nearness blew away the cobwebs and languor that had wrapped his mind in cotton wool the day before.

He told Nat that he would be at the fire with Penhyrddin, and alluded vaguely to the fact that the older man had made reference to the custom of folk staying out for the night. Nat had responded equally casually, saying that aye, it was not uncommon for such things to happen, but as Nat spoke he leaned slightly against him, and the trembling of his arm betrayed his excitement.

The day dawned fair and bright. Jonathan woke before the household was stirring, dressed, and wandered down through the pastures to the cliffs' edge. The clouds had blown clear during the night, and the farm and the surrounding meadows glittered in the early light. The grass was wet and bowed down from the rain, and the earth moist and rich, smelling more of a spring morning than of high summer. He sat for a while on a boulder at the cliff's edge, watching the waves roll in to the shore below him, crashing on the grey rocks standing out from the shore and surging up across the tumbled boulders that lay heaped around the bottom of the headland's sheer cliffs. Cormorants dove in the water and skittered across the surface to take to the air. The *chack-chack* and trill of a bluethroat sounded from the gorse bushes nearby, and overhead a woodlark flashed in the early sunlight and poured out its song in counterpoint. He heard the farm workers hallooing to bring the cows in for morning milking, and started back toward the house.

He ate breakfast with Penhyrddin, and asked about the celebration that night. The men had been gathering the wood for the fire for several days, his cousin said, and the pyre was being built today, as the rain had prevented them preparing it earlier, as was customary. The farm wagons from Trevaglan and the surrounding farmsteads had been pressed into service to haul the wood and remnants of last year's straw up the hill, and the men would place the first layers at the very top, where the fires had been burned since before living memory. The last would bring tins of paraffin to soak the pile. Then Penhyrddin would light it shortly after sunset, with a lamp kindled from the kitchen stove. He was to help in that lighting.

He grew more and more anxious as the afternoon wore on. He hadn't seen Nat all day; in fact, no one had, and Hale, the foreman, had made report to Penhyrddin of his absence shortly after luncheon, while he and his cousin were still at table. Penhyrddin had replied calmly that he supposed Nat had family responsibilities in the village, and that he would speak to him about it the next day. Hale wasn't to worry about it.

Jonathan could not help but worry, and, as the hours passed, fretted about the house and garden until dinner. As the sun began to set, he pinned his hope that his cousin was right, and Nat would join him at the fire itself.

The air was warm and still as he and Penhyrddin set out from the house and walked up the lane toward the road. They were joined by the folk who worked the farm, and, as they climbed the hill behind Mistress Bannel's cottage, people from Landreath village and other farms in the region fell in with them. The crowd walked quietly, some couples holding hands, and the village and farm children running ahead until they were called back and hushed by their parents.

They reached the top of the hill just as the sun touched the horizon. A large crowd had gathered already, mostly the people of the country, but some, Jonathan thought, judging by their clothing, city folk from England—foreigners, Nat would call them—here on holiday. He could see the pile of gathered wood and straw through the crowd. He had expected a haphazard mass, but instead saw a neatly stacked mound, nearly as tall as he, with heavy squared off timbers laid in a rectangle around a central cone of stout branches, all interwoven with vines and flowers. The scent of paraffin was heavy in the air. A breeze stirred, and ruffled his hair.

He scanned the faces of the people assembled, but couldn't find Nat. He swallowed his disappointment, and stood silently as various folk approached and greeted his cousin, spoke briefly of the prospects for harvest or made enquiry about the flocks, and moved on. Then, as the sun slid slowly into the ocean, Mistress Bannel approached them. Her son Justus followed behind her, carrying an unlit torch.

"Good evening, Mr. Penhyrddin," she said, "and to you, Mr. Williams."

"Good evening," Jonathan replied. Again, though he'd spoken to her but once that summer, he had the sense that the woman knew more about him than did anyone in the crowd, even more than his cousin. For the first time, he was relieved that Nat had not come with them; the keen eyes in that sharp face would have laid bare all their secrets within moments, and though she might not speak of them, she would have known.

"Good evening, Moereven Bannel," Penhyrddin said quietly. "I thank you for the use of your land this night."

Mrs. Bannel nodded. "You are welcome here, Andrew Penhyrddin," she said, "and I thank you for bringing us fire this night." She looked again at Jonathan. "And who is this comes with you, then?"

"He is kin to me, my cousin's child," Penhyrddin answered, "and kith to those around."

She nodded again. "Then he is welcome, too," she said. She turned and gestured to her son. He stepped forward and held out the torch to Penhyrddin.

To Jonathan's surprise, Penhyrddin shook his head and gestured that Justus should give the torch to him. He took it, a heavy, twisted branch with one end wrapped with an oil-soaked cloth and its bark rubbed smooth in the center, holding it awkwardly in both hands. He stood, uncertain as to exactly what he was to do with it. Saying nothing, Penhyrddin walked toward the pile of wood and straw, and he followed. They stopped at the edge of the pile, and Penhyrddin turned to him.

"When the sun drops below the horizon," Penhyrddin said in a low voice, "we'll light the torch from the lantern. Then you touch it to the pile."

"Where?"

"Right in front of where you stand," Penhyrddin answered. He nodded toward the pile, and Jonathan saw, on the side nearest him, a tightly wrapped bundle of straw thrust amongst the heavy branches making up the central cone. The heavy timbers were lower here than on the other three sides; he thought he could reach with little trouble.

"Be certain not to drop the torch," Penhyrddin said. "It has been used for all the years of my life, and would bring misfortune should you do so, particularly given that this is your first time."

"Misfortune?" Jonathan whispered, feeling rather silly at the solemnity of those around him. "But it's all superstition."

"To you, perhaps," Penhyrddin said, leaning in close and speaking so softly that Jonathan could barely hear him, "though you may in time come to think differently. But to the folk hereabouts this is most serious, and will color their thinking for the year to come. It behooves us not to tamper with those beliefs, so when it is time, hold tightly, and don't hesitate."

Penhyrddin stepped back and turned to the west, watching intently as the sun slid lower in the sky. The breeze strengthened, laden with the tang of the sea. Not knowing what else to do, Jonathan followed suit, holding the torch in front of him like a cricket bat, the rag end up. Some of the oil trickled down its length and fell on his hand; he brushed it off on his trousers, and angled the top away from him. He glanced at his cousin; Penhyrddin's face was smooth and golden in the waning light, and he seemed younger than his years, and yet older, too—Jonathan was struck again with how little he knew of this man and his history. Any sense of amusement faded with the light, and he felt, stirring somewhere deep inside, a sense of being part of something ancient and unknown, a connection of blood and time and forgotten lore. He swayed slightly, light headed, so he thought, from the smell of the paraffin and oils that drenched the wood behind him.

The last edge of the sun slipped below the horizon.

Penhyrddin turned to face him and opened the lantern. He held out his hand, and Mrs. Bannel laid a braided length of straw in it, which he took and touched to the flame in the lantern. The straw caught and flared, and Penhyrddin held it out as he lowered the lantern to his side. Without conscious thought Jonathan lifted the torch, and Penhyrddin raised the flickering brand and laid it against the rags; blue flames ran out and engulfed the head of the torch. Jonathan stepped toward the bonfire and thrust the torch into the straw.

Fire erupted before him, and he staggered away from the sudden heat, still clutching the torch, its head brushing against the timbers as he did so. The cloth snagged on the timber and tore, and a tendril of flame ran up the shaft along the trail of oil that had dripped down, singeing his hand. He stumbled, and shook the torch, trying to put out the flames. Bits of the torn, oil-soaked cloth came loose and floated down around him in flames, and in a panic, he dropped the torch, then tripped and fell to the ground.

He scrambled back to get away from the fire and the torch, but Penhyrddin had caught it before it struck the ground, and now stood next to him, holding it aloft. A gust of wind stirred the flames of the great fire and the smoke blew in his face, and he coughed. Again a wave of dizziness struck him, and for a brief moment another man seemed to stand in his cousin's place, an older man, shorter, wearing different clothing, rough and ragged. Jonathan coughed again, and his eyes stung from the acrid smoke.

Strong hands took him by the arm and gently helped him to his feet. He wiped his eyes; Justus Bannel held him by the elbow, concern showing in his face. Jonathan shook his head and thanked him—foolish, he thought, as the man couldn't hear. But the man apparently understood his meaning and released his hold, smiling as he did so and offering him a pocket kerchief of rough cloth. Jonathan shook his head and smiled back, hesitantly, not knowing how to indicate that the offer, though welcome, was not necessary.

"A near thing," Penhyrddin said quietly, "but you'll do better your next time." Justus stepped back to stand by his mother, who stood near the fire, apparently impervious to the heat, watching them. Penhyrddin held out the torch, its flame guttering in the wind. "Take it, boy, and come with me."

Hands shaking, Jonathan took the torch—the wood felt hot to his touch—and fell in behind Penhyrddin as he walked away from the bonfire. They climbed a small rise, Mrs. Bannel and Justus following them. The farm and village people stood silent behind them.

"Hold the torch up," Penhyrddin said, "then quench it in the bucket." He gestured, and Justus set a wooden bucket on the ground before them.

Jonathan faced the silent crowd, held the torch aloft with both hands. The only sound was the rattle of the leaves in the hawthorn tree behind him, and the roar and rush of the fire. He plunged the torch into the bucket; the flame vanished with a hiss.

The silence was rent by a cheer, starting at the back of the crowd and swelling until the entire community was shouting. Some of the younger folk broke from the crowd and darted into the twilight, and the rest spread in a circle surrounding the fire.

The flames and smoke billowed high into the darkening sky, and even at this distance Jonathan could feel the heat. Suddenly, one of the younger men dashed in close and plunged a branch into the fire. He danced away, still holding the branch, which now burned with the same bluish fire Jonathan's torch had when first lit. Another man darted in, then another, and another. In moments, a dozen or so had lit torches, and began twirling and spinning them as they danced wildly around the bonfire, forming a single line that wove in and out of the clusters of folk standing watching, cheering them and calling their names. Now and again one would break out of the line and leap and spin, or toss the torch into the air, catching it again as it whirled down toward him. Groups of three or four dancers formed, whirling in the firelight, and circled each other, drawing closer and closer until they merged like globules of mercury on glass. Gradually, one by one, folk, both man and woman, broke off from the smaller groups and fell into the line, stamping and whirling in time to an unheard music, an understood but silent rhythm, until fully half the people present had joined the line and danced with a reckless abandon so wildly different from their daily demeanor that Jonathan would not have thought the change possible.

He watched, fascinated by the sheer, exuberant energy of it. Twilight faded to darkness, and the dancers below became silhouettes against the flames. He sensed, with a dim recognition, the patterns and rhythms that unfolded before him, and more than once found himself swaying in time to their motion, again moved by a part of himself he neither knew nor comprehended, but which responded to the call of the dancers, something primitive coming from the dark and shining depths of his blood, another soul that threatened to shatter the thin veneer of his civilized self, and he longed to hurl himself down the hill and join those half glimpsed shadows around the fire. As they danced, the line stretched and curved in on itself, snaking back and forth in undulating curves like a serpent. They circled the fire once, twice, three times, and the leaders veered off and led the line toward the small rise where he stood.

Arms linked, hands held, the dancers surrounded them, the only sound the gasp of their breath and the muffled drumbeat of their feet flying in high laced boots and beneath long skirts, striking the turf of the down in weird, compelling rhythms. His breath shortened and his heart raced as they circled nearer; his body tensed, and he swayed forward, leaning toward them.

One of the men, one of the leaders, broke from the circle and danced madly in front of them, his feet moving so swiftly that Jonathan could barely follow their motion. The torch smoked and flared as he tossed it from hand to hand and swung it about his head, the flames streaming in the wind of its own making. He skipped past them, and leapt and spun and landed directly in front of Justus. He swung the torch, and Justus stopped it in midswing, the smack of wood on the flesh of his hand loud in the silence. The man grabbed Justus' free arm, and for a moment they balanced each other, like a pair of athletes in a match or soldiers frozen in mid-battle. Then Justus tossed the torch high in the air and caught it as it fell toward him, and pulled the other man with him as he joined in the dance.

Jonathan took an involuntary step forward to follow them, and as he did so, two girls, younger than he, their faces flushed and shining in the firelight, left the line and ran up to him. As the line uncoiled, led by Justus and the other men, the girls danced about him, and then took him by the hands and pulled him toward the fire and the dancers surrounding it.

Startled, confused, Jonathan pulled back. The communion of spirit and flesh he'd felt with the dancers just moments ago was gone, and the thought of joining the spinning, leaping crowd frightened him. He shook his head and shrank back toward Penhyrddin, and the two girls laughed and ran down the hill to join their neighbors.

He stood by his cousin's side, trying to still his trembling, torn between his desire to abandon himself to the wild gyrations of the dancers and his fear of where it would lead should he do so. Over the last weeks he had surrendered, piece by piece, that reserve that had always set him apart from those around him, even from his friends at Eton, but those surrenders had been private and tender, even at their most impassioned. What waited around the fire was different—pagan and extreme, it beckoned to him even as his heartbeat calmed and the sweat that had broken out on his forehead cooled in the evening sea breeze. He shivered.

A figure broke free of the crowd and dashed up the hill.

"Dance with us, Jonny," Nat cried. "Dance with us!"

"What?" he asked. "I don't think—"

"Dance!" Nat said again, gesturing toward the fire. "Don't think, by all that's holy! Just come along!"

"I *can't,*" Jonathan whispered urgently.

"Of course you can," Nat said. "Don't be a dow. There's time and enough for bein' proper all the other nights of the year." He leaned in closer. "Not that you've been too proper of late, mind you," he whispered. He smelled of smoke and wild grass, and Jonathan stepped toward him. "That's a good lad," Nat said.

"No," Jonathan said, his voice still a whisper. He glanced at Penhyrddin, who was talking quietly with Mrs. Bannel some five feet away, worried he might have overheard their exchange. "Where were you today? You're in trouble with James Hale and my cousin because you were gone."

"I had more important things to see to," Nat said. "Don't fratch so. I'll talk over Hale, and Mr. Penhyrddin won't mind, I'm sure." He poked Jonathan in the chest. "I'm his favorite nursemaid, and don't ye ever forget it."

Jonathan shook his head, worried that the conversation was too public, too obvious, to clear in its subtext. "But . . ."

Nat laughed. "You'll but and no and worry yourself to shreds and the night'll be gone." He stepped back, but didn't release Jonathan's arm. "Come, dance," he said softly, his voice low and husky, his desire clear in his eyes. "Join us."

Jonathan wavered. "I . . . can't . . ." he said, his voice faltering. "I don't know how."

"I'll show you," Nat said. "Come with me." He took a step toward the fire.

Jonathan followed him, and as they approached the crowd, quickened his pace to match Nat's. The crowd swept up and surrounded them. Two women pulled Nat away, and Jonathan was alone.

Whirling couples surrounded him, and he stood frozen, frightened once more, desperately looking for Nat in the flashing shapes around him. He turned to run back, but the dancers blocked his way, a shifting wall that offered avenues for escape and then just as quickly took them away. Shoulders brushed his; he shied from them, slowly driven inward toward the fire and its heat. The roaring of the flames was punctuated by hand slapping hand, the rustle of skirts and jackets as the dancers brushed past him, and the steady, rhythmic pounding of feet on the turf.

A couple, hands and arms linked, jostled him as they spun past, and he stumbled toward the fire, only to be caught before falling by a man grabbing his arm.

"Ye dare not stand still, man!" the man cried, holding him by the shoulders. "Why, 'tis the nursery lad!" He laughed aloud; it was Nat's cousin, Tom. "Come to dance with the common folk, have ye?" he asked, and without waiting for an answer took hold of Jonathan's arm. "Then, by God boy, you'd best dance!"

Jonathan tried to pull away, but Tom's hand held his wrist tightly. He staggered as Tom pulled him into the crowd, but Tom steadied him, and he recovered his footing.

At first he could do little except try to keep up as he stumbled along behind; Tom wove between couples and families, following no path or direction Jonathan could discern, but working his way steadily around the fire. They reached the far side, and Tom led him into a large circle of folk close to their age.

"AI *AI AI!*" he cried. "Just look and see what I've found." He pulled Jonathan to the center of the circle, scattering the pairs and quartets that danced there. "The young master's come down to join us." Jonathan pulled loose and rubbed his wrist. The dancers fell back and stood looking at each other and at him, uncertainty in their shadowed faces. Stillness spread out, until all in their vicinity were motionless.

"Comes on! Comes on!" Tom called, and hesitantly, alone or in pairs, a few of the younger people stepped toward them. Tom seized the hand of the nearest, a young man who worked on the farm, and, taking Jonathan's wrist again, began to lead them through and around the watching crowd, all the while crying *"Ai! Ai! Ai!"*

A rough hand caught at his free hand, and Jonathan instinctively tried to pull away, but was held tightly. A fisher lad, perhaps fifteen, but already as tall as he, dressed in rough homespun and wearing a battered cap, held him firmly, and grinned broadly at him; though Jonathan recognized him from the village, he knew neither his name nor his family. More joined them, and soon they formed a line of ten or a dozen, with Tom and him in the lead.

They circled the fire. Embarrassed beyond anything he'd felt before, Jonathan watched the crowd more than he watched his steps; the faces that flashed in and out of view in the variable light alternated between amused and cautiously reserved—he had no doubt that he was the focus of everyone's attention. He tried more than once to break out of the line, but Tom and the boy behind him held fast, and he was trapped in the line and the circle, the people on one side and the fire on the other. He had no way to escape without making a greater fool of himself than he already felt, so he surrendered, and fell into the rhythm of the movement.

As if at some unspoken command, more folk, both men and women, joined the line. Jonathan, sensing himself free of the crowd's scrutiny, began, cautiously and by degrees, to release from his mind the self-consciousness that had unknowingly hampered his feet. His face and hands grew slick with sweat—the fire, though fading, still burned fiercely—and under his jacket his shirt clung to his back and chest. His breath came in short gasps, and he began to revel in the feeling of pure physical exertion. Here, he thought, there were no rules, no strictures of the ball room or dining hall, no careful and austere society, no watchful parents or schoolfellows. There was nothing but the pounding beat of his heart, the harsh breathing of his fellows, the smell of sweat and smoke, and the fading fury of the flames. He harkened to the seed that sprouted, grew, and blossomed in his blood and in his soul, and abandoned himself to the night.

They circled below the fire, the ends of the line joining hands, and with a rush dashed into the center, lifting their hands and shouting aloud. He shouted with them, no words, just sound and exultation. When they pulled back, three men remained in the center, and, as the circle danced around them, began a reel. The other dancers shouted their approval, and Jonathan joined in their cries. When the figure was done, the circle closed on them with wild calls of "Ai! Ai! Ai!" and when they drew back, three women remained and matched the men in their skill, skirts lifted and booted feet flashing.

"Are you ready, boy?" Tom shouted, his face shining with a manic glee.

"Aye!" Jonathan said breathlessly, and when the women had done and the crowd rushed in and fell back, he and Tom and Nat remained in the middle.

As a boy he had learned to dance a country reel, and though years had passed since he'd taken a step, and the dark, smoky meadow was as far removed from his father's drawing room as could possibly be imagined, he didn't hesitate in the least, but threw himself into the reel with an abandonment and passion that suited the place and the people. Nat grinned at him, his face gleaming in the uncertain light, and as they circled in the center raised his hand over his head. Instinctively, Jonathan swung his hand and smacked Nat's; fire ran down his arm and into his gut at that contact, and desire flared and burned, hotter and brighter than the roaring flames of the bonfire.

The circling dancers shouted, and when he and Tom met in the center, he raised his hand first and Tom slapped his, then doubled the movement. Caught off guard but for an instant, Jonathan responded in kind, and the crowd cried out again. When he regained his position at the top of the reel, the circling dancers did not move in as he expected them to do, but instead Tom and Nat started again, this time moving faster, and he matched them as best he could. The swings and slaps, interspersed with stamps and thigh slaps, picked up pace, and the surrounding folk began to clap in time. The rough, untutored movements Tom and Nat made were endowed with a strength and grace unlike any he'd seen at a ballet or ball; his own were a pale imitation. This was feral, wild, a completely uncivilized thing; he doubted that either of the other men knew what any of them was about to do, but simply reacted to the others' advances or led his own. The three men sweated in the firelight, smiling fiercely as they danced—a courtship, a fight, a declaration of friendship and family.

They finished the round, and with a roar the others surrounded them. Hands slapped his back, another took his left hand, and Nat his right. No trio stood in the center now. Instead, the women formed a ring that danced and turned in a counter direction to the outer. The men called encouragement to the women, and the women flirted their responses in return. The silence that had been the rule since the fire was kindled was thoroughly broken, and the bystanders chattered amongst themselves or called to the dancers, joking and jibing, and cheering them on to greater efforts.

Jonathan spun out of the circle and fell to the grass laughing, holding his side. On the next rotation, Nat followed, and they sat on the edge of the crowd, breathing hard, shoulders touching, both laughing and pointing when Tom stumbled and fell, taking the two men on either side of him to the ground. The rings dissolved, breaking into couples—"Courtin'," Nat whispered—or groups of three or four of the same sex, dancing reels and jigs, the disparate parts blending into one messy, exuberant whole. A group of children, apparently delighted at being awake so late at night, played Ring-a-Rosey, shrieking with glee as they fell, and older couples, long married, linked arms and danced past, slowly and intimately. Foreigners—for such Jonathan thought them now—stood aloof, watching the locals' customs with interest and curiosity stamped on their faces. An artist on a stool sketched in a large pad, though how he could see to draw Jonathan could not think.

"We must go," Nat said, leaning in and whispering by Jonathan's ear. "'Tis late enough we've stayed, yet not too early to be leavin', neither."

"Go," Jonathan asked, suddenly sober. "Go where?"

"That's for ye to find out when we get there, now, isn't it?" Nat replied. "Go. Take your leave of your cousin, and tell him what ye will, but be quick." He glanced at the people around them, all still focused on the couples in the dell before them. "Meet me on the path down the hill. We'll go from there." Jonathan nodded.

"Why are ye sittin' off in the dark, Nat," a woman said. Jonathan looked up; Rose Pritchard stood a few feet away, between them and the fire, a silhouette against the dying flames. "Are ye all worn from your day gone away, and too weary to dance?"

Nat stood, and Jonathan scrambled to his feet. "Nout of the kind, Rose," Nat said, brushing off the seat of his trousers. "Me 'n' Mister Jonathan was just in the dance with Tom and the others. Did ye not see? 'Tis not like you to miss such."

"Hello, Rose," Jonathan said.

"There's rarely ought I miss," Rose said without even looking at Jonathan, "as well ye know, but I missed ye today, and I was looking for ye."

Jonathan shifted his weight from one foot to the other, and his old concerns about Rose and Nat reawakened. He did not question that Nat had no desire for the girl, but he was equally certain that she did not know this. And once he was gone in the autumn, returned home and gone up to Cambridge, who could say what proximity and social pressure might not do? Nat had said he'd never loved a man before him, had never felt as he did for him, but he had only touched lightly and facetiously on his involvement with women; Jonathan did not know how deeply those feelings might run, if run they did in any normal sense. Though Nat had laughed off Rose's designs, Jonathan was not nearly convinced that, once he was gone, she might not gain a stronger hold.

"I was lookin' to talk to ye afore this evenin'," she said as she walked over to them. "It wasn't me alone lookin' for ye, Nat,"—her eyes touched Jonathan briefly—"and 'tis no small trouble ye'll get for it, when James Hale's done with ye."

"I'll talk t' Hale," Nat said sharply, "and make it right, if I have to work extra this week t' make up for time spent. There's things as I had to do that bain't no business of his, nor anyone else, for that matter."

Rose clicked her tongue. "Don't be so 'mazed," she said. "I'm just givin' ye warnin' so that ye know what'll come in the mornin'."

"I know well and enough," Nat answered. "Happens so Mister Jonathan's given me word already. Your news is old news, and so no news at all."

"Yes," Jonathan said, interjecting himself into the conversation. "Mr. Penhyrddin asked if I'd seen him today, since Hale and he had not."

Again a slight touch of her gaze, longer this time, and her eyes narrower. She was clearly displeased at his being there, though he doubted that it was for any reason other than her wish to talk to Nat alone, and she was equally clearly trying not to show it in front of him, her employer's relation. "Did he now," she said, her voice low and steady. "That was kindly of him, to take such notice."

"Aye," Nat said, softening his tone, "and kindly it was of you to do so also."

" 'Tis the least I can do," she said. "But will ye not dance again tonight, Nat?" She glanced at Jonathan again and her lips thinned slightly. She seemed to search for the right words. "Is there none you'd dance with?"

Nat laughed. "No, my girl," he said. He pulled off his cap and bowed slightly. "But I'll tell ye this, Rose, that should there be one, she'd have to be so fair as you."

Rose bit her lip and Jonathan could see her frustration in the shifting of her eyes from Nat to him, and away into the night. It burned in the rigidity of her stance and in the way her hands clutched at her skirt. Her voice had been calm and her manner decorous, but she radiated tension like a plucked string.

In a small way he was amused and smug; his continuing presence in their conversation was return in kind for her snubs, which had no power to harm him and only made him more determined to stay. Had she behaved properly and politely, he might have pitied her and spared her his witness of her thinly veiled plea, but as she had ignored him, he ignored her unspoken desire that he leave.

"But now, Rose," Nat said, tugging his cap on, "we'll ask your pardon. I've made promise to see Mr. Jonathan gets home safe, as he's not familiar with that path in the night. Give my best regards to your family, and tell me grammer if she wants ought from Penzance to get word to Tom. Let's go, lad."

Rose stopped him, her hand clutching his sleeve. "Dance with me this night, Nat," she said, her desperation now showing openly in her voice. "Ye must."

"No, Rose," Nat said, gently pulling his arm free. "I'll not dance with no woman this night. I'll keep to myself yet this little while. Bain't my time, I'm thinkin'." He took Jonathan's arm, an unthinkable intimacy in these circumstances, given their company and the difference in their situations. "Come, lad. 'Tis late."

"Your time will come before ye know, Nat Boscawen," Rose said behind them, and they stopped. She stood between them and the fire, a dark silhouette such as she had seemed when Jonathan had first seen her that night, a shadow unilluminated, but with weight and substance. "The time is later than ye think."

"That may be, Rose," Nat replied, "but it'll be a time as I choose, and not others."

"There's not many can say that, Nat," she said, "and least of all you."

A trickle of fear ran down Jonathan's spine, but Nat just shook his head and walked away. Jonathan stood a moment longer. A sense of dread and uncertainty gripped him, though he could not say exactly why. He could almost feel her frustration radiating from her like a cold wind. They stared at each other for a long moment—the woman dark and still, facing away from the light, more threatening in her silence than when she had spoken, and he, lit by the fire, but cut off from its warmth and comfort by her anger. He turned and ran.

"Foolish thing," Nat said when he caught up. "She'd do better to cozy up to James Hale again. He's fancied her since he came here, and all thought she was keeping company with him, too, until she set her cap at me." He shrugged. " 'Tis no business of mine." He led Jonathan along, threading his way through the crowd between them and the path home.

"Will she say anything, do you think?" Jonathan asked.

"What's she to say?" Nat answered. "She ran after me with no thought but her own wishes, and if she tossed over a good man that wanted her in doin' it 'tis her own fault and her own making. It's nout to do with me." He stopped. "Now go tell Mr. Penhyrddin that you're off, and be quick," he said, his voice dropping to a murmur. "The dance and the night has me wanting you that badly, and I can't wait much more."

Jonathan hurried across the meadow to the rise where his cousin and Mrs. Bannel still stood. "I'm leaving," he said in a rush. "I've been in the dance, and I think I'm tired, and I would like to go back and . . . and . . . it's late." He cursed himself silently for his stupidity, for sounding like a child bent on mischief and wishing to remain undiscovered.

Penhyrddin was silent for a moment, a slight smile tugging the side of his mouth. "Indeed," he said gravely. "Then you had best be off." He picked up the lantern and held it out. "You'll need light, though, to find your way. You'll not get lost, will you? You can find the path?"

Jonathan took the lantern and nodded. "Yes, I'll be fine," he said. "It's not far, and, well, no, I'll not get lost."

"Perhaps," Mrs. Bannel said, "you'd do well to take someone as knows the country."

"A good thought," Penhyrddin responded. "Find one of the men from the farm, if you can, and ask him to accompany you. Say that I asked it, and that they can return, if they so wish."

"I . . . I will," Jonathan stammered. *Can it possibly be this simple?* "I'll ask someone. Thank you, sir."

"Take care, lad," Penhyrddin said. "I will see you in the morning, at breakfast, then?"

"Yes, sir," he said.

"Then off with you."

Jonathan walked back, fighting the urge to run. He found Nat where he'd left him, but not alone. He was engaged in what seemed a furious conversation with a man Jonathan had never seen, a broad man, blond and hulking. The two stopped speaking as he approached. Nat's mouth was a thin, hard line, and the big man stood, glowering at him as he walked up. Jonathan could smell liquor on him from where he stood.

"I'm ready to go back to the farm," he said to Nat, uncertain what else to say. "Mr. Penhyrddin asked if you'd be so good as to show me the way in the dark."

The big man snorted. "Oh, aye," he said. "Wolf leadin' lambs, that'll be."

"Shut your mouth, Jack," Nat said tightly. "Ye've got no cause to be talkin' so."

"No?" Jack said. "Penhyrddin wouldn't ha' meant you, unless he wanted someone kitey as my aunt's billy goat." He looked at Jonathan. "Watch yer step lad, lest you end up wanderin' all over the county."

"Shut it, Jack," Nat said, "and get back to yer kin. They'll put up with your gabbin'."

"Ye stinkin' lug," Jack snarled. "Step off wi' me, and away from the boy and *his* kin, and we'll see how much gabbin' ye'll put up with." Fists doubled, he took a step toward Nat.

Before he could swing, Justus Bannel loomed out of the darkness. As big as Jack was, Bannel was bigger, and he caught Jack's arm and pulled him back, almost knocking him off his feet. Jack swung at him, an awkward blow that Bannel deflected easily, catching the other man's fist in his hand. He shoved Jack, who stumbled back, and then he stood, arms folded, and shook his head.

"Justus is right, Jack," Nat said. "Ye know well as any that such isn't allowed here. We'll settle this another day. I bain't goin' anywhere, and neither are you."

"Ye'd best not," Jack said, rubbing his arm, "and if ye do, just know I'll find ye."

"That I do, Jack," Nat said. "I'm lookin' forward to it."

"Ye won't be when I'm done with ye, and all yer new friends won't help that."

"They won't need to," Nat answered. "Let's go, Mr. Williams." He started down the hill toward the farm.

Jonathan took a moment to realize that Nat had meant him, and trotted after, avoiding passing near the muttering Jack. He caught Nat just before they dropped below the crest of the hill.

"Find me?" Nat said as Jonathan fell in beside him. "That eedjit couldn't find his own nose if his finger was stuck up it."

"Who was that?" Jonathan asked. "Why was he so angry?"

"Jack Pritchard, Rose's brother," Nat answered. "He's tight more often than not, and tonight came at me, sayin' how I'd thrown Rose over because I was gettin' above myself, associatin' with the gentry as I am." He nudged Jonathan. "In case ye didn't know, that's you, love."

Jonathan stopped, panic stricken. "God. Do they know?" he whispered. "About us?"

Nat turned back, barely visible in the darkness. "Don't be daft. Of course not."

"Are you sure?"

"Jonny me boy," Nat said. "Do ye think if they thought I was a . . . a Sodom type, he'd want to thrash me for *not* courtin' his sister?"

"N . . . no, I suppose not," Jonathan said, and they started down the hill. He snickered. "I suppose if he did know, he'd want to thrash you for not courting *him*."

"Jack Pritchard?" Nat said, and spat. "Not him. He's too busy shepherding his flock."

"He . . . what?" Jonathan asked, puzzled by the sudden change in subject. "What would that have to do with it?"

Nat laughed aloud. "Oh, me boyo," he said, throwing his arm around Jonathan's shoulders and pulling him close, "you are a treasure and no mistake. I'll keep ye by me always." He squeezed Jonathan's neck, and released him. "Now ye see," he said as they walked carefully across an open field, "when we was all boys, we said that Jack Pritchard didn't know much, but he did *know* his sheep."

"Yes, but . . ." Jonathan said, and then Nat's meaning registered. "Dear God," he said, appalled. "That's vile."

"That's Jack Pritchard," Nat answered, and spat again. "Here, we're coming up on a stile."

"How can you see it?" Jonathan asked.

"I can't," Nat said. "I just know it's there."

"I have the lantern," Jonathan said as Nat steadied him over the stile.

"So I saw," Nat said, and jumped down beside him. "But I don't want to show it yet, not till we're off and out of sight. I'm not much worried about Jack the sheep poker following us—he'll be lucky if he can walk down the hill by the end of the night. But I don't want any other to see us. Most of the folks'll be at the fires, but there might be some about."

"Where are we going?" Jonathan asked.

"Ye'll see when we get there," Nat said. "And with no light and no moon, there's none as'll see us like this." Jonathan started when Nat's hand touched his arm and slid down to his hand, and their fingers intertwined. "Close as we'll ever get to walkin' out together, I'd guess, like normal folk."

Hand in hand they walked down the hill, by unspoken consent circling wide around the Bannels' cottage, though they knew she and Justus were up at the fire. They walked more quickly once on the road, heading away from the village, a direction Jonathan had gone but once or twice in the months he'd been in Cornwall. When they'd walked about a mile or so, as near as Jonathan could tell, they left the road and struck out for the coast. They went more slowly; Jonathan didn't know the countryside at all here, and even Nat seemed less familiar with the land than he had been in the hills and woods around the farm.

Their way led them across more fields and over stone walls and hedgerows, and Jonathan asked again whether they should use the lantern, shuttered but still lit in his hand. Nat said no, that starlight was best, that they'd save it until they arrived, though still he would not say where they were going.

The land here, though cultivated, was more sparsely populated than around Trevaglan. They saw no people, and the few farms and cottages they passed were dark. The ground was uneven and rocky, the soil thin and poor over the bones of the land. More than once Jonathan stumbled and was only kept from falling by Nat's arm in his. The air was warm, and the night silent, though on occasion he could hear the distant murmur of the sea on the rocks. No creatures moved that he could see or hear, and no night bird called. They threaded their way through a small wood, and when they broke clear, they stood at the landward end of a great rock promontory that thrust out into the sea, black and grey in the dim starlight. The breeze was stronger here, chillier, the air fresh and wild.

Here Nat paused, peering into the darkness around them, and Jonathan expected that now, at last, he would ask for the lantern. If they planned to go out toward the cliffs they would need it, so as not to fall to the rocks below. But Nat said nothing, and only took his hand and led him out into the darkness.

At the end of the point the rocks tumbled down to the sea, but Nat pressed on; this time he seemed certain of his place. Two tall stones, black against the dim horizon, stood at the edge of the cliff. They stopped before them.

"This is where we've come," Nat said quietly. "It's an old place, and important to my family. The land was once ours, and still lives in us." His hand brushed the side of Jonathan's face. "Will ye come with me, Jonny?"

Jonathan took Nat's hand in his and kissed the palm. "Yes," he said. "Always."

"Then come."

Nat reached out and touched both of the standing stones as he passed between them, and Jonathan followed. When he reached the edge of what he thought would be a sheer cliff, he was surprised to see that, though the ground fell away steeply, a slope of tumbled boulders lay before him, difficult to traverse, perhaps, but possible, in the daylight. Whether he could do so in the darkness he didn't know, but trusted that Nat would not take him into danger. At the bottom of the slope a spit of rock swelled into a small mount, craggy and dark, surrounded on three sides by the ocean.

A path wound down amongst the boulders, level in places as it cut back and forth across the side of the hill, steep in others, and never wider than one could walk, but surprisingly smooth and passable. When they reached the bottom, Nat took his hand again and led him across the narrow rock that connected the mainland to the smaller mount. This was more precarious: Though the top of the rock was flat and smooth—whether by nature or by the craft of man in some ancient time, he could not tell—the sides fell sheer to the water more than thirty feet below. He walked carefully, his eyes on the dark shape of Nat in front of him, not trusting himself to look down at his feet lest he be drawn to look into the dark abyss on either side.

The sea mount at the end was rugged and worn, with small hardy shrubs clinging in the crevices between the boulders. The path continued around a rock peak and climbed a saddleback between it and a smaller peak at the very end of the land, then through a wide crevice in the living stone. The way here was narrow, the stone disappearing into the darkness above them. Then, with an abruptness that startled him, they turned a corner, and he knew without asking they'd arrived.

At some time in the immemorial past a huge boulder had fallen from the cliff face into the ocean below, leaving a broad hollow gouged from the heart of the mount. The stone walls rose sheer and black on three sides, a wide, irregular circle facing out across the open sea. Across the ages soil had gathered—or had been brought—for the short grass of the downs grew thick here, soft under his feet as he stepped out of the narrow way. He could see little else; the darkness was complete, and he thought that even in the day this would be a shadowed place.

"We'll need your lantern now, Jonny," Nat said quietly. "I'll light the fire. I brought lucifers with me, but 'tis better the flame be brought here than kindled here, and fittin' that you bring it."

Jonathan held out the lantern without a word, and Nat opened its shutter. He saw a tall stone in the center of the hollow, and before it a pile of wood, a miniature of the great bonfire on the hill above Trevaglan. Nat knelt and took a wisp of straw from the pile and touched it to the flame of the lantern. It flared, and he laid it against the kindling at the base of the stack. For a moment Jonathan thought the flame had gone out, but then it steadied and caught. The flames climbed through the wood, but no smell of paraffin or tar tainted the smoke that rose above them. Sweet-grass was mixed with the straw that was bundled beneath the wood, and its scented smoke circled the hollow before being blown clear by the breeze. The smaller branches caught, and the flames climbed high, illuminating the entire hollow with their dancing light.

It was small, perhaps no more than thirty feet across and twenty deep, but in the firelight it seemed large. A single stone monolith, roughly rectangular in shape and taller than he by a good two feet, stood toward the back of the hollow, mute testimony to the devotion and determination of the people of the land, even more than the cromlechs he'd seen in the uplands and the huge boulders that formed the walls of the fogou. What faith or superstition had driven them to carry it here to the very edge of the land and to set it in this inaccessible place he couldn't imagine, but it was a holy thing, he thought, and one unblemished by tourists' prodding and scholars' measuring devices. It was secret and hidden, and, he thought, a fitting witness to their stay.

"Do you like it, Jonny?" Nat asked as he knelt by the fire.

"I do," he answered. "It's . . . I don't have words."

"Aye," Nat said. "I felt that way the first time me uncle brought me and Tom here. I was ten years old then." He rose. "And now I've brought you. We don't come here often any more, and then only after dark. We know that someday outsiders will find it. But for now it's hidden."

"Thank you for bringing me here," Jonathan said. Hesitantly, he took a step into the hollow, and Nat laughed.

"Ye needn't be so solemn," he said. " 'Tisn't a church, for all it feels like one. 'Tis just a place we've always come, and bein' self-ish, wish t' keep it for ourselves."

"Won't someone see the fire?"

"Not unless they're out to sea," Nat answered. "And then

they'll just think they're seein' one of the fires on the hills. We're safe as safe here. Look," he said, pointing to a dark bundle of blankets on the ground near the fire. "It took me some doin', but I've got bedding, and some food, and other whatnots to make us comfortable. God, Jonny! We have the whole night!"

Jonathan crossed the short distance between them and knelt. "It's the shortest night of the year," he said, "so why are we spending it talking?"

Jonathan stretched and sighed. He lay on his stomach on the rough blanket, one side of his body warmed by the fire, the other by Nat, lying on his side next to him. Nat's hand stroked his back gently, from shoulder to the top of his buttocks, and he closed his eyes so that he could concentrate fully on the sensation. He sighed again.

"Am I to take it ye liked it, then?" Nat asked, and kissed his shoulder.

"Mmmmm," Jonathan said. "And I take it you did, too?"

"Of course," Nat said, and cupped his buttock. "How not? 'Tis a grand pleasure."

"Daft thing," Jonathan murmured.

"Not so daft that I don't know what I like and what I want," Nat said, "nor what likes me."

"You needn't be so pleased with yourself," Jonathan said, his eyes still closed. "I'm sure there's others that'd do just as well, if I should bother to look for them."

"Jack the sheep poker, perhaps," Nat said, and smacked him.

"Now you're just disgusting," Jonathan said, grinning, and sat up.

"I can't say as ye didn't deserve it," Nat answered.

"I do like you," Jonathan said, and kissed him, a lingering, gentle kiss. "I love you," he whispered.

"And I, you, Jonny," Nat said. "I don't understand it, God save me. But it's so."

They kissed again, eyes closed, arms wrapped around each other, and Jonathan felt as if they were alone in the world, that no other time, place, or person existed save this hollow, this man, and this love.

"Jonny?" Nat whispered.

"Yes?"

"Will ye . . . will ye pledge t'be mine?" Nat asked. "Like husband and . . . there's no word for it, for what I want." Jonathan opened his eyes, and looked up into Nat's, dark and intent with their desire, yet shadowed with uncertainty. "I said I wouldn't dance with a woman this night, and I didn't lie. And I won't ever. Will ye be mine, Jonny Williams? Now and always, till death and after?"

Jonathan looked away, out into the darkness, uncertain. He knew, somehow, that what Nat asked was different to the pleasure they had shared and the love they had professed of the last several weeks. Those, real as they were, came of chance and the moment, and though they had blossomed and grown into something beyond which he could ever have imagined, were natural responses of the body and the heart, not of the mind.

But to pledge, to . . . to plight his troth, as it seemed to him to be, was a conscious act, a choice, a decision that, once made, could not be undone. He had spent the summer walking paths he had not known existed, and they had brought him to this place, and this question.

And then he looked back into Nat's eyes, and knew that there was no question, and only one answer.

"Yes," he said. "I will."

"When first I thought to ask ye this," Nat whispered, "when we talked about the fire, I remembered words me mother used to say to me dad when I was a boy, though silly I thought 'em then. I made her say it to me over and over, until I had it right." He smiled. "Ye'll not think me silly, too, will ye?"

"Never," Jonathan answered.

"That's a bigger promise than any other ye can make, Jonny," Nat said, and kissed him gently on the forehead, "so I'd be careful."

Jonathan smiled. "Why didn't you have her write it down?"

Nat's face closed. "She's not got her letters," he said shortly. "So she couldn't."

"Then . . ." Jonathan paused. There was only one reason Nat wouldn't have written it out himself. "Then it was kind of her to teach it to you."

Nat relaxed. "Near drove her mad because I wouldn't tell her why I wanted it," he said. "All I'd tell her was I'd thought of it, and like an itch, it wouldn't go away unless she told me it until I had it. Poor thing." He sat up.

A log fell in the fire, and sparks whirled skyward, winking out as they floated on the draft. Nat's body glowed golden in the light, his face in shadow. The wind had fallen, and the hollow was filled with a silent watchfulness.

"Take my hands," he said, kneeling on the blanket. Jonathan scrambled up, and knelt opposite him. "First with faith, and then with life, my troth I'll pledge to thee," Nat said in a slightly singsong voice. "For without faith there is no life, and without life there is no faith, and without troth, there's neither . . . naught." He took a deep breath and let it out. "There, that's the first part, and God help I got it right." He frowned for a moment. "What's the next bit . . . oh. That's right." He nodded and continued. "To bring thee joy and all delight, and banish bitterness, and with sweet sight to dwell as one, to you . . . to thee I pledge my love, my life, my all." He sat back and blew out his cheeks. "Hoo, that's a mouthful, and no mistake!"

Jonathan opened his mouth, but could find no words. "It's beautiful," he finally said. "I've nothing to match it. I'll just fall back on the Church, and I hope God will forgive me." He sat back and took Nat's hands in his. "I, Jonathan Williams, take you, Nat Boscawen, to have and to hold from this day forward, for better for worse, for richer for poorer, in sickness and in health, to love and to cherish, till death us do part; and thereto I plight thee my troth."

"And now you're mine," Nat said, "and I yours."

"Yes," Jonathan said, and hesitated.

"What's the matter, Jonny?" Nat asked.

Jonathan shook his head. "I don't know, actually. I just feel that it isn't sufficient. Not what you said," he amended, when a frown crossed Nat's face, "but mine. They're just . . . words. Words from other people, from the Church, and they just don't seem right, somehow."

Nat drew him close and caressed the side of his face. "We're outside the church, and outside the law, and outside just about everything save you and me," he said, "so we can say what we will, and any bond that's made is you to me, and me to you." He shrugged. "There's nout else."

"No," Jonathan said, "there isn't." He rolled on his side. "There should be. There should be more."

"We can't very well ask the vicar to wed us, Jonny," Nat said. "I think he might object just a bit."

"No, we can't." He stood and walked toward the edge of the hollow, where the ground fell abruptly away to the sea. The air was cooler away from the fire and Nat, and he shivered slightly, his skin raising with the chill. *Church words. Church oaths. Empty and useless.* His father had said those words to his mother and had betrayed them, repeating them to another within weeks of her death. Hollow. They don't mean anything, he thought, and even less when spoken here. He heard the soft brush of Nat's feet on the turf, and leaned back as Nat wrapped his arms around him. For a moment he lost himself in the sheer sensual pleasure of Nat's skin against his, the movement of Nat's muscles underneath as he held him.

"Come back to the fire, Jonny," Nat whispered, "and love me again."

"We should have been born thousands of years ago," he said, softly leaning his head back on Nat's shoulder. "We'd have been warriors, and swore an oath before the gods."

"We're here now, love," Nat said. "Come with me."

Jonathan raised his head. "Yes," he said. "We are." He looked out across the black sea. The church and its empty words didn't exist in this place. Ancient powers lived here, the pagan gods, who knew the strength of the bond between men. His heart beat faster. His people had lived here, danced here as he had, sacrificed on their altars here, loved and fought and bled and died in this land. He heard the sea on the rocks below him, endless and powerful, felt the breath of the breeze across his skin, sensed the cold agelessness of the rocks around him, and the warmth and strength of his lover surrounding him.

"Swear an oath with me," he said.

"What's that?" Nat asked, relaxing his hold.

"Swear an oath," Jonathan said, turning in his arms, "like our people did. Here, in ages past." He stepped back. "A blood oath."

"What are ye talkin' about, lad?"

"Look at us," Jonathan said. "Naked as heathens, just us, we two." He touched Nat's chest. "We've shared our bodies. You've . . . you've been within me, and we've been close to being as one. Be with me again, but . . . but . . . be one with me. One soul. One blood. Swear it with me."

Nat stepped back. "That's foolish, Jonny," he said unevenly. "We aren't boys, spittin' on our hands and slapping palms."

"No," Jonathan said. "We're not boys. We're men, and of the same folk." The hollow was utterly silent except for the faint crackle of the fire. He sensed the stone walls looming over them, watching, and waiting; shadows flickered across their weathered faces. Something was stirring here, rousing itself from a long, deep slumber, and he was caught up in that slow awakening. He gripped Nat's arms.

"Swear an oath with me," he said again.

"Aye, love, I will," Nat said uncertainly. "If ye wish it so."

"I do," Jonathan said. He took Nat's hand and led him back to the fire. "Did you bring your knife?"

"It's here, in the bag," Nat answered, kneeling and picking up his satchel.

Jonathan pulled two larger branches out of the wood pile and placed them in the fire. He sat opposite Nat on the blankets, and the branches crackled and flared as they caught.

Nat opened his clasp knife and laid it on the blanket. "Are ye certain ye want to do this, Jonny? Just come here and let's sleep."

"I do," Jonathan said, and rested his hand on Nat's knee. "Do it now, and then take me and make me yours, always."

Nat picked up the knife. "I can't lay steel to your flesh, love. I can for me, but I'll not cut you."

"Then give me the knife."

Nat wiped the blade on the blanket and handed it to him. The handle was rough in his hands, bone around steel, heavy and unfamiliar. He pressed the point against the heel of his hand, then, biting his lip, cut.

For a moment, he felt nothing, and then as the blood welled out of the cut, dark in the uncertain light, the pain flared up his arm. He gasped and dropped the knife. Nat reached out to him, but he shook his head. "I'm all right," he said. He held out his hands, and the blood dripped slowly into his other palm, one slow, steady drop at a time.

Nat picked up the knife, and quickly cut his own hand, and held it over Jonathan's. Jonathan recoiled slightly, but Nat gripped his hand tightly, and the blood flowed quickly; Nat had cut deeper. The pool grew and spread across his palm.

"Enough," Nat said after a few moments. He pulled Jonathan's cut hand up to his mouth and sucked lightly on the wound, and Jonathan, hesitantly, did the same with Nat's hand as it was offered to him. The blood taste was coppery and strange in his mouth. He'd tasted blood before, his own, when he instinctively put a cut finger in his mouth as a child, but this was different, frightening in a way he didn't fully understand. Nat's fingers brushed the underside of his chin softly, and he swallowed, his throat constricting, the mix of his saliva and the blood burning as it passed through and into his body.

"Enough," Nat said again, and lowered his left hand while still holding his right tightly, the small pool of their mixed blood still cupped in the palm. "Does it hurt, love?"

"Only a little," he answered.

"'Tis the way of such things," Nat said, "of love, of life, and of death. They cut, and we bleed, and only in the sharing of all three do we become one." He gripped Jonathan's hands more tightly. "Are ye certain, Jonny? To do such things is a dark and dangerous path to follow, and more than anything, cannot be taken back. The strongest oaths are made with blood, or so the old folk say, when they say aught of it, and the witches make their darkest spells with it."

Jonathan wavered. The shadows seemed to gather closer around them, in spite of the wood he had added to the fire, and the sense of watchfulness was growing stronger. The standing stone loomed dark and huge behind the fire, and its shadows danced weirdly across the back wall of the hollow. The sea sounded distant now; the crackling of the fire and the harshness of their breathing filled his ears. His head pounded in time with the beating of his heart, and the cut on his hand throbbed. He swallowed.

"I'm certain," he said.

"Then give me your hands," Nat said. Jonathan held them out. "I've no book learnin' of such things, and if there's any here that know such practices, they've not told me." He stirred the blood cupped in Jonathan's hand with his fingers. " 'Tis a good night for this, I'm thinkin', at midsummer when the sun is strongest, and with no moon to watch." He brushed his fingertips across Jonathan's forehead; the blood felt warm and sticky against his skin. "You'll have to find the words, Jonny," he said. "They're your things, words, not mine. Lead, and I'll follow."

Jonathan dipped his finger, and touched the center of Nat's forehead. He knew no oath or promise, but thought back to such stories as he'd read, ghost stories and tales of witches and their spells. "Your head and mind I share, and bind to mine, with trust and knowledge—one word, one thought, one deed."

"Aye," Nat said, "though I've the better part of that bargain,

I think." He touched Jonathan's forehead again. "One word, one thought, mine for yours, bound to me and I to thee."

"Done," Jonathan said. He dipped his fingers again, and brushed them across Nat's shoulders and down his arms, first left then right. "Your arms to hold me, your body to share, tonight and always, I hold for mine."

"Mine for thine, and thine for mine," Nat said as he imitated Jonathan's motions, "I take your body as mine, and give you mine."

"Done," Jonathan said again. He reached toward Nat's face, and gently touched his eyelids. "To dwell in your eyes, to hold you in mine, to see none but you, now and always."

He closed his eyes as Nat lifted his hand, and twitched slightly at the touch on his lids. "Your eyes are mine," Nat said softly, "never to look elsewhere, to hold to me and see me and see into you."

Jonathan opened his eyes, the traces of blood on the lids chill and sticky. "Done," he said. He placed his right palm full down on his left and rubbed his hands together. The cut on his palm still bled, and he rubbed his fingers across his palm, until the whole of his hand was covered. He laid it flat against Nat's chest. He could feel Nat's heart beating, hard and fast under his hand. "I give you my heart, from this moment forward, yours, and yours alone, bound to you, tied to you with love and faith, tonight, tomorrow, until death should us part, two as one, never twain, never divided. I plight and pledge myself to you, thine, thine, and thine again, thrice three times and always thine."

Nat laid his palm across Jonathan's, and smeared most of the remaining blood on his hand. He leaned forward and placed his hand against Jonathan's chest. His hand, slick with the blood, slipped slightly, and Nat moved it back, directly over Jonathan's heart. Their faces were inches apart, and Jonathan looked directly into Nat's eyes, dark unto blackness, deep, fathomless, holding him and frightening him at the same time.

"I take that heart which ye give me," Nat said softly, "and bind it to mine, here, now, and always, from light into darkness, from life into death and beyond, mine and mine always and only, yours and yours only. No more two, but one, tied and bound, and closer than one."

The air around them grew more still, and the light of the fire seemed to fade. All Jonathan could see were Nat's eyes, darkest black and set in deepest shadow. His heart beat furiously, throbbing in his throat. He felt as if a grip was tightening around it, and it gave a sudden, hard, sideways beat, followed by a rapid rush. He grew momentarily lightheaded, and he wanted to stop, to break the moment and to escape, but he was trapped, held, unable to speak or to move.

"No man shall part us," Nat said, his voice barely a whisper, "nor any power on earth and in heaven. I take the oath ye gave me freely, and give mine back. You are mine, and bound to me ever."

"Done," Jonathan whispered.

"And done," Nat said.

"And three times done again."

Nat reached up and held his face, both hands slick on his cheeks, and kissed him. Jonathan kissed him back, softly at first, then with increasing ferocity, his hands first cupping Nat's face, then sliding around Nat's head and tangling in his hair. They broke the kiss mutually, but neither released his hold the other. Jonathan's breath came in short, ragged gasps. Nat's face was blood smeared, his hair tangled, wild and barbaric. A gust of wind swept through the hollow, and the smoke from the fire swirled around them. A flash of movement caught Jonathan's eye, and he involuntarily glanced upward.

An owl circled above them, pale and silent. Startled, Jonathan cried out and lurched forward onto Nat in his fright, toppling them over in a heap on the blanket. When he looked up, the owl had perched on the top of the standing stone, and sat, watching them with wide, unblinking eyes, black in the flat white oval of its face. It clacked its beak and ruffled its feathers, then settled, still as the stone upon which it sat.

"Witness," Jonathan whispered. "It's watching us."

Nat clutched him tightly for a moment, his eyes wild and unfocused, then shook his head. "Damn the thing," he said, and staggered to his feet. He picked up a branch from the fire and hurled it at the bird, but fell short; the branch hit the stone below the owl and dropped into the fire. Sparks flew in the wild breeze, and the owl hissed, then spread its wings and swooped down at them. Nat ducked, and Jonathan flattened himself on the blanket. The owl circled the hollow again, and Nat picked up another branch and swung wildly, missing again by a wide margin. The owl cried once, a wild, piercing shriek, unlike the distant, melancholy calls to which Jonathan had grown accustomed in the weeks he'd been here. The owl banked and floated out over the sea, and Nat threw the branch after it. Its chilling cry echoed again off the rocks, and it vanished in the darkness.

"Damn, evil beast," Nat shouted, his fists clenched at his side. "Witch's soul with wings!" He spun around and faced him. If Jonathan had thought him a wild thing before, he appeared now to be a creature from another time, standing naked at the very edge of the fire's light, his face and body streaked black with blood, his legs bent in a slight crouch, his body tense and vibrating with suppressed fury. He had always seemed to Jonathan to be like a great, sleepy cat, lithe and powerful, aware of his strength but never releasing it. Now the great cat was awake.

Nat crossed the clearing in three steps and, reaching down, caught him by the arms and lifted him effortlessly. Jonathan was, for the first time that night, truly frightened. This blinding rage, erupting from nowhere, Nat's sheer physical strength, and his own complete helplessness terrified him. "Damn them all," Nat said. "Damn their eyes and their ears and their damned prying noses. Damn them to hell and back." He pulled Jonathan into a hard, tight embrace, kissing him, devouring his mouth with his lips and tongue. "You're mine, now and always, Jonny," he said, and kissed him again, his hand on the back of Jonathan's head and his arm around his waist, crushing them together.

Something inside Jonathan's head snapped; terror fell from him like a discarded garment, and he matched the madness of Nat's kisses with a blazing intensity of his own. "And you're mine," he said, dragging Nat down to the blanket. "Forever."

Jonathan opened his eyes, and stretched. His muscles were stiff and sore, and every part of him felt bruised and battered, but at the same time a deep, contented languor filled him. They had made love violently and madly, taking each other with an abandon and frenzy outstripping anything that had gone before. And when they were spent they'd collapsed on the blankets and had fallen asleep, arms and legs entwined, smelling of smoke and blood and sweat. He pulled the blanket close around him and nestled up against Nat.

Nat stirred behind him, and his arm tightened around Jonathan's waist, pulling him close. "Good mornin'," Nat murmured, kissing the back of his neck. "Isn't this grand, to be together in the mornin'?"

"Aye," Jonathan answered. "Though I've slept in softer beds."

"Have ye now, ungrateful thing," Nat said, pinching his arm. "After all the trouble I went to."

"Softer," he said, "but none finer."

"That's more what I should be hearin'." Nat kissed the back of his neck again. "Though I think I know a way to make it even better."

"So I see," Jonathan said. He turned in Nat's arms, and kissed him gently on the mouth. "I think of all your ideas, that's one of the best." He pulled back and smiled lazily. Nat was a sight: His face was streaked with dried blood, soot, and dirt, and Jonathan knew he didn't look much better. "We're a ragged pair," he said. "You should see how you look. A fine mess, the both of us."

He sat back abruptly.

"What's the matter, love," Nat asked, his voice still burred with sleep. "Come back down here."

Jonathan shook his head. The fire was little more than a heap of ash-covered embers, but he could see Nat's face. He looked up. The sky was grey, the stars faded and gone in the brightening light. Dawn came early, he knew, but they had at least an hour's walk back to the farm, and by that time it would be full light.

"We have to go," he said, throwing back the blanket and staggering to his feet. "We'll never get back to the farm before everyone's awake." He dug through the pile of clothing beside the fire for his undergarments.

Nat stretched out, his hands behind his head. "And what if we don't? What's it to them, or to us?"

"Have you lost your mind?" Jonathan asked. He threw Nat's shirt to him. "Here, quickly."

"My, my, you're the teasy one in the mornin', aren't ye?" Nat said, tossing the shirt aside. "I'll have t'remember that the next time." He yawned. "But tell me, love. How will you explain the muck on your face, then, when you've hurried back and all?"

Jonathan stopped in the act of pulling on his trousers. "Dear God," he whispered, stricken. "What will we do?"

"Well, first thing," Nat said, pulling him down, "is t'stop your worryin'." Jonathan struggled to get loose, but Nat held him firmly. "The second, to wash yourself off. I brought a pannick and some water, in case you wanted tea this mornin'. We can use it to wash off, instead. And if you're faint for the want of your tea, you've none but yourself as to blame, seein' how the whole thing was your idea, and not one o' mine."

"There's no time," Jonathan said. "We have to get back before dawn."

"Well, we're too late for that," Nat said.

Jonathan looked up again, and out across the sea. The sky was distinctly lighter now. He scrambled to his feet and ran to the edge of the hollow; the sky was pink in the east, and they would never arrive home before the workers were awake and about the farm. Discovery waited, and exposure. "What do we do?" he said again, turning. "And how can you lie there so calmly?"

"What you have to do," Nat said, hiking up on one elbow, "is get yourself over here and kiss me." Jonathan didn't move. "You'd best be quick, or I'll come and get you. Then we wash up, and for that we'll need the water." Nat sat up and dug into one of the satchels that had lay by the woodpile, hidden in the dark the night before. He pulled out two stone jugs. "I doubt it'll be enough, but we'll be able to wash our faces." He sat back on the blanket. "Of course, we could just go have a dip. There's a path down to the sea, if I can just find it. And then, last, we dress and we go home."

"It will be full day by that time," Jonathan said. He looked at the pile of clothes, dirty from lying on the ground all night, and no doubt reeking of smoke.

"And what if it is?" Nat pulled out a bundle wrapped in white toweling and tossed it to him. "I slipped into your room this week and filched some of your clothes. We'll just dress, and part when we get close. Then just whistle as ye walk up to the house, and should anyone ask, ye tell 'em ye went for a walk before breakfast." He stretched out on the blanket again. "Now. Don't ye think a man so clever as I deserves at least a kiss?"

Jonathan knelt beside him. "At least."

Much to Jonathan's surprise and relief, events turned out precisely as Nat had predicted.

They built up the fire, then clambered down across the rocks and bathed quickly in the sea as the water heated; the salt water stung the cut on his hand. Upon their return to the hollow, they dressed and ate quickly, then struck out across country for the farm. The sun had just risen when they separated on the road, a short distance before the lane to the farm. Nat continued up and around, to approach from the far side by the village path, and Jonathan, hands in his pockets, strolled down the lane to the farm, trying to maintain the air of one who'd simply woke before the sun, and went for a morning turn about the countryside.

His cousin, concern evident in his face, met him in the hall as he walked in the front door.

"Good morning, Jonathan," Penhyrddin said. "I hope you found the bonfire last night enjoyable."

"Yes, sir," Jonathan answered. "I've never seen anything quite like it."

"And you slept well, I trust?"

"I . . . yes, sir," Jonathan said, embarrassed and ashamed for telling a lie, even one of omission.

"Very good," Penhyrddin said. "It's nice to see you up and about so early. Breakfast should be ready shortly. May I speak with you a moment, please?"

Jonathan nodded anxiously, and followed him into the library. He wasn't sure what his cousin wanted to say, but certainly he wouldn't question him more closely.

Penhyrddin crossed to the big writing desk and sat. "I've signed some papers Mr. Fastnedge brought the other evening," he said, "and they'll need to be taken back to him." He took a long yellow envelope out of a pigeon-hole and laid it on the desk top. "After breakfast, if you would, please take this and deliver it. The direction in Chapel Street is noted, and you should have no difficulty in finding it. I've ordered the dogcart to take you after breakfast." He looked at Jonathan, his face quite bland. "I thought perhaps Boscawen could drive you. The Quay Fair is today, and there will be much to see."

Jonathan felt his face flush and burn. "That would be quite pleasant, I'm sure," he said. "I appreciate your consideration."

"Thank you for saving me the journey." He handed Jonathan the envelope as he rose. "Did you hurt yourself?" he asked, frowning.

"I . . . I seem to have cut myself at some point," Jonathan said, covering the cut on his hand. "I must have fallen on the way home last night."

"Have Cook see to it," Penhyrddin said. "We don't want it getting infected."

"Yes, sir."

"I will see you at breakfast, then."

"Yes, sir."

The day was one of unalloyed delight. Nat met him at the gate with the dogcart after breakfast, wearing, in addition to his best shirt and jacket, an aloof and proper manner of a manservant so wildly exaggerated that Jonathan had difficulty not laughing aloud. They maintained their decorum only until they rounded the first bend in the lane and the house disappeared behind the hedgerow; Jonathan laughed first, and Nat held out but a few moments longer. Had their horse not known the way, the outing might well have ended there, for they were helpless with their laughter, but the beast ignored the hilarity behind him, and plodded on.

Having left the horse and cart at a livery stable, they went first to Fastnedge's chambers in Chapel Street. Nat idled outside while Jonathan fidgeted within, first with waiting to see the man, and then waiting while he methodically read every paper in the envelope and reviewed each signature. Jonathan was so impatient he wondered that the man didn't bring out a magnifying glass or a microscope in order to examine them further. Fastnedge finally finished, and, taking far longer to bid his farewells than Jonathan cared to spend, released him.

They strolled up the Promenade and back, ate strawberries in cabbage leaves and heavy cake at the Quay Fair—Nat seemed to know most of the people there, and they drew no small number of curious looks from those—and watched the boating parties on the water. They bought luncheon from a street vendor and carried it to the new gardens, eating in a quiet grove away from the main paths. The warmth of the day and their contentment in each other's company, coupled with the shortness of their sleep the night before, brought on a comfortable somnolence, and they slept for an hour or so before being roused by the gardener.

As they walked back down the hill to the old part of town, Jonathan spied a photographer's shop he had noticed earlier, and, taking Nat's arm, insisted that they have their photograph taken.

Nat argued at first—he'd never had a photograph, and he didn't fancy starting now—but when Jonathan leaned in and whispered that it would be their wedding photograph, and that he was certain that the photographer would give them a sizeable discount on such a happy occasion, Nat started laughing so hard that they had to walk about for another quarter hour until they had composed themselves.

The photographer, a small, reedy man with a thin red mustache, clearly didn't know what to make of the pair of them—the quietly dressed public school man, as his bearing and accent declared him to be, and the farm hand, dressed in his finest, but still roughly clad—but went about his business in a brisk and professional manner. When the photograph was finally taken (no easy task, as they both were subject to fits of laughter and were almost incapable of sitting still, trying the patience of their photographer no end), Jonathan requested two copies to be sent to his attention at Trevaglan. The man noted the direction, Jonathan counted out the shillings asked, and they went their way.

They wandered about the town, poking into shops and ambling down side streets, walking with no destination, talking of this and that or—seeming even more precious to Jonathan—simply walking side by side in silence. As the afternoon drew to a close, Nat went to the livery stable to retrieve the horse and cart, insisting, oddly, that Jonathan stay at the quay and the fair while he did so. Puzzled, he agreed, and gave Nat the money needed to settle the bill, but found little pleasure in the wait. Fully half an hour passed before Nat returned, and though Jonathan had maintained his temper, he was a little annoyed when he climbed into the cart.

They rode in comparative silence out of the town, shoulder against shoulder, the smallness of the seat requiring a closeness they both desired. They wound around the bay with its small towns, and up into the higher land surrounding it. When they reached the top of the cliffs, Nat pulled over and stopped the cart in the shade of a hawthorn hedge, out of site of the road, but commanding a sweeping view of the bay. Tiny in the distance, the boats and their sails spotted the blue surface, bringing the merrymakers to and from the town.

"What's the matter?" Jonathan asked. "Why have we stopped?"

"Nothing's the matter, love," Nat answered, digging in his jacket pocket. "I've somethin' t' give ye is all." He held out a small, cheap, pasteboard box with a dented corner, two inches square, with no markings.

"I . . ." Jonathan said, touched. "I don't know what to say. What is it?"

"Well open it, ye daft thing," Nat said. "That's the best way to find out, now isn't it?"

He lifted the lid of the box and placed it next to him on the seat, then pulled out a layer of soft flannel. Nestled on another piece was a silver ring. He looked up at Nat, tears starting in his eyes. "Oh," he said. "Oh."

"The fool wanted me to just take it by itself, but I made him give me the box and all."

Jonathan gingerly lifted the ring out of the box. It was narrow, with small beads around the edges and a rimpled coil snaking around the center. It was old, he could see, slightly out of true round, and had a nick on the edge, but even with these flaws must have cost Nat a great deal more than he could afford. He thought to say he couldn't accept it, that the cost was too great, but when he looked up to speak, the hope and delight in Nat's face stopped his tongue.

"It's beautiful," he said, and meant it.

It was also too large. Even on his third finger it hung loose; whoever had had the ring made clearly had been a bigger man.

"I didn't think of that," Nat said ruefully. "It fit me well."

"Your hands are larger than mine," he replied, and brushed his fingers over the nearer of Nat's hands. He put the ring back in the box and carefully tucked it in his jacket pocket.

"We can go back, if you like, and see about another," Nat said, though it was clear he did not wish to do so. "There . . . well, there were others, but I liked this one."

"I'll not have another," Jonathan said. He thought for a moment. "I know what I'll do. I'll order a chain, and wear it around my neck. That way I can wear it always, and no one will ask about it." He took Nat's hand. "And it will be nearer my heart."

"You're worse than any poet I've ever heard," Nat said. He looked around, then quickly leaned in and kissed him. "And that's as great a chance as I'll take in the daylight." He picked up the reins and chirruped to the horse, and with a jolt they were on their way.

They didn't speak at all the rest of the way home. Nat held the reins in a loose grip, and Jonathan rested one hand on Nat's thigh, moving it only when they approached a farm or passed a person walking the road, and the other hand stayed in his pocket, wrapped around the box with the ring.

When they arrived back at Trevaglan, Jonathan reported the success of his errand to Penhyrddin, then hurried to his room and tucked the ring into the top left drawer of his chest of drawers, where he had secreted all of his mementos of Nat—some shells, the straw twists from his window sill, a dried sprig of lavender. His father, buying off his conscience by sending his son money regularly, would pay for the chain, he decided. He would order one from a jeweler in Penzance.

When the photographs arrived several days later, he brought Nat's with him the first night they met after, and gave it to him. His own he kept with him as much as possible, placing it in the drawer only when he had no way to take it along. It was the last thing he looked at before he went to bed, and the first in the morning, and on the day it arrived he'd written on the board under the image a single word.

Us.

Cornwall 1906

Jonathan walked into his bedroom, the candle in one hand and the photograph in the other. He placed the candle on his chest of drawers, and automatically reached for the handle of the top left drawer, stopping an inch from it. *What point*, he thought. He laid the photograph next to the candle.

He walked to the window; the fog was still thick and dense, and he could see nothing except the grey swirls outside the panes. Moved by an obscure instinct and an odd feeling of being watched, he reached for the curtains, glancing down as he did so. To his relief, the sill was bare, both inside and, as nearly as he could tell, out. He drew the curtains, not wishing to investigate more closely.

He circled the room, ending back by the photograph. He had burned it. He remembered distinctly that he had done so the day before he departed Cornwall, when he had destroyed everything that was left of that summer. The ring he had lost; it hadn't been in the drawer when he emptied it, though he had been certain he'd put it there after that terrible night. The box had been there, and had joined the photograph in the flames. The next day he had left for Cambridge.

He picked up the photograph, then quickly put it down again. *I've been impossibly rude to Langsford*, he thought with a rush of embarrassment. He started straightening the objects on the top of the chest, counting them as he did so. Langsford had said nothing but the truth, and he'd shouted at him, called him a liar. *Despicable behavior.* He had to speak with him immediately. He picked up the candle and stepped into the hallway just as Langsford arrived at the top of the stairs.

"Langsford," he said. "Please accept my apology. I was shockingly unjustified in my behavior. I'd thought the thing had been lost, but even if it had been, I have no excuse for such language." He faltered for a moment; Langsford hadn't moved since he had entered the hallway, but stood poised at the top of the stair, still and elegant in his evening clothes. "I'm terribly sorry."

"There is no need for this, Williams," Langsford said coolly. "We've both had a most difficult day, and we're both bound to be a bit weary. I understand perfectly."

"No, please, I . . ." he started, but Langsford raised his hand.

"Please, there's no need," Langsford said. "Perhaps we should simply go to bed. I'm certain the whole situation will resolve itself with a good night's sleep." He opened the door. "Good night, Williams," he said, and stepped into his room.

"Good night," Jonathan said to the empty hallway.

CHAPTER 11

"Shall I serve breakfast now, Mr. Williams," Rose asked, "or do you wish to wait?"

"Yes, please, Rose," he answered. "I'll have mine now, and you can bring Mr. Langsford-Knight's to him when he comes down."

"Yes, sir," Rose said, and left the room.

Jonathan crossed from the window and took his seat at the table. The fog was still dense, and he could see little further than a few feet outside the window. A grim, grey morning, matching his mood.

He had slept badly the night before, after he'd finally fallen asleep. Fully half the night he'd laid awake in his bed, listening to the hall clock chime the half hours, torn between the desire to knock on Langsford's door and risk everything and tell him about Nat, about that summer, and about his own feelings. He knew what Langsford's reactions would be—distaste and pity—but as the chimes sounded half past three, even that pity, which he'd so feared, would have been preferable to the gnawing ache, the increasing weight of dread in his heart at Langsford's leaving. Twice he left his bed and crossed to the communicating door between their rooms, and twice he had returned. *Four more days.* At least if he spoke, there would be an end to this misery. An end to their friendship too, in all likelihood, but that was a price he was willing to pay, just to have done with the hiding.

Or so he told himself at half past three in the morning. In

the plain if somewhat fog-enshrouded light of day, he was more pragmatic. He'd hold his tongue, apologize again for his behavior, and enjoy the remainder of the week as best as he was able. He would give orders after breakfast to have his things moved back to his original room, unless Langsford strenuously objected. Their proximity and his own doubt in his ability to maintain his silence were a combination he did not wish to face. He hadn't the strength.

He poured himself a cup of tea. He'd come down later than usual this morning and was surprised that Langsford hadn't arrived before him. He'd heard Langsford moving about in his room and so abandoned the thought of bringing him chocolate again and mending the breach he'd caused with his stupidity the evening before.

His thoughts veered to the photograph again. *Where can it possibly have come from?* That it was his he had no question. Even without the damning word on it, he knew every scratch on the cardboard, every flaw, every small detail. It was the same photograph that he had watched burn.

Or was it?

There had been two, and though he had rarely left his room in the two weeks between Nat's death and his departure, there had been times he'd not been there. Nat's grandmother had been cook at that time. Though it seemed unlikely, perhaps, just perhaps, Nat's mother had found the photograph among Nat's things and had sent it up to the farm with his grandmother, thinking Penhyrddin would send it to him at Cambridge. And at some point, she had put it in the room, and he, without thinking or noticing, had swept it into the drawer, to take it later and burn it, and not his own. His had lain hidden in the drawer, untouched as his books had been on the shelves, until his return. Of course he would not have found it. He didn't open his left-hand drawers; he never had since that summer. And Langsford, hunting for his cufflinks, had opened that drawer by mistake, and had found it. *How had the cufflinks come to be in that drawer?* he wondered. *I never put them there.* But it was the only thing that made any sort of sense, and it increased his culpability for his behavior. An apology was very much required.

He heard a step in the hall, and rose from his chair just as Langsford walked into the room. He was dressed, oddly enough, in the suit he'd worn down the Saturday before, when they'd arrived.

"Good morning, Williams," Langsford said as he pulled back his chair. "I'm sorry if I've kept you waiting. You should have started without me."

"Not at all," Jonathan replied. "I'd just come down myself. I haven't waited at all."

"Very good," Langsford said as he sat and shook out his napkin. "Did you sleep well?"

"I . . . yes," Jonathan said. "I did." He stood for a moment or two, feeling awkward, as if he were a guest in his own house, then sat.

"As did I, as did I," Langsford said. "Would you like some tea? Or do you have some already?"

"I do, thank you. Milk?" He handed it across the table, feeling helpless before Langsford's cheerful normality.

"Yes, thank you," Langsford said. "I always sleep well when the weather's inclement," he continued. "I'm not certain why, but I do." He gestured toward the window. "And shy of a rainstorm, I don't think things could be more inclement than this."

"No," Jonathan said as Meg entered the room carrying a large tray, "I don't suppose it could be. . ."

"Of course, one should expect such a thing in April," Langsford rattled on. "Ah, Meg. Is that toast? And perhaps eggs? You have saved my life. And bacon! I shall be in your debt eternally."

"Now, Mr. Langsford-Knight," Meg replied, "you shouldn't be sayin' such things, though I do know there's nothing like a good breakfast to set me up for the day, and on a day like today, as you were just talkin' of, if you'll pardon me for sayin'."

"I couldn't agree more if I'd said so myself, Meg," Langsford said.

Jonathan was silent as Langsford continued chaffing Meg, and she flirted in return while laying out the breakfast on the side table. The entire situation felt unreal. He very much wanted to find a way to broach the subject of his behavior last night, but of course could not while Meg was in the room.

He studied Langsford more closely. Though he looked well—rested and cheerful—Jonathan sensed a strain in the stream of chatter; he'd lived with Langsford too long and knew him too well to be completely taken in by what Langsford referred to himself as his duchess's dinner companion role. The brittleness of his smile, the rapidity of his conversation, the slight signs of tension around his eyes, unnoticeable except to one who knew him intimately—all indicated that, outward show to the contrary, Langsford had not, as he had said, slept well, if indeed he had slept at all.

"Thank you, Meg," he said when she had finished. "I believe we'll serve ourselves."

"Are ye sure, Mr. Williams?" Meg asked.

"Quite sure, Meg," he answered. "Please close the door when you leave. Mr. Langsford-Knight and I have business to discuss. I'll call for you when we've finished."

"Thank you, sir," she said, and bobbed a slight curtsey at the door as she left.

"That's twice in two days you've saved me from drowning, Williams," Langsford said with a flash of his normal humor as the door closed. "If we continue at this rate I shall owe you my livelihood, my home, and my firstborn child before we've finished."

"I haven't the slightest idea what I'd do with any of them," he replied, crossing to the sideboard. "May I bring you your food? What would you like?"

"Please, don't trouble yourself," Langsford said, the shielded, artificial tone back in his voice. "I'm quite able to pitch in and do my part."

"If you're certain."

"Quite certain," Langsford replied as he turned back the

cover from a serving dish. "Done to a turn. I must say, Mrs. Hale's poached eggs beat Mrs. Galloway's in every category, though I feel rather a traitor saying so." He closed the lid. "And here? Ah, the contributions of our porcine friends. Delightful . . ."

Jonathan helped himself to the food, but didn't try to stem the rising tide of Langsford's chatter. He'd have to stop at some point, and until then there was little good in trying to say anything to his purpose.

"This is delicious," Langsford said when they'd started eating. "I shall certainly mourn Mrs. Hale's cookery when I've returned to London."

"Well," Jonathan said, "you shall have to make the most of it while you're still here. Ask her to prepare anything you like for the remainder of your stay."

"That's something I would like to discuss . . ."

"Really?" Jonathan smiled. "Don't tell me Rose's cooking has seduced you into staying on for another week. Meg will be thrilled, I've no doubt."

"Actually, I'm afraid it's quite the opposite," Langsford said. "I'm terribly sorry to be such a boor, but I'm afraid I must leave before time."

Jonathan laid his fork on the table. "Before time?" he asked. "Before Sunday? What on earth for?"

"It's the Henderson brief," Langsford said. "I must confess to a falsehood earlier. I lay awake half the night thinking about it. I left it with Phillips, but the entire situation is difficult, and we're at a very delicate place in the discussions. I'm not entirely certain he's familiar enough with the complexities to successfully manage. I really must return as quickly as possible."

"How . . . how quickly?"

"This afternoon, if possible," Langsford said, and held up his hand when Jonathan began to protest. "I'm a great idiot, I'm certain, and a terrible inconvenience, but I just can't get it out of my mind. If it won't throw the entire place in an uproar, might Alec drive me into Penzance this afternoon? I'm certain the redoubtable Dawkins will be able to put me up, and I can take the morning train tomorrow."

"Well, no, of course he can," Jonathan said, taken completely off guard by this abrupt turn of events. *Too soon,* he thought, though the night before he'd dreaded having to keep Langsford's company for the rest of the week without blurting out his secret. *Too soon.*

"Thank you," Langsford said, settling back in his chair slightly. "I do so hate to be a bother, but it seems to be my fate this week." He smiled slightly. "Cornwall hasn't been as good to me as it has been to you. It's very kind of you to be so understanding."

They ate in silence for several minutes, then Jonathan laid his fork down again. "Are you quite certain you have to return?" he asked. "Phillips has always seemed to me to be quite capable. You've said so yourself. And they were expecting you to be gone the entire week."

"Of course he's capable," Langsford said. "But I know I won't sleep at all this week, if last night was any indication. I simply can't help it."

"Well . . ." Jonathan said, casting about for any alternative, "perhaps you could send him a wire, or even call trunks. You can speak to him, and see how the matters stand. I'm sure the hotel has a telephone."

Langsford looked momentarily taken aback, then shook his head. "An interesting thought," he said, "but it just won't do. One might send a brief message, perhaps, but to conduct business at this distance over a telephone simply isn't practical. And, of course, the matter is quite, quite confidential. If the operators were to listen to the call—as I'm certain they do—it could prove disastrous. I must be there personally." Langsford took a sip from his tea cup and put it down. "I'm quite decided. I have already packed my things, and I can be gone as soon as Alec is ready."

Jonathan looked out the window—the fog was settling into a light drizzle—then looked back at Langsford. In spite of the lightness of his tone, his face was drawn tightly over his bones; a muscle twitched along the side of his jaw, and his lips were a straight, thin line.

"I'll have Hale prepare the carriage," Jonathan said quietly. "I'll ask them to bring it around immediately after luncheon."

"Thank you," Langsford said, "though the cart will be satisfactory. There's no need for the carriage."

"Not in this weather," Jonathan said. "We'll be far more comfortable in the carriage, and definitely dryer."

"I'm being enough of a bother as it is," Langford said. "There's absolutely no reason for you to go to Penzance and back, just to humor my whims."

"Nonsense," Jonathan said, desperately trying to maintain a calm, natural tone of voice. "I'd always expected to see you off when you left. This is simply moving it forward a few days."

"If the weather were clear, I'd be delighted," Langsford said. "But it's absolutely beastly, as you've pointed out—"

"To hell with the weather!" Jonathan said, his hands twisting the napkin in his lap. He took a breath and continued. "Langsford, if this is a result of my idiotic behavior last night, please accept my apology. I was an absolute fool, and without any cause. The photograph was exactly as you'd said. I must have been mistaken. I was definitely rude, and I'm terribly sorry for it."

"Williams, there's no need for that." Langsford said. "We were both exhausted. Anything you might have said or done is quite forgotten. If you insist on apologizing, then of course I accept it. This business is purely my own foolishness."

"Then for heaven's sake," Jonathan said, "I'll go with you, at least as far as Penzance. If Dawkins has one room, he's bound to have two. I'll stay and see you off in—"

"No," Langsford said sharply, interrupting him. "No," he said again, more softly. "I think it best if I simply go this afternoon, early. The cart is perfectly acceptable. I'll carry an umbrella and borrow a mackintosh, if you have one."

Jonathan looked at him for a long, still moment. Langsford's face was calm, almost cold, with no expression whatsoever. Even his hair, slicked back and looking darker than was its wont, was icy in its perfection. It was the face of a stranger. "Very well," he said. "I'll see to it as soon as we've finished breakfast."

"Thank you," Langsford said.

They ate in comparative silence, speaking only to ask for the salt or to request another cup of tea. When they finished, Jonathan rang the bell. Rose arrived within a few moments, with Meg in her wake.

"Please ask Hale to prepare the dogcart, Rose," Jonathan said, "and to bring it around immediately after luncheon. Mr. Langsford-Knight has been called back to London unexpectedly, and will leave as soon as we've eaten. His baggage is packed, and can be loaded then."

A queer look crossed Rose's face, but she nodded. "What would you like for mid-day, Mr. Williams?" she asked. "And would you like me to prepare something for Mr. Langsford-Knight's journey?"

Jonathan glanced at Langsford, who shook his head. "I don't think that will be necessary, thank you, Rose," he said. "And just prepare something light for us today."

"I'm certain I can find something in the town to see me through the journey, Mrs. Hale," Langsford said. "I'll make inquiries this evening."

"You'll be staying at the White Hart tonight, then?" Rose asked.

"That is my intent, yes," Langsford said, "if he has room."

Again the odd look flickered across Rose's face, fleeting and enigmatic. "My cousin's sister-in-law, Jane, is cook there," she said. "If you speak to Dawkins, she'll prepare you something fitting."

"Thank you, Mrs. Hale."

Jonathan rose. "Is there a fire in the drawing room? It's quite chilly today."

"No, sir," she answered. "Mr. Penhyrddin always preferred the library when the fog set in."

"Very good," Jonathan said.

"I think I shall go back up to my room and lie down," Langsford said. "I am a bit wearier than I had anticipated, and the rest will be welcome."

Jonathan could do nothing but nod. "As you wish."

"Shall I send Alec to light a fire there also, Mr. Williams?" Rose asked. "He'll not be out in the fields today, I think."

"Yes, of course. I will see you at luncheon, then," Jonathan said, and left the room.

He spent the remainder of the morning in the library, sitting by the fire and staring blindly out the window at the fog that shrouded the windows, a book laying unopened and unnoticed in his lap. He roused himself slightly when Meg brought him hot chocolate at midmorning, but when she had left, the chocolate sat as untouched as the book, a thin, hard skin forming on its surface.

Around eleven the drizzle turned to a steady rain, and he watched the drops on the window panes grow, join, and trickle down the glass in thin silver trails. The only sound in the room was the whisper of the rain, the crackle and hiss of the fire on the grate, and the steady, relentless ticking of the mantel clock.

This is how it ends, then. He had no doubt that this was the end, that Langsford was leaving and had little intention of returning in the summer, assuming he'd thought that far in the future. Or, if he did return, it would be in a fashion different to the last ten years of their friendship—pleasant, charming, full of London gossip and news of his family and their friends, but gone from him as surely as he was leaving this afternoon. Jonathan didn't know how he could bear it. He had received his wish—the pain of his parting from Langsford would soon be over—but like that tale wherein the wish is granted, though not as one expected, he would now pay the price.

Langsford knew. There could be no doubt. The photograph had been the final puzzle piece, and once that had been placed—had been cemented in place, in fact, by his own violent reaction to its discovery, though Langsford couldn't begin to understand the reasons behind that reaction—he had fully understood. Had he missed the illumination on Langsford's face when realization finally arrived? Or had it happened after he had left the library, a slow, methodical reasoning, question and answer in Langsford's mind, always precise, always getting to the causes behind the effect, and always making the intuitive leaps of which his colleagues were so frequently incapable. He had always maintained a slight reserve with Langsford, specifically to avoid precisely what had finally happened. And Langsford, sensitive as always to others' sensibilities, was leaving, rather than spend the remainder of his stay negotiating the dangers in what had most likely been, up to that point and in his understanding, an open and frank friendship. His own carelessness and stupidity had created a breach that could not be mended.

Rose called him for the midday meal at one, and Langsford greeted him from the stair as he left the library. Luncheon was precisely what he had anticipated and dreaded: conversation such as he could find at any dinner party in the city on any night in the year, and not one word of it of any interest. They discussed the farm, the train journey, Langsford's family, his own half-brother's progress at school—in short, everything of general interest, and nothing of import. Hale entered the room as they were finishing to tell them that the cart was ready.

"We've loaded your things, Mr. Langsford-Knight," he said, "and wrapped them in oilcloth against the rain. I don't doubt but they'll be fine. 'Tisn't a terribly long ride, and the rain isn't fallin' too hard."

"That was good of you, Hale," Langsford said. "I hadn't thought of that."

Rose appeared in the doorway behind her husband. "I've

brought one of Mr. Penhyrddin's mackintoshes, as you asked, also."

"Thank you, Mrs. Hale," Langsford said, and took it from her. "I'll send it back with Alec, Williams."

"There's no need," Jonathan said. "Keep it, if you think you'll need it in London."

"Thank you," Langsford said formally. "Well, then . . . I suppose I'd better be going."

Jonathan led them out the front door, taking his own overcoat from the tree in the hall as he did so. The rain had actually eased to a heavy mist, and the fog had grown thicker; the front steps were slick with moisture, and drops clung to the spring flowers by the garden path, weighing them down. The cart stood just outside the garden gate, and when they stepped into the lane they saw that the horse was tied to an iron ring set in the stone wall. Meg and all of the Hale children were gathered around the back of the cart. Of Alec there was no sign.

"He said he'd forgotten something," Cassie answered, when Hale asked where he was. "He went back to get it."

"He'd best hurry," Hale said. "We don't want to all be standin' out in the rain. Run and fetch him, Jamie." The boy darted off.

"Williams," Langsford said, and held out his hand. "I will see you in August, God willing, unless you come up to town before. Your room will be waiting, whenever you wish."

Jonathan took Langsford's hand, chill and damp, in both of his. "I do wish you'd reconsider. . . ." He faltered, then took a deep breath. "But of course I understand." He kept his hold on Langsford's hand, unwilling to break this final contact. "And should you wish to come down, even for a weekend, wire ahead, and we'll prepare your room."

"I certainly will," Langsford said, looking him directly in the eye. "I hope it will be very soon."

"As do I," Jonathan answered. They stood there for one frozen moment in the mist, and he forgot the Hale family standing there; he longed, strangely, for that instant on the beach when he had embraced Langsford without any thought except relief that he lived. He wished now, desperately wished, he had spoken that relief aloud and had risked the outcome. One chance lost, and this, his last, impossible. He ached to say more, to beg, to plead, to demand that Langsford stay.

"Wire me that you have arrived safely home," he said quietly, and released Langsford's hand. "And carry my regards to your family."

"I will," Langsford answered, "and please give my regrets to Mrs. Deane." He climbed into the seat as Hale untied the reins from the ring, and looped them loosely through the hook by the seat. "Thank you, Hale," he said, "and to you Mrs. Hale. You've made my stay very enjoyable. I'm only sorry it had to end so abruptly."

"As are we," Hale said, shaking his hand. "And we all hope you'll be comin' back before long."

"We'll miss you somethin' terribly, Mr. Langsford-Knight," Meg added. "And I do hope ye come back and stay for a longer time."

"Hush, Margaret," Rose said.

As they spoke, Alec dashed around the corner of the threshing barn, followed closely by Jamie. Alec had a large, patched rectangle of fabric clutched in his arms: Langsford's kite.

"I'm sorry, sir," he panted as he ran up. "One of the men found it yesterday down by the cliff, and thought it was ours. I forgot to bring it to the house last night." He handed it up to Langsford.

"Here," Jonathan said, "I'll take it and have it shipped to you, unless you wish to pack it now."

"No," Langsford said, and handed it down to him. "Please. Keep it."

Jonathan took the kite and held it tightly against his chest. "Whatever shall I do with it?" he asked.

"Fly it," Langsford said, and his voice wavered, "on the first nice day of spring."

"I will," Jonathan said. "Every year."

"Alec," Langsford said, his eyes not leaving Jonathan's face. "We had best be off."

"Yes, sir," Alec said, and walked around the back of the cart.

"Have a pleasant journey," Jonathan said.

"I trust I will," Langsford said. "I . . . good-bye, Williams."

"Good-bye," he replied.

Langsford glanced toward the front of the cart and started slightly. As he did so, the horse suddenly reared and bolted.

Alec and Hale both shouted. Alec grabbed for the cart, but missed, and Hale shouted again at the horse as he ran after it. Jonathan stood, momentarily horrified, then dropped the kite and ran after them. The other children were screaming behind him, and he heard Rose trying to quiet them.

The cart careened down the lane, weaving from side to side, with Langsford clutching the seat to keep from being thrown off. The cart brushed the hedge, then veered across the lane. The wheel ran up the berm and hit a rock, throwing Langsford from his seat. He struck the hedge and fell heavily to the ground in the middle of the lane.

Jonathan was the first to reach him. Langsford lay on his side, his arm pinned beneath him. He was conscious, to Jonathan's relief, and tried to move as Jonathan knelt next to him. He grimaced as he attempted to sit up, then rolled cautiously onto his back.

"Don't move!" Jonathan said urgently. "Where are you hurt?"

"Other than practically everywhere?" Langsford asked drily. "I'm not entirely certain, but I think I've broken my wrist."

"Dear God!"

"Yes," Langsford replied lightly. "Cornwall clearly is not conducive to my good health." His face grew sober. "Is Alec all right? Is he hurt?"

"You're the only one as is hurt, Mr. Langsford," Hale said, kneeling beside him. "Rose, get some bandages ready, and splints. Alec, Jamie, take that horse back to the stable. Nobody's goin' nowhere today." The boys ran off toward the dogcart, a few yards down the lane; the horse had stopped running almost as soon as Langsford had fallen. Hale looked back at Langsford. "We'll help you back to the house."

"You're getting rather experienced at this, I'm afraid," Langsford said, wincing as he sat up. "I'm in your debt."

With Hale on the other side, Jonathan helped Langsford back to his room. Langsford was limping slightly, but said he felt it was only a bruise on his thigh. They sat him at the writing desk in the corner, and Rose cautiously examined his wrist. Hale left to look after the horse and the cart.

"I don't think it's broken," she said after a few moments, "as the bones feel whole, but 'tis a nasty sprain, and you need to take care. Can you move it at all?"

Langsford tried, his face going white as he moved his hand. "In answer to your question, Mrs. Hale," he said, "yes, I can. Do I want to? No, I do not."

Rose smiled briefly. "I'd not recommend it." She stood up. "I'll bind it, but we should put some cold wraps on it; it'll ease the hurt."

As she moved off to the door, where Meg hovered making concerned noises, Jonathan drew up a chair and sat next to Langsford. "Another exciting afternoon," he said, hoping to match Langsford's earlier tone.

"I must say, Williams," Langsford replied in kind, "you do have the most peculiar notions of how to entertain your houseguests."

"I will try to show a little more care when I draw up the agenda for your next visit," he answered, relieved at Langsford's banter.

"I should certainly hope so," Langsford said. "I'm just thankful that Alec wasn't harmed. I was worried. That is, I was worried between attempts to stay in my seat."

"A few moments more, perhaps, and he would have been in the cart with you and might have had trouble," Jonathan said, "but as it was, he wasn't even near it. Thank heaven, none of the children was."

"I feared he'd been trampled," Langsford said. "He was standing by the horse's head and holding the reins when the damn brute bolted."

"No, he wasn't," Jonathan said, puzzled. "He was quite the other side of the cart from me. He actually jumped for the reins, I think, when the horse ran."

"Nonsense," Langsford said. "I saw him quite distinctly. I was startled myself, that he'd got there so quickly."

Jonathan frowned. What in the world was Langsford talking about? "You couldn't possibly have seen him. He was behind you, behind Rose, also."

"He was, Mr. Langsford-Knight," Rose said, entering the room. "He was never in any peril." She laid the bandages on the table. "Now, if you will, off with your jacket, and roll up the sleeve."

Jonathan, still perplexed, stepped away as Meg and Rose attended to Langsford's wrist. How in the world could Langsford have thought Alec was gathering the reins and standing by the horse, when the boy had barely rounded the *back* of the cart? The fog was dense, true, but this was the first time he'd heard of mist revealing a person, instead of hiding him—and not even revealing, but causing someone to be seen who was in quite another place.

Hale walked in. "The cart's not damaged at all, Mr. Williams, save for the paint being a bit scratched where it brushed up against the hedge," he said. "Rebecca isn't harmed at all, either, though she's acting mighty peculiar. She won't let Alec near her. Damn fool thing."

"That is strange," Rose said, looking up from bandaging Langsford's wrist. "She's not done that before, nor has any beast around Alec."

"Don't I know this?" Hale said. "That animal had best get over it, and right quickly. We've too much work to do."

"Do you think she will be in sufficient condition to take me to Penzance tomorrow, Hale?" Langsford asked.

"I don't see why not," Hale answered. "And if she's still skittish of Alec, I'll drive you in myself."

"You'll do nothing of the sort," Jonathan said firmly, and turned to Langsford. "You'll rest here until Sunday, or until you're able to travel."

Langsford shook his head. "No, I'm afraid that by delaying this long there might be . . . difficulties," he said. "I'll rest tonight—I think a hot bath would do me good—but tomorrow I must leave." He winced. "I think that's quite tight enough, Mrs. Hale."

"That will be all, Rose, thank you," Jonathan said quickly. "I will call if I need any assistance."

"I'll be getting back to my work, then," Hale said.

"I will see you tomorrow, Hale," Langsford said.

"Aye," Hale said briefly, and followed Rose and Meg into the hall, closing the door behind him.

"You most certainly are *not* leaving," Jonathan said, turning on Langsford. "You can't even walk by yourself, as far as we can see. It's absolutely ridiculous to consider travelling until you're able."

Langsford's lips thinned. "Be that as it may, I'm returning to London tomorrow," he said sharply.

"Then I'm coming with you. Good god, man, you can't even carry your own bag."

"You are not travelling all the way to London and back again in order to be my porter," Langsford said. "Hale or Alec will assist me here, and I'll hire a man at the station, or wire Mansell-Jones to meet me there. He can carry them."

"Mansell-Jones," Jonathan said, astonished at the suggestion. "*Mansell-Jones?* If you wired him in the morning, and at every station along the route home, perhaps he'd remember to meet you, but of all people to ask for help, he would be the last I'd recommend."

"Then I'll give him something to remember," Langsford said. "I'll . . . I'll entice him with tales of Cornish ghosts. That will bring him running."

"Cornish ghosts?" Jonathan asked, utterly incredulous.

"Well, tales of extreme atmosphere, then," Langsford said. "It isn't as if we don't have enough material to make up a good haunting. A wire mentioning a remote farmhouse, faces at the window, and mysteriously disappearing figures in the fog will be at least enough to intrigue Mansell-Jones and entice him to the station. He'll be waiting when I arrive."

"Did you strike your head as well as your wrist?" Jonathan asked. "I have little difficulty believing Mansell-Jones to be that gullible, but why on earth are you insisting on leaving tomorrow? My *God*, Langsford, you . . ." He broke off as someone knocked on the door. "Yes," he snapped. "Come in."

The door opened slowly and Alec peered around its edge. "Mother wanted to know if there was aught you needed," he said, "and if I should run fetch Aunt Bannel to look after Mr. Langsford-Knight."

Jonathan stared at him. Nat's worry, there, on the face of a fourteen-year-old boy.

"Mr. Williams?" Alec asked, his voice uncertain.

A face at the window. Figures in the fog . . .

It wasn't possible.

"Williams?" Langsford asked.

Twists of straw on a windowsill. Langsford, falling from a cliff, believing he'd been shoved. A figure by a chair in a darkened library . . .

"Williams, what is it?"

A photograph, burned years before, sitting on the chest of drawers in the next room . . .

Jonathan shook his head. "Nothing of any importance," he said slowly. "Just an odd thought."

"Shall I call for Aunt Bannel then, Mr. Williams?" Alec asked again. "Oh, and you dropped this when you fell, Mr. Langsford-

Knight. I found it after you left."

He dug in his pockets, but Jonathan knew what he had found before he even opened his hand.

"It isn't mine," Langsford said. "I've never worn a ring like that, not to speak of carrying it on a chain."

"The ring is mine," Jonathan said calmly and held out his hand. Langsford looked up quickly, but didn't speak. "It must have fallen from my pocket when I helped you up." The ring burned when Alec placed it on his palm, or, perhaps, it was only in his mind it burned, aflame with memory, intentions, and promises given and broken. He slipped it into his pocket. "You don't need to go for Mrs. Bannel," he continued in that same quiet, rational tone. "I will go myself. I have been remiss in not paying her a call to thank her for coming yesterday. Please ask your mother to bring Mr. Langsford-Knight's tea to him in his room this afternoon." Alec nodded and left. "I'll tell Hale to bring the dogcart around shortly after breakfast tomorrow morning, if you like," he said to Langsford. "You will be able to have a pleasant luncheon at the hotel, I've no doubt."

"I . . . well, yes . . ." Langsford said, appearing startled by Jonathan's abrupt change of mind. "I appreciate your understanding."

"Of course," Jonathan said. "It was rude of me to insist otherwise. If you'll excuse me, I'll call on Mrs. Bannel."

"That's probably not necessary," Langsford said. "It's just a sprain."

"I'll tell her you said that, and let her decide what she feels is the best course of action."

"From what I've seen of her," Langsford said, "I think that is wise."

"I'll leave you to rest."

He pulled the door closed behind him, and leaned against it. The wood against his back was hard, solid and real, and he pushed back harder, feeling the ridge of the panels against his spine. Real. Hesitantly, he slid his hand into his pocket again and pulled out the ring. This, too, was real, as solid as the door behind him. The nick on the edge, the slight deformation of the perfect roundness that it must have had when originally made, the pattern, the metal, the chain from which it dangled, all as real as the straw and the photograph in his room. Indisputable, immutable reality, but the result of that which was impossible, and ridiculous, and, above all, not real.

But the ring hung on the end of its chain, just as it had for the two months he had worn it around his neck. He could feel the ghost of its weight and shape against his chest even now, as he stood in the hallway watching the real thing swing back and forth as it dangled from his hand.

He dropped the ring into his overcoat pocket, and walked down the steps. Taking his cap from the stand in the hall, and his gloves from the table, he crossed through the house and gave his orders to Rose and Meg: tea for Langsford in his room, and for him, and possibly Mrs. Bannel, when he returned.

The fog was thicker when he stepped out of the kitchen into the yard than when they had brought Langsford in. Buildings, trees, and hedges loomed out of the mist as he passed them, and he was careful to stay on the lane, so as not to lose the path and get lost. Sounds echoed weirdly; the voices of the men working in the outbuildings sounded remote but clear, while the sea seemed to rush over rocks just out of his sight.

He brushed his hand along the hedgerow as long as it ran with the lane. The distance seemed far greater than he had thought, and for a moment he believed he was lost, and wandering the fields, but the lane was still dirt beneath his feet, and now and again he caught a glimpse of a tree, or a rock wall. He pulled his coat tightly about him.

He stumbled and nearly fell when he came to the road, that thoroughfare being more worn than his own lane. He stepped directly across to Bannel's cottage, which he could see only as a dark mass in the fog. He could smell the smoke from her fire and hear the discontented squawk of a chicken. He opened the gate, and walked up the path to the house. He hesitated a moment at the door, uncertain whether he wanted to take this step, then knocked.

The door opened almost immediately. Mrs. Bannel stood in the doorway.

"Good afternoon, Mr. Jonathan," she said. "I've been expectin' you these last two days. I have tea ready. Come in."

CHAPTER 12

He stepped across the threshold and Mrs. Bannel closed the door behind him. The room looked precisely as it had fourteen years earlier, and once again he felt the sense of dislocation that had afflicted him periodically across the last few days, a sense of being, not in two places at once, but in two times. And nowhere had this felt so strong as now, here, in this room.

It was an unexceptional room, small, dark, and low-ceilinged. The fireplace dominated the back of the room, set in the whitewashed plaster walls under a large wood mantel. A rough sideboard stood against the wall to one side, a large table in the center of the room. Spindle-backed chairs, mismatched and clearly handed down from an older, finer establishment, stood around the table, which was covered with a rough white cloth. The brick floor was covered in places with rag rugs; a cat lay stretched out on one by the fireplace, and eyed him lazily. Up under the rafters, bundles of herbs were tied to an old ladder made of two slender saplings stripped of their bark. A small doorway led into another room at the back, and another ladder, sturdier and attached to the wall, led to a trap in the wooden ceiling. Pots and pans hung from pegs in the walls up under the eaves. A peat fire burned on the hearth, and the room was redolent of thyme, rosemary, lavender, and smoke.

"How fares your fine friend this day, Mr. Jonathan?" Mrs. Bannel asked.

Jonathan, startled from his memories, glanced over at her. Upon closer examination, he realized that she had changed, to a degree. The lines around her mouth were deeper, and the hair that escaped her cap was white now, instead of the iron grey he remembered. But the hard, dark eyes were the same, as were the sharp chin and the strong nose; she was made of angles, not curves, and no softness ever showed in her face or in her person.

"He has had another accident," he said. "The horse bolted, and he was thrown from the cart. I believe his wrist is sprained."

"Did he now," she said calmly. "A man marked for misfortune, he'd seem to be."

"No," Jonathan said, stung. "No, that's what's peculiar." He walked across the room and warmed his hands at the fire as he searched for words. "Langsford has always been untouched by such things," he finally said. "I mean to say, he has the usual difficulties in life—one cannot avoid those—but this is quite unusual. I know it sounds absurd, but I've always thought him born to good fortune. Everyone has." He shook his head. "I don't know why I'm talking such nonsense."

"'Tisn't nonsense," Mrs. Bannel said. "There are them that are born in a good light, and them that are born in shadow. Your friend? He's as fair as any day of high summer, born to it and will live in it, if those around him don't do him harm." She took an iron kettle off the hearth where it steamed amongst the flames and placed it on an iron trivet on the hearth. "Will you have some tea?"

"Yes, thank you."

"Seat yourself," she said. "You'll want some saffern cakes, too. It will be some time since you've had such." She took two blue and white teacups from a shelf above the window, and set them on the table. "There's no need to worry over your friend," she said as she opened a dented tin and scooped out the tea leaves. "I don't see trouble awaiting him. For all he's a chatterin' fool, he's one such as I said." She poured the boiling water into the tea cup, and then put the kettle back on the fire. "Others are not.

Nat Boscawen was one of those."

Jonathan had reached for the teacup, but his hand stopped inches from the saucer. Nat's name hung in the air like a living thing, and ripples flowed out from the center of it and filled the room. He realized that, although Nat had been foremost in his mind since he had received word of his inheritance, and had been brought before him both in the boy Alec's face and in the weird appearance of articles he'd thought lost or destroyed, no one had spoken his name, or even directly mentioned him, except the Deanes in their naïveté, and Langsford, in his ignorance. He was present in all things, in all minds, none more than Jonathan's own, but none spoke of him.

"He was born for his fate," Mrs. Bannel said quietly, "and there was naught any could do to prevent it, least of all you. Take your tea."

His hand shook violently as he took the cup, spilling the water into the saucer. He put it down on the table quickly. He looked at the fire, biting his lip, tears unexpectedly hot in his eyes.

"He had none to blame but himself," she said, "and none others should shoulder any of it." She moved into his line of sight, and he looked up at her face. He was shocked to see the tears in his eyes mirrored by those in hers, the soft glimmer contrasting strongly with the harsh, set lines of her face. "Least of all you, child," she said gently.

He bit his lip, fighting against the tears. "I don't blame myself for anything," he said, looking at the floor and knowing he lied. "I had nothing to do with it."

"What one knows, and what one believes," she said, "are two different things." He looked up again as she set a plate of cakes on the table next to him. "But often it is we cannot tell the difference."

He was silent. She sat in the chair across from him and folded her hands in her lap. "I know what I know," he said finally, "but not what I believe."

"If that be so," she said, "do you think to find the answers here?"

"I don't know," he replied.

"Then why have ye come?"

He reached into his pocket and drew out the ring on its chain. It gleamed dully in the firelight as it spun in the air between them.

"Because of this," he said.

Cornwall 1892

The following months passed with a lazy, deceptive indolence, June melting into July, and then into shimmering, golden August. The poppies and marigolds glowed in the corn, and the wild roses draped the hedgerows like blankets of softest pink. Jonathan spent his days reading in the shade of the hawthorn trees surrounding the house or basking in the sun on the beach below the cliffs. On Sundays he and Nat would ramble about the countryside, or, on occasion, sail out to Mounts Bay with Tom in the fishing smack. For Jonathan, no place existed except this golden land, no time before, and no future. He lived like a favored dog or cat, petted and content in his life, knowing this day only, and nothing else.

Most nights they met, stealing away to one or another of their hideaways, but never risking staying until dawn. They were nearly caught one night in July when, rather than walking through the fields, they thought to save time by travelling along one of the common footpaths. They heard the group of men, most likely returning from the public house or tavern, only moments before they rounded the bend, and had scant time to hide in the gorse bushes that lined the path. From that time on they were even more cautious, changing the location of their meetings, never going twice to the same place on successive nights, and avoiding the footpaths and habitations of men.

Penhyrddin watched them, Jonathan knew, but since the night of the bonfire he trusted in his cousin's silence and acquiescence, so long as he was discreet and caused no scandal. He repaid this forbearance with caution, never giving cause to jeopardize the freedom he was given, and always being attentive to his cousin's requests and direction. He gradually grew sensitive to Penhyrddin's ways, and watched for subtle hints, sometimes in just the turn of a phrase, as to when the older man would turn a blind eye or, in the opposite case, instruct him to remain at home.

As September drew near, though, and the light began to fade, he grew more anxious. Michaelmas was approaching, and with it, Cambridge. He tried to ignore the shortening span of days, but when the knapweed bloomed at the fields' edges, and the nights grew longer, he was less able to pretend the day wouldn't come that he'd have to leave.

They never spoke of it. If they discussed the future at all—and they rarely did—they spoke of far distant time, and fantastical places, of visiting the Orient, or America, or the Valley of the Nile, places far off and exotic, and as far from their reach as another night spent holding each other until dawn.

Of any other future, they remained silent.

Jonathan dozed in church. The weather this last week of August had been hot and sultry, and the air in the church was still. The vicar's voice droned on in the heat, and Jonathan's head drooped as the lesson wound on its seemingly endless road to conclusion.

He hadn't slept until very late the night before, though not, as was usual, because he had been out. He sat awake and dressed in his room until almost three before undressing and going to bed. He'd been concerned; Nat hadn't come to him or left him word since Monday, the longest time they'd been apart. Nor had he seen him but in passing in the yard, and then at too great a distance to speak. He wanted to send word, but couldn't think of any legitimate ways or means of doing so. Nat had behaved oddly the week preceding this as well; he was short-tempered during the day and almost desperate in their lovemaking at night. More than once he'd smelt of liquor.

The household itself had been disturbed for the past two weeks, also. Rose Pritchard had abruptly left the farm to return to her people in Landreath, and Nat's grandmother had been serving them at table, huffing and sniffing as she banged the dishes down or took them away. Jonathan didn't particularly like Pritchard—he hadn't forgotten her behavior at the bonfire—but he most devoutly missed her table service.

Penhyrddin, too, had been unusually silent. He didn't comment at all on Rose's absence, and when Jonathan asked him directly where she had gone and why, the older man had, for the first time in their acquaintance, shown temper, and told Jonathan to mind his own household, and let him mind his.

These thoughts, and others less domestic and proper in their scope, wandered through his mind as the vicar droned on. His eyes slid closed and he drifted off.

" . . . Nat Boscawen and Rose Pritchard, both of this parish. If any of you knows any cause or just impediment why these two persons should not be joined together in holy matrimony, ye are to declare it. This is the first time of asking."

Jonathan's head snapped up and his eyes flew open. In sheer shock he began to stand, but Penhyrddin gripped his arm and pulled him down.

"Sit still, lad," he murmured. "This is no time for speech."

"What's happened?" Jonathan asked, his throat tight. "What's going on?"

"They're being wed," Penhyrddin answered, "and not a moment too soon."

"But why . . ." Jonathan began, and the import of Penhyrddin's words struck him like a blow. The room spun around him, and he felt the gorge rise in his throat. Black spots danced before his eyes, and he was certain he was going to be ill.

"I have to leave," he said.

"Don't be foolish," Penhyrddin answered.

"I—" He took a deep breath. "I think the heat has been too much for me. I need to get some air."

Penhyrddin looked at him, frowning.

"Please, cousin."

"Go quickly then, and quietly," Penhyrddin said, looking

straight ahead, "and wait for me at the cart."

"Thank you," Jonathan whispered.

He stood as everyone rose for the Creed, slipped into the main aisle of the church, bobbed his reverence, and walked quickly down the aisle. Letting himself out the south door, he sat on the stone bench lining the side of the porch and stared blankly at the tombstones in the churchyard.

Married. To Rose Pritchard. The kitchen maid. In four weeks time, unless for some reason the banns were forbade, or the time shortened. *Married.*

He'd lied. He'd lied all along. He'd lied at the beginning, and he'd lied continuously through the months since. The nights they'd been apart, that Nat had had family business in the village, or had to work late into the evening, or that he had simply been weary—all lies. He thought of where Nat had been—had to have been—and what he had been doing—clearly had been doing—and lurched to his feet.

He made it halfway across the churchyard to a large, granite monument before he was ill, but though he retched and heaved, nothing came up. It sat, festering in his stomach, like poison. The lies, the deception, and his own blindness and stupidity.

He couldn't love her. Couldn't. He'd said he didn't, that he'd loved none but him, had never loved anyone like he loved him. *He loves me,* he cried in his heart. *He said he did. He swore he did.*

He leaned against the worn, lichen-covered tomb. Nat had also said that Rose was nothing to him, that she had chased after him, and he didn't want anything to do with her. And now he was marrying her. Marrying her. *Marrying her.* In a church, in a suit, with the entire village watching, he was marrying the kitchen maid, and they were going to have a passel of brats, one after the other until she died of it.

He thought for a moment of her dying, and wished for it, violently. In childbirth, or a carriage accident, or a fall from the path on the cliffs to the rocks below . . . .

He saw her death clearly in his mind, and then recoiled from that image.

It wasn't her fault. She had done what was natural, what was ordinary—what was, in fact, no different than what he himself had done. He hated her, but she wasn't to blame. He couldn't wish death on her any more than he could on Nat, or any other being. It wasn't in him.

He walked slowly back to the south porch, legs stiff, and sat. *What am I to do? How can I face him again?* Small wonder he'd been gone the last week. He had probably proposed Monday, and she had accepted, and he had been with her. *With her. Every night, been with her.* He started to tremble violently.

What can I do?

He heard the choir start the anthem after the collects; he had to gather himself together. Mercifully he hadn't wept, nor had he been actually ill. He sat up.

He would act as if it hadn't happened. As if the entire summer hadn't happened. He had never considered himself a proud man, but it would certainly be beneath his dignity to acknowledge this pain, this searing, wrenching grief, to the person who had caused it. He had lain with this man, this farmhand, in contravention of everything he had been taught, of everything he had been brought up to believe, had surrendered to common lust with a common man.

No more.

His cousin and he had never spoken openly about it, so there would be no difficulty or awkwardness there. He would meet Penhyrddin for meals, read with him in the afternoon, and sit up after dinner with him, as they always did. His Sundays on the beach or his rambles about the countryside would cease, and if Penhyrddin asked why, he would tell him, quite frankly, he needed to prepare for Cambridge, which was approaching. He would spend his time indoors, with his books, until it was time to leave. One thing was certain: He would leave before the marriage took place.

And when he left, he wouldn't even say goodbye.

He held up his hands; they were steady. He looked up as the door opened and Penhyrddin stepped through, first of all the congregation.

"I'm much better now, sir," he said calmly. "Do you want me to drive home?"

They rode home in silence, and when they arrived at the farm, Jonathan withdrew immediately to his room to change his clothing. Once there, alone, he stripped off his suit and shirt and tie, then grabbed the ring around his neck and pulled it violently off. The chain snapped, and he jerked the top left door open and threw it in, then slammed the drawer shut. He sobbed once, then bit his lip until that pain drove away the greater pain in his heart, then slowly, carefully dressed. *I will throw all the tokens away,* he thought, *or burn them, or bury them,* he didn't care which.

He was calm at lunch, and broached, for the first time, the subject of Cambridge and his departure. He had, he told his cousin, been lax in his studies all summer, and if he was to succeed at all, he would have to start his reading immediately. He also thought, perhaps, that he would leave a week earlier than originally planned, and spend that week with his father and his new wife in Sussex, before going up to Cambridge and before she was brought to bed with her child. Penhyrddin seemed disconcerted by his abrupt change in plans and this unexpected tolerance of his father, but agreed that perhaps that might be a gracious action.

He spent the afternoon in front of the open window in the library, reading Bacon, or Donne, or Shakespeare, he wasn't sure which. What mattered is that the words distracted him, and though they meant nothing to him and were gone from his thoughts immediately, even before his eyes moved to the next sentence or page, they gave him something on which he could focus, rather than the tumult seething in his mind.

Dinner passed in a similar fashion, and after, instead of feigning sleepiness so he could return to his room as soon as darkness fell, he stayed in the library reading until almost midnight, and then retired. Upon returning to his room he crossed to the window; a straw token lay upon the sill. In spite of the warmth of the night, he pulled the casement closed and latched it, fastened the shutters and drew the curtains, then did the same with the other window. When he had undressed and had lain down in his bed he heard a faint tapping at the window. He clenched his fists and bit his lip again, praying that he would just go away, just leave, just go away. After a time the tapping stopped, and he lay there, dry eyed, until almost dawn.

Rose Pritchard came back to the farm that morning. He heard her voice from the hall moments before he walked into the dining room, and so had a brief, all too brief chance to compose himself. He smiled as he welcomed her back, and wished her joy even as he hated her. He wondered how he could have missed the swelling beneath her breast, how anyone could have; she was, to his eye, sleek and fat like a brood mare or a cow great with calf, and he hoped the thing growing in her would be an idiot, or deformed, or die in the moment of its birth.

Unexpected waves of wrenching pain swept him throughout the day, with neither perceivable pattern nor noticeable cause. One moment he was sitting, calmly reading Euripides, and the next he was clutching the book, shaking with the effort to force back the tears. If Penhyrddin noticed anything, he was silent, and if Jonathan had been grateful for his tact before, he was doubly so now.

Odd fancies filled his mind: He would stand up in church when the banns were published the second time—or no, the third and last—and denounce Nat as a seducer of boys and a sodomite, chancing the scandal and disgrace for his revenge. Or instead of going to Cambridge, he would travel to the Argentine, or Australia, or some distant corner of the Empire, and there, unknown to any around him, build his life anew. Or, perhaps, he would be taken ill with consumption, and slowly, painfully die while Nat watched and Rose was forced to nurse him.

Two straw twists waited on his windowsill that night, and he ignored them as he had the one the evening prior, closing the windows and shutters as he had done then. The tapping at the windows went on longer that night, stronger and more urgent, and he was shaking and weeping by the time it ceased. He thought then, in the darkness of the deepest night, of taking his life, of walking out the door and down to the cliffs, and of hurling himself into the sea, to be found broken and dead in the morning on the beach, ending his sorrow where the joy that caused it had begun. He had risen from bed and his hand was on the knob of his bedroom door before he came to his senses. Death like this would benefit no one, and he would not give Nat the satisfaction of knowing how deeply he was hurt.

Why did he come to the window? he thought as he lay back down. Did Nat expect him to go with him again, as if nothing had happened, as if the shattered vows were still intact? Did Nat expect him to wait on his fancy, when he could take himself away from his doting and equally foolish and blind wife, and use him for his pleasure? If Nat thought that, he would learn a bitter lesson.

Exhausted, he fell asleep as light began to show through the crack between the shutters. His sleep was filled with unremembered but unsettling dreams, and he woke wearier than he had been before he slept. He was surly that day, and kept mostly to himself rather than chance showing temper to the others in the house. After lunch, he read in an upstairs bedroom that faced the back of the house. The windows were open and the warm breeze bellied the lace curtains. He lay down on the bed, to rest for a moment, he thought, and for the first time that week, slept soundly and deeply, and woke well after tea had been served. Penhyrddin had come up to call him, so he said, but had let him sleep.

His room was neat and organized when he returned that night. He had, for the last few days, left it more cluttered than was his wont; Pritchard had to straighten it every day, and he took a small, spiteful pleasure in creating more work for her. The windows were again open to the evening breeze off the ocean, and when he looked at the sill he wasn't at all surprised to see three tokens lying there in the lamplight. For the first time he looked out across the lawn, but could see nothing; the moon, though waxing, had set already. The lawn was dark and shadowed, the hawthorn trees black against the grey waste of the land. He closed the casements, and locked the shutters.

The tapping began before he had finished undressing. He stood in the middle of the room, frozen for a moment, then slowly, deliberately undressed and turned back the bedclothes. The tapping was relentless, a quiet, fast staccato broken by moments of silence in which he hoped it would cease, only to begin again.

Finally, though, he heard the whisper, "Jonny, open the window. *Please.* Open the window," and he could stand no more. He had to face this and have done.

He slipped on his dressing gown and crossed the room, then carefully unlocked the shutters and laid them back against the wall. Nat loomed outside the window, a black shadow against the starlit sky. Equally slowly, Jonathan unlatched the window and pushed open the casements. He could smell the liquor before Nat even spoke.

"Yes?" he said coolly.

"Jonny, love," Nat said, his voice slightly slurred. "Why've you kept me waitin'? God, love, I've wanted to see you." He moved to step through the window.

"Don't come in here," Jonathan said sharply. "Have you lost your mind? You're drunk."

"I know, love," Nat said, looking at the ground, "and I'm sorry for it, but I've been goin' mad these last weeks, and it's the only thing helps."

"I should think it would be the last thing that would help," Jonathan said. "What do you want?"

"You, love," Nat said, looking straight at him. "You're all I've ever wanted."

For a moment Jonathan almost surrendered and went to him, so deep was the longing to hold him again, so great the hunger. They stood, eyes locked, deepest black looking into deepest black, and then Nat looked away and down, and Jonathan took control of himself again.

"I should think you have a most unusual way of showing it," he said, his tone biting. "Shall I congratulate you? Doubly? It certainly seems to be in order."

"Jonny, let me explain," Nat said, and stepped closer to the window.

Jonathan stepped back. "I should also think," he said, "that the subject needs no explanation. Pritchard is with child, your child, one assumes, and you are to marry her. It's all very simple." He paused. "And common."

It stung. He could see it in Nat's face.

"I s'pose I deserved that," Nat said.

"Yes," Jonathan answered. "You did."

Nat looked at him again, his misery clear in his face. "Please, come with me, love," he said desperately. "I just want to talk to you, to tell you." He stepped up to the window. "I've been just that mad these last days, knowin' you'd know, and not knowin' what to do about it."

"I can't think of anything you can possibly have to say to me," Jonathan said coldly, "or that I have to say to you, save, perhaps, good night."

He reached for the shutters to close them, and Nat caught him by the arm. "Come w'me," Nat said, pulling him up against the sill, the liquor strong on his breath. "Come w'me and let me talk to you. That's all, just talk. *Please,* Jonny."

"Let go of me," Jonathan said, struggling to get free, angry and frightened. "There's nothing to be said! Let me go—"

Nat grabbed him by the shoulders and lifted him bodily out of the window. Jonathan struggled and kicked, but was no match for Nat's strength.

"Put me down," he hissed, "or I'll shout the house awake, and then how will you explain yourself? Drunk, abducting me . . . have you lost your mind?"

"Aye," Nat said, and released him, "because I've lost you."

Jonathan was silent, not knowing what to say; he could hear the sincerity in Nat's voice.

"Come with me, please, Jonny," Nat said. "I need to talk to ye."

Jonathan wavered. He ought to allow Nat at least a chance to tell his side of the story, he thought, though he was certain he wouldn't believe it. "Very well," he said, grudgingly. "Let me change my clothing. I can hardly go wandering about the countryside in my bed-gown and slippers."

Nat glanced upward, and Jonathan followed his gaze. Lamplight flickered in a window on the first floor, overlooking them.

"There's no time," Nat whispered, and seized his arm again. "Yer robe's dark; ye won't show in the night. Come now."

"Don't be an idiot," Jonathan said, and then gasped as Nat nearly pulled him off his feet and dragged him across the lawn to the gate.

"*Stop* it," he said when they were in the lane, jerking his arm free. "We can talk now."

"No," Nat said mulishly, grabbing him again and pulling him up the lane. "We have to go someplace where we're not disturbed. There's no little amount of talkin' we have to do, and I'll not have some eedjit wandering by and seein' us."

"No, we can't have that," Jonathan said sarcastically. "He might say something to your intended, and then where would you be."

"You stop," Nat said, jerking him upright and holding him by both shoulders. "You just stop that talk."

"You said you wanted to talk," Jonathan snapped. "I don't suppose that included listening, now, did it."

"Stop it," Nat said angrily, and shook him. "Just you shut your mouth unless you have somethin' civil to say."

Jonathan twisted in his grip and pulled himself free. "I can't think of anything civil I care to say to you," he spat. "I'm going back to my room."

"The devil you are," Nat said. "You'll come with me if I have to carry ye there an' back again."

Jonathan turned to run back to the house, but Nat caught him and pulled him along the lane until finally, realizing he would never break loose, he relented and followed, stiff and silent. When they reached the road, however, and it became clear where Nat was headed—up into the hills to the old ruins—he stopped abruptly.

"No," he said. "Not there."

"Sssssssssst," Nat hissed. "Keep quiet. Old lady Bannel can hear an ant fart six miles gone."

"Then perhaps we shouldn't have come this way," Jonathan whispered furiously.

"Aye, we should," Nat said. "Just keep still."

Infuriated, but feeling helpless to resist, Jonathan stumbled along behind him. They circled quickly around the cottage and down the ravine, crossed the stream, then up the other side. Far more quickly than he wished they were picking their way through the old ruins. The gorse and brambles snagged at his dressing gown, and he cursed to hear it tear when he pulled it free. When they reached the low, dark mouth of the cave, Jonathan stopped.

"We're here," he said sharply. "Have your say, and be done."

"Come inside," Nat said. "Please, Jonny."

"No," Jonathan said. "I detest this place and I always have. I'm here, and I'll listen, and there's no one else in this godforsaken country, so you needn't worry about being overheard."

"I'll not talk until we're someplace as none can find us," Nat said obstinately.

"Very well, then," Jonathan said. "Have a pleasant night."

He tried to leave, but Nat grabbed his arm, gripping him so tightly that the pain made Jonathan wince, and pulled him in close. "I'll not let you go until you've heard my say," Nat said. "We'll stand here all night, if we have to, and you can damn well explain that to old man Penhyrddin."

"Let me go," Jonathan said between clenched teeth.

"Not until ye've heard me out," Nat said.

Jonathan cursed himself for agreeing to leave the house. Nat was stubborn at best of times, but now, no little bit drunk and determined on his course, Jonathan was certain he was perfectly capable of keeping them standing in the middle of the fields all night.

"Fine," Jonathan said. "You have ten minutes to speak your piece, and then I leave. Now let me go."

"Fair enough," Nat said, and released his grip.

Jonathan dropped to his knees and crawled into the tunnel. The place smelled dank, but not as dead as it had on occasion. A candle guttered in a niche just inside the entrance, and another at the bend in the main passage. He scrambled to his feet, brushed his knees, and without waiting for Nat, walked down the length of the tunnel. Light glimmered from the mouth of the side chamber, and he ducked through the low entry arch. This space was warmer than the damp of the main chamber; the embers of a fire glowed on the rough hearth, and two lanterns burned, casting a dim but steady light. The ticking mat and its blankets were tucked up against the wall, as always, with the jug of water they kept sitting on the ground by it. Another, smaller bottle lay corked and on its side, next to that.

He turned and crossed his arms over his chest as Nat came into the chamber. Nat started to reach for him, but he took a step back and held up his hand. "Say what you brought me to hear," he said.

"I just want to hold ye whilst I'm tellin' ye," Nat said. "If I'm holding you, everythin' will be all right again."

"I am not," Jonathan said in the iciest tone he could muster, "in the habit of embracing men whose affections are engaged elsewhere. Nor do I intend to start."

"My affections aren't . . . *God,* Jonny, no, I don't love her. I never did."

"I'm sure that will come as quite a surprise to her family and to your child, when it's born."

"I didn't never love her!" Nat ran his hand through his hair and began to pace around the room. "I didn't, I swear. She started talkin' sweet to me in the spring, and chasin' after, and we . . . we . . . we only were together once or twice, and it weren't anything but a fun bit of play, I thought."

Jonathan felt the gorge rise in his throat at the thought of Nat lying with her, and tears started in his eyes. He fought against them, angry at himself for weakening. "A fun bit of play," he said, cutting through Nat's protests. "You seem skilled at that. But then, you'd told me so at the beginning." Shaking, he fought for calm. "I should have taken that as fair warning."

"Not you, Jonny," Nat said, reaching for him again. "Love, just let me hold you once, just make things right again. You're different. We are. We've always been."

"Really?" Jonathan said, stepping back again. "I'm so very flattered." Nat flinched, and Jonathan felt a small, hot flare of pleasure in the pain he had inflicted. "I'll remember that on your wedding day."

"I don't want to marry her!" Nat cried. "I never did, never, but they've been at me, night and day for weeks, her mother, me gran, her father and her brothers, all the time since she told them the baby's mine. They've been at me until I can't see straight. Even Penhyrddin, he said he'd have to sack me if I didn't do right by her. I didn't know what to do or say, and I couldn't tell ye about it. Dear God . . ." He stopped and held out his arms again. "Help me, Jonny, please. Please, make things right again."

Jonathan had gone numb at the mention of his cousin's name. Penhyrddin had known, or had guessed, about him and Nat, and had done nothing to prevent or stop them, and so, Jonathan had thought, sick at his own naïveté, had approved in a quiet way. That he had practically forced Nat to wed Pritchard was unthinkable. But it had happened.

"There is nothing to be done," he said in a still, chill voice. "Things will never be right again."

"Don't say so," Nat said. "We can do something, you and me,

we can think of something. We're bound, we're tied, we *love* each other."

"There is nothing to be done," Jonathan repeated, the cold spreading from his voice down into his chest.

"We can leave, we can run away," Nat said, and began pacing again, "like we talked of. We can go to . . . to Australia, or America, or Italy or some such place, somewhere no one knows us, we can go. I can work, we can find some work, you have your schoolin' and such, and I can work, until we can find some way to live."

"No." The world was against them, against their kind, and in his folly and dreamy-eyed innocence he had thought they could conquer it. And even if they did leave, if he abandoned everything and everyone he knew, there would always be this betrayal between them, the child left behind, and the smallest, cancerous thought that—

"Did you lay with her after you'd been with me?" he asked in the same flat, dead tone.

"Did I . . . what?" Nat asked, gaping.

"Did you lay with her after you'd been with me?" he said more loudly. His heart started pounding, and the ice in his chest melted into furious anger, anger at Nat for destroying his trust, at Pritchard for being the vessel of that destruction, at Penhyrddin for forcing it to be so, and at himself for being the greatest fool of them all, for thinking that it could end in any way but this. He had seen it all, and he had willfully ignored everything but his own blind folly. He hated himself and he hated them, and he wanted nothing more than to strike out at them all.

"I . . . no," Nat stammered. "I never did!"

"I don't believe you," Jonathan said, the biting arrogance back in his tone. "I think you did. I think you did all this time. Did you use to lie with her and laugh about the poor motherless boy, following you around like a puppy dog or a little lost lamb?" He laughed bitterly. "A little lamb. Maybe you and Jack the sheep poker aren't that different after all."

Nat went still. "Don't say such things," he said.

"Why not?" Jonathan said. "I don't see much difference, except that I'm the sheep." He lifted his chin. "This is what I get for fornicating with a common farmhand."

"Jonny . . . don't."

He smiled a slow, mocking smile. "A common, *illiterate* farmhand."

He didn't even see the blow coming before it struck him. He was suddenly sprawled on the floor, the side of his face numb. His ear rang, and he felt a trickle running down his upper lip from his nose; the coppery taste of blood filled his mouth. He lay for a moment, stunned, then looked up at Nat, standing over him.

"You . . . you hit me," he said.

Nat dropped to his knees next to him. "Oh, God, love, God, Jonny," he said. "I'm sorry, I didn't . . . but . . . I just don't know what's gone on in my head, and I didn't mean to. I'm sorry, love."

Pain burned across Jonathan's face, and tears trickled from his eyes. "You hit me," he said again, and choked back a sob.

"No, love, no," Nat said, and lifted him and held him. "I didn't mean it, no, love. I'm sorry."

For a moment, Jonathan lay loose-limbed in the warm strength of Nat's arms, the familiar feeling and deep comfort banishing all thought and memory. But when Nat's lips brushed the top of his head, he stiffened.

"No," he said, trying to push away. "*No.*"

"Just stay here safe with me," Nat said, "and everything will be all right."

"No," he said, struggling to get free. "Let me go."

Nat held him tighter and started kissing him on his forehead, his eyes, his face. "Don't, love, don't, if we just stay, just let me show you, I'm sorry for it all." Nat pulled him up and kissed his mouth.

Jonathan twisted his face away. "No!" he cried. "Stop it. Let me *go.*"

"Please, Jonny," Nat said, sobbing, as he dragged him toward the mat. "You belong to me, and me to you. Just be with me, and you'll see, and everything will be right."

"No!" Jonathan shouted, squirming and kicking. "Stop!"

Nat pushed him onto the mat. "Don't, Jonny, don't," he said, tears running down his face. "You'll see, we'll be like we were, it will all be good again. It has to be." He pinned Jonathan's arms above his head and straddled his hips. "I love you," he said, his voice breaking.

Jonathan squirmed under Nat's weight, but couldn't get free; for the first time that night he was truly frightened. He pulled and twisted, but couldn't break loose. Nat bent down, his breath reeking of liquor, and kissed him hard, pushing his head into the blanket. Nat shifted his grip slightly, holding both of his arms in one hand, and when he started fumbling with the sash of his robe with the other, Jonathan panicked. He bucked and heaved, trying to sit up. Nat shoved him back with his free hand, then continued pulling at the knot in the sash. It came loose; Nat tore the robe back and fumbled at the nightshirt beneath it. Jonathan lurched, terrified, and pulled one arm free, striking at Nat, trying to shove him away. Nat hit him again.

"Don't, Jonny," Nat sobbed. "Don't make me hurt you." He ripped open the nightshirt. "Just let me love you again, please, God." He pulled at belt of his own pants.

"No!" Jonathan screamed. "Let me go! Don't touch me." He wrenched his arms free and beat at Nat's face. Nat reared back, and with a heave, Jonathan tore loose and tried to crawl away. Nat fell on him, crying, and pinned him to the mat, pulling at his clothing.

"Just love me," Nat cried. "For the love of God, for us, for me, Jonny, let me love you!"

Jonathan screamed when Nat entered him. The pain ripped through his body, making his legs go numb and burning up through his gut in increasing waves. He screamed again when Nat pulled out and thrust in again, a tearing, burning, blinding pain. He scrabbled at the mat, trying desperately to pull away, to get away, to escape, but Nat gripped him tightly by the shoulders and pulled him back, thrusting again and again, sobbing as he did, and saying over and over, "Just be mine, be mine, be mine again," in a hideous, ripping repetition.

He made one last effort, shoving back against Nat, trying to topple them both over backward, but he was weak and numb from the repeated assault. Nat hit him again and he collapsed, his face driven into the coarse straw-filled cloth. Nat held him down by the neck, sobbing louder, begging him not to fight, not to leave him, not to end it, end them, end everything, each time driving him into the ground.

He struggled weakly, but there was no fight left in him, and he started weeping too, softly, helplessly, lost and terrified. The pain had passed to numbness, and he felt little except the impact of Nat's hips on his buttocks, and the grinding of the mat against his face. He wept, whimpering, "No, no, please, no," and feared he would die before it ended.

Nat shuddered and cried out as he spent himself inside him, and Jonathan sobbed and clutched at the cloth. Nat fell on top of him and lay there, breathing heavily. Jonathan lay still, too numb to move, terrified that anything he did would spark another attack. He felt Nat start shaking, and then, with a convulsive howl, roll off him. He wept quietly as he heard Nat stagger around the chamber, screaming. Crockery shattered against stone, and the shards and drops of water sprayed across him. He moved feebly, curling into a ball and covering his head.

For a brief, ghastly moment, the room was silent. Then he heard footsteps slurring across the floor, and felt Nat drop on his knees next to him. He shuddered, but when Nat touched him gently on the shoulder, he screamed and recoiled, clutching the rags of his night shirt around him, his back against the rough stone wall.

Nat knelt on the edge of the mat, his face twisted in pain and streaked with tears, dirt, and blood. "Oh, God," he said, "what have I done to you, love, what have I become?"

"Go away," Jonathan whispered.

"No," Nat said, and crawled toward him. "Let me help you."

"Go away!" Jonathan screamed. "Never come near me!" He grabbed at the second jug and hurled it at Nat, striking him in the face. *"Go away,"* he screamed again.

Nat fell back on the floor and lay there, weeping, before slowly crawling across the chamber to the entry. Clawing at the stones, he pulled himself upright, and turned and looked back. Blood trickled from a gash on his forehead.

"I," Nat said, and choked. "I'm sorry."

"Go away," he sobbed.

Nat picked up a lantern and stumbled out of the chamber into the darkness.

CHAPTER 13

The chamber stank of liquor and shit and blood. Jonathan didn't know how long he lay curled on the mat, shaking and crying, but when one of the candles guttered and went out, he pushed himself to his knees. He felt his bowels loosen, and he frantically pulled up his robe and shirt, and then squatted as they emptied themselves on the floor. He staggered to his feet and fell against the wall. His head spun, and he stumbled and fell to his knees and vomited. He crawled across the floor, cutting his hands on the shards of crockery, until he reached the lantern. It felt light, as if it had little fuel left. He fought off another wave of nausea to stand, and leaned against the wall. He had to get back to the house, he had to bathe, he had to hide what had happened to him. He had to hide.

He wasn't certain he could make it to the entrance.

He stumbled toward the passage and stepped on a piece of the broken crockery and fell, barely keeping from smashing the lantern on the ground. Groping in the shadows and under the blankets, he found his slippers and pulled them on; his foot was bleeding from the cut. Clutching the lantern, he crawled across the room and into the short tunnel to the main passage.

He stopped at the entrance, terrified that Nat was waiting for him. He held his breath, listening, but heard nothing. Slowly, cautiously, he peered around the edge of the stones.

The candle at the bend in the passage still burned, and he could see nothing. He crept into the main passage, and, hugging the wall, made his way toward the entrance. The candle there had burned out, and he froze, listening, but again heard nothing but the soughing of the wind across the tunnel's mouth. He chanced the lantern, and the tunnel was empty.

He crawled into the warmth of the outdoors and drew the clean air of the night into his lungs in great, heaving gasps. After the fœtor of the cave it felt like a plunge into icy cold water, clean and astringent. He lay face down in the soft green turf, clutching the grass and weeping softly. He could think no coherent thought except that he had to get away; the horror of the assault had numbed his mind as the blows had his body.

A rustle in the grass near him jolted him to his feet, but he could see no one in the dim circle of lamplight. His heart raced, and though he thought it unlikely that Nat would return, he could not chance that he might.

He quickly lost himself amongst the stone walls and pits on the hill top, stumbling over rocks and low-lying shrubs and wandering through the maze of tumbled stones that made up the old village. Though he knew the place was no larger than the farmstead itself, he could not seem to find his way out; each path seemed to double back on itself, or lead to a blank wall. The lantern did him little good, but he clung to it, the one island of light in a sea of darkness. Finally, by chance rather than design, he came upon the opening in the ring wall of the village that opened to the fields beyond.

He staggered down the hill, concentrating on putting one foot before the other, numbly avoiding all thought except those governing the simple motions of walking. The trek across the fields seemed an endless nightmare. Owls called in the trees and hedgerows, and small creatures rustled through the tall grass; every sound terrified him, and at each he crouched in the grass, covering the lantern's light until silence again surrounded him. He crawled over the stiles separating the fields, and squeezed through narrow gaps in the hedges, losing a slipper in one and unable to find it, even with the lantern's light.

He moved even more cautiously when he struck the footpath to the ford. He could find his way home now, he was certain, but the path ran near old lady Bannel's cottage, and he didn't wish to be seen by anyone before he could sneak into the farmhouse. He entered the belt of trees by the river, and crept from tree to tree, as silently as possible, hiding at every imagined sound or sight.

He crouched in the underbrush near the stream; the log bridge was the only way across, and he was almost too frightened to take it. Though only ten feet long at most, he would be utterly exposed and have no way to escape, should anyone chance to be out this late and come upon him. When he finally nerved himself to cross, he clutched the rail, barely lifting his feet from the log, so as not to risk his balance. Caution availed him nothing. A bat or some hunting night bird fluttered by his head, and he gasped and spun, lost his balance, and fell into the stream below.

The stream was low with the season, but the chill of the water struck him like a blow, and he lost his grip on the lantern. He landed on his knees in the shallows, and, terrified at the noise he'd made, floundered quickly back to the shore and ducked under the overhanging bank. He shivered there, listening for any sound above the rippling of the water over stones, but when he heard nothing, he cautiously crept out into the stream again.

The ravine was drowned in utter darkness; the blackness of the moonless night was complete under the canopy of the trees and brambles that overhung the streambed. The water at midstream rose to his knees, and he bent quickly and scooped some and rinsed his face. The cold stung the cuts, but he felt better and scooped more. He scrubbed his neck and hair, trying to wash the smell and the blood out of them. He pulled open his robe and nightshirt, and splashed water on his chest and stomach and legs, rubbing them violently, trying to get the scent out of them, the feel of the mattress ticking off of his skin, the feel of Nat holding him down out of his mind.

He fell to his knees and ducked his head completely under the water, shaking with the cold, but desperately wanting to be clean. He scooped up sand and mud from the stream bottom, and scoured his arms and chest, his legs, and his buttocks. He realized he was crying again, but couldn't remember when he had started, or if indeed he had ever stopped. Sobbing harder, he scooped more mud, and sand, and pebbles, and rotting leaves and sticks, anything that might make him clean. He scrubbed feverishly at his face, shoving it below the surface to rinse it, only to start again, face, chest, back, every inch he could find or reach, then going under, and wailing each time he broke the surface.

Light fell on his face, and he staggered back, falling in midstream. Someone stood on the bank before him, holding up a lantern. He clutched at his robe and scrambled for the far bank, and the figure held up the lantern to show his face. It was Justus Bannel.

Not knowing what to do, he cowered against a tree stump on the opposite bank, too frightened to run in any direction. Justus took a step onto the bridge and Jonathan panicked; he tried to claw his way up the bank to the top, but Justus stopped and held out his hand, palm forward. Jonathan froze; Justus gestured for him to follow, walked a few feet up the path, and waited.

He hesitated. All he wanted was to be in his room, in bed, with the door and windows locked and bolted. He didn't want to see anyone, to talk to anyone. Justus—massive and silent, an unknowable force—terrified him.

Justus retreated a few more steps and held both hands low, again palms out, and again gestured for him to follow. Jonathan took one tentative step across the stream, then another, and Justus smiled and gestured again.

He reached the other side of the stream and started to climb out, clinging to the bushes and tree roots that projected from the bank. He struggled and slid back, and Justus stepped toward him. He panicked again and scrambled back across the stream, trembling against the far bank once more.

Justus stopped immediately. He placed the lantern on the path, and, again holding both hands out, backed away from it. When he reached the edge of the circle of lamplight, he stood, hands folded, and waited.

Warily, Jonathan waded across the stream again and climbed the bank. He crouched on the path, afraid to reach for the lantern or to get any closer to the bigger man, but when Justus retreated a few more steps, he followed, and picked up the lantern. Justus nodded and pointed to himself, then pointed down the path. He gestured that Jonathan should follow, then walked slowly away.

Holding the lamp more like a weapon than a light, Jonathan trailed behind him. The cut on his foot throbbed, and he couldn't walk quickly, but he also didn't want to be too near Justus if he had to try to escape him. He kept his distance, but followed Justus over the small ridge and down the footpath toward the cottage.

When Justus reached the yard, he didn't go through the small gate at the back, but circled around front. Jonathan hurried after him, to keep him in sight, but Justus was standing waiting by the front gate when Jonathan limped around the corner. He opened the gate and walked up the path to the front door. He patted the door, and gestured for Jonathan to follow.

Jonathan stood at the gate, irresolute, then shook his head and put the lantern down. He backed away, but Justus opened the door and stepped through. The room inside glowed with faint lamplight, and Jonathan could see a fire burning in the hearth. Justus stepped back farther and held his hand out and down, inviting Jonathan in.

Jonathan took a timid step forward, then another; Justus smiled and nodded, then turned and walked over to the fireplace. Jonathan picked up the lantern, and cautiously crept up the garden path to the doorway. The scent of turf smoke and herbs wafted out on the warm night air, and the smell of cakes or bread recently baked. Jonathan sniffed, stepped onto the threshold, and looked into the room.

The old woman sat in a chair beside the fireplace, and Jonathan darted back into the darkness. Justus, he believed, meant him no harm, but his fear of the woman overwhelmed him, and he retreated a few paces toward the gate. He stood in the middle of the path, torn between the warmth of the fire and its possible comfort, and the powerful need to be home and hidden. When neither Justus nor his mother moved or spoke, he crept forward to the doorway again, and peered around the jamb.

"Come in, child," Mrs. Bannel said in a low, quiet voice. "There's food and drink if you wish, or quiet and warmth if naught else."

Jonathan shook his head and huddled against the door. He was frightened of being indoors and having no escape, particularly here, with people he didn't know and whom he didn't understand.

"Do as you wish, child," Mrs. Bannel said gently. "But you're welcome here, now and always." She looked at Justus and made a motion with her hand, and he nodded and left the room. Jonathan stayed in the doorway, and in a few moments Justus returned with a large kettle, which he placed near the fire. He left again, and Jonathan heard the splash of water. Justus returned with a bucket, which he poured into the kettle, then left and returned with another. He hung the kettle over the fire and retreated to the far corner of the room.

Mrs. Bannel rose—Jonathan retreated a step—and lifted a large crockery mug off the shelf. Without even looking at him, she placed it on the table and crumbled some herbs into it. She lifted a tea kettle out of the coals and poured the steaming water into the cup, and replaced the kettle in the fire. Crossing to a battered old wooden cupboard, she took out a round of cheese. She cut a several small slices and placed them on a dish and laid it on the table. She picked up a poker and lifted out a small door set in the bricks of the fireplace, set it down, and drew out a loaf of bread, which she sliced and laid with the cheese.

The yeast smell, stronger now, enticed him, and he sidled into the room, his gaze flicking between Mrs. Bannel and Justus. She paid him no attention at all, but set about replacing the oven door, and Justus nodded toward the table. Keeping close to the walls, he slipped around the room and into the chair.

The bread was warm and fresh, and he crammed it into his mouth, surprised at how hungry he was. Though it hurt to chew, he finished the slice quickly, washing it down with sips from the mug, which, to his confusion, didn't contain tea, but a bitter liquid, flavored with mint. The cheese was hard, and difficult to eat; he pushed it aside and reached for another piece of bread.

Mrs. Bannel sat in the chair opposite him, and he reared back, startled. "Finish," she said, "and drink. It will help the pain."

He ate a second slice of bread and pushed the plate away. He started as Justus approached him, but the big man stopped several feet from him and held out a blanket. Jonathan took it and wrapped it around his own shoulders, holding it close around his neck as he sipped from the mug; the hot liquid warmed him, and his shivering lessened. Justus sat next to the fireplace.

"Will ye let me look at ye, Mr. Williams," Mrs. Bannel said softly, "and tend to your cuts?"

Jonathan looked at her sharply, and she returned his gaze calmly. He shook his head.

"I know that you're probably more accustomed to doctors and such," she said in a conversational tone, "but I can bandage a cut as good as the next, and perhaps better than some." She rose, and Jonathan clutched the mug tightly, ready to throw it if she approached him, but she simply crossed to the cupboard and took out a bottle and several crockery pots. "I'll not try to force you, no, but such cuts and bruises as you have might turn bad." She laid the pots out on the table and returned to the cupboard. "Be certain when ye get back to Trevaglan that you have Mr. Penhyrddin call a doctor for ye. He'll be wantin' to himself, no doubt, when he talks to ye on the morrow." She took a bundle of white cloth out of the cabinet and laid it on the table.

Jonathan put the mug down. He hadn't thought of that. He was no doubt scraped and bruised, and if he came down to breakfast in such a state, his cousin was certain to ask questions and insist on a doctor. He started shaking again, frightened of the questions the doctor would ask; he didn't know how he would answer them, or if he could avoid them. He looked up at her.

"Shall I see to ye here, then?" she asked. "I'll send word with Justus to Mr. Penhyrddin that I've done so, and he'll not bother with a doctor, lest I say."

Jonathan nodded.

"Come sit by the fire here, then," she said, and moved a chair. He stood, steadier on his feet than he had been, and sat in the chair. She lit a candle in a holder, and gently took his chin in her hand. He flinched at her touch; she withdrew her hand and waited. He nodded, and she again touched him gently, turning his face first one way, then the other. Then she stood upright.

"'Tisn't good," she said, "but 'tisn't bad as it looked at first. Much of it's dirt, and we need to get you washed." She stepped back. "Are ye hurt elsewhere?" she asked.

He hesitated, then nodded.

"Then I'll need to look," she said, "and we'll need to bathe you."

He shook his head violently, appalled at the concept of undressing in front of a woman, and looked away, unable to meet her eye.

"I understand," she said, and he looked back at her. She seemed neither offended nor even concerned. "Would ye let Justus help ye, then? I'll wait in the other room."

He stood abruptly, knocking over the chair, and backed away. Embarrassing as disrobing in front of her would have been, to be alone and naked in a room with Justus—or any man—terrified him. He couldn't do it . . . and then realized he would have to do just that, should his cousin insist on a doctor. He stopped, torn between terror and mortification, unable to move.

"Ye wouldn't be the first man I've seen down to the skin," Mrs. Bannel said, "and like as not you won't be the last. I shan't look for lookin', Mr. Williams."

Clutching the blanket even more tightly, he nodded quickly—*best to have it done, and done at once,* he thought—and was surprised when she drew near to see that tears glistened in her eyes. He had thought her incapable of shedding them.

"We'll close the door," she said, "but we'll leave it off the latch, and you can leave any time ye need." She touched his shoulder gently. "Ye're safe now, child."

His throat closed, and he felt a cry building in his chest. He fought it, but when the tears started to run down his cheeks it burst forth in great wracking sobs; he couldn't move, and his entire body shook with his weeping. Mrs. Bannel took him gently by the arm and led him to a chair, and he put his head in his arms and cried.

She was unexpectedly gentle with him across the next hour, undressing him slowly, and waiting whenever he reacted or objected, and then proceeding when he was ready for her to do so. It was an hour of humiliation and comfort blended in equal parts; the embarrassment at disrobing assuaged by the warmth of the water and soap she used to bathe him and the sting of the ointments she rubbed on his injuries. He stayed close to the fire and its warmth, and moved as she instructed him, turning when she asked, standing and sitting when she required.

Her manner was matter of fact, without a shred of false sympathy or condescension; he felt at one point that she would probably have treated an injured horse with the same deftness of hand and steadiness of voice as she did him, and under their influence he slowly relaxed and felt, as she had said, safe.

She spoke little save to explain to him what the ointments were she was using, and instructing him which of his cuts were the more serious and why. She said she would send some pots with him, so that he might care for them himself until they were healed, but if he should need her, he had but to send word and she would come at once.

When she was finished, she wrapped the blanket around him and sat him by the fire. She poured a small amount of liquid from the bottle into a glass and handed it to him.

"'Tis hawthorn berry and honey wine," she said, "and it will keep you warm on the walk home." He took it and sipped; it was both sweet and pungent, and smelled of summer nights. She sat opposite him, and folded her hands on the table. "Will ye tell me now as to what happened to ye?"

He looked at her dark eyes, in which dwelt no sign of tears now, just watchfulness and a hard, firm question. He knew he could not tell her, could never tell her or anyone what had happened to him. He had no idea what he would tell his cousin in the morning, how he would explain his absence or his injuries, but he had no intention of telling the truth. As for now, he looked away from the old woman and shook his head.

She said nothing, and the silence lengthened between them. He felt her wishing him, willing him to explain as surely as if she had been leaning over him and asking him over and over the same question, but he refused to answer, or even to acknowledge her stare.

"Well, then" she said finally, "if ever comes a time ye will, just come, and I'll hear what ye'll tell me." He looked back at her and, after a moment, nodded.

She rose. "Ye can borrow a Justus's shirt and breeches t'get ye home. Shoes also, and though a sorry fit they'll be on ye, 'tis better than sendin' ye home wrapped in a blanket." She looked at Justus and pointed to the ceiling, and touched her arm. He nodded, and climbed the ladder and through the trap. "I don't know whether I'll be able to wash the dirt and such out of your things," she said, lifting them off the hook by the fire where they had been hanging. "But I'll send them to ye . . ."

"Burn them," Jonathan said.

She turned and looked at him, and slowly inclined her head. "Aye. Perhaps 'tis best so."

Justus climbed down the ladder, carrying a bundle of cloth. The clothes were ridiculously large on him, and he had to tie the waist with a length of cord to keep the trousers on. The boots were impossible; in the end she wrapped his feet in lengths of cloth and tied them, as it was but a short walk down the lane to Trevaglan.

When he was dressed, she tied a small bundle of pots with the different ointments in them, and then wrapped it in a sling he could wear over his shoulder, rather than chance dropping them on the walk home. He clung to the blanket the entire time, and when he reluctantly returned it at the doorway, she shook her head.

"Wrap up in it warm and safe," she said. "Justus will see ye safe home. If ye need me to come, have Mr. Penhyrddin send word, or come yourself. Come after dark, if ye wish none to know."

"Thank you for your kindness," he said, and, after her nod, walked to where Justus stood by the gate, holding the lamp.

They saw no one on the short walk down the lane to the farm, and no lights shone in the farmhouse or the outbuildings. His window still stood open, and he quickly scrambled over the sill and into his room. He struck a match, and lit the lamp sitting on the chest of drawers, and stood for a moment, disoriented; he had somehow expected it to be different, changed, destroyed, but of course, it was none of those things. He looked at the clock on the mantel. He had been gone a little more than five hours.

Someone rapped on the windowsill, and Jonathan whirled, horrified, but it was Justus. He touched his forehead with his hand; Jonathan nodded, and Justus disappeared into the night.

He crossed quickly to the window and closed and bolted the casement, then locked the shutters and drew the curtains. He undressed quickly and put on clean undergarments and a nightshirt, and stuffed Justus's clothing under the bed. He'd find a way to send them back in the morning, or, God forbid, take them himself. He crawled under the covers and blew out the lamp.

What am I to do? he thought. How could he explain the injuries? And how in the world would he face Nat? He couldn't avoid him forever, he knew, though if he stayed in the house he would run much less risk of chance encounters. He doubted Nat would try to speak to him again, but he didn't know nor could he think what to do should they meet again face to face.

The horror and ruin of all that they had been beat at him. Had he brought it on himself, he wondered, mocking Nat as he had? Had they been doomed to such tragedy from the beginning? Was this God's punishment on them both for their sin, the magnitude of the punishment matching the joy they took in committing it, their foolishness in thinking that they had fooled Him as well as the people around them?

He didn't know.

He lay awake, dry-eyed and numb, through the chiming of the hours, and the few hours of darkness left him slipped away. He grew more frightened as those brief hours passed; discovery waited with the day, and he didn't know what waited with it. Seven o'clock passed, then eight. No light entered his room, and he lay in the warm, close darkness, dreading the moment when someone would finally call for him. At half an hour past eight he heard footsteps approaching his door, and discovery was upon him.

The knock was brisk and abrupt, and not the quiet tapping he had anticipated. Confused, still uncertain, he didn't answer, and the person knocked again, harder this time. Again he didn't answer, hoping that whoever it was would assume he'd gone out, and leave him more time. But the door opened.

"Jonathan?" Penhyrddin asked. "Are you still in bed?" Jonathan could see him outlined against the dim light from the corridor, but he didn't answer. "Jonathan," he said again, his tone urgent. "Wake up."

"I'm awake," he answered, his voice shaking.

"I have to speak to you," Penhyrddin said, crossing to the window and pulling back the curtains. "Good God, you have the shutters locked."

"Don't," Jonathan said desperately as Penhyrddin fumbled at the catch. "Please leave them closed."

"Don't be foolish," Penhyrddin said, and laid back the shutters. "I have to speak to you and can't —" Penhyrddin stopped and stared at him, a look of distress growing on his face. "Dear God boy, what in heaven's name has happened to you?"

"I . . . I fell," he said.

"Fell?" Penhyrddin repeated. "Fell?"

"Yes . . . I . . ." Jonathan stammered, "I went for a walk again last night, and I . . . I f-fell."

Penhyrddin glanced at the door, then looked back at Jonathan. "Stay right here," he said. "Don't move, don't leave this room, and above all, don't answer the door for anyone but me." He crossed the room quickly and left, closing the door behind him.

Jonathan stared at the door in confusion. Of all the responses he could have imagined, this was perhaps the last. Had he questioned him more closely about where he had been, he would have been hard pressed to have answered. Had Penhyrddin reprimanded him for not taking greater care as he had warned earlier, he would have been contrite. But this precipitous departure and the peculiar warning not to leave the room alarmed him. He threw back the bedclothes and crossed to his mirror.

It was worse than he had imagined. The left side of his face was swollen, dragging the side of his mouth down. A livid reddish-purple bruise under his eye reached halfway down his cheek, and a cut ran back from the corner across his temple. Blood, red and shocking, filled one side of his eye. His lip was cut, and an abrasion discolored part of his forehead. Small cuts and scrapes covered his face, and his skin was red and mottled.

He had no idea why it didn't hurt. He reached up and touched his cheek, then his eye, and finally his forehead. The mark on his forehead was sensitive, and once he had noticed it, ached dully, but the rest was simply numb—hideous to see, indeed, but strangely free of pain.

He looked at his hands. They, too, were covered with miniscule cuts and scrapes, as well as deeper cuts on the palms, and dark bruises circled his wrists. Shaking, he unbuttoned his nightshirt; his entire body was similarly marked.

He heard footsteps in the hallway again, and scrambled back into his bed, pulling his blankets up around his neck. Penhyrddin walked in without knocking and locked the door behind him.

"Where were you last night?" Penhyrddin asked without preamble.

"I . . . I was out, as . . . as I do, walking," Jonathan said.

"Where?" Penhyrddin asked. "And where did you fall?"

"I . . ." Jonathan thought furiously. He couldn't say exactly what had happened, clearly, but had to say something. He had to lie, and lie convincingly.

"Quickly, boy, this is important."

"I walked up and behind the house, to . . . to the hill where the bonfire was," he said in a rush. "I fell, I, coming back over one of the walls." This was thin, he knew, but he couldn't think of anything better.

"Were you anywhere near the cliffs?" Penhyrddin asked.

"The cliffs?" Jonathan asked, his astonishment genuine. "No . . . I . . . no, I was back in the hills."

Penhyrddin's tension eased slightly. "Did anyone see you?"

Should I say? he wondered, utterly confused. If he lied, and Mrs. Bannel sent word asking about him, his cousin might question him more closely about how he came by his injuries. "Yes," he answered, and the older man stiffened.

"Who?" he said harshly.

"Mrs. Bannel," Jonathan said. "And her son. I . . . I was lost after I fell, and he found me, and she took . . . took care of my cuts."

Penhyrddin exhaled. "Then that's good."

"Sir," Jonathan said, "what has happened?"

"I have some very bad news," Penhyrddin replied, taking the chair and sitting by the bed. "It will be particularly upsetting to you, I am afraid. Two men from the farm found Nat Boscawen this morning. He had fallen from the cliffs below the farm and into the sea. He was drowned. They found his body on the beach. I don't know any easy way to tell you."

"Oh," Jonathan said, looking at his hands. "Oh."

Nat? Dead? That wasn't possible. Of course he was alive. He'd been all too terribly alive last night. He couldn't be dead.

"I know you two were great friends," Penhyrddin said, "and this is a terrible shock to you, and to everyone."

"Yes," Jonathan said blankly. "It is."

Nat couldn't have fallen off the cliffs, even drunk as he was. He'd been worse; Jonathan has seen him so himself. It wasn't possible.

He looked up. "Are they certain?"

Penhyrddin frowned. "Yes, they are. Quite certain. Why do you ask?"

"It just doesn't seem possible."

Penhyrddin's expression eased again. "I know. It's difficult when one so young is taken, and so unexpectedly."

"Yes."

His head felt light, as if he was going to faint, and a numb, sick feeling spread from his stomach to his throat, and choked him. *Dead. Nat. Dead and cold on the rocks. It couldn't be.*

Penhyrddin sat back. "The funeral services are in two days' time," he said. "Given your friendship, it is natural that you would want to attend—"

"No," Jonathan said sharply, looking up. "No. I don't know that I should like to."

Penhyrddin looked taken aback by the vehemence of Jonathan's tone. "Indeed," he said. "I was going to say, perhaps, that given your injuries, it might be better if you stayed at home." His eyes narrowed slightly. "Are you not in the least interested in what happened?"

"Do you know what happened?" Jonathan asked. Nat was dead. Dead. *Why are you doing this to me?* he thought frantically. *Why prolong this?*

"To a degree," Penhyrddin replied. "He had been drinking in the village last night, a celebration, no doubt, of his coming nuptials. Drinking rather heavily, it would seem."

Jonathan flinched. "And then?" he asked. He didn't want to know, couldn't bear to hear, but he was desperate to have this interview over.

"And then, later, he said he had to leave, and struck off, so the men said, in the direction of the farm." Penhyrddin leaned in. "Are you certain you didn't see him?" he asked urgently. "See him, or anyone else?"

"No, cousin," Jonathan said desperately. "Please. I didn't."

Penhyrddin bit his lip. "Were you anywhere near the cliffs last night? Any time at all?"

Jonathan shook his head violently. "No," he said. "No. I never went near them."

Penhyrddin nodded. "Very well, then." He rose, and tucked the chair back under the desk. "Dear God, I'm sorry, with all of this I didn't even think. You look, quite honestly, terrible. Are you in very great pain? Please forgive me."

"No," Jonathan said. "I . . . I quite understand. A little fall and some bruising is nothing in comparison." *In comparison to Nat. Dead. Lying broken on the rocks by the sea.*

"This is more than a little bruising. I'll send to Penzance for the doctor and have him look at you."

"No," Jonathan said quickly. "I don't need a doctor. Mrs. Bannel said she thought not, and that you could send for her, if I should need any assistance."

"Are you certain?"

"Yes," Jonathan said. "I'm quite certain. I frankly would prefer that no one see me looking like this."

Penhyrddin nodded. "As you wish. I quite understand. I'll bring you some breakfast myself, in that case," he said. "We're making shift with a woman from the village. Pritchard and Cook are both mourning, of course."

"Yes," Jonathan said. "Of course." 'Me Gran', Nat had always called her, and now with another child to mourn. "Is there anything I can do?"

"No, but thank you," Penhyrddin said by the door. He looked suddenly weary. "We will manage quite well, I'm sure. Rest, and we'll talk more later this afternoon."

Jonathan lay back after Penhyrddin had closed the door. Nat was dead. The enormity of it overwhelmed him. He thought back to his shock when he had received word that his mother had died, and it seemed distant and grey. He had wept, he remembered, and had mourned, but he couldn't recall if he had felt this enormous, soul-numbing cold. He couldn't imagine it. Dead. Fallen from the cliffs. Dead.

Fallen.

He started to tremble. The last thing Nat had said, before he left him there in the cave, was that he was sorry. The last thing *he* had said, was for Nat to go away. To go away.

Nat couldn't have. He never would. He would never, no matter how desperate, or unhappy, or wracked with remorse, take his own life.

I'm sorry.

Go away!

He couldn't think of that, wouldn't, but instead would put it from his mind. He wouldn't think at all, he wouldn't feel, he would simply—

He stared up at the ceiling, his eyes dry and burning.

He spent the next two weeks so, rarely leaving his room, except to bathe or use the necessary, or when his room needed to be cleaned. In the latter case, he would retreat to a bedroom on the second floor and waited until all was complete. His cousin gave out the story that he had influenza, and he used this to cover the time until his departure for Cambridge.

Rose Pritchard and Cook returned to Trevaglan after the funeral, but he never saw them prior to his departure. Which of them cleaned his room, he did not know, nor did he care; he spent his time trying to read, or simply staring listlessly about the room. He never looked out the windows no matter where he was; on one side of the house lay the hills, and he couldn't bear to look at them, and the other the sea. He was trapped between them, between his agony and his loss, and he couldn't look either in the face.

They left Trevaglan before dawn the day of his departure; Penhyrddin drove the cart himself, and Jonathan's face had healed enough that the worker who held the horse while he came from the house couldn't see the slight discolorations or scabs that remained. His eye itself was still fiercely red, but even that was beginning to fade.

The night before he had slipped from the house and walked down to the low spot in the cliffs, where the rocks overhung the water, and there cast a small bundle into the sea. In it he had wrapped all the straw dollies Nat had left on the windowsill that summer; he had saved every one, except those that appeared the last three nights. With them were some shells, a dried flower, a small twig with a leaf—remembrances he had collected and treasured, tucking them in the top left drawer of his chest of drawers. The photograph of the two of them he had burned in the grate in his room. He had put it in the fire face down, unable to look at it again, unable to watch them both disappear in the flames. All that was missing was the ring; he had searched for it when it was missing from the drawer, thoroughly searched the entire room, but never found it.

Cornwall 1906

"And now he's come back," Mrs. Bannel said.

"You can't possibly believe that," Jonathan said, startled into incivility.

He had methodically told her all of the strange occurrences that had transpired since their arrival, much as Langsford had so lightly listed them after the accident with the cart. He also explained the meaning behind the items he had found—the straw dollies, the photograph, and the ring—trying at first to be reticent, but gradually sacrificing discretion for the need to tell someone what had happened that summer, and though he didn't like the old woman, though she unsettled him still with her silences and her piercing questions, there was no one whom he trusted more to keep his secrets.

"I don't know as how my believing is the question," she said, "or if you believing is."

"I believe in many things," he said, "but I cannot say I believe that ghosts exist."

"Then why have ye come?" she asked.

He was silent. Why had he come? For explanations of things that seemed to be happening? To safeguard Langsford from someone or something that seemed to wish him harm—this was the reason he had been repeating to himself all afternoon. Or, perhaps, to answer the ages-old urge of Man to confess, to seek expiation and forgiveness, *and,* he thought bitterly, *lay my own ghosts to rest in their graves.*

"Because I need help," he said, "and I don't know where else to turn."

Mrs. Bannel leaned across the table and patted the back of his hand. "'Tis the first wholly honest thing ye've told me, child," she said, "and fair time it is ye did." She sat back. "Now tell me true. Is this haunt real?"

"I . . . no, of course not," he said. "It's coincidence and imagination."

"That wasn't your first thought. What was it?"

He looked away from her and into the fire that burned in the grate, unwilling to meet her gaze. "My first thought was 'I don't know.'" He shook his head and looked back at her. "But it isn't possible."

"The smallest question," she said, "the smallest doubt is all the seed needed to grow the tree. Jealousy between a man and wife, now, needs nothing but a coincidence, a look, and imaginin' for it to become real. Is this so very different?"

"Of course it's different," he said. "One is a subjective emotion, and the other an objective reality."

"Do ye know that?" she asked. "Can ye? Behind those words lies either a world of difference, or no difference at all." She leaned in again. "Was your oath real?"

He felt his face go flush. "Yes," he stammered. "It was."

"And ye spoke those words, as ye said."

"I . . . yes, I did."

"And do ye not believe in the power of words?"

"Nonsense," he said. He stood and walked to the fireplace. "They were just words. Oh, important words, no question, and they meant the world to me then, but they were just words."

"Words have power," she replied. "Power to give life, or to cause death. Never doubt that there's power in words, young man. Your friend can tell ye that, if he's ever seen a judge don the black cap from the bench." She rose. "Enough about words, and enough words. Ye've come to me for help. Do ye wish my help, or do ye not? I'll warn ye, there's a cost."

For the first time that evening, he smiled. "Like in the old stories?" he asked. She nodded. "Then what's the cost for your help?"

"Two things," she said, "one small and one great. First, that when you've done as I instructed, you return and tell me that you've done so. I lay that upon you: Come to me and tell me yourself. Do you agree?"

"Well, yes, of course, if you wish," he said. "I agree."

"Good," she said. "And the second, that when this is done and past, and Nat sleeps quiet at last, as I think ye wish him to do, ye come and live here at Trevaglan Farm, as was intended from the day ye first saw it."

At this he hesitated. He hadn't decided whether he would settle permanently at Trevaglan, though anything holding him in London now seemed irrevocably lost. He knew he could, in all likelihood, simply say yes, and then do as he wished, but somehow, here, in this dark and shadowed room, with the queer old woman standing opposite him by the fire, he knew that he would be held accountable for what he promised, as he was being held to account for what he had promised fourteen years before.

"Yes," he said. "This will be my home."

"Done," she said. "Now, to the business at hand. There's reasons that a haunt comes back, and then there's reasons." She crossed to the cabinet where she'd kept her ointments years ago, and looked over her shoulder as she opened the doors. "Did y'know that they say that the old village is haunted now? And that none dare go near it after darkness, for fear of the uncanny wailing and crying that man hears?"

"No," he said, shaken. "I'd not heard such things."

"I thought not," she replied, taking the jars and herbs and laying them on the table. "But it gives me thoughts now, as it's given me questions before. In this, I'm thinkin', there's two things that have brought the spirit to plague you." She looked at him queerly for a moment. "Or, perhaps, three." She nodded, then went on gathering different items from the shelves, never hesitating at the cubbyholes, deft handed and certain, always picking decidedly from the pile of objects stowed there without searching or pause.

"First," she said, as she sorted the items—candles and herbs, lengths of twine and bits of cloth—on the table into separate piles, "is the one that seems most clear: he did ye great harm, and it haunts him now as he haunts you and yours." She looked at the items, cocking her head. "Hmph." She returned to the shelf. "And that lets us know where ye must go to do what ye must do."

"No," he said abruptly. "That is out of the question." He couldn't go back to the hill. He couldn't go back to that room, that horror, and live it again. It was impossible.

She turned and fixed him with the hard, dark stare that had so unnerved him as a young man. "I never promised that it'd be an easy thing, now did I?" she said. "Such things never are. If ye haven't the strength to face your own past, child, ye haven't the strength nor the right to any future. You've agreed to do what needs to be done, and asked my help. I've given it. The fire is lit, Mister Jonathan, and there's no quenching it now."

"I don't understand why I have to go to a place so abhorrent to me, to appease a ghost that I don't even believe exists," he said, feeling the flutter of panic around his heart.

"Ye don't go to appease," she said. "Ye go to banish, and to lay it." She crossed and laid her hand on his arm. "Ye don't go for him, child. Ye go for yerself." Again, she gave that queer look. "And for those that ye love, and that love ye back."

That I love, he thought. Langsford had taken greater harm than he in all the things that had happened. Should he fail to have the strength of will to see this thing through, and should this be true, against all that was sane and practical, then Langsford was the one at risk, and that was not something he would chance. And, he realized with fear leavened with ironic amusement, he had taken the fatal step of believing it to be true.

"Very well," he said quietly. "I go."

"Second," she said, "is that ye both swore to be bound till death and after—you're certain that those were the words? Ah. And this, ye see, tells us what ye have t'do, when ye get where you need to go."

"I don't understand."

"Of course ye don't, ye great ninny," she said, and for the first time ever he saw her smile, the briefest twitch of a corner of that stern, hard mouth. "If ye did, would ye be here?" She scanned the items on the table again, and nodded. "An oath is a bond, as is marriage, and any such vow. When ye made that oath, ye tied your souls together, and it's that knot that needs t'be cut, to sever the bond that ties ye. A blood bond, no less. Poor fools." She shook her head

"I didn't know," Jonathan said. "I had no idea."

"The young never do."

"I . . . I loved him so terribly," he said, blinking against the tears that burned his eyes.

"I know, child," she said in the same gentle voice she'd used years before. "I saw it then, and I see the ruins of it now. And that's why, when ye asked, I answered."

"What must I do?"

"You have t'cut the knot that binds the two of ye as lovers," she said.

"But . . . I don't know what that is. What do you mean?"

She reached out and took his hand. "You have to cut the knot," she repeated, then turned his hand over and tapped on the underside of his wrist. "You must do it this night, and then you'll be free."

CHAPTER 14

Jonathan pulled his cap tightly down over his head and leaned into the wind. The break in the stone wall was somewhere just ahead, he was certain, though the darkness and the weather made any landmarks all but invisible. He hoisted the satchel with the supplies that Mrs. Bannel had given him and trudged on, keeping the stone wall close on his right.

He'd spend most of the afternoon in the cottage. The old woman had told him precisely what it was she wanted him to do and to say, making him repeat it over and over again until he had it to her satisfaction. He had felt ridiculous at first; words chanted and herbs sprinkled in the flames at specific times, then at the end, the cutting of the cords she had tied about his wrists.

When he had returned to the farmhouse, he'd gone straight to his room, and had laid out his clothes for the evening. He had, to his horror, found another token on his windowsill, but instead of filling him with dread, it had steeled his resolve. He didn't know who had placed it there, or how, no more than he knew how the photograph had appeared for Langsford to discover, but whatever the cause, he was determined to cut it out, to excise it, and to have done with it.

He worried at the cords again, as he'd done through dinner and all the long trek across country. Coarse red twine, they chafed under the cuffs of his shirt and his borrowed oilskin. The rain had settled in shortly before dark, a steady, monotonous drizzle, not enough to require an umbrella, but more than sufficient to cause discomfort. Now and again an icy drop penetrated his clothes and trickled down his back.

The dark grey of the wall gave way to black, and he lifted his lantern; he had reached the gap. He prayed that he could find the opening to the cave itself; he was determined, if he was to do this foolishness, that he would do it properly. Mrs. Bannel had clearly believed every word and action she had taught him, and in the course of the afternoon that belief had infected him, and now held him totally under its sway.

He pushed through the bushes that had grown in the gap, and broke into the ruin itself. "Three rings 'round, then straight on and down," he murmured, and caught himself up short; it was a rhyme Nat had taught him to help him find his way to the fogou when he had to come by himself. The words brought Nat suddenly near, and for the first time, Jonathan was frightened of more than his memories.

The wind seemed less within the enclosure of the walls, and the rain more sullen. The place seemed watchful, filled with eyes. Gritting his teeth, he walked forward until he came to the first low circular wall of what had been a hut, ages before. He circled it to his left, then picked up the second, which he circled to his right. A gap, just a few feet, and then the third, right again. When he reached the break in that wall he walked forward into the darkness and up the hill, holding the lantern high, for all the good the dim flame did. One pace, two, three, four . . .

The ground fell away before him, and he slid down the slight bank. He leaned forward and held out the lantern. There, almost hidden amongst the bushes, lay the mouth of the fogou.

He stood, staring at it, willing himself to move forward, but his body refused. Flesh and bone were at war with mind and thought, and the battle was over, he thought, before it had truly been joined. He couldn't do it. He had been foolish even to agree to it, foolish and superstitious. There was nothing for him to do but go back.

He heard a stone clatter and fall, and he whirled, shuttering the lantern as he did. He stood frozen, but there was no other sound. The sense of watchfulness he'd felt when he first broke into the ruin increased, and he again felt the shiver of fear whisper around him. He turned back to the darkness at his feet. There was no other way out but going through this. He tightened his grip on the satchel and crawled into the tunnel.

The entry passage was shorter than he remembered, and he was into the main passage before he had expected. He scrambled to his feet and opened the shutter on the lantern; the tunnel stretched before him, dark and dank, unchanged in the years since he'd been there, or, indeed, for centuries before. He walked slowly down the center of the way and around the bend. The tunnel was empty.

He stopped again opposite the entrance to the circular chamber. It looked both ominous and curiously devoid of threat—a dark opening to a darker place, and a hole in the wall of an ancient tunnel. Without hesitation, almost without thought, he ducked and walked through, then held up his light.

A bundle of cloth lay against one wall—the tattered and worn remains of the mattress and blankets they'd brought. They'd been scattered about the room, most likely by animals, and smelled of mold and rot. The lamplight glinted on shards of pottery that lay amongst the rags. There was nothing else. He stood in the place of his nightmares, and it was an empty room.

A tear ran down his cheek, and then another. Years spent, fearing a place that held nothing, a great empty chamber of stone, and the only horror in it was in his mind.

He brushed away the tears and put down the lantern and the satchel. He'd come here to do a task. Best to do it, and be done with this place forever.

Langsford squinted into the rain and cursed himself for being a fool.

He had spent the afternoon in his room, vacillating, caught between a frantic urge to escape back to London and a deeper need to stay with Williams. Three times he had crossed the room, determined to walk down the stairs and talk frankly and openly with Williams. I have little to lose, he thought. *When one has nothing, what can one lose?* And three times he had stopped at the door, and then returned to his chair and the book of ghost stories.

Dinner had been queer. He had gone down early, but to his surprise he found Williams was out; Meg said he hadn't returned after leaving to see Mrs. Bannel, shortly after lunch. He fretted in the library until Mrs. Hale called him for dinner. He quickly set aside any thought of conversation. During the meal Williams had been quiet, distracted, and when he had asked a direct question about Mrs. Bannel, had looked at him as if he hadn't known him, or indeed, as if he wasn't even there.

Williams had retired immediately to his bedroom, and Langsford to the library, where Meg, full of prattle and gossip at finding him alone, had served him coffee. He had dismissed her rather brusquely, and was brooding in front of the fire, when he'd heard Williams' door open, and Williams descend the stair. When he heard the front door open, he stole into the hallway in time to see Williams slip out, closing the door behind him.

He'd hurried to the drawing room, and from the window watched Williams walk down the front path and out the gate, then disappear up the lane. Curious, he'd just turned to go back to the library when a light caught his eye; someone crossed the yard from behind the barn, and followed Williams up the lane.

Now thoroughly uneasy, he donned his borrowed mackintosh and hat and followed them both. He was careful to remain unseen—not that anyone could see more than ten feet in this gloom—but was nearly caught when he'd arrived at the high road; the man with the light was standing behind a tree, watching the Bannels' cottage. It was Alec.

Now more confused than alarmed, but increasingly curious, he huddled under the lee of the hedge until the cottage door opened, and Williams appeared in the rectangle of light, carrying a lantern and what appeared to be a sack. He ducked behind the hedge when Williams walked to the gate—he had no idea in the world how he would explain his presence—but when Williams didn't appear, he looked again, just in time to see Alec vanish around the corner of the hedge surrounding the cottage.

He'd followed them both through a ravine, across an extremely perilous bridge, and up through the fields and hedges, only to lose them when he was completely lost himself.

He stood in the rain, debating whether he should press on with little chance of finding them, or re-trace his tracks and return to the farm. A flicker of motion ahead caught his eye, and he instinctively ducked, though none could see him, he was certain. He crept forward, but saw no light; another hedge and a dark field lay before him. He climbed the wall, hampered by his injured wrist, and again caught a flash of movement out of the corner of his eye, but again could see no one. He walked in the direction that the person had gone—or seemed to have gone—and thought to call out, asking direction or help, but stayed his tongue. The night had grown eerie, and whether from reading the tales in the book, or from some atavistic place in his being, he felt the stirrings of fear.

He spun suddenly. Had that been a sound? A sigh? A laugh? Or merely the wind whistling through the hedges he knew lay in that direction? The sense of being watched that had dogged him since coming to Cornwall returned, stronger and more unnerving than it had ever been. Against all reason, he knew that it would be more dangerous and difficult for him to return than to press forward, and he turned his face to the wind, and trudged on.

The ground rose from the fields to the hills, and more than once he slipped in the wet grass and fell to his knees, only to clamber to his feet and keep walking. He no longer thought where he was going, but just walked on, following the will o' the wisp of motion, and fleeing the watchfulness behind him.

Abruptly, a stone wall loomed out of the darkness; tall and ruined, it wasn't a hedge, but something older and larger, a ruined house or building. He thought of the mines that dotted the Cornish countryside, and proceeded more slowly. He followed the wall up the hill, and when it came to an end, he pushed his way through the brush surrounding it, and passed into the open space beyond.

It was the place of his nightmare. A low stone wall curved away before him, just as they had in his dream. He turned to run, but to his horror, he had somehow lost his bearing; instead of the low bushes he expected, the stone wall stood before him, as high as his head, blocking his way. He tried to climb over it, but the stones were slick; his shoes found no purchase on their mossy surfaces, and his single arm could not support his weight. He fell to the ground, pulling one stone with him, narrowly missing being crushed beneath it when it fell.

He tried to follow the circuit of the outer wall back to the opening, but lower walls blocked his path, and, as in his nightmare, he was forced inward, toward the center of the ruins. A scream, distant and muffled, sounded from higher on the hill, and he cowered down behind a wall, every hair on his arms standing on end. Another scream, louder, and then another, louder still, cut through the wind and rain, and he knew, not believed, but *knew* that something walked the ground between the stones, and he felt a growing sense of horror, of dark things moving in the ruins, of spirits called and unleashed—every dark story he'd relished as a child or that had amused him as an adult was upon him, and he groped without thought or direction, searching for an escape.

Jonathan crumbled the herbs Mrs. Bannel had given him and dropped all but a handful of them into the small teapot that bubbled on the spirit lamp before him. He was stiff from kneeling, but as nearly as he could tell, he had done everything as she had directed: lighting the three tallow candles, drawing a circle in the earth floor, saying a brief prayer before each action; folly, he was sure, but he doggedly, mindlessly followed her directions, and with the adding of the rosemary, rue, and dried hawthorn berries to the water, he was almost finished. Feathers—black raven, grey dove, and white swan—lay scattered on the floor around him, and smoke from a small fire of twigs and charcoal filled the air of the chamber. He scattered the last of the herbs into the fire; they sparkled and flared as the flames consumed them, adding their scent to the steam rising from the kettle.

He dug into the satchel and pulled out the last item remaining: a long, narrow dagger in a leather sheath. She had showed it him in the cottage; though it was old and its handle worn, the blade was razor sharp on both sides. He gingerly pulled it from the sheath, and the steel gleamed wickedly in the flickering light. He dipped it in the boiling water, then passed it through the fire. The flames spat and hissed as the water dropped on them. He lifted it before his face—

Nat knelt in the entrance to the chamber, not ten feet away, half in shadow, half in the uncertain light of the candles.

Jonathan's heart lurched, and he staggered back against the rear wall of the chamber. *Not real*, he thought, *this isn't real. He can't harm me, he can't touch me.* He swallowed, and held the knife in front of him; Nat faded back into the shadows.

"In the name of the Father," Jonathan said, his voice shaking, "and of the Son, and of the Holy Spirit, I bid you be gone, back to the grave whence you came, and come never here again to torment those that live. God alone can pardon you; find peace in His mercy, and forgiveness for your sins, and balm for your soul in His grace. In the Father's name, Amen."

Shadows still lurked in the entry, a glimmer of motion.

Sadness and grief almost overwhelmed him, and he clutched the knife tightly. One last task, one more thing to do and to say. He shifted the knife to his left hand, and slid the tip under the cord around his right wrist.

"*Thine for mine, and mine for thine*, I pledged you," he said. "My heart I bound to you, my life I tied to you, my soul I knit to yours." He turned the blade; the edges lay against his wrist and the cord. "Those knots I cut, those ties, I cut, that pledge, I cut, and all that binds us still. Once one, now twain." A tear rolled down his cheek. "I loved you, and I know you loved me, but you're gone, and gone, and gone again, love. Let me go, as I do you." He choked down a sob. "I don't hate you now, Nat, I don't. But I can't love you, and I can't live with this any longer. Farewell, and farewell, and three times farewell. Peace to your soul, and to mine." He slid the knife forward, feeling it scrape against the cord, tight against his wrist.

The thing in the shadows moved.

He pushed back against the wall, sawing desperately at the cord. It parted as Nat stood in the entry, dripping wet, and holding out his hands.

Jonathan screamed and quickly switched the knife to his other hand. Nat stepped toward him, and he screamed again and kicked at the spirit lamp. It tipped over, and the paraffin spilled across the floor, soaking the ragged remains of the blanket. He thrust the knife at the cord on his left wrist and felt the blade slice into his flesh as he desperately cut at the cord. Nat's mouth moved, and he stepped forward again, but if he made any sound, Jonathan couldn't hear for his own screams.

A blue flicker of flame flashed out from the fire, and the pile of rags, soaked with the paraffin, ignited. Nat backed away from the flames, and Jonathan hurled the knife and his lantern at him, and dashed for the entrance. He crawled through and ran blindly up the main chamber. He struck the wall hard, and fell backward, stunned, but crawled forward when he heard rustling sounds in the darkness behind him.

He groped desperately at the walls and sobbed with relief when his hands met emptiness, and he smelled the fresh rain and felt the clean air before him. He crawled out the tunnel and into the night, and staggered to his feet and tried to run, to get away, to flee whatever horror waited under the ground behind him. His head spun, and he felt dizzy, but he staggered on. He tripped and fell, and the breath was knocked from him, but he clawed at the ground and crawled on. The ground dropped away, and he tumbled down the slope, coming to rest against another wall. Clutching at the stones, he stumbled forward a step, then two, but a pit opened before him, and he stepped on empty air and fell into the dark.

Langsford crouched beneath the stone wall. The screams had cut off suddenly, but the ensuing silence was more ghastly than the horror of their sound. He waited, torn, uncertain whether he should find the man screaming or flee into the night.

"Jonathan," he said aloud, and stood.

Jonathan was out there in this nightmare. He—or Alec—was the source of those dreadful sounds, and Langsford couldn't leave, couldn't run, while one or the other was lost in this hell of stone and rain and wind.

He clambered over the wall behind which he had sheltered. The cries had come from farther up the hill, and he climbed and clawed his way upwards, scrambling over the low stone walls and tearing through the bushes. He had no thought but to find him, if he had to search every inch of this maze on his hands and knees. A light appeared suddenly before him, and he fell back with an oath.

"Who's there," a boy cried, his voice cracking with fear.

"Alec?"

"Oh, God, Mr. Langsford-Knight," Alec sobbed, scrambling down to where he lay on the ground. "It's Mr. Williams, sir. He's hurt, and I can't carry him."

Langsford struggled to his feet. "Hurt? Where is he? Take me to him."

"He's here, sir," Alec said, and climbed back up the slope. "He's just here. Can you follow?"

"Of course I can," Langford said. "Hurry, for God's sake."

Hurt. Langsford's heart pounded as he followed Alec around the stones and bushes littering the hillside. *Please God,* he prayed, *don't let him be hurt badly. Let it not be as serious as the boy seems to think. I'll promise anything. Just let him be alive.* Alec paused, then jumped down into one of the shallow pits that littered the ruins and held up the lantern.

Jonathan lay on the ground, on his side, covered with Alec's patched mackintosh. His face was pale in the lantern's light, and his eyes closed. Sick with fear, Langsford knelt next to him and gently turned him on his side. His face was cold, and Langsford tore back the mackintosh and pulled open the coat and shirt underneath.

His heart still beat. It felt weak, distant, but he was alive.

"Help me," Langsford said. "Help me carry him out of here."

He slid his arms under Jonathan's shoulders and lifted, but his wrist gave out, and Jonathan slid back to the ground.

"Run," he said, looking across at Alec. "Fast as you can, but go safely. Get some of the men, and bring them up here. Bring a cart, bring a sling, bring anything you can. Just be quick."

"Aye, sir," Alec said, and dashed away and up the hill.

He spread Alec's overcoat on the ground, and slid Jonathan onto it, then tore off his own and laid it over him. He tucked Jonathan's arms under cover, and felt warmth on his hands. Pulling them back, he held them up to the lantern. They were covered in blood.

"Oh, dear God, no," he said, his stomach knotting. "No, no, no."

He held the lantern close and examined Jonathan's wrists. Both were bloody, but he couldn't tell how badly they were cut. Frantically, he searched his pockets for anything to use as a bandage. His handkerchief he used for what looked the worse of the two, and his tie for the other. He bound them as tightly as he could, then tucked the coat close around him.

"Don't die," he whispered, and brushed the hair back from Jonathan's too-pale face. "Please, please, don't die. I couldn't live if you died. I can't." Desperately, he looked around, knowing that help would be long in coming, but unable to stop himself.

Alec stood at the top of the slope, his shirt reflecting the dim lamplight.

"Damn you to hell, boy!" Langsford shouted. "Don't stand there like a fool. Get help, I said. Go, damn you!"

Alec lifted his hand, and vanished in the darkness.

Trembling with rage, Langsford sank to his knees. If Jonathan died, he would make the boy's life a living hell, him and every member of his family, and all the people on the farm. He turned back, and touched Jonathan's face. How could he have thought of leaving? How could he ever go? How could he live if he lost him now?

Jonathan stirred, and his eyes fluttered open. "Alayne?" he asked. "How are you here?" He slipped his hand from under the coat and touched Langsford's face.

"Don't," Langsford said, his heart in this throat. "Don't move. Alec's gone for help. Don't move."

"I'm so cold," Jonathan said, and his gaze drifted away. "So cold."

"Shall . . . shall I hold you?" Langsford asked. "That might warm you."

Jonathan smiled and closed his eyes. "Yes," he murmured. "Yes, please, I'm so very cold."

Shaking, he gathered Jonathan into his arms, and held him tightly against his body. "I'll hold you until help comes," he said. "I'll keep you warm and safe." He felt Jonathan's breathing deepen. "I'll always keep you safe," he whispered.

Jonathan opened his eyes. "Will you?"

"Yes, Jon. Always. I promise you."

Jonathan smiled again. "I'm glad. I love you so very much. Did you know that?"

Langsford's heart pounded so hard he thought it would tear from his chest. "No," he said quietly. "I didn't know."

"And now you do," Jonathan said. "I'm glad."

"So am I," he said, fighting back tears. "I love you, too."

"You do?" Jonathan asked, his voice barely a whisper.

"Yes," he replied, "I do." And he leaned down and gently, tenderly kissed Jonathan.

Jonathan smiled when the kiss ended. "I always will love you," he said, his eyelids sliding closed. "But I'm so very tired. Will you hold me while I sleep?"

"Yes, Jon," Langsford said, and kissed his forehead. "I will."

Chapter 15

"Will he be all right?" Langsford whispered.

"This one?" the old woman asked, and smoothed the counterpane. "Ye needn't worry about him. Would take more than that to kill him."

Langsford sat on the edge of his chair, unable to relax. He had changed quickly when they had brought Jonathan back to Trevaglan, and hadn't left his side since.

They'd sat huddled under the stone wall for what had seemed an eternity, until Alec had appeared over the edge of the pit with Justus Bannel, who had picked Jonathan up and carried him as lightly as if he had been a child. His mother had met them at the gate as they passed and had gone with them to the house to see to Jonathan's injuries.

Jonathan had been restless at first, stirring and crying out, sometimes with his eyes closed, sometimes wide and staring. He'd batted at the air in front of him, crying out Nat's name, and weeping. Langsford had gone pale at that, and only noticed later that Rose Hale had left the room.

Jonathan had gradually calmed, and he had sent Meg, Alec, and Hale to bed. Justus left shortly after. Mrs. Bannel had stayed, bathing Jonathan's head and murmuring softly. Her touch seemed to calm him, and he slept.

"I'll sit with him," Langsford said, "if you wish to return home. Or you may stay here, if you prefer."

She nodded and straightened. "'Tis a short walk, and Justus will wonder if I've succumbed to your charms, should I not come home until mornin'."

"I . . ." Langsford stammered. "I'm sure he'll not think—"

"Hush, child," she said as she drew her shawl about her shoulders. "I'm but chaffin' ye, and 'tis somethin' I think ye'd best become accustomed to."

He smiled at her as he rose from his chair. "I certainly hope I shall. I cannot thank you enough for what you've done. I don't know what I can ever do to repay you."

She reached up and touched his cheek. "Live long, and dwell in joy, child. 'Tis all I want from thee." She left the room, closing the door behind her.

He sank into his chair. Dwell in joy, she had said. Could he? He knew he couldn't leave the next day—that would have been impossible now, even if Jonathan hadn't made that shattering admission in the ruins on the hill. He couldn't blot the images from his mind: Jonathan, covered in blood, pale, soaking wet on ground, Alec screaming in the wind that he needed help, Jonathan waking and touching his face with that cold, bloody hand and saying . . .

Would Jonathan even remember it?

He watched Jonathan sleep through the deep of the night, the lamplight glowing softly on his face, his hair dark against the white pillows. How could he not love him? But how could he stay? He looked at the rain streaming against the windows. What would his family say, his friends?

"Don't leave me, Alayne," Jonathan said softly.

Langsford turned; Jonathan's eyes were open.

"I . . . no, Jon," he said. "I won't. I'll be here all night if you need me."

"Don't ever leave me," Jonathan said. "I couldn't bear it."

"I'll be here through the week," he said, his throat tight. *Please, don't go any farther.* "I'll wire London and take another week, until you're well."

Jonathan shook his head slightly. "Unless you can tell me you don't love me," he said, "don't ever leave me."

Langsford opened his mouth to speak, but no words came out.

"Last night you said you did," Jonathan said. "Have you forgotten so soon?"

"No," he answered. "I haven't forgotten."

Jonathan smiled. "Nor have I." He held out his hand. "I never will."

Trembling, Langsford took Jonathan's hand in his. "I hope you never do. I'll never stop."

"I'm glad," Jonathan said, his eyes closing. "And we'll never part."

"Never," he said, and held Jonathan's hand while he slept.

Rose pulled the door to the kitchen closed behind her and walked slowly down the passage.

"Nat, don't!" he had cried in his delirium. *"Stop, God, please, stop…"*

What memory had he been reliving? What unnatural thing had he done—had they done—that could be worse than what she first suspected, than what she had known in her heart, that could cause him to cry out so when he so clearly had gone back to that time in his mind? Can it have been worse than that which she relived when the winds howled around the corner of the cottage, and voices cried for her in the night? She would have pitied him, had she not despised him so.

The kitchen was dim, lit only by the one lamp they had left when they had taken him upstairs. Where in God's name had they gone, and to what end? Why was Alec out in the storm with them, to return with that Langsford fool, and Justus Bannel, carrying Williams in out of the night like a soldier carrying a wounded comrade?

She stirred the fire in the stove and moved the kettle to heat more water. Aunt Bannel would want it boiling for her teas and brews, no doubt, to nurse him back to life and to health. Bitterly, she wished her luck with that; he'd lost no small amount of blood and was soaked clear to the skin. If he didn't die of his wounds, he was bound to fall ill, and that would carry him off. She shivered. She'd never wished anyone dead before.

Dead. He would be dead, and maybe, just maybe, her long sorrow would die with him. He had caused it all, brought them all to ruin, and had gone, leaving her with a child in her womb and a husband she'd never wanted. If he had never lived, had never come to the farm, Nat would have never turned from her, and she would never have—

Voices sounded in the passage, and footsteps on the flagged floor.

"Rose," James called. "Will ye be makin' some tea now? We need some for the hero of the day." He entered the room with his hand on Alec's shoulder.

"I'll fix it for him meself," Meg said, bustling in behind them. "We've heaven to thank and your son, Rose, that Mr. Williams and Mr. Langsford-Knight are safe, for certain they'd have never found their way home themselves, had he not been along." She hurried off to the pantry.

"Aye, that we do," James said, clapping Alec on the shoulder. "He brought them home safe."

"Justus it was that brought him," Alec said, blushing. "Mr. Langsford-Knight and me, we couldn't lift him."

"It was good fortune, then, that you found him," James said.

Alec nodded. "He found us, as if he were lookin' for us. I wasn't half way back when I met him comin' through the fields. He knew just where he was goin', as I couldn't tell him anything."

"'Tis his gift," James said. "Justus knows when man or beast is in need, and finds them faster than any."

"I'd like to know what you were doing out there, following them," Rose said.

"I wasn't, Mum," Alec said. "I was comin' in from me chores, when I saw Mr. Williams goin' out. I was worried, so followed him, t' make sure he'd be safe, it bein' night and all."

"What place had ye doin' that?" she asked sharply.

"You . . . you told me to keep eye on them, and to show them places and to keep near," Alec said, looking frightened. "I was just doin' as you said! And . . . and . . . it's lucky I did!"

"It would have been better had ye left him out there t'die," Rose said bitterly.

"Rose!" James said, catching her by the arm. "Keep such thoughts behind your teeth! Mr. Williams is owner and master here now, and I'll not have ye hazard our place here with talk like that."

"I begged you t' leave here before he came," she said fiercely. "We needn't stay and work for that creature and his kind."

"'His kind'?" James said, releasing his grasp. "What foolishness are ye spoutin'? He seems a good man, and one who takes interest in the doin's of the farm. He's naught like ye said before he came, but just as I recall him—bookish, yes, but so was Mr. Penhyrddin, and ye had no quarrel with him."

"I had no quarrel until he died and left us all in the hands of that man upstairs," Rose spat. "Nor with you, save that you're blind to what he is and what he'll do to us all, if he stays here."

"He'll stay here, God willing," James said. "He needs t' be, as well you know."

"We'll see about that," she replied, and turned back to the stove. "We'll just see."

"What have you done, Rose," James said, his voice hushed. "What are ye doin'?"

"I'm doin' naught that concerns you, James Hale," she said. "Old sins cast long shadows, and if he lives in those shadows, there's none to blame but he if they come home to him. If Mr. Williams can't face those sins and leave here, 'tis neither doing nor fault of mine."

"Sins? What sins can he have?"

"Causin' the death of a good man," she said bitterly, "and leaving all here in the wreckage of that death."

"Good man?" James said, scorn evident in his voice. "Nat Boscawen was a troublemaker who got drunk and walked off a cliff. There's your good man for ye."

"Have a care, James," Rose said, her voice low and dangerous. "You'd best not talk on that which ye know naught about."

"I know that he was a rascal and a wastrel who didn't do his fair share of work, and used Williams to get away with it!"

"*Used* him? Used *him*?" she said, spitting in her fury. "You're blind as well as foolish, if that's what ye think."

"Not so blind as you, if you think Nat Boscawen was a good man," James shouted, then mastered himself and laid a hand on Alec's back. "I'm sorry, lad. I didn't mean to cause you grief. I shouldn't talk so."

"It's nothin' I didn't already know," Alec said, resignation evident in his voice. "'Tis no secret to me or anyone. Like as not I bain't the only bastard he fathered hereabouts—"

"No!" Rose said, grabbing Alec's arm and shaking him. "That isn't so. Don't you ever say that again, or anything like! He was a *good* man, and he'd have been a good father to you."

Alec pulled away from her. "I *have* a good father," he said, "and *he's* a good man. You've never spoke of him that sired me, but he wasn't a good man. He did something terrible to Mr. Williams. I don't know what it is, but he spoke of it all the way home. And . . . and Mr. Williams don't like it when I'm around, I can see that, and it's because I look like him. Everyone says so when they think I can't hear them. But I can! I can. And I won't do it anymore. If he hurt Mr. Williams, then I'm glad he's dead and gone. I'm glad, just as I'm glad I don't carry his name."

Rose slapped Alec across the face, hard, and he fell back against the wall, shock clear on his face. "What would you know of it?" she shouted at him. "All I did was for you, and you repay with this, bringing back the man who ruined your father and drove him to his death? And then takin' his side against your own blood?"

"Rose!" James shouted. "Don't be saying such things!"

"What I say to my son and what I don't is no business of yours,

James," Rose said angrily, "not where this is concerned."

"Our son," James said, his jaw clenched.

"*My* son, and well you know it," Rose snapped, "and not a day there is you don't remind me of it."

James's face turned red. "The only one reminds you of that, Rose, is you yourself."

"You and every man and woman in the village and here around," she said, the long anger in her finally boiling over. "There isn't a one of ye that doesn't! If he hadn't died—"

"The best thing Nat Boscawen ever did in his life was die," James shouted, "and if he hadn't have done it you'd know that now, for all the misery he'd have brought ye."

"And how would ye know that, bought man?" Rose asked.

"You watch your tongue, Rose," James said, stepping toward her with his fists clenched.

"What will ye do?" Rose taunted. "Strike me, if ye will, and in front of the boy, and let him see what kind of man ye truly are."

"Mum!" Alec shouted. "Stop it!"

"Go right on," Rose said, grabbing Alec and shoving him at James. "Tell your *son* how ye married his mother and took a dead man's place, and earned fifty pounds in the doin' of it."

The accusation hung in the air like poison and Rose reveled in finally having an object on which to vent her anger and frustration.

"Dad?" Alec asked uncertainly.

James had fallen back a step, his face pale. "I married ye because I loved you, Rose, and for no other reason," he said, his voice shaking. "I always did."

"Ye married me because Penhyrddin paid ye t' do it," Rose said.

"That money was for the child and sits in the bank to this day," James said, his voice rising. "That money will be Alec's when his time comes. You were part of all that talk, and know it well. That wasn't why I married you."

"You married me because your own greed and lust blinded

you to the truth."

"Mum!" Alec cried, tears on his face. "Please stop!"

"Blinded ye to the fact that I wanted another man, and he wanted me. There's not once in all these years that I haven't thought of him while I was layin' with you."

James picked up the old rocking chair and hurled it across the room. "Damn you, Rose!" he shouted. "Damn you t' hell. I've lived fourteen years with Boscawen's ghost in my bed and in my house, and I won't do it no more. You'll sleep no more by my side. You hate this place so? Well then, suffer in it, because I'll no longer have you near me nor my children. You'll sleep in this house this night and every night hereafter, because I'll have none of ye."

"And good riddance to you!" she screamed back. "If there's any good come out of this, it's that I won't have to bear you any more brats. We'll take that money and go, and that's the last of it!"

"No," Alec said.

"What?" she said, shocked into silence.

"I said no. I'll not leave. This is my home, and my place is here. I'll not leave."

"You have no say in it," she said sharply. "You'll go where I say."

"No, he won't," James said, putting his arm around Alec's shoulder. "He stays here with me. He's my son, and I'll not let you take him from me."

"And how do you expect to keep him?" she jeered. "*Your* son! There's not one hereabouts doesn't know the story of his birth, nor how I married you just to give him a name."

"And proud I am that he carries it," James said, "as all around here know, too. He's my son, and so all the church records say. I'll not let you take my son when you leave, and if ye try, I'll have the law on ye."

"No," she said, suddenly frightened. "You can't take him from me. He's my child."

"So are the others that lie sleeping nearby," James said quietly, "and you'd have left them without a thought. I don't know what you've been about these last days, Rose, but you'll do it no longer." He reached down and took Alec's arm. "Come lad. The sins of the father might be visited on the children, but not this time, not if I have any say." He opened the door and looked back at her. "Nor the sins of the mother."

"Alec . . ." she cried.

Alec stood for a moment on the threshold, his tear-streaked face in the lamplight a ghastly, terrifying echo of Nat's the last time she'd seen him. He just shook his head, and closed the door behind him.

She stood in the middle of the kitchen, stunned, staring at the door. *What happened? What did I say?*

Mechanically, she crossed the room and took the teapot from the shelf and placed it on the table. The water was boiling in the kettle, and she moved it away from the heat. She reached above the stove and took a mug off its hook. She looked at it for a moment, the chipped mouth and worn and crazed glazing, then threw it across the room to smash against the row of dishes lined along the wall above the windows.

They've all left me, she thought. *He's turned them all against me.* She pulled another mug down and threw it to shatter against the pantry door. "No," she said, and stormed across the kitchen. "No, no, no, no, no!" she shrieked, punctuating each scream with a thrown plate. He'd turned them against her, made them hate her, had taken what was hers—what she'd spent her life building—and corrupted it. Poisoned it. Destroyed it.

"It's all your fault!" she cried, hurling a tin of flour to explode against the wall by the back door. "Your fault, *your fault*, *YOUR FAULT!*" Just like before, just like then, and now she faced an even greater loss and shame. Cast out by her husband, who'd sided with him—*with him*—and taken her son. Her child. *Her son.* Her son and Nat's, the only thing left of his that she had. "He's *mine*, damn you," she shrieked, smashing a bowl on the floor. "You'll not take him, too, like you took his father!"

She raged about the kitchen, screaming and smashing the crockery, hurling pans to clatter against the wall, until finally, exhausted, she sank to the floor and sat, sobbing.

"Mine," she wept. "Dear God, no. Not again, not again..."

"Nat Boscawen was never yours, Rose Hale," Aunt Bannel said behind her.

"What would you know of this, Moereven Bannel?" Rose asked wearily, not even looking around. "And what say do you have in it?"

"Say and enough," the old woman said. "Say and enough." She walked into the kitchen, picking her way over the wreckage on the floor. She righted the old rocking chair, then, adjusting her shawl about her shoulders, sat and folded her hands. "Margaret Berryman," she called. "You come out here!"

The pantry door opened slowly and Meg, pale and shaking, peered out. Rose lowered her head and closed her eyes. The story would be all over the county by morning, and all of the gossiping wives, those who'd whispered for years about her oldest son, would feast on her like kites on a dead lamb.

"You'll take yourself to bed now, Margaret," Aunt Bannel said, "and you'll not speak one word of what was said here this night. If you do, you'll answer to me, and greatly you'll rue it. Do you understand?"

"Yes, Mistress Bannel," Meg said in a frightened voice.

"Then go. You'll clean this tomorrow," she said, waving her off.

Meg bobbed a curtsey and fled up the passage.

Silently, Rose took the large kettle off the stove and filled the teapot, feeling Aunt Bannel's cold, hard eyes watching her. She placed the kettle on the stove and turned to the pantry.

"Put some mayweed in the water," Aunt Bannel said. "It will be good."

"I was just going to fetch it," Rose said.

Aunt Bannel nodded. "You were always clever, Rose," she said. "'A great pity you weren't always wise."

Rose stopped in the middle of the floor, but instead of the anger she usually felt at the old woman's carping, now she felt only a cold and empty sadness. "'Tis an old story, Auntie," she said without looking at the other woman, "and one I'm weary of havin' told me."

"There's none that tells it so often as you do," Aunt Bannel replied, "though you may never say a word of it."

"And how am I not to tell it to myself," she said bitterly, turning, "when I saw the fruit of it every day, in my own child's face, and in the looks of the people of the village? Even Margaret, that has no room for talking. If I was a fool, was I not a fool with cause?" She walked to the pantry and took the mayweed from the shelf. When she turned, Aunt Bannel stood in the doorway.

"Ye may have had cause, child," Aunt Bannel said, "but ye didn't have eyes. Ye didn't see what was there before your face, what everyone else knew and no small number told ye: He wasn't for you, and you not for him."

"He was mine," Rose said, brushing past her, "had he not been taken from me."

"He was never yours, Rose Hale," Aunt Bannel said sternly. "He belonged to another. He always did, and well you know it."

"He did not," she said. "I'll not have such things said in this house."

"Aye," the old woman said, settling into the chair again. "Words give things power, give things life. You know more than most that's true."

"I did naught that was wrong," Rose said defensively.

"You did naught that was right, neither," Aunt Bannel said, "and dearly it's cost you."

"You've done the same for others," Rose said, turning on the old woman, her anger rising, "and often enough."

"But ne'er for myself," Aunt Bannel replied. "And ne'er one that was taken of another."

"That wasn't so!" Rose cried.

"It was, and ye know it," Aunt Bannel snapped, rising from

her chair, "as ye knew it then, when ye said those words and spoke those soons." She paced across the room, and Rose fell back before her. "I taught ye myself! Did ye think me so old and feeble that I wouldn't know when you'd lifted your hand to snare him?"

"Snare him?" Rose flared. "*Snare him?* Snare that which was mine by right, and father to my child? If I lifted my hand at all, it was to save that which was mine from that which turned his heart."

"None turned his heart, Rose Hale. It was never yours to begin with, for all your wantin' it, and when it was given, it was given freely to one who returned it."

"Given?" she spat. "Taken by an unnatural thing, against all laws of man and God! Do ye think I didn't see? Didn't know? I saw them sneakin' off, sneakin' off to be together, when he was called to be mine!"

"I'm marryin' ye," he'd said, *"and damn ye to hell for it, you and all your kin."*

"When did ye see them, Rose?" Aunt Bannel asked, stepping toward her.

"That night," she snapped, "the last time I seen him, and he's sneakin' off with that man, that *thing* that took him."

"Treasure that child," he'd said, his face twisted with hatred and streaked with dirt in the lantern light, *"for it's all ye'll get of me."*

"Where did ye see them, Rose?" Aunt Bannel's voice was calm, insistent, pressuring her to speak.

"You'll keep away from him!" she'd screamed. *"You're mine, and I'll not have you be with that creature!"*

"From the window," she answered, seeing them clearly in her mind. The kitchen around her faded, and she was once again at the attic window looking down at two shadowed figures slipping away across a black garden.

He'd struck out at her, struck and missed, and she'd shoved him away…

All of her suspicions, then, had been true. The glances, the smiles, the unconscious touches, the thousand small ways they betrayed themselves to one who was watching. She'd seen them all, and understanding had slowly dawned on her—understanding and anger.

Shoved him and he'd fallen and hadn't even tried to catch himself. He was frozen in her mind, always, staring at her, shocked as he stumbled backward.

And now, after all these years, that man had come back, come back to rouse memories from their slumber, to wake old pains, to make her relive over and over the devastating horror of that night.

For one moment he hung there in the air.

His fault, now as it was then. His fault.

Then he smiled, and was gone.

"What did you do, Rose?" Aunt Bannel's voice sliced through her memories like a beacon through a dark night.

"I did *nothing!*" she shrieked. "I did nothing!"

"He was never yours, and he never would have been, Rose Hale," Aunt Bannel said, leaning over her where she sat on the floor, sobbing. "He was bound to another, heart fast to one who loved him in return, and nothing ye could do would have changed that. All ye could do was destroy it."

"I'm not sorry," she said, staggering to her feet. "I'm not sorry, and nothing you can say will make me so! It was *wrong!* It was wrong and none can say otherwise!"

"Leave this place." Aunt Bannel's voice was chill and hard. "Leave this house, and don't come back. There's none left that will speak for ye, and there's none to blame but yourself."

"No," she whispered. "I can't." *All for nothing. All of this, for nothing...*

"Ye must," Aunt Bannel said, stepping away from her. "Unless ye can wash clean the poison that lives in your soul, there's no place for ye here. You'll do none any harm here this night or tomorrow, and I'll watch to see that it's so."

Aunt Bannel crossed the room and opened the door; the chill

night breeze swept through the room, and Rose shivered.

"May ye find peace, my child," Aunt Bannel said. "I don't know where ye will, and I can't see how it will come to ye, but I pray it will."

She closed the door, and Rose was alone.

Jonathan put his teacup down on the bedside table and stretched in the morning sunlight. He was still weary, but rested and at ease as he hadn't been since coming to Trevaglan. Langsford—Alayne had been sitting in the chair next to him when he woke, and had kissed him.

Kissed him. It had been an unimaginable joy.

Someone knocked on the door.

"Come in," he called.

The door opened and Rose entered.

"I'm giving my notice, sir," she said, closing the door behind her.

"What?" Jonathan asked, shocked, sitting up against his pillow.

"Yes sir," Rose replied. "And as soon as I pack my things, I am leaving."

"But your husband," Jonathan said. "You—"

"What James does is his business, sir," she said, "and what I do is mine, and after today, none of yours."

"But what . . . why?"

"Because I hate the sight of you," she said quietly, but the words were laced with venom, "and I'll not stay another day under a roof that shelters you. You poison everything you touch, you unnatural thing, and I'll not stand for it another minute."

Jonathan fell back against his pillow, appalled by the loathing in the woman's voice.

"You killed the father of my child, and I've had to live with the shame and disgrace of that ever since."

"That's enough, Mrs. Hale," Langsford said from the door to his room. "Leave here immediately."

"And you, poor man, think you that you love this creature? I saw it sure in your face, the same look as my Nat had, and he died of it." She whirled on Jonathan before either of them could speak. "Why? Tell me why, you devil's brood! Why did you bring such grief? What did I ever do to you? What did *he* ever do to you!"

"He raped me."

Jonathan wasn't even aware he'd said the words aloud until he saw the look of shock on Rose's face.

"*No,*" she breathed.

"Yes," Jonathan said firmly, pushing upright. "He came to my room, and he dragged me off to the ruins."

"Jonathan," Langsford said quietly. "Don't—"

"No, Alayne. No." He threw back the covers and climbed out of the bed. "Three days after your banns were read, when I wouldn't come to him, he came for me, and he raped me."

Rose staggered back against the door. "It isn't true," she cried. "You're lying!"

"When I wouldn't come to him, as I had every night that summer, he came for me."

Sobbing, Rose slid to the floor. "No, no, no, no, no . . ."

"Every single night," he said relentlessly. "And when I didn't because I learned you were with child and he was to marry you, he took me, and he raped me, and he left me there."

Rose curled in a ball, and he leaned over her.

"He raped me, and he left me there, and he went to his death. Don't talk to me of grief or shame, Rose Pritchard. I've lived with that shame every day, every night, every waking minute for fourteen years. *Alone.* I had no family, no husband or wife or children to love me through it. No one. Alone." He turned, strode across the room, and picked up the straw token he'd found the day before. "How many, Rose?" he said, grabbing her hair and pulling her head back so she had to look at him. "How many of these did he leave on your windowsill that summer?"

"I don't know what you mean," she sobbed.

He shoved her away and stood. "How many did you leave on my window this week?"

"None! I did nothing!"

They stared at each other for a long, charged moment. "You killed him," he said in a low voice, as certain as if he had witnessed it himself, and Rose flinched. "You found out about us. You found out and you waited for him and you killed him."

"*You* killed him, you filth!" she spat back at him. "You ruined him and poisoned his heart. You killed him sure as if *you* pushed him off that cliff yourself, and may the devil take you for it."

"You're discharged," he said coldly, and turned and stared out the window. "I'll write you any recommendation you want, only get out of my sight. Get out of my house."

He heard her stagger to her feet, still gasping for breath, and heard the doorknob turn and the door close behind her. The room was silent.

She had destroyed him—destroyed them both—in a last terrible act of vengeance, destroyed any chance he had, as he had destroyed hers. There was a nightmarish symmetry to the entire affair; they were both ruined by their own pasts, their own passions, and their own failures. He couldn't bear to turn and look at Langsford.

"I'm sorry you had to witness that," he said. "I don't know what possessed her to say such things." He bit his lip. "Or me. I'm terribly sorry. I understand, of course, if you feel you must leave, or . . . or restate anything you've said."

"You were mistaken about one thing," Langsford said calmly from behind him. "Two, actually."

"Indeed?" Jonathan tried to keep his voice from shaking.

"Yes," Langsford said. "You said there was none that loved you through all those years, and that you were alone. You were quite mistaken in that."

"You heard the things she said . . . the things I said . . ." He shook his head. "I cannot ask you forget them."

"The only thing I would have you ask me forget," Langsford said, "is that I waited until last night to tell you I loved you. And the only thing I would ask *you* to forget, is my foolishness in waiting so long to do so. Are those things too terribly much to ask?" He felt Langsford's hand gently touch his back, and he turned. "Can you deny me those two small requests?"

Jonathan looked up into those blue eyes, so familiar, yet so strange in their nearness and utter vulnerability, and felt the last of his defenses and fears fall away. "God help me no, I cannot," he whispered, and pulled Langsford to him.

The kiss lasted a moment—an eon—and every sensation was seared on his mind and body: Langford's lips, hard on his own, the feel of Langsford's body pressed against him, Langsford's hands on either side of his face, holding him. He slid his arms around Langsford's back and ran his hands up through his hair. He brushed his tongue lightly against Langsford's lips and felt him tremble. No wonder, he thought he felt weak himself, and was shaking with desire and tenderness. They broke the kiss, and stood clinging to each other, and gasping for breath.

"We can't," Langsford whispered. "The door . . . and your hands—"

He pulled Langsford's mouth down to his own, and kissed him gently, delicately, each kiss causing Langsford to gasp and shiver.

"Do you think," he murmured breathlessly, and kissed, "that I care"—another kiss—"who finds us"—two kisses—"or if my hands hurt?"

"N-No," Langsford whispered. "I don't think so."

"And I hope," he said and kissed again, "that you don't mind either." He began to unbutton Langsford's waistcoat, kissing him on the chin, and then the throat as Langsford's eyes closed and his head fell back.

"No," Langsford said, his voice barely audible, "I don't."

The waistcoat slid to the floor, and he ran his hands up over Langsford's chest and around his neck. Langsford leaned down and pulled Jonathan in tightly against him, kissing him deeply. It was more than he could have imagined, more than he could have thought possible—all of his years of longing had not prepared him in the least for the reality of holding Langsford in his arms, tasting him, touching him. He started trembling, and his knees buckled.

"Are you all right?" Langsford asked, holding him up.

"Yes," Jonathan said, smiling up at him. "I have never been more so. I'm just a little—"

Langsford kissed him gently on the forehead. "Perhaps you should lie down for a while, until you're rested."

"Perhaps we should," he whispered.

Epilogue

Rose disappeared two weeks later.

She had left the farm that day as she told Jonathan she would, and had gone back to her people in Landreath. They met her at the door with stony faces and cold silence; they had had enough of Rose Hale and the gossip about her. Meg hadn't heard much when she'd listened at Jonathan's door that morning, but she'd heard enough, and as the tale spread, so did the silence that met Rose wherever she went in the village. One morning, when her mother went to wake her, she was gone.

In the years that followed, the legend grew of the Fair Rose of Trevaglan Farm, who killed her lover because he was untrue, and then died of a broken heart. She was cursed for the crime by the witch of the downs, they said, huddling over tankards of ale in the pub or around a kitchen stove on a winter night, and was doomed to wander the cliff path, weeping for her lover and crying out his name. The people of the village eventually shunned the old path and found another way to the farm, for to meet the Ghost of the Cliffs of a moonless night was a certain harbinger of death, like the Bean Sidhe of Ireland or the Barghest, the black hound of the Yorkshire Moors.

That tale was still in the future. The day after Rose disappeared, her mother went to Trevaglan to ask of James Hale if she had returned to him. She had not. Jonathan made inquiries at Penzance and Falmouth, and as far afield as Truro and St. Ives, but found no word of her. And when Langsford traveled to London later that summer to close up the flat and move at last to Trevaglan, he sought out people her family knew in London, but none had any news of her. She had simply vanished.

Alec stayed at the farm with James Hale and worked there until the Great War broke upon Europe and the world. When the call came he went, and was wounded at the Somme, losing a leg to an enemy shell. He returned to Trevaglan to recover, and it was there he met Jonathan's niece one summer's night when she had come to visit her uncle. It was there they fell in love and there they married, to her mother's horror and Jonathan's delight. And when Jonathan died some fifty years later, and Langsford, worn by time and his grief, followed him in death less than a year after, it was Alec's younger son who inherited Trevaglan Farm and all of its secrets.

Cornwall 1906

The bonfire on the hill behind Breawragh Cottage had burned low, and the last of the revelers had returned to the village. The moon had barely shown as a sliver in the twilight, then vanished, and the stars burned in the black vault of the sky. Golowan's Eve had come and gone once again, the first in fourteen years that Jonathan had not been wracked by memories.

He and Langsford stood on the rise above the fire, with Aunt Bannel and Justus beside them. The crowds had been small this year; the old ways were passing, and with them the beliefs that had knit the people of the country down through the centuries.

"We should go," Jonathan said, unexpectedly sad at the thought of time slipping away.

"Not yet," Aunt Bannel said. "There's one thing more that needs t'be done."

A man and a woman, hand in hand, walked into the dim light of the glowing embers that remained from the great fire that had burned for hours. Another pair appeared from the woods and two more, old and bent, made their way up the hill.

"'Tis the nursery boy come home again," one of the men said out of the darkness.

"Tom?" Jonathan called. Could it possibly be?

"Aye," Tom said, and strode up the hill. He was older, balding, and worn with the passage of time, but his grip was strong, and his smile wide. "And glad I am to see ye."

"And I," Jonathan said.

"Tom, mind your place," Mrs. Bannel said. "And the rest of ye, too." The six folk, some familiar to Jonathan, some not, formed a circle around them.

"You've come a long journey, Jonathan Williams," Aunt Bannel said, "and have come home now, and here to stay. You've joined yourself to the land, and stand heart and heart with those that love ye."

Jonathan glanced at Langsford, silent beside him. *And those I love.*

"There's a sayin' here that so long as one of the peculiar gentlemen in our land live at Trevaglan, the country will be blessed, and all flourish." She took his hand, and placed Langsford's in it. Instinctively, he pulled back, as did Langsford, and Mrs. Bannel clicked her tongue. "Ye needn't worry, children," she said. "There bain't any here as will give ye away. Take hands."

He heard Langsford laugh quietly next to him, and felt the brush of his hand. He reached and took it in his, and they stood hand in hand together.

"Are you here to wed us then, Auntie?" Langsford asked.

"I may be," she said, "I may be. I doubt the parson'll be marryin' ye any time soon, but he don't hold sway here this night. I do. Hold out your hands."

He looked up at Langsford, who simply shrugged, and they held out the hands they had clasped together.

She held up a length of ribbon. "Green," she said, "for the land and for the spring, and for all things that grow and flourish." She deftly slipped it around their wrists and tied it in a knot. She reached up both hands and touched them each on the cheek.

"They say if ye jump the fire on Golowan's Eve, ye'll be protected against witches and evil for the rest of the year." She glanced over her shoulder at the embers. "Of witches I think ye needn't fear, but blessings should be taken where ye can find them." She looked back at them. "Well? What are ye two duffers waitin' for?"

"Should we?" Langsford asked.

"Would you argue with her?" Jonathan answered.

"Not for the world."

"Then jump with me," he said, and, hand in hand, they ran down the hill, and leaped.

Acknowledgements

Writing is a solitary endeavor, but not something one can do entirely alone. Many people had input—direct or otherwise—into this book, and without them it would not have happened. I'd like to thank my friends John Butterfield, Susan Amber Springer, Lisa Drostova, Carolyn Segal, Sherwood Smith, Sandra Leipelt, Kathleen McKay, Shawn Wacker-Smith, and my sister Julie, all of whom listened patiently as I blathered on and on about this story, and who gave input and unconditional support throughout the process. Special thanks go to Ken and Lynette at The Highlands in Guerneville, who provided the best writing environment one could ask for. Also, thank you to my very patient and long-suffering editor, Lisa Clancy, who gently nudged me along the way to publication. And finally, two people without whom this would not have been remotely possible: Deborah Doyle, who spent hours discussing and debating story points and character details, and strongly shaped the people and events depicted here, and Erastes, Brit Crit and wielder of the Keep Writing Whip, who believed in these people and this story before I did, and whose morning emails of "WHERE ARE THE WORDS?" kept me moving when I might have stalled out. Thank you all, folks. I couldn't have done it without you.

About the Author

A San Francisco Bay-area resident, **Donald L. Hardy** lives on an elderly but adorable sailboat with a very conversational schnauzer named Schultz. He moved from the East Coast, where he had lived since childhood, while trapped in the grip of a midlife crisis of biblical proportions. He is currently considering embarking upon pirate raids on uninhabited islands in the Bay in his free time.

He began writing after moving aboard and dumping his television and has gradually expanded his output. *Lovers' Knot* is his first published novel.

When he isn't writing—or catering to the demands of Schultz—he can be found onstage or in rehearsal at the Butterfield 8 theater company in Concord, California, usually performing in Shakespeare with a twist. On certain weekends, he's an avid Renaissance (Faire) Man—proving that even when he's offstage, he's onstage.

He has discovered, in the writing of this biography, that speaking of himself in the third person is strangely appealing, and is struggling with his desire to break into the royal first person plural. He fears he may fail, and so will end, lest he offend even more.

Please visit him at *http://www.donaldhardy.net.*